KT-151-418

Libraries**West**

4 4 0179415 1

THE SECRET
SHE KEPT IN
BOLLYWOOD

TARA PAMMI

A CINDERELLA
FOR THE PRINCE'S
REVENGE

EMMY GRAYSON

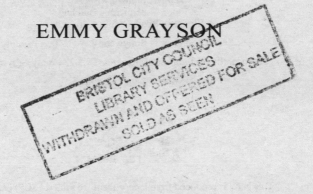

MILLS & BOON

First Published in Great Britain 2022
by Mills & Boon, an imprint of HarperCollins*Publishers* Ltd,
1 London Bridge Street, London, SE1 9GF

www.harpercollins.co.uk

HarperCollins*Publishers*
1st Floor, Watermarque Building,
Ringsend Road, Dublin 4, Ireland

The Secret She Kept in Bollywood © 2022 Tara Pammi

A Cinderella for the Prince's Revenge © 2022 Emmy Grayson

ISBN: 978-0-263-30082-6

05/22

MIX
Paper from
responsible sources
FSC® C007454

This book is produced from independently certified FSC™ paper
to ensure responsible forest management.
For more information visit www.harpercollins.co.uk/green.

Printed and Bound in Spain using 100% Renewable Electricity
at CPI Black Print, Barcelona

THE SECRET SHE KEPT IN BOLLYWOOD

TARA PAMMI

MILLS & BOON

CHAPTER ONE

SOMETHING MOMENTOUS will happen today. Follow your heart bravely. Anya Raawal stepped out of the car, the little line from her favorite astrology app running circles in her mind. From the moment she'd opened her eyes this morning, Anya had felt the change in the energy around her. Even her quick call to the astrology pundit she consulted with every month had shown that Saturn was leaving some part of her chart and was going to grant her a departing boon.

Several years of tormenting her with health issues and the loss of her beloved grandmother—who'd been more of a parent to her than her real ones—and the cranky universe was apparently going to give her a gift.

Anya was *so* ready for it—whether that was a new creative challenge that would push her to her limits, an old friend walking back into her life or she'd even settle for Mama finding a new hobby that would stop her from trying to set up Anya with yet another "perfect" man.

Sighing, she gestured at Salim Bhai to drive off. A major problem with having staff who had seen you skin your knees and soothed the bumps with Band-Aids and hugs was that they all saw far too much of things she wanted to keep private.

She didn't mind their concern, for the most part. To be

honest, she was more than grateful for the staff who had more than once stepped in as caring, concerned adults when her famous movie-star parents had been far too busy with their very messed-up, mostly public, marital dramas and ego wars.

It had been Salim Bhai's wife Noor, and Anya's grandmother who'd nursed Anya back to health from a serious case of blood loss after giving birth to a baby girl at eighteen and from the spiral of depression she'd gone into after giving her up for adoption.

But today, she couldn't stand the extra scrutiny. Nor for them or any of her family to mock her for her beliefs.

She walked up the steps of the luxury five-star hotel where the rehearsals were happening for their production company Raawal House of Cinema's next blockbuster. Her brother Virat was a critically acclaimed director but also often a beast on set.

Now, with his wife Zara, back to work after giving birth to their son, rumors were that his rudeness had reached new heights. So there was no reason for Anya to be here today.

As the head costume designer for the period movie, she wouldn't be needed at the rehearsals. But it was as if there was hook in her belly, pulling her toward this meeting. She knew she was being even more eccentric than usual. That her deep belief in all things cosmic bothered her eldest brother Vikram, to no end.

But it was her chosen madness, her comfort blanket, and she was loath to give it up. It wasn't that she waited for some kind of sign from the stars, but that she believed in listening to the universe.

She breezed in through the front doors and took the lift, refusing to be thwarted by the idea of her bossy, overprotective older brothers focusing their unwanted attention on her. Hopefully, their respective wives—God, how she adored her two sisters-in-law, Naina and Zara—would tell her two big brothers to stick their big noses out of Anya's business.

The security in the lobby of the twenty-second floor waved her in. Anya ducked into one suite after another, absorbing the energy of the room and then walking out when it didn't resonate with her. There was something here… she could feel it thrumming through her veins.

She walked into the biggest suite on the floor to find her brothers, Vikram and Virat, and her sister-in-law Zara and a number of other team members.

A small makeshift dais had been created out of the raised sitting area.

Anya waved at her sister-in-law, who'd looked up from the script when the girl on the stage caught her attention. The movie was about a warrior queen that Zara would be playing, and the younger girl had been cast as the teen version of the queen. While Anya hadn't met the young actress chosen for the role, she'd already started researching the time period and had begun sketching out her wardrobe. Sooner or later, she'd meet her. Especially since both her brothers had sung the praises of the girl's natural talent on stage.

Her name was Meera Verma—daughter of the now-late Rani Verma, one of the most celebrated actresses of Bollywood more than a decade ago. The actress had retired from Bollywood and public life to raise a family and had never returned.

The girl was reading lines from the script in her hand, her voice deep and loud, her plump face illuminated by the overhead lights.

Anya walked closer to the stage, her heart racing so fast that she could hear the echo of it in her entire body. Even thirteen years later, she couldn't forget that beautiful face. Those large distinctive light brown eyes—catlike eyes of the man that had fathered Anya's child—were almost too big for her round face. And then there were the wide pink lips and the dark little finger-width mole that made a slash through the girl's left eyebrow…the one imperfection in her baby's face which had only made her even more perfect in Anya's eyes.

The very baby girl that she'd given up thirteen years ago, the baby she hadn't been strong enough to look after—not mentally, not physically—the baby who'd stolen a piece of her heart in the couple of hours that she'd been held in her mother's arms…this young actress was her daughter.

Meera… The girl's name was Meera… Her daughter's name was Meera.

That's what the universe had brought her here for?

To show her the baby that had been a piece of her heart all grown up?

To dangle the girl in front of Anya when she couldn't be a part of her life, when she couldn't claim any kind of relationship with her?

To make Anya's torment that she had struggled with for thirteen years, even more sharp and painful?

A huge sob built through her chest, sucking out all her breath, leaving her shaking.

Somehow, Anya managed to walk out of the large sitting room, her eyes full of unshed tears, careful to not catch any of her family's eyes.

Her heart breaking all over again…even after all these years.

Simon De Acosta was not a fan of the movie industry and everything it entailed. He'd seen firsthand the high accolades and the low reviews and broken contracts and nepotism at play and the wreckage it had created within the fragile but brilliant mind of his wife Rani. He would never forget the number of years she'd paid her dues in minor roles, forever trying to stay on the right side of powerful men who pulled all the strings.

After several years, Rani's perseverance had finally borne fruit and she'd reached the heights of fame even she'd only dreamed of. But by then, it had done indelible harm to not only to their marriage but also her mental and physical health. Their failure to conceive had broken her down even more.

The only saving grace had been the arrival of Meera in their lives—she'd wrought the miracle that Simon had tried to achieve for years. At only a day old, Meera had gotten her mother to slow down. At a month old, she'd gotten Rani to quit the long hours and the brutal pace— even though her career had been at its peak—and retire.

No lifestyle where she disappeared for weeks on a shoot and he also traveled internationally for work would work for her precious baby girl, Rani had announced with that focused fixation that had often unnerved Simon. But he'd been more than happy to go along with her decision. With his real estate business at a place where he could dictate his own lifestyle, they'd moved to Singapore immediately. Even their marriage had had a second life breathed into it after years of conflict created by two ambitious, demanding careers and the strife and pain caused by their failure to conceive a child.

Until Rani's restlessness had begun once more three years ago and things had begun to fall apart. All over again.

And now, eighteen months after losing Rani in a car crash, he was back in the city of Mumbai with Meera in tow. He'd done his best to persuade Meera to turn away from Bollywood but acting was in her blood, just as it had been in Rani's. It didn't matter that she was adopted.

Simon rubbed a hand over his face and stepped out of the lift into the expansive lobby. It seemed like he'd only blinked twice, and in that time not only had Meera been scouted at a shopping mall of all places, but the acclaimed director Virat Raawal himself had given her a screen test and called her his next incredible find.

Since losing Rani, it was the first time Simon had seen Meera excited about something. Neither had he been able to argue with his thirteen-year-old daughter's wisdom that without her mom, their home was not a home anymore, nor were they any more than automatons surviving each bleak, empty day.

He'd been so wrapped up in his guilt and grief—two emotions that fed each other—that he hadn't even noticed that Meera's grades had been suffering or that she'd retreated from a vibrant social life.

This was a good move, he reminded himself now. It wasn't healthy for him or Meera to be so…isolated as they'd been the last eighteen months. Now, he just needed to find someone trustworthy to watch over Meera for the next few months during the preproduction and the shoot, especially when he traveled for work.

He'd already interviewed several agencies but Meera, being thirteen, hated almost every one of the candidates they'd met. His wife had raised Meera to be not only a well-adjusted, independent girl but also confident in her own decision-making.

For the next few weeks, though, Simon was determined to spend every spare minute their schedules afforded with Meera. He checked his watch. It was six in the evening, which meant Meera wouldn't finish for another hour at least. But he would hang around. He needed to get to know

all the members of the production team despite his irrational aversion for the industry. Even the powerful Raawal
brothers of whom everyone sang litanies of praise.

Simon was about to walk into the rehearsal suite when
he saw a woman kneeling on the floor in the small circular lobby tucked at the end of the corridor.

With Mumbai's skyline visible through the high glass
windows, her long neck and slender back were clearly
delineated. A faint light spilled into the small sitting area
hidden from the view of the long corridor that opened into
the various suites. Her shoulders were shaking, her head
bowed as if weighed down by insurmountable grief.

Should he walk away?

Rani used to tease him mercilessly for his unmodern
instinct to help damsels in distress. But he couldn't just…
ignore the woman, could he? Especially now, when he was
the father of a teenage girl and had to hope that someone
would show her a kindness if she needed it, under any
circumstance.

Stopping at a short distance from her, Simon crouched
down with one hand on the sofa behind him. "Miss, is everything okay?" he whispered, trying to make his broad
form shrink into something less threatening. Which was
nearly impossible.

The woman raised her head, her gaze full of shock
and…grief. Grief that he'd seen in his own reflection far
too much these past eighteen months and recognized only
too well.

The woman was young, barely late twenties maybe.
Large brown eyes, followed by a distinctive nose that was
too big for her face and a wide mouth…not classically
beautiful like Rani had been. But the strong, stark lines
of her face and the stubborn resolve to her pointed chin
tugged at him.

He didn't dare look below her neck for something about her was ringing all the bells in his body, waking up a hunger that had been choked by grief and guilt even before Rani had died.

Despite the warning, his greedy senses nonetheless registered the smooth expanse of golden-brown skin left bare by the deep square neck of the woman's white top. Thin lace shimmered at the neckline kissing the upper swells of her breasts. She was tall and slender and yet curvy in all the right places—voluptuous. Her hair was jet-black with golden highlights in it, cut stylishly to frame her face. The silky ends moved with her baby-bird-like movements as she tilted her head.

What the hell was wrong with him?

The last thing the woman needed was a forty-three-year-old man to be checking her out while she was in the middle of what was clearly a panic attack. Simon exhaled roughly, willing his traitorous body to calm down. And yet he couldn't help but enjoy the slow hum of attraction simmering beneath his skin. It had been so long since he'd felt anything like it.

Tears had drawn rivulets over her sharp cheekbones and pooled around her mouth. She stared at him and yet, Simon knew she hadn't really registered his presence. There was a blankness in her eyes that terrified him to his bones.

"Hey, I'm Simon," he said in a soft, steady voice. "Are you in pain? Should I call for a doctor?"

The woman shook her head. A fat tear dropped to her chin and disappeared down her neck and into the blouse.

"Okay, that's good," he said, settling onto his knees, keeping his hands on his thighs where she could see them. "I'll just sit here for a while with you, yeah?"

She didn't nod but he saw her shoulders relax.

He waited like that for a few minutes before prompting, "Is there anyone I can call for you? A family member?"

She shook her head very emphatically at the last. Was she in danger from them? His blood roared at the very idea. "Okay. That's okay."

Slowly, she scrubbed a hand over her face.

Simon braced himself for her to walk away. He was after all a total stranger. And yes, he had to brace himself because suddenly he didn't want her to leave. Not until he spent a little more time in her company while she pulled herself together.

"Whatever help or comfort you need, big or small, I'd like to help. Whenever you're ready, that is," he added.

"Can you turn back time?" she said at last, in a voice turned husky by her tears.

Her question struck him deep in his heart, pricking the guilt button, reminding him of how helpless he'd felt faced with Rani's dissatisfaction with their life together. It didn't matter that Rani and he had fallen out of love with one another in the last few years. She'd been a part of his life—his best friend, his investor, his lover—for more than two decades. Her loss was raw and real. He settled back against the sofa, his fingers steepled on top of his knees. "That's a question I've asked myself so many times. But all the wealth and power in the world can't help anyone to do that."

She scrubbed her hand over her face once again and mirrored his pose against the coffee table. Their feet sat parallel, almost touching—his booted and hers pink toed and sandaled—as did their knees. It was impossible to not notice her long legs and toned thighs bared by dark denim shorts. Or her smooth golden-brown skin. Or that her every moment, every turn of her head, every lift of her limb was imbued with a languid grace.

"It's a stupid question, isn't it?" she scoffed. "We assume that if we can go back into the past, we'd make different decisions." She inhaled sharply and her mouth stretched in a watery smile. "But the truth is we can't make different decisions." She looked at her laced fingers, and then looked up. "At least I wouldn't have. Couldn't have. But I still revisit it as if I had different choices."

Simon leaned his head against the sofa and closed his eyes. He knew exactly what she meant. The last, bitter fight he and Rani had engaged in still kept him up most nights.

Her solution to breathing new life into their marriage, to restore her increasing dissociation from him and Meera had been to suggest they try to conceive through another round of IVF again.

It had been unacceptable to him.

Maybe she'd forgotten what trauma she'd put her body and heart through the last time, but he hadn't. Even his argument that she was nearly forty and that kind of stress on her body might send her mental health into decline like the last time hadn't helped. His refusal and her pushing that it was the only solution had festered and blazed and grown like a resentful wound until it had burst into a bitter, hateful fight the very night she had stormed out and then died in a car accident.

Could he have changed anything about the last few years of his marriage with Rani? When Meera and he hadn't been enough for her? What if he had agreed to her plea to try IVF again, even though it hadn't worked when she'd been much younger and had nearly been the end of them? What if they hadn't argued that last day so bitterly before she'd driven off? Would she still be alive today?

Those questions tormented him almost every waking moment.

"Nothing will ever," he said, opening his eyes and coming back to the present, "stop us from wishing we could act differently." He exhaled. "There's only striving for acceptance for the choices that have been already made."

She lifted her lashes and met his gaze properly this time. As if she was finally seeing him—this stranger, a man who'd stopped to chat with her. Noticing things about him. Listening to the pain behind his words. "You understand," she said simply.

He gave her a simple nod. Despite the heavy tone of their musings, Simon noted her sudden alertness as she watched him. The stifled gasp as she became aware of him.

Still, her gaze swept over him, quick and greedy and heated, just as his had done earlier. A bare few seconds but he felt it all the same. Maybe because of the artlessness of it. Maybe because she wore her shock at her reaction to him so openly on her face. He could almost pinpoint the moment her mind registered the darkly potent electricity arcing between them. Her knees shifted in a jerky move, as if to get away from him, but boxed in between the coffee table and the sofa, her long legs fell back against his. Even with his trouser-covered legs, Simon felt the weight of them like a shock to his system.

Long, thick lashes flicked down in shyness but that stubbornness he'd noted in her chin brought them back up. Simon could see the very second she decided she wouldn't let grief win. Saw her wonder if she could use their mutual attraction to dig herself out of whatever had brought her to her knees.

Watching her fight the shadows of her grief was sexy as hell. Every muscle in his body tightened in an instantaneous reaction. The urge to stay here, the urge to do more than talk was...so strong that he fisted his hands at his sides.

"I'm... Angel," she said, stretching out a hand over their

touching knees. The echo of tears was still in her voice but there was also a raspy huskiness now.

"Simon," he said automatically, not reaching out to take her hand.

If he thought she'd be hurt by his reluctance to touch her, she proved him wrong. She simply kept her hand there, a brow raising in her beautiful face, throwing down a gauntlet. Calling him on his sudden aloofness.

Hell, he was a forty-three-year-old man and he was scared of touching this fragile beauty? Was he that dead inside?

Simon took her hand in his, and felt the jolt go up his arm, and all the way down through his body to his groin. Her fingers were soft and slender but full of calluses. He rubbed the bridge of her thumb with the pad of his, marveling at how deliciously good even the simple contact felt. How life-affirming. He wanted to touch her more, everywhere, wanted to smooth out the furrow between her brows with his thumb, wanted to bury his mouth in the sensitive crook of her neck and shoulders.

Her light brown eyes widened, her nostrils flaring with an indrawn breath.

He dropped her hand, the contact igniting a fire inside him he knew he couldn't quench. "If you don't need anything else—"

"Thank you for your kindness," she said, her voice suddenly dripping with a formality he disliked immensely. Even though he'd forced her to it with his own withdrawal. "I should go. Before someone sees me."

"It was nothing," he said, at a loss for words. All the questions he wanted to ask were too intrusive. All the things he wanted to say to her…didn't bear thinking, much less saying out loud. Not with their adult-rated content.

One hand on the sofa behind her, she quickly pushed

up to her feet and Simon followed. To find her swaying on her feet, her skin pale and drawn tight.

He clamped his hands over her shoulders, frowning. "You're not all right."

She pushed away from his hold, her eyes on his mouth. "I just stood up too fast and I haven't eaten anything all day."

He scowled. Even as every inch of him was aware of her body, her movements, her expressions. She was tall and slender and yet curvy at her breasts and hips. Vulnerable clearly but also strong. "It's six thirty in the evening."

She bit her lower lip. "I had other things on my mind. More important things."

"Let me take you to dinner then," he said, the offer bursting out of him before he thought it through. This woman was dangerous to his peace and yet, he wanted her company for just a little while longer. "Let me take care of you."

"I don't need another man to tell me I need looking after. I have enough of those in my life. I need…" She tugged at the strap of the cross-body bag that fell between her breasts, making them more pronounced. "I should go. Thanks for…everything."

He should've let her go then. Instead he clasped his fingers over her wrist in a gentle movement, contrary to how his pulse zigzagged almost violently through him. "What do you need, Angel?"

Suddenly, she stood close, her front to his side, almost grazing him. Almost…but not quite. She was only a couple of inches shorter than him, so her breath hit him on his jaw, her gaze sliding to his mouth and then upward in a blatant gesture. "Someone who'll listen to what I say *I* need. Someone who'll give me what I need." She stared into his eyes, challenge glinting there. In seconds, that

naive fragility had transformed into pure temptation with
a spine of steel. A scornful smile split her mouth. "It's not
you though. I can already tell you're one of those men who
doesn't really see me. You're someone who loves playing the knight, someone who deals in honor and duty but
doesn't really like getting his hands dirty."

God, the woman had his number down perfect. Hadn't
Rani been just as resentful of him that he wouldn't give
her what she wanted? Hadn't he tormented himself wondering if he should've just given in, even when he'd known
it would end in total disaster?

Was she right that he'd refused Rani because he hadn't
the emotional energy to love her as she needed to be loved?
Because he'd simply assumed that he knew better?

That this stranger could pierce him so easily, that she
challenged what he'd assumed was honor grated like the
scrape of nails. "You don't know what I can do for you,"
he said, his voice low and deep and far too commanding to
use on a woman he'd found in distress. A stranger, at that.

There was no doubt that he was temporarily out of his
mind.

And yet…she didn't look at him as if he was losing his
mind. As if he was being a creepy stranger hitting on the
woman he'd found in tears. As if his sudden demand for
her to let him in, to let him do something for her was anything but…utter madness.

"Ask me," he said, his blood full of a deafening hum,
his heart punching away at his rib cage as if it had just
stuttered back to glorious life.

"Anything?" she said sensually, turning toward him.

Simon cast one look at the closed door of the rehearsal
suite and nodded. Reaching for his hand, she laced her
fingers around his. Clinging to him, certainly but also
full of resolve. And then she dragged him after her—this

woman, this stranger he'd met no more than twenty minutes ago—and he followed.

He knew what she wanted. It was irresponsible and scandalous and reckless and… But it was also like coming awake after decades of slumber.

It was being alive for a moment in time, knowing that the future was nothing but a long stretch of emptiness and silence. Nothing but guilt and grief ravaging him. And Simon decided he wanted this moment. After three years of struggling with Rani's restlessness and disillusion with the life they'd built, after months of loneliness even when she was lying next to him, after the hollow powerlessness of not being able to give her what she demanded, this woman's naked desire for him was a soothing benediction he hadn't known he'd needed.

A stringent reminder of his own wants and needs.

A much-needed human connection.

He would indulge her and he would gorge himself by giving her whatever she wanted.

CHAPTER TWO

IT WAS NOTHING but sheer madness.

Her brothers were behind a closed door not a few hundred feet away. Her daughter…one she couldn't claim, one she couldn't hold and touch and love openly, not in this lifetime, was also behind that same door. The very thought threatened to bring Anya to her knees again.

And she was dragging a stranger—a man who'd shown her only kindness—along with her into all this crazy. This reckless woman wasn't her.

But if she didn't do this, if she didn't take what he offered, if she didn't grasp this thing between them and hold on to it, it felt like she'd stay on her knees, raging at a fate she couldn't change, forever… And Anya refused to be that woman anymore.

It was as if she was walking through one of those fantastical daydreams she still had sometimes when her anxiety became too much. The one where she just spun herself into an alternate world because in actual reality she was nothing but a coward.

Now, those realities were merging, and the possibility that she could be more than her grief and guilt and loss was the only thing that kept her standing upright. It took her a minute to find an empty suite, to turn the knob and then lock it behind them.

Silence and almost total darkness cloaked them. A sliver of light from the bathroom showed that it was another expansive suite, and they were standing in the entryway. Anya pressed herself against the door with the man facing her. The commanding bridge of his nose that seemed to slash through his face with perfect symmetry, the square jaw and the broad shoulders...the faint outline of his strong, masculine features guided her. But those eyes... wide and penetrating, full of an aching pain and naked desire that could span the width of an ocean...she couldn't see those properly anymore. Without meeting those eyes, she could pretend this was a simple case of lust.

Simon, she said in her mind, tasting his name there first...so tall and broad that even standing at five-ten, she felt so utterly encompassed by him.

Simon with the kind eyes and the tight mouth and a fleck of gray at his temples. And a banked desire he'd been determined to not let drive him.

But despite that obvious struggle, he was here with her. Ready to give her whatever she wanted from him.

What did she want? How far was she going to take this temporary madness?

His arm lifted, his hand moving toward the light switch next to her head. Anya captured it with her own and his big hand encompassed hers. The contact sent a jolt through her, the rough scrape of his palm, the tight grip of his fingers a lifeline she couldn't let go.

"Don't," she whispered, all her courage deserting her as fast as it had come, leaving her cold and shivering.

Her knees shook and he moved closer, his hands on her arms gently holding her up. "It's okay, Angel," he said, in that deep, bass voice that resonated through her body. "You're okay."

Anya bent her head and found his shoulder. Slowly, she

nuzzled her way across to his throat, and tried to breathe. His fingers instantly moved to her neck, wrapping around her nape, tethering her in the here and now, while she hyperventilated.

"I've never done anything like this before," she offered lamely. Letting the real world intrude in here too, allowing rationality and common sense and all kinds of noise back into her head. But none of those could save her from the pain. Nor even offer comfort. Only he could, only this could...

A bark of a laugh fell from his mouth—more self-deprecating than anything else. "And you still don't have to do anything you don't want to, Angel. Nothing matters other than this moment—not the past, not the future."

She breathed in deep and the most decadent scent— his skin and cologne—filled her lungs. That lick of desire flared again, cutting through the loop of thoughts her mind wanted to drown her in.

Awareness inched back into her body, his rock-hard thighs anchoring her when she let herself sway forward, the heat of his body cutting through the chill pervading her skin, the warmth of his breath coating her forehead, tickling the hairs at her temple...her body coming alive in a way she hadn't known in so long. "There's only now," she said, her resolve coming back.

The pad of his thumb found the sensitive hollow of her jaw below her ear. "Yes." One long finger pressed against her pulse, his touch shifting from tender and protective to something darker and demanding and...possessive. "Now, will you tell me what you truly want, Angel? We're alone in the dark and I have nothing to guide me but your words. Nothing to guide my actions but your wishes. There's no honor, no duty, no playing the hero. I'm here to do your bidding."

Heat flushed through every inch of Anya's skin at how easily he'd transformed from a kind stranger to this…seductive man. At the delicious promise in his words. At the easy way he'd made this all about her.

Lifting her head, she inched her hands toward him. They landed somewhere below his chest. Slowly, she sent them up his torso, loving the taut, muscular feel of him under her fingers, relishing the strong thud of his heart, and then she clasped her fingers at the nape of his neck.

The ends of his silky hair tickled the tips of her fingers. Stretching up on tiptoe, she leaned in until her mouth found his jaw—stubbled and rough and oh so delicious against her lips. "I want you. Everything you can give me, everything you want from me. I want us both satisfied and limp and incapable of thought."

"Everything I can give?"

"Yes, Simon."

She loved his name on her lips. She loved the sense of freedom it gave her, the curl of feminine power his groan sent through her lower belly as she articulated every dark thought that had bloomed into life the moment her eyes had met his. "I want to forget what I gave up. I want to forget how empty my life feels if I let that loss take over. I'm sure you think I'm being hysterical."

His hand covered her mouth. "I don't. The moment I looked into your eyes, the moment I saw your grief, I saw myself. I know exactly what you mean, Angel. I've mourned too."

Anya kissed his palm. "Then indulge us both. I want to feel alive. I want nothing but pleasure."

His mouth found hers with another searing groan.

A blinding wave of need blazed into life in every pore at the contact. All the scenarios she'd played out in her head in the span of a few seconds, all the suppositions and

assumptions she'd made about this sudden attraction…
everything turned to dust, everything left behind by the
instant, consuming heat of his touch.

Her body slammed into his. She moaned as her breasts,
already heavy and begging to be touched, flattened against
the hard breadth of his chest. His fingers around her neck
tightened as he nipped at her lower lip, demanding access.

Anya opened up obediently and then he was licking into
her mouth with a demanding eagerness that dialed up her
own hunger. They kissed as if this was their last kiss, not
their first. As if they already knew each other's darkest
desires. As if they knew how to give what the other needed
and demanded without restraint or shame.

His other palm kneaded her hip, pressing long fingers
into her willing flesh. Then he moved them up her sides,
stroking, learning, tracing, inflaming her while his mouth
soothed and licked and laved.

When he left her mouth for a much-needed breath, Anya
sank her fingers into his hair and pulled him back. Out of
pure, clawing instinct to be closer to him, she lifted her leg
and wrapped it around his hip. His hand was at her thigh
instantly, holding her up, and then he brought his lower
body against hers. Her sex clenched deep and hard at the
flutter of his fingers at her inner thigh.

The urgent press of his erection against her groin made
a curse rip out of her mouth so filthy that Anya saw the
flash of his white grin in the darkness. So full of wicked
want that she thrust up against him in a mindless search
for more. It was as instinctual as breathing, this need to
rile him up into the same frenzy, to drive him toward the
edge where she was ready to free-fall. The next time her
hips met his, she stayed there, relishing the hard length of

him against her lower belly, reveling in the raw proof of what she did to him.

It was his turn to color the air around them and he did it in such explicit detail that Anya blushed far more than from anything they'd done so far.

Her back slammed into the door behind her but somehow he had his palm pressed up between the door and her back before she could be hurt. He was everywhere—in her mouth, on her skin, curling into a deep want in her very muscles.

"I can keep kissing you like this until the night comes to an end," he said, licking a languorous path over the shell of her ear, kissing his way across her jaw to her mouth, every hard contour of his body pressed up against her.

"More. I need more."

She felt his smile against her mouth and it was the most sensuous thing Anya had ever experienced. Dampness gushed between her thighs and she moaned, wanting his fingers there. Wanting whatever he'd give her there.

He pulled away from her, the rhythm of his breaths shallow. "I found you falling apart not that long ago. I don't want to take advantage of you, Angel."

"I thought you weren't playing the knight anymore."

His mouth quirked up on one side, his fingers tracing her sensitive lips. "It's called simple decency."

"And if I tell you that I need this? That I don't want the past to be the only thing that defines me, that I'm making my pleasure a choice? You could leave me feeling worse than before." She lifted his hand to her mouth and kissed the rough palm. Then she brought it down her neck to her breast. "Or you could see this all the way through," she said, pure resolve and naked need in her tone.

His fingers cupped her breast, kneading, teasing, making her breath come in short pants. She arched into his touch, her spine all but melted desire. "As you promised."

"I will stop the moment you change your mind."

"Don't stop, Simon."

"As you wish, Angel."

The pop-pop of her buttons as he ripped more than a couple made her shiver with anticipation. Clever fingers pulled down the flimsy lacy cup of her bra and then his bare hand covered her breast. "Protection," he whispered, even as his fingers drew mindless circles around the taut nipple begging for his attention.

"Condom in my bag," she murmured, writhing against his clever fingers, a damp flush coating her skin. Moaning, she arched into his touch. "More."

That's all she had to say. In the next breath, his mouth was at her breast.

Anya let out a long, deep groan that seemed to be ripped from the depths of her as he played with her nipple using the tip of his tongue and then drew it into his mouth.

On and on, switching between both breasts, until she was writhing against his body, and crying out. "I won't be of any use to you if you continue like this," she warned, her voice ragged.

He took her mouth in a slow, soft kiss this time, his hands deserting her breasts to move down. His fingers fluttered over the small curve of her belly to the seam of her denim shorts. "That's the point of this. I don't want you to do anything but enjoy this. All I want is for you to tell me what you want."

"I want it all," Anya said, hiding her face in the warm crook of his neck.

His fingers undid the button and the zipper of her shorts and then slowly, oh so slowly that she could hear the roar of her heart in her ears, he sneaked them in. Ever so gently, he traced the lips of her sex.

Anya licked the hollow of his throat, and nipped at his skin, begging silently with her own caresses.

And then his tongue thrust into her mouth in an erotic kiss as he drew her shorts and panties down her hips. They dropped to her ankles and she carefully stepped out of them. "Damn, you're wet for me."

Anya flushed, loving the rough texture of his words even more than the smooth caresses of his fingers, learning every inch of her sex. "Widen your legs," he whispered at her ear and she did. "More?"

"God, yes."

One long finger thrust into her and then two all the while his thumb played at her sensitive bud. Anya banged her head against the door, release hovering at the edge of her skin, shimmering just out of reach.

She had been here at this point, so many times, frustrated beyond measure at not pushing off, her body so desperately craving the release. She'd stopped trying when she'd realized she needed a sense of intimacy with someone else in order to climax but that was the very thing that scared her. And now...now she was here with Simon and all she wanted was to lose herself in the pleasure he was giving her.

She thrust her hips in tune to his fingers' play, chasing them mindlessly but her climax stayed out of her reach, sending frustrated tears to the back of her eyes.

A groan left her mouth as the peak started slipping away.

His lips were at her temple, instantly soothing, brushing so gently that she wanted to burrow into him. "Shh... Angel, it's okay." He flicked at the damp tendrils sticking to her forehead, his breath ghosting over her skin like a cool caress. "What do you need? Whatever you need…it's yours." He didn't say it arrogantly, but with such a stark promise in his voice that Anya opened her eyes.

The darkness was no barrier with the way he looked at her, the way he devoured every nuance of her expression.

"I don't know," she whispered, shedding the last layer of vulnerability, stripping herself completely bare.

No one had seen her like this. No one had ever known her like this. There was strength and power and a bone-deep pleasure in giving this to him in a corner of darkness, this man who'd seen her at her lowest and cared enough to stay. When he simply stared at her with that infinite patience he seemed to have, she bit her lip. "I don't… I don't have a lot of experience with men. Or achieving orgasms."

He licked the tip of her mouth, a wink and a smile flashing at her. The smile was wide and wicked, and Anya had never thought a smile could taste like such pure acceptance and unfettered joy.

Counterpoint to that smile, his finger curled deep inside her, hitting a point so deep and pleasurable that she cried out in ecstasy. It was unlike anything she'd felt before, the barrage of pressure and pleasure that coiled there. "That's not a problem." His mouth was against hers again, lazily sipping, licking, his other hand stroking over her neck. "Because it means we get to try so many things. Where are you most sensitive?"

Anya cupped her breasts even as fiery heat coated her cheeks at the dark satisfaction in his eyes. But there was no space for modesty or shyness here, no space for shame. Only pleasure.

"Ahh…my favorite too," he said with a roguish smile and then his mouth fluttered down from her pulse, nipping the slope of her breast so that the tiny bite of pain made the pleasure of his fingers moving inside her that much sharper and delicious and then his tongue was at her nipple again.

"I love how lushly you fit in my palms, how wet you are for me," he said, between licks and nibbles as if she were his favorite sweet. In the dark, Anya saw his wicked eyes glint with satisfaction as he licked his finger. "How sweet you taste to me, Angel. I feel like a randy teenager just imagining how good you'll feel around my shaft... how hungrily you will swallow me whole."

"More words," she said, leaning into him and stretching her thigh higher so that he could go deeper. The ache was building again, faster and more powerful, threatening to shatter her. For the first time in her life, Anya was not afraid. All she wanted was to fragment, to forget, to fly in this moment, be free of the past and the future. "Please, Simon," she whispered, burying her face in his neck and pressing her open mouth against his skin. He tasted like salt and soap and something woodsy and she wanted to devour him whole.

"I love how you reached for this...for me when you could've simply walked away. I love how you dared me to give you what you want. I love how you pushed me to have this, Angel, have you."

Anya's fingers reached his groin and he let out a deep groan as she traced the outline of his erection with her fingers. But he didn't stop the torment of his fingers or his mouth, building her climb all over again. So well that she was panting when she said, "I want you inside me when I..." Her breath shuddered in and out as once again her release fluttered closer. "Please. This whole thing will shatter once I climax. The real world will intrude...and I'll run away. From you. From myself. I... I need this. I need you inside me. Now."

"Are you sure, Angel?" he asked seriously.

"God, yes. More than anything," Anya answered and with steady fingers, slowly, undid his trousers.

Somehow, they managed to find the condom in her bag. She heard the sound of the package tearing, saw him roll it up his length and then he was kissing her again. With such gentle reverence that she knew she wouldn't forget it for years.

"Tell me one last time what you're thinking," she demanded. "Tell me."

One hand cupped her hip and jerked her away from the main door of the suite toward the wall. Anya flushed, knowing that he was the only one thinking rationally here. And she liked it. She liked being the wild one, the aggressor, the one who took risks and pursued her pleasure boldly. The one who wasn't afraid to trust him and herself, for once.

"I'm thinking this is the most irresponsible thing I've ever done in my life." A hard kiss to her mouth. "It's also the most alive I've felt in years. You're like a sweet benediction from heaven, an earthly reminder that I'm not dead inside." His fingers at her inner thigh opened her indecently wide. "And I'm never going to live like this again."

Anya felt the head of his erection flicking against her core, and she gasped anew. Sensation zinged and pooled in her lower belly, her entire being stretched taut at the cusp of explosion. The dark was a cover for things she wouldn't have dared ask for in daylight, but the dark also converged every ounce of her being at her sex, damp and ready for him.

"I'm thinking," he continued, feeding himself into her wet heat, inch by tormenting inch, his words a raw whisper at her temple, "that I'll never have another encounter like this." Anya buried her face into his neck at the sharp sting of his invasion. His long fingers on her buttocks, he stilled and waited until she urged him on with a hard kiss. "That I needed this more than I could ever put into words." His voice sounded rough and guttural as he thrust in a little more. "That I'll never meet another woman like you, someone who'll make me this insane." They both groaned when he was lodged all the way inside her. "Someone who'll make me glad that I gave in to temptation for one magical instant."

Hands clenching his rock-hard shoulders, Anya breathed in shallow gasps. Not her imagination, not the one encounter she'd had with Meera's father all of fourteen years ago, nothing had prepared her for the achy fullness that filled her body or the desperate need for release. Her thigh muscles ached at how wide his hips pushed them, her arms burned at how hard she clung to him and that made the pleasure of him inside her that much sweeter.

"You okay, Angel?" he asked, his voice so deep and hoarse that she adored it.

The sharp sting was already receding, and Anya jerked her hips experimentally.

Simon's fingers tightened on her hips, his ragged exhale coating her jaw.

"If it hurts, tell me. We can stop. Now."

She shook her head and searched for his mouth in the darkness. His lips were sweet and soft when she found him. His kiss possessive and alternating with sexy little nips of his teeth. "No...you just...you feel like you're lodged here," she said, dragging his palm to her breast. "I... I'm so very glad to have met you, Simon." He did something with his hips—a swivel and a thrust that made her head bang against the wall, her eyes roll into the back of her head. "And not just because you can do that," she said, giggling.

"I love tasting your smile, Angel," he whispered, mirroring her very thoughts. His hips retreated a fraction before he was pinning hers to the wall again. Anya huffed out a shallow breath, her spine melting. "Now hold on to me, yeah?"

"God, yes."

And then he was thrusting into her hard and fast, while his thumb stubbornly stayed at her clit, applying counter-pressure. His mouth was at her neck, his teeth dragging over the sensitive skin there and it was all too much. Anya wrapped her hands around his shoulders and just hung on.

Each thrust against the wall rattled some picture frames she couldn't even see and it only added to the symphony of sounds they made together. He drove her higher and higher, the pressure in her belly tightening.

"You feel amazing, Angel," he groaned, and she swore that with each movement of his body he hit every single pleasure point in hers as if he could weave magic.

Head bowed against his shoulder, Anya came in a sudden rush of such pulsating pleasure that she let out a keening cry. He took that into himself, soothing her and kissing her even as he ravaged her and Anya had never been more aware of, or more in love with her own body than at the moment.

Now that it gave him such pleasure, now that he held it with such reverence. Now that it could send his powerful body shuddering as release crashed into him. His broad shoulders shook as he came with a final thrust that pinioned his hips to hers, his fingers digging into her hips.

Anya hung on, for what felt like eternity, her face buried in his shoulder. But it could have been no more than a few breaths.

"Are you all right?" he asked, his exhale playing with the damp tendrils of her hair sticking to her temples. His chest rose and fell against her, his muscles around her still shuddering from his release.

She nodded, unable to conjure words.

"I'm going to—" she looked up, and his gaze met hers, steady and reassuring even in the dark that surrounded them "—set you to rights, okay? I need to leave soon but we can stay here, like this, for a little longer." He traced the edge of her mouth with a thumb. "Yes, Angel?"

His tenderness threatened to tear her apart. She didn't want him to leave. She wanted to stay in this darkness with him, breathing in the scent of their sex in the air, cocooned in the warmth and secure embrace of his body. "I'm fine," she said, finally. "Do you mind if I leave first? Like I said, I don't want to be found on this floor."

He acknowledged her request with a nod. Slowly, he released his hold on her, his hand moving away from her thigh. When he pulled out of her, Anya drew in a sharp breath at the slight sting. But it had nothing on the emptiness she felt.

He noted her discomfort, this man who seemed to miss nothing, planted a soft kiss on her lips and then righted her clothes with a gentleness that made tears pound at the back of her throat. When he released her from the fortress of the wall and his body, she swayed, her thighs trembling. Instantly, he pulled her toward him until she was leaning into him again.

"I've got you," he said, his hand on her back, his tone tender.

Time passed too swiftly then, and Anya knew she'd get into real trouble—the kind of fuss that her older brothers specialized in—if she didn't get away now. One look at her and they would know everything that had just happened—both the grief that was already inching its way back around her heart and the thoroughly reckless but desperately needed pleasure she'd just indulged in.

With a stranger at that.

With the entire production team two doors away.

She pushed out of his hold and he immediately let her go. Her knuckles tightened around the strap of her bag as if it could somehow steady her fluctuating emotions. Hand on the doorknob, she turned toward him and pressed a soft kiss to his jaw. The stubble tingled her already sensitive lips. "Thank you, Simon, for giving me what I needed. For seeing the real me. I'll never forget…tonight," she amended at the last minute.

And then she was walking through the corridor, into the lift and jumping into a taxi without looking back. She trembled all the way home but there was not a ray of regret inside her for what had happened. Her body ached in a way she wanted to cherish and her smile lingered for a long time even after she let herself into her flat.

Even after she sank into her sheets without having showered, because she wanted to smell Simon and his masculine scent all over her skin for a few more hours.

Today, she'd lived a little.

Today, she'd carved a moment's happiness for herself.

Today, she'd trusted herself and the universe and she vowed to try to be a little braver every day.

CHAPTER THREE

ANYA HID OVER the next three days.

Not licking her wounds in private so much as bracing herself for the next time she'd run into…her daughter. The next time when she couldn't simply run away, but would have to chat with her as if she were any other actress for whom Anya was designing a wardrobe.

For a hot minute, she considered telling her brother Virat that she had to drop out of this project. He wouldn't like it one bit—his creative vision and hers clicked so well usually—but he'd respect her wishes.

But for one thing, it would bring all of her family's scrutiny down on her head. Despite the passive-aggressive dynamics of her brothers' relationship with their parents, in this one thing, they all seemed to agree unanimously. That Anya must be protected, even if it meant invading her privacy and trashing the boundaries she'd tried very hard to set with her interfering family.

And for another thing, how long would she hide? What if Meera became a staple of the industry? How could she bear to lose the little time she had to get to know the girl who held a piece of her heart?

The fourth evening, she arrived at the bungalow that had once belonged to her grandparents. Now it was the home of her brother Virat and his wife Zara, where Zara was throwing a small, intimate party.

She'd show her face, play with her toddler nephew and her infant niece, chat with her other sister-in-law, Naina, about the screenplay she was working on, smile at her parents, hug her brothers and leave.

The first half hour of the party, Anya did just that—she caught up with her family and the four close friends Zara had invited. She was even proud of herself—showing her face in polite society as if she were a normally functioning adult, when two unprecedented things had taken place not four days ago in her life.

The last time something like that had happened she'd fallen pregnant at eighteen by a man nine years older than her—a fortune hunter who'd specifically targeted her and then left her when he'd realized he wasn't going to get a slice of the Raawal pie—and she'd retreated into her shell for the next few years. Of course, giving birth, almost dying and then giving up her baby girl had been the most traumatic experiences of her life.

But after the thoroughly scandalous episode she'd indulged in, she felt as if she had finally wrested back some control over her own life. She even felt a little hopeful for her own future.

Lounging on the divan, Anya was laughing at something Vikram and his wife, Naina, said when Meera walked into the sitting lounge.

Dressed in a cotton crop top and high-waisted jeans, her smile so broad that it hurt Anya to look at the girl's face, Meera was palpably excited as she waved at everyone.

Fisting her hands at her sides, Anya fought the urge to run away again. A fake smile pasted to her lips, she forced herself to draw breaths in, counting them in her head. She almost had it together when a dark figure, so broad and tall that Anya blinked, materialized behind Meera.

It was *him*...the stranger who'd given her a slice of paradise.

Who'd belonged to her for a tiny blink of time.

Simon...was here at Zara's party. And he was clearly with Meera.

Why?

A deafening silence descended in her ears, her heart beating a frantic tattoo as Zara walked up to greet Meera and Simon. Through it all, Anya could hear the girl's voice chattering away excitedly.

Papa...she was calling him Papa. Meera was calling him Papa...

The man Anya had had sex with under the cover of darkness, the man she'd poured her heart out to was... Meera's father.

Her baby girl's adoptive father.

God, how had she let this happen? Why was the universe trying to destroy her again?

Anya shot up from the divan, adrenaline pounding through her making flight the only choice left to her. Just as the two of them accompanied by Zara reached her.

"I can't tell you how excited I am to finally meet you, Ms. Raawal," Meera said and Anya stared at her animated face, her throat so tight that it hurt to swallow. "Zara di said you'd come in during the rehearsal, but I must have missed you. I can't tell you what a fan I am of your latest line of clothes for teens." She tugged at the seam of the jeans she was wearing, rocking on the balls of her feet. "Do you know how impossible it usually is for me to find jeans that fit me so well? Just because I'm tall and curvy and..."

"Give Ms. Raawal a chance to respond, Meera," said a

deep voice behind the girl. The voice that had whispered the filthiest things in her ear four nights ago.

Heat swarming her cheeks, Anya found her gaze colliding with his. He knew her identity but he didn't reveal it even by the blink of an eyelid.

She should be thankful. She was thankful. But the spiral of her thoughts wouldn't cease… What did he think of her? Would he forbid her from seeing even the little of Meera that she'd hoped for? Would he think her a bad influence?

"I'm Meera De Acosta… Well, Meera Verma for the industry," the girl said, puncturing Anya's spiral. "I'm the daughter of…"

"Rani Verma, I know," Anya said, through numb lips. "I'm excited to meet you too, Ms. Verma. My brother's been singing high praises of you."

"Please, call me Meera. Especially since you're going to create my wardrobe for the movie and I'm going to pester you a lot."

Anya smiled, despite the spectacular spiral her life was going into. It was impossible to stay unmoved with the girl's adorable smile and easy excitement coming at her in overwhelming waves.

"This is my dad, Simon," Meera said, shifting to the side.

"It's nice to meet you, Ms. Raawal." He sounded as if they'd just met.

She should follow his lead and simply pretend too. Act like it hadn't been a big deal. After all, she was an adult and she hadn't done anything wrong.

But all her warnings and reassurances didn't help.

She stared at his hand stretched out between hers, long fingers with bluntly trimmed nails. Corded wrist with hair sprinkled. That hand had touched her everywhere. Those fingers had pleasured her so intimately. Those powerful thighs had held her against the wall while he... God!

She'd had sex with her daughter's father, had ruined any chances she might have had of being in Meera's life—even temporarily. It was a twist worthy of one of Vikram's blockbuster movies that Virat teased him about so mercilessly.

"Anya?" She heard Zara's voice as if it was coming from far away.

Her vision swam and her breath felt choppy. But before she hit the floor, Simon was there. With his broad shoulders, and concerned eyes, and strong hands holding her tightly.

Their eyes met and Anya saw his concern and his questions.

"I'm okay," she whispered, loath to draw anyone else's attention. Especially her brothers'. "I just need some air."

He nodded and let her go. But not before his jaw hardened and he whispered back, "We're going to talk soon, *Angel*."

This wasn't the kind stranger or the seductive lover. This was a different man—more demanding, terse, even.

Anya pasted a smile onto her lips and turned to Meera. "I'm feeling a little unwell this evening, that's all," she offered, tears prickling at the back of her eyes.

Glad that she'd kept her composure, she walked away. And didn't miss the sensation of Simon's gaze on her back determined to probe to the depths of her soul.

Straightening her spine, Anya made the decision at that moment that she would tell him about Meera. She'd had enough of the damned universe playing games with her.

She was going to tell Simon the truth—for no other reason than that he deserved to know. And because Anya wanted to trust him with the secret she didn't want to carry around alone any longer.

Simon found her on the terrace, her body limned by the moonlight, a couple of hours later. It was ridiculous that he'd spent the last hour chasing her shadow in every corner and nook of the expansive bungalow.

It was ridiculous that he'd barely exchanged any more than cursory greetings with the Raawal brothers—his entire reason for attending this dinner.

It was ridiculous that he was so concerned about her, a stranger no less, about the stark shock in her eyes when she'd spied him, that he hadn't been able to think of anything else. Ridiculous that he'd left his daughter in the company of Zara and lied that he needed fresh air. Not that Zara had believed it.

But he wanted to talk to his Angel.

Ms. Anya Raawal, he corrected in his head. He'd simply reassure her that he didn't mean her any kind of harm. Make it clear that he had no wish to continue their association. It was a few moments of madness—done with and never to be repeated again. His steps made no sound on the smooth marble floor, but he saw her shoulders tense.

She turned around, her motions jerky, her eyes red rimmed but steadily gazing back at him.

"Are you feeling better now?" he asked, stopping a few feet from her, loathing the very idea of spooking her.

She stared at him, aghast, before she attempted a smile. But he could tell it didn't reach her eyes. It didn't make them sparkle. It didn't remove the stress lines etched around her mouth. "You have to stop asking me that, Simon. Stop…showing me that concern of yours."

"I will, Ms. Raawal," he said formally, and saw her eyes widen. "As soon as you tell me what's wrong with you."

She would say she was fine, and he would nod and that would be that. But she didn't say anything. The silence went on and on, picking up more and more weight until it was nearly unbearable.

For the first time since he'd walked in and seen her, he put his shock and other inconvenient emotions that had been plaguing him aside. Tried to look at the puzzle that was Anya Raawal objectively.

It couldn't be seeing him again that had caused her such shock. When he'd caught sight of her, she'd been sitting on the divan. Her legs folded under her, laughing openly with her family. He hadn't been able to look away. And so he'd seen the laughter turn to shock when she'd spotted Meera. But it was only when she'd seen him behind Meera that it had turned to panic. Just like that day at the hotel.

So what had spooked her then? Again?

"Did someone try to harm you at the hotel? Is that person here today too?"

She didn't laugh at his dramatic conjecture. Her eyes improbably wide, her skin stretched tightly over her cheekbones, she said, "No. Nothing like that."

"Then what is it, Angel?" he said, his words more demanding than they had any right to be. "What keeps sending you into such stark panic? Have you told anyone about it?"

Her chin lifted. "No. Because it's no one else's business but mine," she said with a thread of steel he hadn't heard before.

So there was something then.

He should walk away, his gut said. Leave her to her mysterious problem. It was none of his concern. Nothing could come of further entangling himself with her. Especially now that he knew that she was not some nobody who would disappear into the night as she'd hinted. Now that he knew she was a mainstay of the industry with all her connections and her successful career.

She was Anya Raawal, the sister of the powerful and, by her own admission, overly protective Raawal brothers. She was also fragile and far too young for him.

One scandalous escapade—one forbidden encounter—was more than enough.

And yet, Simon stood there, caught between his usual common sense and the utter irrationality of wanting to be near her. Of wanting to figure her out. Of wanting to help her. "Not even your brothers?" he taunted.

"Especially not them," she said with just as much vehemence.

He moved toward her, giving her enough time to slip away.

Her fingers tightened over the sill behind her, her face turning up toward him in challenge.

He reached her but didn't touch her. Just being near her, breathing in the scent of her made his skin hum. He knew she felt the instant pull too in how her eyes widened. The madness that was already beginning to demand that he taste her lips just once more. "What did you give up all those years ago?"

"Who were you mourning?" she demanded, tilting her head up to look at him, baring that neck that he wanted to kiss all over again.

"Rani, my wife. She died in a car accident eighteen months ago," he said softly. His guilt dulled right now by the puzzle he was trying to solve. By this woman who upended his thoughts and emotions with her mere presence. "Now you answer my question, Angel. What did you give up?"

Tears pooled in her big eyes and her mouth trembled. "You're not going to like it."

"But you want to tell me," he said, going all in on instinct. He could see it in her face now—this had something to do with him. The inevitability of it had been written on her face the moment she'd seen him tonight and lost all color in her face.

A sudden dread twisted his gut when she didn't deny it. He was about to back off, about to walk away from this woman who'd already made him behave so unlike himself when she looked up at him.

A lone tear fell down her cheek and she wiped it away roughly. "I gave up my baby girl thirteen years ago. I…" She took a deep breath, somehow containing the huge sob that threatened to tear her apart. "I never imagined I'd see her again. I…didn't even realize until I saw her four days ago that she still holds a piece of my heart. That I've been carrying around this love for her here—" she pressed a hand to her chest "—that would create a void in my very life."

Her grief and revelation came at him like a punch to his throat. He stepped back, his thoughts an incoherent, terrified jumble. "You saw Meera at the rehearsal."

She nodded, her chest heaving out a shuddering breath, but not crying. "I did. That mark she has through her left eyebrow… I'd know her in my sleep. I held her for a while before they took her away."

Simon took another step back, feeling as if the ground was being ripped from under him. "Did you know who I was? Did you know she's my daughter?" he demanded in a cold voice that was so unlike him that he hated it.

Her flinch told him how outlandish his accusation was. How much of a lie it made of everything they had shared. A desperate curse flew from his mouth and he thrust a hand through his hair. "Sorry." He kicked a pillar like a youth trying to work his temper out. "God, I'm so sorry. Of course you didn't know. That's why you looked as if you'd been kicked in the gut when we walked in together earlier."

Damn it, he should've never returned here with Meera. Never taken the chance on someone knowing her. But Rani had been the one who'd arranged everything with the adoption and he hadn't minded as long as she was happy. As long as they had a child to love.

A teen pregnancy, that's all they'd been told. A teen... He turned around, seeing the woman he'd thought so fragile, anew. "You...you had to have been so young."

"I was barely eighteen when I gave birth."

It hit him square in his gut. God, she'd been just a few years older than Meera now when she'd gotten pregnant, no more than a girl herself. He couldn't even imagine what it would have been like to be pregnant at that age. The man who was responsible... Every protective instinct in him roared at the very thought of a man who'd take advantage of a teenager.

"What happened to the man who fathered Meera?"

"He was a fortune hunter out for what he could get. He was nine years older than me, and he lavished me with attention I was desperate for. You see, I'd always had anxiety—even as a child—and it grew worse in my teens. The public nature of my parents' marriage, the constant media attention, the articles and interviews wondering if I was the talentless hack of the family...it made me such a ripe target for him. All he had to do was whisper a few empty promises and I gave myself over."

"He was a predator then. And no one can blame you for his actions. Not even yourself."

Something flickered in her eyes, making Simon want to pull her into his arms. Hold her again. Instead, he waited in silence, knowing she wanted to say more, holding the space for what had to be painful recollection.

"By the time I was ready to give birth, my mental health was at its worst. Not to mention I was anemic and far too thin. I couldn't trust my parents to keep my stuffed teddy bear safe let alone a baby," she said with no rancor, "Vikram was working night and day trying to dig us out of a financial pit and keep Virat from spiraling out of control, and my grandmother…she had her hands full keeping me alive and sane. I… I fought it so much back then but I'd have harmed Meera more if I'd kept her. I wasn't fit to be a parent."

"You don't owe me or anyone else an explanation, Anya. Not for taking such a hard decision at such a young age."

"I want you to know that I gave her up because I wanted a better life for her," she said, her expression painfully earnest. "Not because I didn't love her."

Simon nodded, swallowing the ache her confession had lodged in his own throat. But whatever she'd gone through—however terrible it had been, it was in the past. As clinical and awful as it sounded in his mind, it wasn't his problem. Anya…and her grief weren't his to handle. Not that he'd proved himself any good at that when it had come to his wife.

He was only responsible for Meera and her well-being, thank God. Not this fierce but fragile woman.

"That choice meant she became our daughter, mine and Rani's," he said, without tempering the possessive claim in his voice. Without looking at the woman who seemed to wear her heart in her eyes. And in doing so weakened his resolve. "Rani adored Meera and gave up so much for her. Meera's her daughter, even more so than mine, I think."

"Of course she is," came Anya's voice, resolute and composed. "I didn't question that, not for a second."

Simon jerked his head around. But there was only calm

acceptance in her eyes. Something about it steadied his own racing heartbeat.

He studied her—the composure she'd gained, the calm demeanor—and marveled at the strength of her. And yet, her grief was like a crackle of charge in the air, a shield she used to keep everyone out. He knew, without doubt, that she hadn't shared the news of her discovery with another soul. Not her brothers, not her sisters-in-law, not a friend.

And yet she'd told him.

Perversely, the trust she'd showed in him made his voice sharp as he said, "What do you want from me, Ms. Raawal?"

If she was hurt by how formal and terse he suddenly sounded, she didn't show it. He was beginning to realize that he had been a temporary escape for her, yes. But nothing more. Her attraction to him and everything that had followed between them meant very little in the bigger scheme of things like discovering the baby she'd given up.

As it should be.

"Nothing. I want nothing. Meera's adorable and funny and talented and well-adjusted and happy and above all, she's your daughter. I would never do anything to jeopardize her happiness, her sense of security. Ever."

He nodded, amazed by the strength of her will, by the grace with which she'd pulled herself together. "But? Because I'm sensing one," he said, a thread of anger in his tone.

But it was at himself, not her.

Was he already infatuated with this woman? Was it because he'd had sex with her, broken his years of celibacy with her that he was so tuned into her? Was it that for the first time in years his emotions were so sensitive to a particular woman's? Was it because she'd made him feel alive like no one else had in such a very long time?

Rani had always teased him that he was oblivious to all the emotional undercurrents in a room, that it took an elephant stomping around for him to realize that something was wrong. And yet, with this woman, he sensed and understood every nuance of emotion, every rise and dip of her mood. Worse, he was left only to admire her.

"I didn't plan for any of this," she said, a hint of steel creeping into her own tone now. "I didn't sit down and think... Gee, what am I going to do if I run into the precious baby I gave up thirteen years ago? Will I just idly stand by and watch her walk around without knowing who I am to her? Or hmm...will I mess everything up further by having wild, against-the-wall sex with her hot silver fox dad? Hmm...let's go with the second option because my life isn't exciting enough." Her chest was rising and falling by the time she finished her tirade, her beautiful brown eyes blazing with temper.

Simon laughed. So loudly that a couple of birds resting on the sill flew away.

She stared, stunned.

"Hot silver fox dad?" He'd never been able to flirt in his entire life and yet, that's what came out.

Her cheeks pink, Anya scowled at him. "I'm glad one of us finds this funny," she said with a sudden primness that he wanted to unravel all over again. Then she sighed. "You have to believe me that I didn't..."

"Don't, Anya," he said, her name falling off his lips so easily. Just once more, he promised himself, liking the taste of it on his tongue. "You don't have to apologize. Not to me or anyone." He thrust a hand through his hair, still feeling out of balance. "Neither do I forget for a single second how hard this must be for you. But damn it..."

"Can I ask you for just...one thing?" she said softly.

Simon nodded, knowing that he would agree to the

most outrageous demand of hers if she looked at him like that with those big brown eyes and that ridiculously wide mouth and that earnest and somehow fierce expression.

"Please...don't change your plans because of me. Don't take her away from here because I'm here too. Don't let what happened between us...change your mind. All I want is to—" she looked up, as if the sky held all the answers "—to just see her for the few months of the shoot. I... I'd be content to just see her around the production schedule. I'm already..." Her throat bobbed up and down as she swallowed. "I'm so relieved and happy that she's been so well loved. I couldn't have asked for a better home for her. It's the one thing that makes all of the pain worth it."

"Meera's well-being matters more than anything to me." It was a reminder to him as much as it was for her. "I wasn't happy with her being here in the first place," he said, even though he hadn't decided to confide in her. "I... I don't like how this industry will prey on someone weak or young or innocent given a single chance."

"I'll keep an eye on her," she said, color blooming in her wan cheeks. "Without betraying who I am to her, I promise. My brother's production team is the safest place for her and I'm already on-site for the next few months as the costume designer. No one will question my presence around her. If it helps, you can even tell... Meera that you've asked me to keep an eye on her. That way, we're not deceiving her about my interest in her."

"Isn't that an added burden for you?"

She shook her head. "I'd have offered to do that for any young girl that came into the industry if I could. I was taken advantage of in my teens, remember. And that was despite my keeping a mostly low profile. Vikram regrets it to this day that he wasn't able to protect me better. Standing on the other side today, I can understand his pain after all these years."

Look at the two of them, being all adult and responsible and polite about this...

Simon wanted to believe it could stay mess free like this. That it wouldn't get all tangled in emotions. That this damned attraction between them, the intimacy they'd already shared wouldn't muck up everything again.

He gave her a nod and turned to go. Almost at the door that opened into the stairway, he said, "Why did you tell me?"

"What do you mean?"

"One would think I'm the last person you'd tell that you're the biological mother of my child. So why did you do it then?"

"I told you, I didn't plan for any of this."

As she walked toward him, Simon couldn't help but note the grace with which she moved, the core of steel beneath those tears and that panic. Beneath the fragile air that surrounded her, there was so much more to this woman. And that strength teased and tugged at him.

"Why shouldn't I tell you? This is your daughter I'm talking about. After that night, I feel as if..."

"It was just sex, Ms. Raawal," he said, infusing every ounce of remoteness he could manage into his words. "Damned good sex but that's all it was."

She tilted her chin. "I know that. But you were kind to me. That means whether you like it or not, I trust you. And I'd never do anything to hurt Meera. Or you."

That she added him in that vow made a pulse of emotions spear through him. When he just stared at her, she snapped, "Is there a reason you came after me tonight? The stranger you took against a wall in the darkness?"

Satisfaction glinted in her eyes at his continued silence.

Their non-answer hung between them, more powerful than any words could conjure. "Maybe that's the very reason I couldn't keep it a secret from you. It felt like…playing games. I hate playing games with anyone's feelings. Especially when the stakes are this high." She rubbed a hand over her face, her jaw tight. "And God, I'm so tired of fate screwing me over. Again and again. This time, I'm going to drive this, not chance, not fate, not the past."

She walked past him, her head held high, leaving the scent of her skin lodged in his nostrils, and in his very lungs. And as much as he wanted to deny it, Simon knew he would never be able to think of her simply as the woman he'd had sex with in one moment of madness. Nor simply as the woman who'd given birth to Meera.

She was so much more than the sum of those things.

But he admired her too much already. For any of this to remain as uncomplicated as they both wished, he had no choice but to stay away from the woman. As much as was humanly possible.

CHAPTER FOUR

"YOU DON'T LIKE my dad, do you?" asked Meera softly, panting while she walked fast on the treadmill.

The nib of Anya's pencil broke with a sharp click at Meera's sudden question. Anya took her time putting the pencil down and closing her sketchbook before she looked up at the chatty teenager.

Simon's matter-of-fact instructions to Meera that Anya was her unofficial companion when he wasn't around had been met with delight by the teenager. For some reason Anya didn't understand and could only marvel at, Meera considered Anya cool. In the last few days, Meera had thrown innumerable questions at Anya—about the Raawals, their stature in the industry, Anya's connections, her friends, her hobbies and which Bollywood star she currently had a crush on.

Anya had started showing up at the luxury hotel every morning, content to work on her sketches and designs while Meera finished her lessons in swordplay, archery and then wrapped up the rehearsals. If Virat thought it strange that Anya, who usually always preferred to work by herself until her sketches were ready for his input, was showing up at the preproduction every day, he didn't ask her any questions.

Despite her resolution that she'd see this time with her

daughter as a gift and not get too attached, Anya knew she was more than halfway in love with the girl. There was something incredibly brave about Meera, much like the warrior queen she was playing in the movie. She seemed to breeze through life, informed about most things and intent on learning the rest.

Every day when their work ended, they'd eat while discussing any suggestions Meera had received from Virat, then she'd work out for about an hour. While her brother hadn't asked that Meera lose weight—Anya and Zara and Naina would have slaughtered him if he'd dared—he did want her to tone up to make the athletic swordplay and the fight scenes as authentic as possible.

If Meera's unending enthusiasm occupied Anya's day, thoughts about her dad consumed Anya's nights. If Simon's studious avoidance of her was anything to go by, he had no such problems.

"If it takes you this long to answer me, maybe I'm wrong and you do like him," Meera said, pulling Anya back to the present. Her hair pulled away from her plump face, the dim light in the gym casting half of it in shadows, she looked so much like Anya's mother, Bollywood's yesteryear superstar Vandana Raawal, that her breath caught in her throat.

"I don't know him well enough to like him or not like him," Anya said, courting diplomacy.

"It's just that," Meera said, huffing, "I've noticed that you…get very tense every time he comes around to pick me up. And Dad hasn't been himself lately so if he's said anything to upset you—"

A fierce heat claimed her cheeks. "Your dad and I hardly talk for him to offend me in any way."

"He doesn't like me being here—you know…getting into acting, I mean," Meera continued, thankfully ignorant of Anya's blush. "So if he did say anything to you about the Raawal House of Cinema or the movie industry, please don't take it personally." Meera wiped her face. "I don't want to lose you as a friend, Ms. Raawal. And not just because you're going to make me look like an amazing warrior queen. I just... I really like you."

Anya's chest tightened. "Of course you won't lose me. I'll be your friend for as long as you want," she added. "Nothing your dad says or does would change that, Meera."

There were so many questions she wanted to ask Meera but Anya rationed herself every day. Because she knew the risk of investing more and more of herself into this relationship. She knew that Meera would inevitably move on once this film was over, and when she did, she'd walk away with another piece of Anya's heart.

Despite the silent warning to herself, she couldn't stop asking, "What made you so interested in acting? Your... mother?"

She wasn't using the girl to satisfy her curiosity about the woman who'd owned Simon's heart. She wasn't.

There was an ache in her wide eyes as Meera thought of her mother, but there was also joy there too. "Partly, yes. You know she retired before I was born. So I wasn't really immersed in that world growing up. But I loved watching her movies. Dad and I would pick one every Friday. She knew so much about so many people in the industry. She always indulged me when I asked for all the behind-the-scenes details and gossip." Meera hit Stop on the treadmill and grabbed a towel. "But at school, I seemed to naturally gravitate toward drama and dance. I just love everything about acting, you know? I mean, I'm adopted, so it can't be in the blood, but it definitely comes from somewhere."

Anya gasped. "What?"

"Oh, yeah, I'm adopted," Meera said, without even an

ounce of anxiety in her tone. "Mama and Dad told me when I was seven. It didn't really make much of a difference to me. They *are* my parents."

Anya nodded, swallowing the knot in her throat. If she needed any proof that she'd done the right thing thirteen years ago, here it was. Her daughter was strong and well-adjusted, even with the loss she'd suffered at such a young age.

"I can imagine what your mother must have been like to have raised you to be such a wonderful girl," Anya whispered softly. From everything she was learning from Simon and Meera, Rani sounded like she'd been a wonderful woman. No wonder there had been such pain in Simon's expression every time he mentioned her.

Meera smiled. "I like to think she'd be proud of me. But I worry about Dad. He didn't really want to move back to Mumbai. I twisted his arm. But I did it as much for him as for me."

Anya knew she should stop this line of discussion immediately. Especially since just the mention of Simon's name had her pulse racing. She wanted to know nothing more about the man who already occupied too much of her thoughts and emotions. The man who'd brought her out of her shell.

The man who'd made her want so much out of life all of a sudden.

But when she looked at Meera, it was clear that the girl was desperate to share her worries with someone. "Why do you say that?" she prompted softly.

"He's been so lonely since Mama died. I know it's only been eighteen months, but I've never seen him so...withdrawn and grumpy as he's been recently. I struggled a lot in the beginning too. But he was wonderful to me. He didn't even get angry with me when he learned my grades were slipping. I feel as if he's still stuck there emotionally. I knew we had to get out of that empty flat and make a fresh start. So I made a huge ruckus after we met Virat sir at the mall. I whined constantly that Mama would never have said no to me, never would've stopped me trying... and that's when he finally agreed." A sheepishness filled Meera's face. "I kinda manipulated him. But I don't feel too bad about it, you know? I did it for his own good."

Anya laughed at the girl's innate confidence. "How is bringing your dad here for his own good?"

"Well, for one thing, he has some distant cousins here. More importantly, his business partner and closest friend lives here. Ms. Sampson has visited us a few times after Mama died. I mean, she's definitely not who I want for a stepmother but..."

"Stepmother?" Anya said, aghast. "Your dad's marrying again?" The question burst out of her before she could judge the wisdom of asking the teenager about her dad's love life. Her heart was racing, her thoughts already spiraling into a loop.

Had Simon been in a relationship when he and Anya had...had sex that first night? Was he with her, even now, while Anya was obsessing over him? God, why was she obsessing over him?

It had been a moment of madness—utterly pleasurable madness, but still. Knowing now who he was to Meera, she could never indulge with him like that again. Not when she was finally albeit slowly coming out of her shell after all these years.

"I don't know," Meera said, tugging her hair back. "When we went to dinner on our second day back here, she was hinting pretty hard about how well-suited they are. And to be honest, whenever he sees her, Dad does cheer up a bit. I mean, it's not how Virat sir looks at Zara di or Vikram sir at Naina di," she added with a dreamy sigh and Anya giggled.

Her powerful brothers—known to be ruthless and caustic and brilliant—turned into completely different people around their wives. Their marriages had truly taken on a dreamy Bollywood-esque fairy-tale quality in the media for how real and passionate they were. Something Anya couldn't even imagine for herself. That kind of love needed utter surrender and vulnerability and a kind of bravery she'd never had.

"But his marrying Ms. Sampson has to be better than him being lonely, right?" Meera asked morosely.

"You don't like her?" Anya said, frowning. Maybe she had no right to be jealous over some faceless woman, but she had every right to worry whether this woman would be kind to Meera as a stepmother.

"Not at all," Meera said without hesitation. "For one thing, she treats me like I was…six instead of thirteen. And she pretends all this interest in me in front of Dad but I can totally see through her. Pfft…she's not that good of an actress. She forgets I have Mama and Zara di for reference."

Anya couldn't help smiling at the girl's phrasing and took her hand. "Meera, it's not your job to worry over—"

"What's happened? Meera, what are you worrying about?" came Simon's deep voice behind them.

Releasing Meera's hand, Anya turned. Dressed casually in a light blue V-necked sweater and dark denim, Simon instantly dominated the vast gym area, his rugged masculinity in contrast with the overtly muscular look that was all the rage on cinema screens right now. The gray at his temples, the laughter lines around his mouth, the easy confidence with which he greeted everyone—from her brothers to the errand boy on set—made him the most potently real man Anya had ever met.

Meera scrunched her nose when Simon bent his head. "I'm all sweaty, Dad."

Simon kissed her cheek anyway. He cast Anya a quick but such a thorough glance that it sent a shiver down her spine before asking again, "What's got you worried, Meera?"

"Oh, just Virat sir's feedback today," Meera said without blinking. "If anyone can get me to quit acting, it's got be him."

"What?" They both responded though Simon's question came out in a thunderous growl. "Do you want me to talk to him?" Anya said, turning to her.

"God, no, I was just joking," Meera said, making a face. "Stop looking like that. Both of you. Everyone in the industry knows he's incredibly forthright when it comes to work. I've just got to grow a thicker skin." She turned to her dad. "I'm going to grab a quick shower." Meera looped her arm through Anya's, innocently fluttering her lashes at them. "Maybe Anya can join us for dinner?"

"No."

They both responded at the same time and with such emphasis that Meera's eyes went wide. "You know I thought I was imagining it, but I'm not. Why do you guys dislike each other?" she said, her tone suddenly petulant enough to remind Anya that she was a teenager who always wanted to have her own way.

"I don't dislike Ms. Raawal," Simon protested, his gaze holding Anya's. While every inch of his posture backed up his words, his eyes...his eyes said something else altogether. But Anya lacked both the confidence and the courage to call him on it.

"I've got to finish those initial sketches tonight," she mumbled, patting Meera's arm. "You just reminded me how Virat gets when he's in the thick of a project."

Hands on her hips, Meera turned her stubborn gaze to her dad, demanding an answer.

Simon sighed. "I haven't seen you much this week, Meera. I'd rather it just be the two of us this evening."

A whisper of dejection pinched Anya but she pushed it away. With Simon, she could always at least count on honesty. Grabbing her gym bag, Meera walked toward the bathroom.

Simon instantly switched his cell phone on, not even a little bothered by the cloud of awkwardness and tension swirling around them.

Anya stepped closer to him. The scent of him instantly made her belly tighten with longing. Both physical and... otherwise. Holding her spine straight took a lot of effort when all she wanted to do was to melt into his broad strength. "I need to talk to you."

Simon sighed, switched off his phone and tucked his hands into the pockets of his trousers. His whole "I'm bored with this conversation already" attitude made anger pour through Anya. "Yes, Ms. Raawal. What is it?"

"Don't 'Ms. Raawal' me as if I'm another teenager bothering you."

She sighed, instantly regretting her curt tone. He wasn't acting any differently from what they'd agreed to be going forward—polite strangers.

But this suave, remote Simon...made her feel so unsure of herself. "That night...when we..."

He raised a brow, an unholy light suddenly shimmering in his eyes. "When we...what?" he teased.

"When you and I..." Anya said, licking her dry lips and casting a quick glance in the direction that Meera had gone in, "when we had—" she lowered her voice to a bare whisper, but it took another swallow to get the word out "—*sex*, were you...already in a relationship with someone else?"

The thread of humor in his beautiful eyes disappeared. His thick brows knotted into a scowl and the step he took toward Anya had her backing up against the wall.

He swore. "Stop acting as if you're scared of me."

"Of course I'm not," she retorted, feeling hot all over.

"Is that why you scurried off and hid in the bathroom for five minutes last time I picked up Meera?"

So he had noticed that. "I'm just…" She rubbed a hand over the nape of her neck. "Being near you does a number on me, okay?"

That answer burned away the quick flare of his temper. But a shimmer of a remote coolness remained. "Are you asking me if I was cheating on someone with you, Angel?"

His frigid tone was answer enough and still, some wild, wanton part of Anya didn't want to release him yet. Because she had a strange feeling that she had a hold on him just then. He didn't like that she could think him capable of something like that. "It's just…" She swallowed Meera's name, feeling heat creep up her cheeks. "Something made me wonder."

When the glacial coolness in his eyes didn't thaw, Anya pushed at his chest with her palms, a strange belligerence rising up in her. "It's not my fault if I did wonder, is it? We barely knew each other and ever since…you've been acting as if I'll proposition you if you so much as look at me. I thought with everything that happened, we were friends at least."

"You're even more naive than I assumed if you think we could be friends after what's happened." His voice softened, as if he was trying to not upset her delicate sensibilities. That in turn only angered her.

"So you weren't cheating then? You weren't with anyone else romantically?" she probed shamelessly, wanting to know if he was in a relationship with Ms. Sampson now.

"No, I wasn't. Even when Rani and I were married…" He exhaled roughly, biting away the rest. "And that ends this discussion."

Anya's curiosity about his marriage, about his loyalty to his wife, about everything related to him, basically, went up another notch. "I'm sorry if I implied you were capable of infidelity."

"You're forgiven," he said with an ease that said he'd grant her anything if she just stopped talking to him.

"But I do have something else important I want to talk to you about. Why don't we meet during lunch tomorrow here at the hotel? Meera and my brothers will be busy. My suite is out of everyone's way and we can—"

"Are you asking me over for an afternoon quickie, Angel?"

"What?" Her pulse raced at the very idea, her body softening at the picture her overimaginative brain painted immediately. Quickie or not, this time she'd make sure there was a bed available. Definitely.

Simon tapped her shoulder, grinning wickedly. "I was just kidding."

"I know that. And of course I'm not inviting you for a—" she lowered her voice again "—quickie."

He shrugged. "I can't have lunch with you tomorrow. I'm…busy."

"Simon, this is—"

"Good evening, Ms. Raawal," he pronounced stiffly in a raised voice.

Anya looked behind her to see Meera had just emerged from the bathroom at the other end of the long gym. She pressed a hand to Simon's chest and leaned closer. He straightened from his relaxed stance, tension swathing him at her touch. She bent and whispered, "So you're available for the quickie but not to talk?"

Without waiting for his answer, Anya pulled away, a feral satisfaction flooding her at his stunned gaze. Pasting a beaming smile to her lips, she bid Meera a quiet good-night and walked away on trembling knees.

Before the infuriating man tempted her to more unwise actions.

She was playing with fire—and thank God he hadn't called her bluff. No way could she do the casual thing with him again. But she also didn't remember a moment where she'd felt so alive in her entire life.

Long after Meera went to bed, Simon poured himself a drink at the bar and wandered toward the terrace attached to the penthouse. The night was balmy and muggy with a storm in the making.

Despite the fact that the penthouse at the hotel—one of his own group—was the height of luxury, he didn't like the temporariness of it any more than he'd liked the empty silence of their home in Singapore over the last year and a half. It smacked of uncertainty. After growing up with a single parent who'd dragged him up and down the country in search of work, Simon didn't like not having a solid home base. They could choose any one of his residences in a number of the big cities in India, but this was where Meera wanted to be now.

Where she was thriving.

Yet the fact that Meera was thriving in an overwhelmingly demanding industry, in a new city, amid strangers, was, he knew, in no small way thanks to Anya's calming, serene influence. Not even ten days had passed since they'd met and already he could see her stable hand guiding Meera's impulsive nature to make better choices.

And just like that, the real source of his unease became crystal clear. It had less to do with the fact that his

life and Meera's were in a flux right now and more to do
with the woman who'd just walked into their lives like
Mumbai's monsoon season.

Even the smallest interaction with her began a clam-
oring in his gut for more…

His muscles tightened at the memory of Anya's palm
pressed against his abdomen not a few hours ago. The
subtle jasmine scent of her as she'd bent her head and
taunted him. The tease of her hair against his jaw, the
naked desire she'd let him see in her eyes for a split second…

So you're available for the quickie but not to talk…

The raw, wanton pleasure they'd shared that first evening together was never far from his mind. But when
Anya stood close to him like that… Simon wanted far
too much. Not just of her, but of himself, of his life. Desires and dreams he'd written off long ago reared up again
now, slithering hungrily through him.

If he hadn't spied Meera emerging from the bathroom,
he didn't know what he'd have done at Anya's husky
challenge.

No, who was he kidding?

He knew exactly what he'd have done.

He'd have pressed the saucy minx against the wall and
captured those pretty lips with his. He'd have kissed the
hell out of her right there, uncaring of who might walk
in—her brothers, Meera, the entire damned world for
all he cared. He'd have dragged her up to another one of
those shadowy corners and proceeded with the quickie
that they both so badly wanted. Then he'd have taken
her to her bedroom and spent the whole night proving
to her that this fire between them wouldn't die with one
orgasm or ten.

Clutching the metal sill of the balcony tight until his

knuckles turned white, Simon willed his rising libido to calm down. There was no release for him coming anytime soon. Especially not with the one woman he wanted.

And he couldn't even blame her because he was the one who'd brought up the idea of another round of sex in the first place. He'd wanted to shake her up. Wanted to have a little petty revenge at the fact that she'd dare think so little of him that he'd be unfaithful to anyone he cared for. So he'd tugged the one thread that seemed to bind them together. Just her and him. Selfishly, he'd wanted it to be the thread that had nothing to do with Meera or how desperately Anya wanted to be a part of his daughter's life.

The look in her eyes when she'd asked if he'd made her a party to cheating, the way it took her so long to say the word *sex*…it was a good reminder that Anya Raawal was the last woman he could have a temporary, secret affair with.

And that's all he could offer her. Not counting the fact that between her brothers and his daughter, it wouldn't remain a secret for too long.

She wanted to be part of Meera's life, not his. She was far too young for him, and by her own admission, she'd barely dipped her toe into romantic relationships. "Made for love and marriage" might as well have been stamped on her forehead for how generous hearted she was, how achingly lovely she was.

Eventually, she'd want things he didn't want to give, couldn't give another woman. Like marriage and children and…love. Eventually, she'd look at him as Rani had looked at him at the end—with resentment and anger and bitterness. It had eaten away at them both like acid, killing any love they'd once felt for one another.

Even the thought of that bitterness in Anya's eyes, hurt pinching that lush mouth…was unbearable.

He couldn't afford for history to repeat itself. And this time with a woman who was even more fragile and innocent than Rani had ever been.

CHAPTER FIVE

ANYA STUDIED THE carefully curated pictures on Leila Sampson's social media feed, anxiety and something else rising up within her belly like an impending storm. In the last month, every fourth picture that had been posted was of her and Simon. In a variety of his hotel locations, the latest in Thailand and Seychelles.

While none of them were intimate poses—and a dark emotion that tasted very like jealousy gripped Any at the thought—it was clear that, whatever the nature of their relationship, Simon was spending every spare moment with the other woman.

The last few weeks had been bad enough in terms of how distracted she'd been at work. Predictably, Virat had torn her initial sketches into shreds—literally and figuratively. For the first time in her life, Anya wasn't able to give her all to her work.

If it was only because she was spending more time with Meera, Anya could have made her peace with it. But she couldn't ignore the fact that a large part of her brain was occupied with Simon and what was becoming increasingly obvious—whatever he'd claimed before, the man was now getting serious about Leila Sampson.

And ever since Leila had been caught coming out of a couture wedding gown designer's studio after a personal

consultation, Anya had had trouble sleeping. The gossip
was all over social media.

Millionaire widower looking for love again?
    Once the big love of our beloved star actress Rani
Verma's life, real estate magnate Simon De Acosta's
back in Mumbai to keep a close eye on his daughter Meera Verma's acting debut with the prestigious
Raawal House of Cinema!
    As if that wasn't exciting enough for us, Simon
has a new lady love. When questioned about their
plans, real estate heiress Ms. Leila Sampson revealed
exclusively to us that things are moving fast between
her and Simon. But what kind of woman would have
the guts to fill the shoes of the brilliant, beautiful
and beloved Rani Verma?

Despite all the stern lectures she'd given herself to stay
out of Simon's private life, Anya had to do something. The
man had left her no choice at all.
  If he was determined to marry a woman without considering Meera's future happiness, then Anya would remind him that he'd gotten his priorities all wrong. And for
Meera, who'd innocently told Anya where Simon would
be, she would even venture out of her shell and accost the
man at one of those parties that she usually avoided like
the plague.
  Desperate times called for desperate measures.

The party hadn't been as boring and nerve-racking as Anya
had assumed it would feel. She'd run into a couple of familiar faces and found it easy, even effortless to catch up.
People who'd asked after her latest designs, about when
she was traveling again…friends she'd kept at a distance

because she'd thought all their interest in her was only because she was a Raawal.

Of course, there were opportunists and social climbers and even predators in the industry, but how had she become so distrustful of everyone? So afraid of her own shadow? Why had it taken her this long to step back into her own life and look outside of its margins?

She didn't know if it was because she'd discovered Meera, or because of the bold step she'd already taken with Simon, but Anya felt this new...fizz of excitement in her belly for all the possibilities that were suddenly open to her.

But not for a second did she forget why she was at the party. All evening, she'd kept an eye on Simon and Leila, the possessive way the latter had clung to Simon. There was a familiarity in how they talked to each other but not once did Anya see him give the other woman his undivided attention. He also never touched her like he had Anya. So why was he marrying her then?

As the party wound down and guests began to drift into smaller groups, Anya, like an unscrupulous PI or journalist shamelessly followed the couple into the beautiful gazebo set in the expansive lawn. String lights and paper lanterns hung from trees, making the garden a perfect destination for lovers. And yet the argument that Anya had sensed brewing between the couple all evening finally seemed to blow up. The stiffness of Simon's gestures as he faced the other woman took away the last hesitation Anya felt in interrupting them like a crazy groupie.

Neither did she miss the irony in the fact that she was judging Leila for clearly marking her territory when it came to Simon when Anya herself was this close to stalking the man. Of course, her primary motivation was

Meera's well-being, she convinced herself. Though she was beginning to wonder if there was a lot more to it than that.

Refusing to back out now, Anya moved toward him. "Simon…" She forced out a laugh which sounded utterly fake to her own ears. "It is you."

His head jerked in her direction, searching for her in the darkness. The planets had to be on her side because Leila Sampson's cell phone trilled at that moment. With one glance at her phone, then at Simon, she left.

Heart racing, Anya felt his gaze move over her face, then do a quick once-over of her body as if he was tracing the contours with those rough fingers. That single glance was enough to start a powerful hum beneath her skin.

She watched greedily as his long, powerful strides covered the distance between them, moonlight gilding the breadth of his shoulders, the tapering of his hips, the muscled thighs. Revealing him bit by bit, unwrapping him bit by bit, for her very own pleasure. Around him, Anya felt like a feral, possessive creature. A feeling she didn't want to trust but couldn't ignore either.

Hopefully hiding the intensity of her awareness, she beamed at him. Because she knew, on an instinctive level, that Simon should never know how much she longed to kiss him again. How much she thought of him, how much she liked herself when she was with him.

"Ms. Raawal," he said, a hint of humor pulsing beneath the stiff formality of his address. His white linen shirt lovingly molded to the broad span of his chest and there was so much of him she longed to reach out and touch.

Her fingers twitching, Anya cursed herself for the non-intimacy of their one-night stand. She'd gotten no chance to explore his gorgeous body at all. "Fancy seeing you here tonight."

"I should be the one surprised," he said, his eyes gleaming. "Meera informs me—frequently and volubly—that you strictly avoid this kind of gathering."

"Meera's right. But I've long been a fan of Ustadji's music so I made an exception tonight."

"I noticed how lost you were to the music," he said, surprising her. She hadn't known he was aware of her presence even. He rubbed a finger over his brow and almost glared at her. "It seems you draw people to you as effortlessly as the rest of your family." The humor lingered in his tone but there was something sharp in that statement that reminded her of the man who'd granted her everything she'd once asked for under the cover of darkness.

That small shift in his tone made liquid warmth unspool in her lower belly. At the simple knowledge that he'd been as aware of her throughout the evening as she'd been of him. "If you're talking about Ustadji's son asking for my phone number," she said, heat rising in her cheeks, "that man is an irresistible poet in addition to the soulful music he produces. Magic in his fingers and words."

"And?"

Anya pulled the edge of her shawl tighter as it slid from her shoulders. "And what?" she said, sensing the energy between them shift and grow. Becoming more than that constant hum.

"Are you going to take him up on his offer?"

Anya so desperately wanted to flutter her eyelashes and play coy. But it was more than her aversion for the limelight that had kept her from acting. She was bad at dissembling. Bad at playing games and pretending. Bad at acting as if she could just forget that night with him had happened.

"I enjoyed tonight more than I'd expected. But I'm not sure about…seeing him again."

"Good."

The emphasis in his word reverberated in the air between them. It felt like he was throwing a gauntlet down and it set her teeth on edge. Her spine stiffened and she realized maybe it wasn't a bad thing to be like her brothers. They were arrogant and determined but they were also brave and loyal and hid hearts of gold. And it had taken them every single ounce of that courage to win their wives.

While Anya wasn't looking for love, this thing with Simon…this relationship they were having without calling it so, needed all her wits. Maybe she needed to own up to having a little Raawal blood in her. Maybe it wasn't all a bad thing after all.

"I might change my mind though," Anya added, her voice low. "I know I should stop hiding so much, live life a little more. The last time I did that, I found it extremely… *rewarding*."

He stepped toward her, sucking out all the oxygen from around them. At least that's how it felt to her lungs. "Do you plan to go out and have a *rewarding* experience every time the fancy strikes you?"

"Maybe. No, the answer is yes. Definitely yes."

"Is that such a good idea, Ms. Raawal?"

Anya took another step, feeling as if she was sitting at the very top of a roller coaster. About to drop off the edge. She knew she was going to scream, she knew she was going to have the time of her life, but there was only a little fear. Mostly, there was this…violent excitement in her limbs, anticipation a ball in her chest.

She reached out and delicately flicked the edge of his collar, as if she was dusting off a leaf or a petal. Barely touching him but wanting to claim a small part of him. "Maybe you shouldn't be butting into my life while you call me Ms. Raawal in that forbidding tone?"

Tension rolled off him in waves. "I have no right to forbid you from doing anything. But as someone who's aware of the distressing discovery you made not that long ago, in fact as the only one who knows of it, I'm more than entitled to caution you."

"And what is the caution you think I should exercise?"

"You should be careful with whom you…associate, Angel. You're in a vulnerable place."

"Associate…hmm," Anya said softly, a thread of hurt winding itself around her heart. "So having sex with you is okay even though you were a stranger but it's wrong to do it with someone who's not you?"

His nostrils flared but his voice stayed low, steady. "That's not at all what I said. Even as an outsider to the industry, I know the kind of games Ustadji's son is known for. You were lucky with me. Not every stranger is going to be…"

"As generous and giving as you were?"

"As harmless as me." He pushed a hand through his hair, his frustration translating itself to Anya. He obviously didn't want any kind of relationship with her, but he didn't want her to be friendly with any other man? She shouldn't have been able to understand that but strangely, she did.

"You said Meera was your priority right now," he added.

"If you're worried that I might turn into some kind of bad influence on Meera, you should…"

His fingers landed on her chin, tilting her up to meet his eyes. Just the tips of two fingers and yet, she felt the contact all over her body. "I don't think that at all. I… I'm only thinking of you. Damn it, I feel responsible, Angel. For you."

Something about the possessive gleam in his eyes, the firm grip of his fingers, the scent of him filling her nostrils, her very lungs, goaded Anya. "What shall I do then, Simon? Lock myself away for another decade? Or should I just call you when I need a reward for good behavior?"

Simon pulled away his fingers, as if her words burned him. "Why are you really here tonight, Anya?"

"I've something important to say to you," she said, trying to find her way through the dark. They were moving farther away from the gazebo and the fairy lights.

"Talk then," he said, his hand immediately grasping her elbow when she stepped onto an uneven path.

A cold breeze flew past and Anya pulled the shawl around her neck tighter. Instantly, Simon pulled her against his body as if he meant to shield her from the elements. By the time they reached the outer edge of the gardens, hidden from the other guests, her resolve that she was only doing this for Meera's sake weakened.

Whatever he saw in her face, Simon's mouth tightened. "You're nervous."

Anya scrunched her nose. "A little."

"Did something happen with Meera?"

"No," she hurried to reassure him. "Well, there's the thing with one of the young light boys but I dealt with it."

He scowled. "What is the thing with the light boy?"

"A harmless crush."

"For God's sake, she's only thirteen. What did he do?"

"He? He did nothing. She's the one who keeps finding reasons to talk to him. If you didn't know this about her already, she's bold as brass."

Mouth pursed tight, Simon looked like he still wanted to find the light boy and straighten him out.

"Meera's fine," she repeated. "We all went to get ice cream together. I sat at a different table and they talked for a little bit. She has no friends of her own age here yet, Simon. This is good for her."

"You're not a parent. You don't know that."

Anya flinched. Just because she'd spent the better part of three weeks with Meera now, didn't mean Anya knew everything about parenting. But try as she might, his words hurt.

He raked a hand through his hair and grabbed her wrist gently. "I...didn't mean that the way it sounded."

"I know that," Anya said softly. Why the hell was it so easy to trust this man? Why him when he clearly didn't want to have anything to do with her? "It has come to my notice that you're getting serious about Ms. Sampson," she blurted out, reminding herself why she was here.

"And who brought you this notice?"

His dry tone made Anya flush, but she went on. "Apparently, she and you are planning to buy a villa together... and she's getting an exclusive designer wedding gown designed for her."

Simon's gaze turned inscrutable and Anya had no way of knowing if he knew of it already.

Had he already proposed? Had they even set a date?

Dark and bitter, jealousy twisted her gut as she considered the possibility that soon even thinking about Simon when she went to bed alone, when she tried to imitate his caresses would be forbidden, since he'd belong to someone else. Even this easy camaraderie and strange intimacy they shared—despite his determination to keep her at a distance—she'd have no right to enjoy.

"And where did you see this?"

"On Ms. Sampson's social media."

His thick brows rose. "You've been spying on her?"

"I went straight to the source instead of listening to the media's speculations, that's all."

One corner of his mouth twitched and Anya had a feeling he was enjoying her discomfiture too much. But at least he wasn't angry, thank God.

"And now you've accosted me at a party to what? Congratulate me?"

"I thought someone should tell you that Meera doesn't like her at all. In the role of a stepmother, that is." When his silence began leaching away her courage, Anya just plowed on, her genuine concern for Meera overtaking her innate resistance to the rude way she was barging into his personal life. "And more importantly, she thinks Ms. Sampson neither likes her nor cares about her."

"And you're the expert on Ms. Sampson now?"

Anya didn't miss the fact that he hadn't denied her claim. "I simply choose to trust Meera's judgment. As you very well know, she's desperate for you to be happy. She even mentioned that if marrying Ms. Sampson is what it takes for you to be happy, she'll bear it. But I don't think that's fair at all. She's just thirteen, she lost her mother not eighteen months ago and she's handling a new career in another country. She shouldn't have to put up with a woman who only pretends an interest in her on top of everything else."

His fingers cupped her shoulder, his mouth flat. "Wait, go back. Meera wants me to be what?"

Anya sighed, relief crashing through her. It was clear that he had no idea of Meera's concerns for him. "Meera's worried about you. She talks of you and your loneliness and how…lost you've been the last year and a half. She totally adores you, Simon, and thinks Rani's death has… changed you in ways she doesn't understand."

His jaw tightened as he released her. His gaze cut away from her as if he didn't want to share even a bit of his grief with her. "I lost my wife in a car accident. It should change me."

Anya's chest tightened. But there was more than simple grief there. "I'm not questioning why she feels like that. And I didn't mean to pile on any guilt. I'm just…"

"Sharing one evening with me doesn't give you the right to interfere in my life."

His words, delivered in a cold, flat tone, landed hard. As he'd meant for them to. "But being someone who loves Meera unconditionally, someone who's desperately wishing for a chance to be part of her life permanently, I have the right to ask. I have the right to point out that you might be making a wrong decision," Anya rallied valiantly.

"Neither Meera nor you know what it's been like for me." He glared at her, as if daring her to argue. "As for the matter of Leila, not that it's any of your—"

"If anyone should be Meera's mother, it should be me. And we both know that at least the sex between us would be fantastic!"

He rounded on her, his jaw slackened incredulously.

Anya clamped her hand over her mouth, her pulse racing madly all over. She hadn't realized what she meant to say until the words had just popped out. Until her brain grabbed them out of air and conjured the image of a future that teased Anya's imagination. She waited for a thread of fear to filter through. The thought of a future with a man—someone who could break her trust all over again, someone who would only see her for what he could get out of her—had always terrified her before. And yet nothing came when she thought of Simon and Meera in her life. Nothing but an unbidden, unwanted thrill shooting through her.

"Is that a proposal, Angel?"

Embarrassment made her skin heat. "It's not what I meant to say but it's better than you marrying a woman who barely tolerates Meera, isn't it?" Anya retorted, bristling. "No other woman in your life will love Meera more wholeheartedly than I already do. And if you're also getting married for regular sex—hello, ding-ding-ding…? We have a winner there too," she said, moving her hand between them. "I don't have much experience with men, as you know, but the kind of chemistry we have... I think it should work for even the irregular kind of sex too."

"What's irregular sex? How long have I been celibate for? Did they invent a new kind of sex while I was away from the dating scene?"

Her cheeks were on fire and he was laughing at her now but still, her determination and desperation wouldn't stop the words from bubbling over. "No, I mean just not traditional sex. But like fun sex. Not that what we did at the hotel was traditional... In fact, I think it kinda straddled the line between traditional and fun..."

"Thank the Lord! For a moment there I was afraid of what I'd missed!"

Anya swatted him. "You're making fun of me!"

His eyes were wide pools of laughter; his broad chest shook with it. He looked so breathtakingly gorgeous when he laughed like that she only half minded that she'd just made a complete fool of herself. "You're making it irresistible not to."

With a gasp of outrage, she turned and threw her hand out almost losing her balance. He caught it and tugged. The momentum made her stumble and he caught her too and before she knew it, Anya banged her hip into his front. His curse was loud and colorful in the quiet garden as her nose bumped against his jaw. Still he didn't let her go. "Are you hurt?"

The corded strength of him surrounded her, taking her breath away. "Only my ego," she said softly, pressing her hand to his jaw, wanting desperately to soothe him. Wanting to touch him all over. Just once, God, just once, she wanted her hands all over him—over every hard contour, every solid sinew, every tight muscle. She wanted to rake her nails over his broad pecs, test the give of his ridged abdomen with her teeth. She wanted to mark him all over until the thought of every other woman—the ghost of his ex, and his very current business partner—was driven from his mind.

The strength of her possessive instincts sent a flurry of alarm through her. And still, she couldn't pull away.

"Are you?" she asked, her thumb moving to the sharp jut of his prominent cheekbones and over the hollow underneath.

"Of course I'm not hurt." His fingers grabbed her wrist to stop the motion but stilled. "Except you are making me lose my mind."

She bit her lip, her fingers relishing the raspy sensation of his evening stubble. "I didn't mean for this—"

"Stop touching me," he muttered. Perversely, a second before his mouth covered hers.

His lips were hungry and desperate and hard but only for a few seconds. Wrapping her arms around his muscled back, Anya pressed herself into him in silent surrender. Instantly, his kiss softened, his caresses gentled, transformed into something else.

Tender and hot and…exploratory. He tasted her, tempted her, teased her without the urgency that had swamped them in the darkness at the hotel. Fingers buried in her hair, her body arched into him so that she could feel the imprint of his growing erection against her belly. He riled up her passion and soothed it all at the same time in a devilishly thorough kiss.

It was the first kiss they should've had if Anya's discovery about Meera hadn't plunged her into a kind of temporary madness. This was a "do you want to do this with me" kiss. His lips were soft and yet firm, pressing forward and then retreating, inviting her to play, inviting her tongue to dance with his. Inviting her to enjoy just this moment with him.

They kissed for what felt like an eternity to her, Simon pulling away just when Anya needed her breath and pressing her down onto a stone bench. And then coming back before she could recover her equilibrium. The lazy swirl of his tongue inside her mouth, the soothing strokes of his hands over her back, the way he peppered her jaw and neck with his kisses before finding his way back again to her sensitized lips, there was no destination, no rush to do anything except savor this moment. To just be.

Clinging to him like a jasmine creeper to the wall, Anya gave in to the delicious torment. And it was exactly what she'd needed from the moment she'd discovered he was Meera's adoptive father. From the moment he'd become forbidden to her. From the moment she'd realized they were now connected by something that neither of them had chosen, that whatever had happened between them already was the most they could ever have.

She'd needed to know that Simon still wanted her. After everything she'd revealed, after everything that had passed between them. And he did want her. This kiss told her that beyond a doubt.

The realization unraveled the tangle of her own emotions. She wondered if, in her heart of hearts, this was what she'd come here for tonight. If the ridiculous proposal of marriage that had fluttered onto her lips was her subconscious telling her she wanted far more of Simon in her life. That her interest in him had so much more to do with him as a man than simply the fact that he was Meera's father.

Not a month ago, she'd been content to hide, to live her life in the margins.

And now, now it seemed all she wanted to do was jump straight off the cliff.

Because there was no doubt, she reminded herself even as every inch of her body ached for his complete possession, that indulging in the idea of Simon as some kind of romantic partner—even a temporary one—was nothing short of jumping off a cliff to a very messy end.

Anya was the softest, sweetest thing he'd ever kissed. A shaft of moonlight crossed her face in a beam, highlighting the swollen plumpness of her lips. Even that wasn't enough of a reminder to stop Simon. One arm cupping the nape of her neck, he lapped at her lips until she gave in one more time. She sank into the kiss with a soft moan that reverberated through him, warming up every limb, waking up every dormant need.

Her fingers tugged at the lapels of his shirt, her mouth pulling back from his just enough for her to speak. "How can you kiss me like this and think of marrying another woman?" Vulnerability sparked in her question, in the soft, curious slant of her eyes.

With a pithy curse, Simon wrenched himself away from her. Pulling her knees up into her chest, Anya stayed on the stone bench, looking painfully innocent.

His body was shaking and incredibly aroused, his breath coming in shallow spurts. "I'm sorry," he whispered. "For kissing you like that. For acting like a thorough hypocrite."

She gave him her sharp profile in reply.

He wished she would berate him for acting like a rogue. Worse, for blowing hot and cold on her. Instead, when she spoke again, her voice was a sweet whisper. "I like it when you kiss me. It makes me feel brave, different, wanted. As if—"

"It was a slip. And it doesn't change anything, Angel. You and I can have nothing more than Meera in common. And that's enough of a complication as it is."

He saw the movement of her Adam's apple, the thread of hurt she tried to hide. "You keep saying that. But it doesn't mean I can't enjoy it when I overwhelm your reason."

He smiled despite everything, the open admission sending warmth through his veins.

She straightened to her feet. The loose V-necked top she wore hung on her slender frame and yet, she looked so starkly sensual that Simon's pulse beat erratically. Dark skinny jeans molded to her long legs. The cashmere shawl hung at her elbows, a flimsy protection against the cool night. Her beautiful eyes glimmered in the faint moonlight, resolve etched into her stubborn features. "You never answered my question."

"For God's sake, I've no intention of ever marrying again. I've barely recovered from the last time."

She took a step back, her gaze wide and searching at his blunt admission. Could she see that what she thought was grief in his eyes was actually crippling guilt? "You are...not marrying Leila then?"

"No."

"Oh."

"Would you like to take back your oh-so-romantic proposal now?" he asked, enjoying her discomfiture far too much.

Her fingers tightened around the edges of her shawl. "Yes, I think so."

He pressed a palm to his chest, curving his mouth in a mocking laugh. "Wow, first the assumption that I'd marry anyone without first considering Meera's happiness. Then the withdrawal of your proposal. You came packed tonight, Angel."

"I'm sorry for assuming you wouldn't consider Meera, but everything pointed to..."

Simon thrust a hand roughly through his hair. "Look,

Leila is my oldest friend and business partner. Which, believe me, has given me enough insight into her character.
I'm aware that she has no interest whatsoever in Meera.
And while I don't hold it against her, I'm also aware it
would make her a very poor choice of wife for me. Despite what she thinks."

"So she does want to marry you?"

"I'm not answering that, Ms. Raawal."

"Ms. Raawal? Are we really back to that again? And
why not answer me?"

"All you need to know is that no woman will try to push
you out of Meera's life. No woman, other than her mother,
has a claim on her affections. Now, I'd prefer it if could
you untangle your emotions about me and Meera in your
head." He sent her a confused face a hard glance, carefully
picking his words. "It would be nice if you stopped throwing yourself at me just to remain close to my daughter."

"That's an awful thing to say!" she gasped.

He remained silent, his blood pounding in his ears.

Outrage sparked in her eyes as she covered the distance
between them. "If you must know," she said, poking him
in his chest, her hair mussed from his fingers, her mouth
swollen and pink, looking so delectable that it took all he
had to not throw her over his shoulder and steal her away
all over again, "what I want to do with you has nothing to
do with Meera. It has nothing to do with logic or self-pres-
ervation or common sense. And it terrifies me to my soul.

"What I want with you is…simply you. I want you for
you, Simon. For your kisses. For your kindness. For the
generous, honorable man you are even when that results
in you pushing me away. God help me, I don't know how
to stop this wanting."

Before Simon could respond to that heated declaration,
she stomped away from him, her back rigid, her steps sure.

For long minutes after she left, he stood there, his ruffled ego soothed by her passionate declaration, his body tight and hungry for release, his emotions in as big a tangle as their old string of Christmas lights in Meera's hands.

He'd had no problem rejecting Leila's suggestion that they wed earlier that evening, or holding out against her rational arguments when he'd refused. But deep down in his soul, Anya Raawal and her…horribly awkward but endearing non-proposal tempted him.

She tempted him. To no end.

No one made him laugh like she did.

No one made him come alive like she did.

No one made him want to abandon the little common sense he had left in him and simply seduce her, take whatever she was willing to give him.

For once, Simon wanted to be totally selfish and damn the consequences to hell. He wanted the joy and unfettered pleasure Anya Raawal brought to his life by her mere presence.

He wanted to be the Simon he'd glimpsed in her eyes.

CHAPTER SIX

THE LAST THING Anya had expected when she walked into the MahaRani suite at the beautifully renovated luxury hotel—historically called the Palace of Mirrors—in Udaipur for the shoot location was to find her brothers and Simon waiting on her.

It had been a surprise when the production coordinator had directed her to this hotel when her brothers and the crew were staying closer to the set a few kilometers away. Not that she had any complaints about a stay in the luxurious hotel—even Vikram with all his reach hadn't been able to book this suite last year when he'd wanted to impress Naina.

Until she had stepped into the beautiful foyer and realized the hotel and its recent renovation from a dilapidated palace was one of Simon's recent projects.

The suite she'd been accorded was vast, luxurious, with a private courtyard and a pool in the back. A gazebo, assumed to be the secret meeting place of two local lovers, sat on the edge of the beautiful pool like the pendant on a pearl necklace. As a history buff, there was nothing she liked more than to study local history, mine the rich folktales, try to see the past come alive through clothes and architecture and weaponry that had once been used.

With Simon standing on one side of the sitting lounge,

both her brothers on the other, and Zara and Naina sitting on a luxurious settee in between them, it was as if one of the local battles was about to take place in this very suite. She didn't even have a moment to marvel at the thick Persian rug under her feet or the classy royal procession wallpaper design that gave the suite an utterly elegant, almost royal look.

Dumping her handbag and overnight bag on an armchair that had heavy dark wood and modern upholstery in a perfect marriage of old and new, she stole a surreptitious glance at Simon first.

Seeing him here in her suite, three days after she'd made that foolishly passionate declaration about how much she wanted him, after they'd shared such a raw, needy kiss was shock enough. But to face him with her brothers watching on... Anya rubbed a hand over her temple, more than physical exhaustion catching up with her.

With all the decisions she'd been making recently, she had known that some version of her brothers butting in would happen soon. But she'd naively hoped for it to be later rather than sooner.

She'd barely slept in the last three days. The costume designs she'd been working on for Zara and Meera had finally clicked. With Virat's demand for perfection in every small detail, they were nowhere near finalized. But he had said "brilliant" to her, and that was high praise indeed. After his approval, she'd gone into a frenzy with her production team to get them finished in time for the costume rehearsal. She'd been working long hours at her workshop, where she worked with some of the best seamstresses and tailors in the country.

It was a world of its own—her sanctuary when reality became too much for her. And maybe, just maybe, she'd also been hiding from her own desperate need to see Simon again.

Anya had no doubt that Naina's and Zara's presence was to corral her brothers' inclination to be overly protective of her. No one else dared to try, much less succeed.

"What? Is there something on my face?" she barked at her brothers, her crankiness coming out at impending family drama.

This was her fault. She'd let them cocoon her and cosset her for far too long. Now, they'd have trouble accepting that she could think and act for herself.

"Why didn't you tell us?" Vikram demanded.

Virat simply studied her.

"Tell you what?" Anya asked.

"Have you looked at any social media recently, Anya?" Zara asked in a soft, concerned tone.

Her heart thudded against her rib cage, fear snaking through her veins like tendrils taking root. "Not at all. I've been at the workshop. There's barely any internet connection there and I like it like that." Her hands shook as she unraveled the scarf from around her neck. God, what had they written about her family now?

"Is it about Mama and Papa?"

"No," Virat spoke finally. "It's about you."

About her? About her and who? What about her?

Her gaze instantly sought Simon. Broad shoulders leaning against the French doors, he simply watched her.

"Simon? Is it bad?"

"Depends, Angel." He didn't sound angry but there was a tightness to his mouth. And the fact that he'd called her Angel instead of Anya or Ms. Raawal in that formal tone of his…helped her draw a breath. "I tried to contact you but you weren't picking up."

"I don't usually check my cell phone when I'm at the

last stage of production. They know what it's like," she said, pointing to the four gazes shifting between her and Simon, all of them having clearly registered his nickname for her. "Why were you looking for me?"

"Because I think you and I should deal with this. Just the two of us. Not the entire damned world." The dark look he sent her older brother might have felled a lesser man.

Vikram simply glared back at Simon.

"Anya, we don't want to interfere in your private life. Your brothers just want to know if everything's okay, that's all." Naina's soft, calming voice couldn't hide the thread of curiosity beneath or the warning she was issuing her husband. "To reassure themselves that this latest social media stunt hasn't upset you."

Anya flushed as she realized she'd walked halfway up the suite toward Simon. As if he were her true north.

She was not all right. Her knees were shaking and there was already a cold sweat breaking out all over her skin. She was close to falling apart. "I don't care who's here, Simon. Will you please…" Her breath turned choppy as a ghastly thought stuck her next. "Is it…to do with Meera?" she asked in a soft whisper, covering the distance between them. "Do they know about her? Oh, my God… I promise you I didn't tell anyone. Not even my family. How did this…? How is she? Does she hate me?"

Simon's hands clamped down firmly, reassuringly on her shoulders, pulling her out of the spiral. "No, sweetheart. She doesn't know. No one knows," he said, an instant softening in his eyes. "Only you and me, Anya. Not anyone else."

A shuddering exhale left Anya, but the shivers continued. She wanted to drown in the depths of these eyes, wanted to burrow into his heart and stay there.

"Why didn't you tell us that you were…seeing him?"

Vikram clearly still had a PhD in overprotective non-sense. Still, Anya could see the real worry in his eyes. "I'm not seeing him so much as… Wait, how do you even know that?"

"So you *are* dating him?" Vikram pounced on her.

"Simon, what exactly happened?"

"Someone caught us on a cell phone. Kissing on the bench in Ustadji's garden. The pics are all over the damned internet."

Pushing away from him, Anya fished her cell phone out of her handbag and typed in her own name in the browser. Something she never did. Ever. Pictures of her and Simon—three different angles—of her sitting across his lap, plastered to him while they were lost in a passionate kiss, his broad palms all over her back, her arms clinging around his neck…

Her gaze moved over the write-up, her heart in her throat.

Anya Raawal's secret affair with Simon De Acosta!

Apparently Anya Raawal—the usually reclusive member of the powerful Raawals—has cracked the code to get to the rich, successful Simon De Acosta: building a friendship with his daughter Meera Verma.

It's no secret that the two have been spending a lot of time together on the set of Raawal House's latest production. Their unusual friendship had been noted by more than one team member. Looks like clever Anya knew all along that the way to the property tycoon's heart is through his daughter…

Her phone slipped from her hand and fell onto the carpet with a loud thud. "They make it sound so bad. As if I befriended her to get to you, as if I…" Tears knocked at her throat. "Meera…has she seen this? Did she ask about it? Please, Simon, what did you tell her? Did you tell her it's not like that? Does she hate me now? What should I…?" Her knees gave up and she sank to the floor.

"Shh…breathe, Angel." Simon's deep voice cut through the loop. A mere second later, he was there, weaving his arms around her. He pulled her into his lap as easily as if she were a child. Muscled arms hugged her; a warm mouth bussed her temple until all she felt was him.

And still, the spiral of her thoughts continued.

Did Meera hate her now?

Would she never want to see her again?

Would she lose her baby girl already?

The thoughts were like tips of poison poking at her and she struggled to draw in a breath. Her chest felt like there was a large rock pressing down upon it.

"Look at me, Anya. Look at me." Simon's voice was pure possessive demand and Anya automatically followed it. Let him tug her out of the dark hole.

Dark eyes captured hers and held. His fingers gripped her jaw firmly, his breath coating her skin in warm strokes. "Tell me three things, Angel, three things you can see and smell and touch."

"You," she said, tears pouring down her cheeks, "I see you." She rubbed a finger over his brow. Over the dominating sweep of his nose. Over the tension lines around his mouth. Her chest rose and fell on a shuddering breath. "The scent of you is in my pores and I like it…" She stroked her hands over his broad chest, the thick nap of his sweater cool and soft under her fingers. His heart thudded under her palms, his muscles clenching at every touch. "I can feel you… And my hands can't get enough."

But the panic was like a monster waiting to swallow her

down given a moment's thought. She raised her teary gaze to his, desperate to make him understand. "You know it wasn't like that, Simon. I would never use any child like that, especially not her." A sob fought to break through her words. "I would never use you to get to her either. I… hate how the media can ruin things like this… I hate how they corrupt everything."

His arms were like a vise around her shoulders now. "I know that. Look at me, Angel." He was a shimmery vision through her tears as Anya tilted her face. His brown eyes were full of trust, his mouth rising up at one corner in a familiar gesture that stole her breath. "I know you, Anya. Trust me right now if you can trust nothing else."

Something in his tone beat away at the spiral, as if he were truly her knight. Her hero. Anya bent her head, burying her face in his neck. She counted to ten, breathing in the male scent of him. "What does she think of me now? What did she say?"

"She saw the posts, yes. In fact, she was the one who said I should call you. That you wouldn't have seen it. That I should talk to you, warn you, before someone else told you."

Anya laughed through her tears, her words a blubbery mess. "Meera is so precious, Simon. You should be very proud of her."

"She is and I am. It was you who reminded me that she has a solid head on her shoulders. She doesn't believe any of the trash they wrote about you using her to get to me. I asked her if she wanted to talk about it, and she said she wants to talk to us both. In her words, she's dying to get all the gossip from you. She's fine, Anya, I swear. Look at me."

Anya looked at him—at the face of this man she'd propositioned for sex, the man she'd blurted out her most precious truth to, this man she'd accidentally proposed marriage to in a moment of madness. And yet he was here. Whatever she threw at him, he caught her. He held her as if she was the dearest thing to him in the world and he... Her breath fluttered for a whole other reason as she saw her reflection in his deep brown eyes. "I'm sorry for losing it so spectacularly."

He shook his head while pushing away sweaty tendrils of hair from her forehead. "The last few weeks have been a lot, Angel. Falling apart is nothing to be ashamed of."

"I did my best to see you where we wouldn't be interrupted, Simon."

"Hush, I know that. If someone's been irresponsible, it's me. I'm the one who turned that discussion into something else, the one who kissed you in public. I'm the one who didn't see how much Meera was worrying over me. I didn't realize how tuned in she was to my own emotional state. You...made me see that."

"So maybe we could say we're rescuing each other?"

One corner of his mouth tilted up. "You could say that."

"You know my idea that you should marry me is beginning to sound better and better," Anya blurted out too loudly, intent on lightening the mood, wanting to tease him.

The atmosphere in the sitting lounge shifted into something else then, the tension ratcheting up even higher than before. There was no chance her brothers and their wives hadn't heard that remark.

Anya closed her eyes and cringed.

Simon's quiet laughter shook his arms and shoulders and her body. She opened her eyes to see him shaking his head.

"I'm so sorry," she mouthed, loving the wide smile

curving his mouth. Loving how he shielded her from even her family's gaze until she was ready to face them.

"No problem. This will give me a chance to take on your older brother."

She gasped. "God, please no. Don't give him a reason to dislike you, Simon. Any more than he probably already does," she said, lowering her voice now when it was too late.

She pushed back from his warm embrace, even though she didn't want him to let go. Pushing onto his feet in a smooth move, Simon pulled her up. Anya swayed, but only for a moment. Fishing out a tissue from her handbag, she wiped her face and turned to face her family.

The concern in her brothers' grief-stricken faces, the shock in their tight mouths, brought fresh tears to her eyes but she held them back. God, all the years she'd hidden away, all the years she'd refused to live her life to the full, she'd only compounded their guilt. "I'm sorry you had to see that. But I'm fine. Really, I am," she said.

Virat studied her and Simon before saying, "Meera, is she our—"

"Yes," Anya said, cutting him off. "But I don't want to talk about that. I don't want even a whisper of it leaving this room. I don't ever want Meera to be hurt by any of this. She's our first priority." Something she spied on her brothers' faces made her soften her tone. "It's enough that I know her, that I can see what a brilliant girl she is. Enough that she knows me too, and that she considers me a friend."

They all nodded. Whatever flicker of sympathy and worry there had been two seconds ago in her brothers' eyes turned into a flare of pride. But of course, she should have known her older brother wouldn't stay quiet for too long.

"You can't marry him just because he is...her father,"

Vikram said, coming to stand by her side. "We don't know anything about him."

"And how do you plan to stop me, bhai?" Anya said, at the same time that Virat said, "It's her life, bhai. At least, she's finally living it."

Vikram's scowl disappeared. He regarded Simon with fresh eyes. "For one thing, don't you think he's...too old for you?"

Anya looked at Simon. His expression curious, he raised his shoulders, as if saying, "This is all yours." But he didn't remove his hand from her shoulder, to remind her he was right there with her. As if they were part of a team already. His quiet strength at her back made her feel as if she could take on a mountain. "This from the man whose wife is twelve years younger than him," Anya said, winking at Naina. And for all the years he'd tormented her with his overprotectiveness, she added, "Old or not, he serves my purpose. Believe me, I've already taken him out for a test drive."

Simon laughed again, sending vibrations down her spine. It was deep and from the belly and the most wonderful sound she'd ever heard.

Now both her brothers looked like they wished they'd never had to hear that. Had never provoked her into saying it.

"Good for you, Anya," added Naina while Zara whooped and the three of them burst into laughter. Her brothers watched her, mouths agape.

"As much as I loved seeing your sister putting you both in your place, we're not actually getting married. That was never under...consideration," Simon said diplomatically.

How could she not like him when he tried to save her pride, save her face even with her own family? How could he not see how irresistible his kindness was?

"Anya has more than proved to me that she has nothing but Meera's happiness at heart. Meera and she have already grown close. I ask that you stay out of this. I would not have you hurt Meera in any way with your interference. Even if she's your…" He never finished the thought. But he regarded Anya for a second and added, "Or Anya, for that matter."

If her brothers thought it wildly out of line that he was warning them to be careful with their own sister, they didn't bat an eye. In fact, she thought she saw a glint of respect dawn in her older brother's fierce gaze.

Like recognizes like, Anya thought, with a roll of her eyes.

"But now that our… *Meera* knows about whatever it is between you two, or some version of it," Vikram said, "where does this go?"

"That is for Anya and me to decide. And for you to go along with, whatever our decision," Simon said, his statement nonnegotiable and delivered just as bluntly. It was clear Vikram had met his match in Simon.

"You're okay with all of this?" Virat asked her, and there was more than one question in there. There was concern and worry but there was also faith in his eyes—in her. In her capabilities. In her choices. In her strength to keep standing through this.

Overcome by a sudden impulse, Anya hugged both her brothers. They'd long taken the role of her guardians, thanks to their parents' neglect and far too public marriage problems.

Her older brother especially had had all of her family's financial burdens thrust onto his shoulders when he'd been barely eighteen. "Yes, I'm good. I mean, it was really hard when I saw her for the first time…but I'm dealing with it well now. I can do this, bhai."

"I can't believe I didn't realize that Meera's that baby girl I held all those years ago." Vikram held Anya's wrist, his face wreathed in pain. "I'm sorry I didn't do more to keep her in your life, Anya. I'm sorry that I had no other choice but to urge you to give her up—"

"No, I'm the one who should beg for forgiveness," she said, for once able to see the past clearly. This talk had been long needed. For all his faults, Vikram had always looked out for her and Virat, who were several years younger than him. And in return, all he'd gotten was resentment from both of them. "I resented you so much for so long and you didn't deserve any of it."

Her oldest brother squeezed her shoulders until she fell into his arms. "You don't owe me anything, Anya. I know I'm pushy and arrogant sometimes, but I've always only wanted the best for you and that sweet baby. You were so fragile when you were carrying her, and that was before you lost so much blood after the delivery…all I wanted was to protect you as much as the baby."

She looked up and the awful guilt in his eyes, perversely, made her stiffen her spine. "I didn't understand for a long time how much was on your shoulders back then, bhai. You were trying to dig our finances out of a hole by revitalizing the Raawal House of Cinema, and at the same time trying to get Mama and Papa to behave and keeping Virat out of trouble. And through it all, you looked out for me. You looked out for that baby girl when I couldn't, when no one else would."

She wiped her tears and smiled. "And now…have you seen what a beautiful, brave, talented girl she's grown into? Have you seen what a wonder she is?"

When he nodded and smiled through his tears, Anya went up on her toes and kissed his cheek. "I'm sorry that I never thanked you. For myself or for finding such a loving family for her. So I'll say it now, bhai. Thank you for looking out for me. Thank you for looking out for my baby. I was not ready in shape or form to be a mother." Anya swallowed the lump of grief in her throat. "You made a hard decision and you became my villain. But you never wavered. I can't thank you enough for that."

Tears in his own eyes, her brother wrapped those long arms around her. There was no need for words as they stood like that for countless minutes.

Anya sighed, feeling as if another wound that had festered for so long had finally begun to heal.

Feeling as if the past had loosened another painful claw from her present.

Feeling free and whole and light for the first time in years.

CHAPTER SEVEN

"I'M SORRY YOU were pulled into all that family drama," Anya added, feeling awkward in the suddenly empty suite. Her brothers and their wives had left and for the first time in…forever, Anya felt as if she were a new person. A different person.

In a way, she felt relieved that they all knew. They knew what Meera was to her. And they knew that, whatever the future held for her, Anya could look after herself. For the first time in years, she'd come out of her shell and she was taking up space in her own life.

And they knew that Simon cared about her.

She wasn't going to delude herself that it was anything romantic or even close to love, but the fact was that he cared about her. Just as she did about him. And she held that knowledge close to her heart like a lick of flame giving out constant warmth in even the darkest patches of night.

"I wish I could say I don't understand where they're coming from. But I do." Simon rubbed a hand over his face. "I know how it feels to see a loved one suffering and be powerless to help. How…it eats away at you. How it makes you seem harsh and unyielding when all you're doing is trying to help."

The little glimpse into his past sent a shock through Anya. She wanted to know everything about him—about this man who had a great capacity to love, clearly, but didn't want to.

"Simon, what are you talking about?"

His gaze was distant. "Rani… I didn't always give her what she wanted. And she resented me for it."

"How…how do you mean?"

"Let's just say I let her down. Especially when she needed me."

His revelation startled Anya. From everything Meera said, she'd assumed his marriage had been perfect, his wife a paragon of perfection she could never compete with. And yet, he sounded as if he blamed himself for Rani's unhappiness. How? Why?

Curiosity gnawed at Anya, but she was loath to intrude. Especially after her family had just done so in such a spectacular fashion. "I can't believe that you would ever have hurt her, Simon. What did you refuse her?" When his jaw locked tight, Anya tried to pick up the thread of their conversation. "I…never realized how hard it must have been for bhai back then. How heavily it weighed on him that he couldn't do more for me," she said, pointing her shoulder at the closed door behind her.

"You weren't much more than a child yourself," he said gently. "I can understand Vikram's helplessness even better now. His need to hover around you." He handed her a bottle of water and she took it gratefully. "You look tired."

She felt her gaze on her face as she tipped it up and drank it in one long gulp. "I was working straight for three full days. That might have triggered the panic partly too."

"Does it happen a lot?"

"Not frequently anymore. I haven't had an episode since the night I discovered who Meera is and before that it was some years ago."

"But it happened a lot after you…gave her up?"

Anya nodded, squeezing the bottle of water in her hands. "Before too."

She didn't like thinking about that period of her life at all. It was like a nightmare waiting to sink its claws into her again. But she wanted to share it with Simon. She wanted to put it to rest finally.

"I was sixteen when I met…him. We used to meet in secret. I badly needed an escape and he provided it. Outwardly, my family was the uncrowned royalty of the industry. But it was all hollow inside. My dad's gambling habits and Mama's three gigantic investments into reviving her career meant we were close to being bankrupt. They'd already ruined Vikram and Virat's childhoods with their constant public breakups and reunions. And Vikram… he was trying to hold it all together, trying to keep Virat from running away. My grandmother did her best to look after me. And this man…he gave me sweet words and false promises."

Simon's fingers rested on her wrist, as if to keep the ache of it at bay.

"I didn't even know until I was too far along that I was pregnant. And then when I did find out I hid it from everyone. It became this strange obsession I began to focus on. That man was long gone. Especially after I told him that our wealth was nothing but a smoke screen." Anya rubbed at her eyes. "Sometimes I see Meera and I think… God, how naive was I to just fall for a predator like that?"

"From everything I gather, you didn't have the easiest childhood. The tales of your parents' escapades are still talked about now. It's not a jump to believe you were looking for some attention and fell prey to the wrong guy. Meera, on the other hand…"

"Has had the most wonderful upbringing. And she has you uprooting your life and moving to another country just so she could try her chance at acting. If I ever decide to have a child again, that's the kind of…" Heat climbing her cheeks, Anya let the words fly away from her lips.

"Shouldn't you consider that before you throw proposals willy-nilly at the first man you like?"

Anya tried to not take his brusque tone personally. "What do you mean?"

"That you should know what a man can give you and can't give you before you propose." He sighed and closed his eyes. "Rani and I lost entire years trying to conceive. She went through so much, mentally and physically. Our relationship never quite recovered." She saw his Adam's apple move, as if the admission was still painful. "You should know, Anya, marriage and children and love…those aren't things I believe in anymore."

Her heart thudded at the flatness of his words. He wasn't simply warning her away. There was a well of pain in his heart. "I didn't mean to bring up painful memories for you." She cleared her throat, trying to make her way through the tension between them. "Simon, about having a child… I was daydreaming. Until you…and Meera came along, I never gave a thought to the shape of my future. I had no particular dreams."

"When did you tell your family about the pregnancy?" he asked, cutting her off.

Anya wanted to push the issue. Tell him what she'd realized in the last three days. That she'd take a casual affair with him in the present. For however long it lasted. Especially now that Meera knew a version of the truth about them. But the tight lines around his mouth made her back off.

"I didn't tell them," Anya said, picking up the thread of her own past. "I collapsed one evening—my blood pressure was dangerously high—and Vikram found me.

I don't think he or Virat recovered from that for a long time. I know they blamed themselves for not looking after me better."

His dark eyes full of understanding, Simon simply listened. And for him, because she wanted him to know this, Anya went on. Just this one time. "I got medical attention after that but things really didn't improve. My body and mind felt so…disconnected. And I went into a very deep depression."

"And after you gave birth?"

Anya sighed. "That was another disaster. I lost a lot of blood and nearly went into a coma. Vikram spent the weeks leading up to the due date talking to me about adoption. Promised that he had a friend who'd reassured him that the baby would go to parents who absolutely wanted her. He spent hours and hours with me, telling me I was too young, too unwell. That it was a responsibility I just wasn't ready for, and that I needed to look after myself first.

"I finally relented—especially after the doctor told us that it was going to be a difficult birth. I held her for a little while, looking at her darling little face, but I was still hemorrhaging so they had to take me away."

Simon clasped her hand in his.

"When I became conscious two days later, she was gone. That depressive episode continued for a long time. For years, the only thing I remember feeling was this…irrational anger toward Vikram. But he never held it against me."

"So you're saying I should give even more credit to the far-too-full-of-himself Vikram Raawal?"

Anya smiled, her heart warming up at the fact that that's exactly what Simon intended to do. "His heart's always been in the right place."

His thumb traced the plump veins on the back of her

hand. "I'm glad he looked after you. What you went through...was incredibly hard. Rani would've wanted me to thank you for giving us such a wonderful gift."

"It didn't feel like that at the time. I didn't even have time to bond with her properly...it felt like my heart was breaking."

He nodded, his deep brown eyes searching for something in hers. Before Anya could figure out what it was, he let her hand go. "Thank you for sharing that with me. I can't imagine how painful it must be to talk about it."

His words felt formal, practiced, as if he was establishing distance between them again. As if he needed to pull back from the intimacy her shared secret had suddenly woven around them.

"What are we going to tell her?" Anya asked, feeling super tired but determined to get this over with. "Should we say I had...kind of a breakdown and you had to play my knight in shining armor? That it wasn't romantic so much as an obligation? That you..."

He scowled so fiercely that she clasped her elbows in opposite hands. "What?"

"There's no obligation between us, Anya. Sooner or later, she's going to realize that I'm insanely attracted to you."

Simon wanted her. Maybe even with the same desperation that she wanted him. But he clearly wasn't happy about it. In fact, sometimes Anya got the feeling that he was downright angry that it was *she* he'd found himself drawn to.

She didn't understand that. Because not once had he ever hinted—by word or gesture—that he didn't like her. That he didn't respect her.

After dealing with emotionally closed off men—her father and even her brothers to an extent—for most of her life, Simon's openness and honesty was like a breath of fresh air. And yet...the more he learned about her, the more he seemed to want to pull away.

Slowly, he extended his hand toward her face, as if he didn't want to spook her, and waited. Only when she nodded did he clasp her cheek in his broad palm.

Holding his gaze, Anya leaned into the simple touch. Her breath stuttered as the pad of his thumb rubbed back and forth. Again and again. He didn't lean in or pull her toward him, didn't turn the touch into something sexual. Neither did he let her go. For long minutes, they stood like that, her thigh leaning against the side of his. Her lungs full of his woodsy scent.

She wrapped her fingers around his wrist. "One day you push me away—" she nuzzled her face into his palm, loving the rough abrasiveness of his skin, learning the length and breadth of his blunt-nailed fingers "—the next...you're holding me through a panic attack and threatening my brothers to watch themselves around me or else."

His brows pulled into a line. As if he was realizing only now how his actions could be perceived. "Kindness and decency don't make me into a suitable romantic partner for you. I think that's what Vikram was trying to tell you."

"And yet, those are the qualities I rarely find in most of the men I know." Releasing his palm, Anya rubbed her hands over her hips. She had to give them something else to do. "Also let's not forget sex appeal," she teased. "That really clinches the deal for me."

His laughter thrummed through her spine, pooling low in her belly.

"I shouldn't have distracted us from the topic of what we'll tell Meera."

"I won't make you look weak to her just so we can get

out of a sticky situation. You never needed rescuing, Angel.
Not even the evening we met."

"What did I need?"

"Someone to simply stand by your side. Someone to
remind you that you'll come out of that too."

Anya wondered if he could hear the thud of her heart,
if he could see in her face that she'd fallen in love with
him at that moment. Just a little. "You want to tell her the
truth then? That how we met was as strangers screwing
against the wall?"

"Damn, you're blunt when you're angry."

Anya shrugged, enjoying the dark strip of color at the
crest of his cheekbones. The man's face was full of rough
planes, and broad strokes. As if the sculptor had stopped
midway because he'd realized this face was better off raw
and unfinished.

"I… I'm not ready to talk about my questionable decisions with my daughter. I might never be ready."

Anya pouted. "Just so you know, I'm officially taking
offense at being called a questionable decision. That's the
meanest thing you've ever said to me."

"I will present you with a more appealing term then."

"Simon, what if I were to make you a different kind of
proposition? One that could both distract the media and
also give us lots of mutual orgasms along the way?" She
had no idea where her boldness was coming from. While
she wasn't desperate for just any man, she wanted to live.
She wanted to have fun, she wanted more pleasure, she
wanted to share more moonlight kisses with him.

God, she'd done enough hiding for one lifetime.

Interest gleamed in his eyes and she felt as if she was
going to float away on a high. "You think you could handle a purely sexual relationship?"

"I'm thirteen years younger than you, old man. Our

generation is all about the casual. And for the sake of the complete honesty that we've both always engaged in, I won't know if I can handle it unless I try it, right?"

He let such a filthy curse fly that her battered confidence soared. A strange knowing fluttered through her heart, however much she tried to deal with rational facts. That their fates were tied together. And by more than Meera. There was a reason the universe had pushed her into Simon's path. A reason Simon had wandered out into that corridor instead of ignoring her distress.

She just…had to have faith in it. And in herself.

"So…what's your answer? Do we put on a fake relationship for show, or am I allowed to touch you for real?"

His mouth curved into a lazy smile that drew grooves around his mouth. "You're quite bloodthirsty beneath all that fragile softness, aren't you, Angel?"

Anya pouted. "I mean, I understand not accepting my ridiculous marriage proposal but if I'm forced to suffer through a bout of celibacy, especially when I'm the most horny I've ever been in my life, then yes, it's going to make me feel better if I can punish you for it."

He dipped his head, as if to hide his expression. "Why do I have the feeling even your punishments are going to be enjoyable?"

"I'd hate telling Meera any kind of lies, Simon."

He clasped her cheek, his expression gentle and yet somehow consuming. "Then we'll tell her the truth."

"Which is?"

"That we like each other." A glimmer of smile broke through and she felt drenched in its warmth. "But that neither of us is in a hurry. That we're just simply exploring what might be. That should work until the shoot gets wrapped up."

"Okay," she said, leaning her forehead against his shoulder. "You think one of us will be ready to move on by then, don't you?" Anya prompted, wanting to know the truth.

He shrugged.

Anya sighed. "Will you promise me that—"

He broke her off with a hard, fast kiss to her lips that sent her blood pumping despite her exhaustion. His forehead rested against hers, his breath warm against her skin. "Nothing that happens between us, or doesn't happen will affect your relationship with Meera." He traced a path under her eyes with the pad of his thumb gently. "You look shattered. And that was before you saw the news."

"I feel it," she said, giving in. "It's always like that during the week rushing to rehearsals or the shoot. I'd like nothing more than a bath and then to crawl under the sheets."

"Sure you won't fall asleep in the bath?"

The question made her flush. "I don't think so."

He tapped her cheek. "Okay, go get out of these clothes. You have to take better care of yourself, Anya."

"Sir, yes, sir," Anya threw behind her shoulder, warmth blossoming in her belly. She didn't doubt for a second that Simon was extra concerned right now after witnessing her panic attack. But still, his care felt like a childhood blanket wrapped around her. They'd had sex and yet, there was a true intimacy in the small things, in everyday life that she wanted more of. "I will do my best to satisfy you."

She heard his laughter behind her and her own mouth curved into a broad smile. Just talking to Simon—even about the most painful part of her past—made her heart sing, her body thrum. When she came back to the bathroom in a thick, fluffy robe that barely covered her thighs, the bathtub was filled with hot water, the scent of jasmine oil rising up from it coiling through the air, with a few candles lit up around it.

Simon stood at the door, his gaze firmly staying on her face. "Don't fall asleep in there, Angel. We have connecting rooms. I'll be back to check on you."

"Connecting rooms?" Anya said raising a brow. "Whose idea was that?"

"Mine." From the wicked light in his eyes, he knew exactly what she was thinking.

"So you knew how this was all going to play out?"

"The second I saw the headlines, yes. I knew how it would affect you and I planned to keep you close." He waited, as if worried he'd find complaints from her over his highhanded behavior. "That was before I realized your brothers would interfere. I didn't want you to think you were alone in dealing with this…just because I…"

"Just because you rejected me?"

"I rejected your ridiculous proposal as you called it. Not you."

Anya walked toward the bathroom and came to a standstill in front of the door. "Ahh…that means I'll just have to find the right angle to tempt you."

Surprised delight shone in his eyes. "If you don't want me to see you naked, Angel, you better get out of the bathtub fast."

"And you think that's going to make me get out quickly or stay in for longer?" She looked at him wickedly over her shoulder, her fingers lingering on the knot of her robe. "You're confusing reward with punishment, Simon."

She had the ultimate reward of seeing his eyes darken before she closed the door on him and leaned against it, her knees shaking.

Who'd have known the Raawal boldness would come in so handy one day? And she was only getting started.

CHAPTER EIGHT

SIMON FOLLOWED ANYA'S voice to Meera's room across the corridor and pushed the already-open door ajar. If they were not on the production set or the rehearsal halls, he would always find Anya and Meera together either at the small cafe in the neighborhood village or in one of their rooms.

In the two weeks they'd been in Udaipur, the three of them had already settled into a routine. Despite the unpredictability of a production set in progress, delays in schedules, problems with supply chains, somehow Anya made it easy for not only Meera but for him to find some kind of stability.

Much as he wanted to, Simon couldn't deny the fact that she'd made herself indispensable to both of them and not for any selfish agenda of her own. Not for any other reason than the fact that she cared about Meera and him.

He'd seen her work ten to twelve hours each day, coordinating last-minute fittings and repairs based on rehearsals of the fight scenes, redesigning a part of the men's armor because some of the leather belts had been lost in delivery, and still she always made time for Meera in the evening.

Every small thing Meera needed, from help with rehearsing her own lines to dealing with a fever on the very night when Simon had been out of town for an overnight trip, dealing with his daughter's first heartbreak—apparently the punk light boy had found a girlfriend in the catering company—Anya was ever ready, with infinite patience and calm demeanor and quick-witted answers that satisfied even the sulky teenager that Meera could sometimes be.

As he watched her move around Meera's room picking up all the myriad things his daughter scattered about, a tight knot emerged in his chest. He forced himself to exhale, forced himself to examine the source of his tension.

He'd been waiting for a break in that soft, generous smile.

For a fracture in her sunny temper where she'd say she needed a break from Meera or him or both.

For the dream to lose some of its shine in the dirty patches of reality.

For her to get restless or bored or annoyed…which, he knew, would've been completely fair. What struck him was how he'd been comparing her to Rani and that was unfair to both women. For all he'd assumed she was fragile, Anya had her feet solidly on the ground.

If Meera was busy with something, Anya asked Simon if he wanted to have dinner together. If she was going on a day trip to play tourist and visit local spots on the one day Virat had decided he didn't need her, she asked him if he'd like to come along. If Simon happened to be working late—which he mostly had to because he still hadn't completely decided if he wanted to make Mumbai his new HQ—she dragged in her portable sketching table and her box of pencils and loose paper and worked alongside him in silence.

While Vikram's PR manager put a tight quality control on what was leaked from the movie production site by the crew, a few pictures of him and Anya had made it to the social media sites. After the first baseless rumor, apparently, the media and the public were now quite fond of him and Anya as a couple.

And despite his resolution that he'd not send her mixed signals, that he wouldn't take advantage of her generosity, Simon had complied with most of her suggestions. Basically, because—for all the lies he told himself—there was no one else he wanted to face over the dinner table. No one he wanted to chat with whether it was about Meera's future or art, or even his own business.

The woman was driving him out of his mind, just as she'd promised she would. And after just spending an entire day in Thailand, bored to death at meetings and parties, Simon had begun to question why he was denying himself this spot of happiness and pleasure.

"Oh, God, Anya, do we have to go through this again?" Meera whined, bringing his attention back to the scene in front of him.

Dressed in a loose skirt and a shirt that she'd knotted below her breasts, Anya was taking Meera's measurements. The groove of her spine bared by the shirt called his gaze every time she moved. "We didn't actually discuss this, Meera. I simply mentioned it to your dad and you. Before either of us could decide, you went ahead and okayed the interview."

Meera did the whole "rolling her eyes and blowing a pent-up sigh" routine. "I heard Vikram sir tell you that it's better to get in front of this, instead of letting the media drive it. And Virat sir said he agreed."

It was Simon's turn to sigh. His daughter had a huge crush on both her uncles. Thank God she thought anybody older than twenty-one was gross.

"Yes, that's true," Anya said, her tone still worried but firm. For all her unconditional love for Meera, she never let the teenager treat her like a pushover. "But my brothers conveniently forget that they've spent their whole lives being the media's darlings. And they're men so they've always been given more leeway." Anya sighed. "Not that they didn't have their own challenges. I'm just saying they...don't know what it is to be a young girl who's unwillingly thrust into the limelight and is measured against her illustrious mother whether she wants to compete or not."

Meera stilled, her eyes wide in her face.

"I don't mean to infer that your...mother was anything like mine," Anya said hurriedly.

"I know," Meera said, her eyes full of understanding that felt far too mature for her age. "Okay, let's go over everything ready for the interview next week. On the condition that you'll let me wear the Louboutins Zara di gave you for your birthday gift."

Anya's eyes widened. "I haven't even taken them out of the box, you greedy girl. Plus they'll be too big for you."

Meera wiggled her foot in front of Anya's face. "I checked. I'm almost the same size as you. Also, we have identical-shaped feet."

Her hand on Meera's foot, Anya stared. A shadow crossed her face before she recovered with a big smile. "Fine. You can wear them. Once."

Meera threw herself at Anya with a whoop and almost sent them both toppling to the floor.

With a strength he wouldn't have guessed she held in her slender form, Anya righted Meera and herself and they settled safely on the floor and leaned against the bed.

Simon stayed at the door, unwilling to interrupt the scene.

"They'll ask about working with my brothers," Anya said, her tone serious. "They'll dig for stories about your mom. And just when you're relaxed enough, when you think you're doing well, they'll pounce with a question about me and…your dad."

"To which I'll say my dad's single, Anya's adorable and it's nobody's business," Meera said with a teenager's confidence that she could storm through every obstacle in her life.

"They'll almost certainly ask what you think about having me as your stepmom." Before Meera could reply, she continued. "I'm sorry that we've put you in—"

"My dad's happier than I've seen him in a long time, Anya. Why are adults so…thick?"

A deep sigh gusted through Simon. His daughter had gotten to the punchline far faster than he had.

Her mouth falling open, Anya seemed taken aback by Meera's confident announcement. "I grew up with parents who didn't care how their antics in public affected us. So if you're upset, that's perfectly valid."

"Anya, for the last time, I'm not upset."

"Okay. That's good. Because I'd hate it if you were."

"And I'd never think you're trying to replace Mama. If you do marry Dad, we'll be more like…friends."

Anya frowned, as if realizing that she was fast losing control of the situation. "Please remember we told you that—"

"I knew something was going on between the two of you long before anyone else," came back Meera. God, his daughter had a smart mouth on her. "Even before you were caught smooching in public."

Cheeks pink, Anya spluttered. "First of all, we weren't smooching in public, we thought we were alone, and second of all…" Anya seemed to have realized what she'd betrayed for she slapped her hand over her mouth. "This is inappropriate."

"I agree. Now if only that stunt master who keeps flirt-

ing with you realized he's got no chance against my dad."
Pride dripped from that last sentence.

Simon pushed the door open, unwilling to swallow his
curiosity. Unwilling to just watch from the sidelines any
longer. "Who's this guy hitting on my girlfriend?"

Meera squealed and threw herself at him. "Dad, you're
back."

He kissed the top of his daughter's head, while his gaze
met Anya's over it. A soft pink crested her cheeks, her eyes
wide and beautiful. "I finished the meeting early in Thailand. So who's this guy?"

"Oh, he thinks he's a total stud, Dad," Meera said, rolling her eyes. "But don't worry. Anya only has eyes for
you."

"Hey," Anya protested, throwing a scarf at Meera, that
fluttered to the ground midway. "Stop spying on me for
him."

"Well, neither Dad nor I want to lose you and everything's fair in love and war."

Simon laughed. "So much for your trust in your old
man, huh?"

"I don't know how it was done in your generation, Dad,
but in this new era," Meera said cheekily, "you actually
have to spend time with your woman if you want to keep
her. Especially someone as hot and in demand as Anya."

When Simon would've swatted her on her shoulder, she
slipped away from him with a grin. "Now, I have to be off
before Virat sir bites my head off again."

She was off and out of the room, like a storm, leaving
a tense silence behind. Simon closed the door and clicked
the lock into place. He stood leaning against the door,
watching Anya as she collected the assortment of papers
and clothes they'd strewn around.

"How long is she going to be out this afternoon?"

"Rehearsals and then archery class and then stunt practice…at least three hours."

"Good."

She sucked in her breath in a soft gasp.

"Are you into this…stunt master stud?" he asked into the silence.

Frowning, she looked up. "No. I don't change my mind about who I want in a matter of days."

"Is he bothering you?"

"Not at all. I think he's more in awe of Vikram than he is genuinely interested in me. He keeps asking a thousand questions about him. He's awkward and clumsy, even worse at flirting than I am."

"And yet he's poaching on my territory?"

She raised a brow, her chin tilting up. "What am I? A pheasant for him to steal?"

"What you are, Angel, is…mine," he said, loving the taste of it on his tongue.

Without waiting for her answer, he walked across the room and locked the connecting door into his room.

Then he went to the king bed, sat down on her side and proceeded to remove his shoes and socks. He pulled his dark gray shirt out of his trousers and undid his cuffs. He unbuttoned his shirt all the way through and then, only then, did he look at the quiet woman still sitting on the floor.

"Come here." Now that he'd decided he wanted her, his control was hanging by a thread. For all that she'd boldly asked him to go to bed with her, he knew how inexperienced she was. He didn't want to spook her by showing how desperately he needed her, didn't want to scare her even though all he wanted was to devour her whole.

Her teeth bit into her lower lip. Her gaze landed on his chest and then skidded away. "How did the trip go?"

Feeling devilishly wicked, Simon shrugged off his shirt completely and went to work on the waistband of his trousers. He'd never been more thankful for all the hands-on construction projects he took on, for his body had remained lean and fit. "As well as could be expected."

He'd undone the button on his pants when she whispered, "Simon?"

"Hmm…yes, Angel?"

"What…what are you doing?"

He gave her his hand, and she took it. Pulling her up, he tugged her until she fell into his lap. "I'm calling myself all kinds of names."

Her fingers landed on his bare shoulders. Then boldly moved downward. The smattering of hair on his chest seemed to consume her attention for she ran her palm up and down his chest, her mouth falling open on a soft gasp. If she felt an ounce of the pleasure that coursed through him, he didn't blame her. "Why?"

"Because I went to a meeting in Thailand when all I wanted was to be inside you."

Her hand stilled, her gaze colliding with his. "Oh."

He grinned and took her mouth in a hard kiss. "I would like to formally accept your proposition, Ms. Raawal."

A cute little frown tying her brows, she raked her nail across his nipple. He hissed and hardened against her bottom and her eyes widened. She wriggled, the wily minx, and his erection responded by showing its eager appreciation. Her words were a raspy whisper across his skin. "I've made you so many propositions, Simon. Which one is it that you're accepting?" Bending her head, she licked a path from his neck to his nipple before she flicked the flat bud with her teeth.

His self-control dissolving like a mist, Simon launched her backward onto the bed. He was on her in seconds, his substantial weight held up on his elbows. Her legs fell away instantly, forming a welcoming cradle for him. He let his hips fall, grinding his erection into her sex. His eyes rolled back in his head when she chased his hips with hers with a needy groan. "This proposition, Angel."

Head thrown back, she arched into him. Her fingers gripped his biceps, and she pushed her head up to meet his lips. With a raw groan, Simon let her tongue into his mouth. She seduced him with her tongue, with soft nips, with hard licks, until he was grinding on top of her like a teenager.

With one hand, he pushed up the flowing skirt she wore, loving every inch of the silky-smooth skin he discovered with his fingers. He bit back a curse when he found a flimsy thong, already damp with wetness. He bent his head and kissed the pulse racing at her neck.

"Angel?"

"Hmm…"

"I need you now."

"Okay, yes."

"I want hard and fast and…"

Fiery pink coated her cheeks but she nodded. "Yes, okay. But then after, slow and lazy."

He grinned and licked her lower lip. "You sound like you have your priorities all set."

"I have a list I've been composing, Simon. All the things I'd do to you, with you, if I ever got my hands on you."

"Yeah?" he said, pushing the thong away, wondering what kind fate had dropped her into his lap.

"Yes. If you have anything you want to add to the list, just let me know."

Holding himself off her, Simon pushed his trousers down. His erection jerked up into his belly, hard and already beading at the tip.

Her gaze wide, Anya traced a line down his length. Up and down until all he could hear was his own heartbeat in his ears. Then her finger rested gently on the soft tip, before dipping into the drop of his release.

And while he watched, his tendons jutting out with pressure, she brought the finger to her mouth and licked at it. Her gaze when it met his was darkly carnal, wicked and full of delight.

"God, this is going to be over before we've even started if you look at me like that, Angel."

"I want to lick you here, all over," she said, fisting his shaft. Moving it up and down with enthusiasm if not expertise.

Simon thrust into her hands, blind need driving him. The thought of that lush mouth wrapped around his erection pushed him that much closer to his release. "Some other time," he managed before he used his free hand to push away the flimsy thong. Gently, he traced the lips of her sex before dipping his finger at her opening. Wetness coated his fingers. She was ready for him, so ready. "Now, Anya?"

"Yes," she said, thrusting her hips up.

Taking himself in hand, he covered up with a condom and thrust into her wet warmth in one go. And didn't stop until he was all the way inside her.

The tight clutch of her sex was the sweetest torment he'd ever faced. Her gasp sent a flutter through his nerves, making him impossibly harder inside her.

Simon kissed a path up her neck to her mouth. "Did I hurt you, Angel?"

She turned to him, her eyes dark with desire, her nostrils flaring. Her fingers moved from his hips to his buttocks, her breathing shallow. "I have imagined your weight bearing down on me so many times, Simon. Of having you move over me. So give me more of you."

A pang went through his chest and he shook his head. "I'll crush you."

"No. Please, Simon."

He let her feel a little more of his weight. Her feet wrapped above his buttocks, her thighs stretched wide. A feral grin curled her lips and he kissed her deep and hard, taking more than giving.

Then he pulled out and thrust back in. Her head moved up on the bed and she wrapped her fingers around the headboard. "Do that again, but faster."

"Hell, you're ruining me, Angel," he muttered before he gave her what she wanted. What he needed too. But he didn't want to go over the edge without her. "Undo that knot. I want to see your breasts."

Breath falling in sharp staccato, she complied with his demands. He roughly pushed away the flaps of her shirt and her bra. Her dark brown nipples were plump, her pulse fluttering away at her neck.

With her hair in disarray, her clothes still on but baring everything to his gaze, she was his fantasy given life. He bent and licked and sucked the nipple into his mouth, each moan and thrust of her body sending a tingle down her spine.

Then he took her hand from his abdomen and brought it to the swollen nub at her core. Her eyes wide, she looked down at the erotic sight of his fingers holding hers, pressing, caressing, flicking the tight bundle of nerves. "Keep that up, Angel," he whispered, praying he wouldn't disgrace himself. "I want to feel you clench around me, Anya. I want to feel everything my body does to you. And keep your eyes open."

With the raw command, he upped the tempo of his thrusts.

Their gazes held as he used her hard and fast, the intensity of their building climaxes, the thud of their hearts, telling them it was going to be even better than last time.

That the remaining few weeks weren't going to be enough. That there was nothing casual about this at all.

Soon, pure pleasure overtook any rational thought and Simon roared as her climaxing muscles milked him hard and tight and he fell apart in her arms.

He held her long after she fell asleep.

It shouldn't have been this easy. This simple. She shouldn't have been able to sneak into his head, his thoughts this easily.

But she was there, without question. She made him laugh. And she made him want. And she made him… realize how lonely he'd been for a long time. She made him realize that he'd sort of given up on himself too. But he wasn't sure if he'd ever have the courage to trust his heart again.

Or trust himself with her happiness.

CHAPTER NINE

I T WAS PAST eleven when Simon knocked on the connecting door between his and Anya's four days later. Again. Nothing but silence answered him.

While she hadn't told him herself, Meera had let it slip that it was Anya's birthday. Simon couldn't wait to see her face when he revealed the small surprise he'd planned for her at the last minute. It had shocked him, his overwhelming desire to do something for Anya, his own excitement while he'd arranged the surprise, the depth of his need for it to be something special. As special as her smile, her joy she so easily shared with him and Meera.

But today of all days, he'd been stuck in meetings for hours and when he'd finally returned to their suite, both Anya and Meera had been gone.

After waiting for more than a couple of hours, he gave up on the pretense of work. He wouldn't be able to concentrate anyway until he knew Anya was safely in her bed. Or his, where they'd been spending the last few days. Every moment they could manage, like young lovers stealing away from adults.

In their case, it was any time they were afforded by Meera's and Anya's rigorous schedules. At forty-three, Simon wasn't into instant gratification nor should he have the stamina for it, but God, Anya made him feel wild in his skin again. After that first lazy afternoon they'd spent in bed, after which they'd both fallen asleep together, he'd wondered if he was going through some kind of midlife crisis. If that was the reason Anya appealed to him so much.

Just the question had left a horrible taste in his throat.

However many reasons and excuses he'd tried to explain away the madness in his blood, this wild obsession with her, nothing fit.

It was just all her.

Her laughter. Her sensuality. Her generous heart. Her... unending energy to try everything she claimed she'd missed out on for so long. Her sweet, soft body that she gave without inhibitions even as he pushed them both to the edge and then careened right over it.

How long would it last though? How long before Simon let her down too?

Feeling far too restless in his skin, he pushed up from his seat and pulled on a sweater. He'd simply walk to the set. Vikram had security guards posted all over the location and through the walkway between the site and the luxury hotel where Anya, Meera and he were staying but he still felt a thread of anxiety in his gut when she wasn't back in her room.

Just as he was used to worrying over Meera. It had no rational basis; he knew that much. And he didn't right now care beyond that.

He heard the laughter and shouts before he entered the makeshift tent that had been erected for the crew to rest during outdoor shoots on hot days. Bending his head to get through the low arch, he walked in to find a center table decorated with cake and candles and balloons. There were almost fifty crew members circulating with drinks in hand.

Simon was about to ask Vikram—he and the older

Raawal had made peace of sorts—when he saw the flash of a smile and an elegant hand with a leather strip in it that he knew was Anya.

She was standing with a young, brawny actor—the same so-called stud that Meera had talked about before. Simon knew because he'd gone on set the next day to find out. The man clenched his arm so that his muscled bicep was on glorious display while Anya was checking the leather thong on the arm straps that were part of the costume.

Every time he flexed his bicep—and he did it a few times—the strap loosened and Anya tried to buckle it up again. With a laugh, the actor pointed to the same kind of bands he wore on his wrists, ankles and even thighs.

It was the first time in his life that Simon felt the taste of possessiveness and jealousy curl on his tongue.

"She's not as fragile as she looks."

He'd been so immersed in watching Anya that he hadn't even realized that Virat had walked up to him. "I know that."

"Then why do you look at her with such wariness in your eyes?"

Simon stayed silent for a beat too long to deny it.

Apparently, Virat was more discreet than his brother for he didn't push Simon. "I've never seen Anya this happy. This…excited about life in general. Her work has reached a new level of brilliance. I never did believe in the whole 'suffering creates better art' nonsense."

Simon swallowed his token protest and waited. He hadn't even realized he needed to hear this. Hadn't real-ized how deep and raw a wound Rani's silence and her unhappiness and her retreat had carved in him.

As if sensing this, Virat continued. "I can't tell you the number of years Vikram and I spent trying to get her to celebrate her birthday in a big way, to coax her out of her shell. And yet, this year, she ordered the cake and balloons for herself, and she invited the crew. She's even invited our parents when she usually tries her best to avoid them. I think my sister's finally celebrating who she's become."

Simon could see the joy written plainly over Anya's face. Something that made his own chest expansive and full. "That could have been to do with finding Meera again."

Virat turned to face him and Simon was forced to do so too. As much as he liked to keep the Raawal brothers at a distance—the reason being how protective he felt about not only Meera but Anya too—he'd discovered in the last fortnight that he genuinely liked both men. For all they'd been born with silver spoons and a legacy, they had also borne a lot of burdens along the way and had hearts of gold. Their choice in wives spoke most volubly for both of them.

"You and I both know that's only half the reason, Simon. Neither Vikram nor I can overlook the fact that you made the hardest thing in her life easier for her to face. That you've been supportive and kind during every step of the way for Anya. I can't tell you how grateful we are to see her this happy, and to see Meera flourish."

His heart felt as if it might explode out of his heart. "I only want Meera's happiness. And… Anya's."

"And yet you still doubt that it lies with you?"

Simon said the words that had been sitting on his chest like a bag of rocks for days now. Even weeks. "Anya has been through a lot already. She's told me about her anxiety and I've seen her panic attacks. She's still so young and—"

"And you think that somehow makes her less of a person?" Virat bit out, jaw tight. "Did I mistake you for a better man, Simon?"

"Of course it doesn't make her any less. She has so

much to give despite everything, such fire and courage...
don't think for one second I don't see her as she really is,
Virat." Simon searched for the right words. "But you have
to understand that I... The thought of having her happiness in my hands, the thought of hurting her in any way...
the very thought of being the reason Anya loses out on
something she truly deserves..." Simon hated speaking
the words aloud but he did it anyway. He needed the reminder these days. "I hate to agree that Vikram's right, but
I am older than her and there are some things that my life
experience has taught me to be wary of. Some things that
I'm incapable of giving at this point in my life. I'm jaded
and at the risk of sounding like a quitter, I'm not sure I'm
the right person to deal with...fragile things. That young
show-off, as much as I hate him pawing at your sister, is
probably a better man for her than I am."

"No wonder my brother likes you so much beneath all
the bluster he aims at you... You're both cut from the same
overprotective, overthinking cloth." Virat looked at Anya,
who'd clearly noticed them chatting and was heading their
way. He bent forward and gripped Simon's shoulder hard.
"Don't undercut her like that. Not when she's just found
her wings. There's nothing more arrogant than assuming
you're responsible for someone's happiness. Especially
when it's the woman you just admitted to seeing and admiring. Don't coat your cowardice, your fears with her
imagined flaws, Simon. Believe me, I did that once, and
I almost lost Zara."

Simon stared at Virat's retreating back, his words re-
verberating through him.

Was it arrogant to believe he would become responsible for Anya's happiness if he took this any further? Was
he doing her an injustice thinking he knew better for her

than she herself did? Was he wrong about the state of his marriage to Rani there at the end too?

He scrubbed a hand down his face just as Anya tapped him on the arm. "Hey. Is everything okay? Did Virat say something he shouldn't?"

Simon faced her and shook his head. "No. I think I got a dose of why the critics call him a blunt but brilliant filmmaker."

She didn't look convinced but she nodded. "What are you doing here? Meera's spending the night with Zara's sister who's visiting. I checked on them again before I came down."

"I came to find my errant girlfriend."

The bright shine in her gaze went straight to his head. "Yeah?"

"Why didn't you invite me to the celebration?" he said, waving an arm in the direction of the cake and the balloons.

"I know how much you dislike hanging out with the movie crew. I didn't want to force you to do it after-hours too."

He tapped a finger on her scrunched nose, wanting to touch her again. In many more places. In a spot where they weren't surrounded by gorgeous young men and their brawny bodies.

"How many times are you going to have to fix that joker's armbands and thigh bands and calf bands? Have you wondered if maybe he's breaking them on purpose so that you will admire his bulging biceps and fix them for him again?"

For a second, Anya blinked, confusion apparent in her eyes. And then she laughed. Loud and bold and drifting up from her belly. Her already-wide mouth widened and her too-big nose flared and she was so beautiful that it stole his breath.

At some point during her laughter she'd tucked her arm through his and leaned against him. Simon tried to remind himself that she was probably only doing it for the avidly watching crowd. But he knew that was a lie. Just as it was a lie that he had wrapped his other arm around her because it was the gentlemanly thing to do when she was clinging to him.

Simon knew most of the heads had turned toward them under the marquee now. Not surprising because they'd gathered to celebrate Anya. Also not surprising because, while they were meant to be a couple, neither of them had embraced in public. Her brothers and sisters-in-law and even her parents—all of them were staring with such shock in their eyes.

Reaching out with her hand, she pushed a lock of hair from his forehead. "Are you jealous of that muscly actor, Simon?"

"A little," he admitted. "No. A lot, actually."

Something stirred in her liquid gaze. And this time, it went straight to his shaft.

She patted a hand over his chest, as if she was dusting something off his sweater. But he knew she wanted to feel the thud of his heart. As if she knew its beat was already rushing in his ears anytime she was near. "Don't be. He can't handle me."

Simon knew she was half joking but he wanted the answer anyway. He wanted to hear it in her words. "How do you mean?"

Her smile didn't quite disappear but she sobered. She knew exactly what he was asking. "Do you think he'd have asked me what I needed when I fell apart after seeing Meera? Do you think he'd have held me, kissed me, made me feel alive at the worst point of my life? Do you think he'd have shown such care when I told him I'd got pregnant and given up a baby when I was a teenager? Do you think he'd have given me a second glance if I weren't the Raawal brothers' sister?" She pressed against him, her arms going around his neck just as soft music burst through the speakers. Stepping onto her tiptoes, she whispered at his ear. "Do you think he'd see beneath the pretty shell and the wealthy accessories to the real woman with her anxiety and her flaws and her tainted past, Simon?"

His hands went around her waist as if they belonged there and Simon pressed his mouth to her temple. Her confidence and her words resonated through him.

They swayed slowly to the music. The minx knew that he was putty in her hands.

Simon pressed another kiss to her temple. "Happy birthday, Angel." Most of the attending crew had turned away from them.

"I know what I want from you."

"Anya…" he said, injecting a warning into his tone. Her "marriage proposal" had become a running joke between them. Every time he tried to corral this thing between them into some semblance of a temporary affair, Anya teased his retreat by asking him to marry her.

The joke was on him though. Because marriage in itself was not what bothered Simon. He had no idea when it had happened but tying himself to Anya for the rest of their lifetimes didn't bother him at all. He would give her that if it guaranteed her happiness. If it meant he'd never let her down as he'd done with Rani.

But no such guarantee existed in the world.

She lifted her gaze to him and bit her lower lip. "You won't accept even on my birthday?"

He softly pinched the curve of one hip in his hand.

Loving the tight dip of her waist and the flare of her hip. Neither had he missed the fact that she'd filled out a bit in the last few weeks. Since he'd first seen her. She'd lost the gaunt look and he liked her even better like this—healthy and thriving and happy.

She gasped softly. "Fine. I was going to settle for a few kisses and one orgasm."

Simon swallowed. Desire and laughter were twin ropes, tightening in his lower belly, curling his muscles tight. He wanted to tell himself he was too old to separate lust and liking, but it would be another lie to add to the pile he was telling himself. "Hell, woman, you're killing me."

More people left the tent, leaving only her family around. Simon held her through two more songs, more than content to just touch her. And hold her. It was enough for his heart to know that she was his.

"My brothers... I trust wholeheartedly. But Papa and Mama... I'm not ready for them to meet you and muddy this up, Simon. Why aren't you rushing me away like a frantic lover?"

Simon raised a brow and she giggled. "This was your celebration. I don't want to hurry you away from it. Especially after Virat reminded me you don't often do this."

Surprise flitted across her face.

For once, Simon wasn't sure what she was thinking. "I appreciate that you didn't invite me because I'm not a huge fan of the industry." Her eyes big in her face, she nodded. He rubbed his thumb over his cheek. "But you and Meera are a part of this world. I'm more than happy to support you both when you need me to be here."

Simon didn't realize how it sounded until he said the words. But neither did he want to take them back.

She tugged at the collar of his shirt, her mouth trembling. "You're... I..."

"Anya, are you okay?"

She looked at him through a tremulous smile. "I was done a couple of hours ago. All the celebrating I want to do now is with you."

Simon stared at her, another piece clicking into place.

For months before her accident, he'd tried to break through the wall that Rani had pulled up between them. He'd been nearly driven out of his mind trying to work out what would make her happy. About how to build a bridge back to her. Worried about losing her all over again. In the end, her infuriating demands and her silent rejection of everything he'd tried had killed the love he'd once felt for her. Long before she'd decided to go back to acting and try to revive her career, their relationship had died. But then she'd died before she could set her plans into motion.

And here was this woman…who wore everything she felt on her face.

Who asked outright for what she wanted of him.

Who was turning him upside down by her mere presence.

His assumption that she was too fragile like Rani, that she'd fall apart at the smallest obstacle, that she wouldn't know her own mind…disintegrated into dust at his feet.

She was nothing like Rani.

And the realization loosened the tight thread of fear he'd clutched to him ever since she'd set those beautiful brown eyes on him. Maybe Virat was right. Maybe thinking he'd been wholly responsible for Rani's happiness was only his arrogance and worse, his fear talking.

"Where are we going?"

To give herself credit, Anya had tried to bury the question for the entire fifteen-minute ride on the helicopter that Simon kept at the luxury hotel and that he himself had piloted. But it was a little past midnight and she'd thought they'd be in bed.

Instead, he'd tugged her outside, talked on the phone with his arm around her and then said, "Let's go," which instruction she had blindly, happily followed. Of course, he'd asked her if she'd trust him to fly her safely, after rattling off the number of hours that he had piloted for.

Anya stepped out of the chopper now, taking in the restored palace in front of her with wide eyes. She'd studied the history of the city and the kings and queens that had ruled it in majestic splendor. Which was why she knew that the small palace in front of her—small being relative in comparison to the huge, sprawling one that they were currently shooting the movie in—was the only one that had stayed under the ownership of a reclusive royal who'd refused any price tag for the government or any other millionaires.

Clasping her hand in his, Simon simply pressed another quick kiss to her temple before saying, "You'll see."

Anticipation bloomed in her belly as they mounted the steps toward a smaller entrance instead of the grand, wide entrance. A uniformed servant dressed in traditional clothes bowed his head and then bade them to follow. Her mouth progressively fell open as they followed him through corridor after corridor. Priceless art hung on the walls, and there were decadent rugs, and antique furniture casually strewed about the palace. While she wanted to linger and learn the history behind every piece, Anya simply followed along.

After what felt like a ten-minute walk, they were shown into what might once have been a woman's boudoir. For the vast room was covered in mirrors all around her, with several open archways leading into different corridors.

Her gasp was loud as Anya walked around, seeing their reflections grinning back at them.

And still, the best wasn't over yet.

Divans of different sizes and heights were placed between the open archways. Each covered with clothes, leather armor, weapons, jewelry.

"What is this place?" Anya asked, feeling as if she was standing at a different time and place in history.

Raising her hand to his mouth, Simon grinned. "It's a private collection. A friend of mine owns it. This palace actually belonged to the famous dancer who was supposed to have been the lover of the king."

"The king who owned the other palace where we're shooting?"

"Yes. Did you know both the palaces are connected through a secret passageway? Although I've heard it's been a century at least since it's been blocked."

"He kept his lover here?"

"Yes. Apparently, she hailed from an enemy clan."

"Or he simply wanted to have his cake and eat it too?" Anya replied, grinning back at Simon.

"Possible," he answered, letting her hand go. "But the clothes and the jewelry and the weapons…they're all centuries old. I thought you would enjoy seeing the collection."

Anya threw herself at him, joy bursting through her chest.

For a second, Simon was stiff around her. Then she heard his laughter and his arms surrounded her. Feeling vulnerable and yet as if she might burst apart, Anya pushed away. "How long do we have?"

"He's having the collection moved permanently tomorrow morning. So I'd say we have a few hours. We can't take any pictures or copy the designs."

"Of course," Anya said, awe filling her throat. "You don't mind if I spend a couple of hours here?"

Simon shook his head. "Be my guest."

After that invitation, Anya didn't hesitate. She let the ornate jewelry, the lavish handmade *lehengas*, the starkly beautiful hand swords and knives dazzle her, carry her away to another time.

It was past three in the morning when she walked up to Simon and told him she was ready to go. This time, no servant walked them out. Dawn was still an hour or so away but the courtyard where Simon had landed the chopper was littered with lights to show the way.

Anya pulled Simon against a wall and kissed his mouth, pouring all the emotion that wanted to burst out of her into the kiss. They were panting when they broke apart.

"What was that for?" Simon asked, his grin wide, his eyes dancing.

"Thank you so much for taking me. For knowing how much I'd appreciate seeing something like that before it forever disappeared into someone's vault."

Simon rubbed the curve of her lower lip, still smiling. "I'll admit to doing it for completely selfish reasons."

"Yeah? What might those be?"

"To win one over all the young studs on the set that keep swarming around you."

Anya laughed so hard that she was afraid her heart might burst out of her. She pressed her face into his neck and licked the salt of his skin. His erection, as if in reward, hardened against her lower belly. "All I want is you, Simon."

With a hard sigh, Simon tugged her toward the chopper, his gaze promising any number of delights.

CHAPTER TEN

OUT OF ALL the things Anya had been terrified that the interview host would ask Meera, she hadn't imagined in her worst nightmare that the thing that would shatter the young girl's easy confidence and expansive faith in the world would be to do with Rani Verma.

With the fact that Rani had apparently signed on to a large project with Raawal House of Cinema—of all the production houses in the world—in what was supposed to have been a huge comeback, a mere three months before her death in the accident. Or the awful rumor that on the same trip to Mumbai, Rani had also visited a high-profile divorce lawyer, according to a source close to the late actress.

Hours later, she couldn't still believe the utter malice in pouncing on a thirteen-year-old and asking her such an intrusive question about her dead mother in what was supposed to have been a fun interview. No wonder Simon hated the thought of Meera in the midst of such a toxic culture.

Her steps felt leaden as Anya remembered the stricken expression in the girl's face.

It had been clear that Meera had had no idea that her mother was returning to Bollywood, or that she had signed on to such a major blockbuster project that she'd have been on a production site for at least nine months.

But Meera had recovered fast, and said it should be no

surprise that a talent like her mother's would have come back to the silver screen sooner or later. As for the divorce, she'd said, those were just horrible rumors. Her mouth had been trembling, but her gaze was resolute.

The moment the camera had cut, she had rushed away from the temporary set in search of her father. Anya had followed silently, not wishing to intrude on such a private moment. But wanting to be there in case Meera needed to vent.

For hours after Simon learned of the interview, father and daughter had been behind closed doors in Meera's room.

Anya drifted through the courtyard and then back into the lounge outside Meera's bedroom like a cursed ghost, wanting to go in but so, so afraid that she'd be seen as an unwelcome intrusion. That when it mattered, she'd always be on the outside looking in on father and daughter. Because her foolish heart ached for Simon as much as it did for Meera.

Had Rani and Simon been on the cusp of separation?

Was that why Simon always seemed so reluctant to even broach the topic of his marriage?

I didn't give her what she wanted and she resented me for it... I let her down...

Simon's words pinged through her until useless thoughts spun around and around in Anya's head. She felt an irrational anger toward a woman she hadn't even known for casting such a large shadow over Meera's and Simon's lives. The moment the thought crossed Anya's mind, she knew she was in deep trouble.

But the truth was that his marriage to Rani—whatever it had been like—cast a pall on Simon's present. Maybe even on his future. On their future. And she wanted to know what she was up against. But she was also afraid of rocking the boat, of pushing Simon when the topic was clearly taboo for him, of losing what little she had with him.

It didn't matter that she'd spent every single night in the last week in his bed. It didn't matter that they'd crossed over all the lines Simon had wanted to draw between them. Her thoughts went in circular directions, her statement that she'd keep it casual biting at her.

After what felt like a long while, Simon stepped out, looking at his phone. His features were taut with tension. Still, a soft smile curved his mouth when he found her standing there.

Relief swept through Anya in waves and she cursed herself for the fear beneath it. Was it fair to herself if she was this scared of things falling apart so easily?

He lifted the phone. "I was just about to call you."

"Is she okay?"

"She's been better," he said, and Anya could have hugged him for telling her the truth. "But she will bounce back."

She nodded. "I want to touch you."

He knew what she was asking. The weary look in his eyes was replaced by warm appreciation. "You don't ever have to ask."

Anya threw her arms around him and hugged him so hard that she could feel his heart thundering away against hers. It was selfish to think of their relationship in the midst of the heap of hurt Meera was facing but she'd been terrified that he'd push her away. That he'd blame her in some kind of convoluted way. For a moment, she'd forgotten that Simon wasn't that kind of man. "I'm so sorry this happened."

He pressed a kiss to her temple, his own arms tight bands around her. "You're the last person who should apologize. You've been trying to warn Meera and me both that something like this would happen. This is all my fault."

There was such anger in his voice that Anya jerked her head back to look at him.

A thread of fear wound through her heart. "You might not like hearing this but I'm going to say it anyway."

To her surprise, he laughed. A serrated sound that half vibrated with anger. At himself, she knew. He clasped her cheek roughly before he said, "Don't ever change, Angel."

Her heart kicked against her rib cage. At the emotion in those words. At the tenderness in his eyes.

"Tell me," he said, releasing her.

"Rani was so adored by fans and the industry alike that with even a whiff of this news existing somewhere in someone's mind, it was bound to come out."

"So you're saying I messed this up too."

"Did you know she was making a comeback?"

"Yes," Simon said, biting the single word out. "I knew that she had signed with someone but not who. It was her exit plan from our marriage."

The flat tone of his words said more than the words themselves. "Is that what you...fought about?"

A bitter smile twisted his mouth as he held Anya's gaze in a challenge. "You think I'm such a small man as to begrudge her her career?"

Anya's heart ached at the pain etched into his features. "No. I'm just...trying to understand."

Understand you, and what hold your marriage and Rani still have on you...why you look so tormented by this.

But she said none of those things.

"God, I made mistakes enough," he said, his gaze distant, "but I never stood in the path of her career. Not even when it ruined her mental health. We just never got a chance to tell Meera before the accident happened. She wanted all the logistics in place first. She was looking at schools, interviewing nannies... Rani intended to use the movie shoot as the first phase of our separation. She was determined that none of the upheaval would hurt Meera in any way. Whatever was happening in her mind, in her own life, she was a good mother to Meera."

"So you didn't know she'd signed with Raawal House, specifically?"

"No. Nor did she do me the courtesy of telling me that she was considering a comeback before she signed. Our relationship had already…fallen apart when she told me her news. After the fact. I just didn't believe it at first… I was so angry."

For her leaving him?

Had he still loved her when she'd left him?

No, from the first moment, all she'd heard in his voice was guilt. And he was too honorable to play with her if he still loved Rani.

Anya touched her fingers to his arm, gently shaking him out of his reverie. "Then it was bound to get out, Simon. At least now we can look at it this way—the worst is over. If we can just get Meera through this…they can never do anything more to damage Rani's memory for her."

He rubbed a thumb against her cheek. "God, what did I do to deserve you in my life?"

"I'd like to think we both deserve each other," she said, other words fluttering on her lips. "Not in the usual horrible way it's meant. In a good way."

His smile widened. "I got that." He exhaled harshly. "Meera wants to see you. Will you talk to her?"

"Of course I will."

He pulled her to the small lounge at the end of the corridor, his hand at her lower back. "I've told her that I knew about Rani signing that project. That we'd been waiting to have all the logistics in place before we gave her the news. But that her mother had passed away before that ever happened. All of which is more or less true... And the other part..." His gaze had that far-off look again. "I can't destroy her mother's memory, so I've told her that it was all a lie built off the fact that her mother was returning to her career. I think she wants some reassurance from you."

Anya nodded. "For all she didn't blink when they threw that at her, she's only a girl."

He gazed at her for a while, his thoughts inscrutable, his fingers never not touching her in that way of his. Her shoulders, the nape of her neck, her back, his broad palms stroked her. Anya let the touch soothe her, aware that that's what he was doing too.

Then he pulled her to him with a rough groan, and kissed her. Hard. Long fingers buried in her hair tipped her head up for his pleasure. His teeth nipped at her lower lip, and when she opened, he swooped in with his tongue, stroking, licking, until their breaths were a harsh symphony. It was possessive and rough and feral and Anya reveled in every moment of it.

He leaned his forehead against hers, his breath choppy. "I've wanted to do that all day."

Anya licked her lower lip and gasped, the tiny sting making the pleasure singing through her body all the more potent.

Simon's gaze followed the movement. His breath feathered over her in rough strokes. "Damn it, Angel. I'm sorry I was rough."

Anya rubbed a finger over his lush lower lip and shook her head. "You've never done anything with me that I didn't enjoy thoroughly, Simon."

"For once, I don't want to share you with Meera. I want you for myself. I want to forget this entire day happened. I want to bury myself deep inside you. I want to run away from all this..." His arm wound around her waist and tugged until she was pressed against him. Her breasts felt heavy, achy when he crushed her to him. "And you would be the perfect escape. The perfect place to land, Angel."

Anya buried her face in his neck, the raw admission spreading through her limbs like molten honey.

Only an escape, Anya. You're just a temporary pleasure for him. Not a partner he'll share his hurt with, his life with, the nasty, doubtful voice inside her head whispered, but she shushed it up.

When he released her, she said, "I'll ask Naina and Zara over after we're done talking. Meera loves hanging out with all of us." She hesitated a beat and then asked, "Where will you be?"

"I'm going to get drunk and maybe punch one of your brothers for not vetting that reporter enough. For not telling me that it was their house Rani had signed on with."

Shock made her mouth fall open until Anya realized he was joking.

"Don't worry. I'm aware that I'm looking for someone other than myself to blame. But they should serve my purpose for a little while."

"They can take it," she said automatically, her head full of a hundred questions.

"All joking aside, I do think Vikram could have dropped a small hint to me in our conversations."

"And you?" Anya asked, despite knowing that she should let him go. "Have you ever recovered, Simon?"

Instant tension swathed his features, the tender lover of moments ago all but gone. "From what?"

"From the fact that your wife saw a divorce lawyer and didn't tell you?"

He laughed bitterly and thrust a hand through his hair. "Remember how you asked me if I could turn back time that first moment we met? I wish I could, because damn it,

I'd have made better decisions. First I hurt Rani and now, what I drove her to, is hurting Meera."

With that, his gaze turned to the dark night beyond the balcony. He'd kissed her, held her, he trusted her to look after Meera, but it was clear that he wasn't going to share his deepest pain with her.

Before she begged him to explain why there was such guilt in his eyes, Anya forced herself to walk toward Meera's room. He didn't need her probing into that wound right now. Didn't need her to bring up the guilt and pain that twisted and pulsed beneath every word.

At least with Meera, she knew that she'd be able to allay her fears, to show her how much she loved her.

Orange light was filtering through the sheer silk curtains in her room by the time Anya returned to her room. While she'd caught more than a few hours of sleep in Meera's queen bed, she felt bone-tired and lethargic like never before. Either she was getting anemic again—she made a note in her calendar to call her GP—or her body was telling her to slow down.

She had been pushing too hard this last month so she'd informed Virat that she was taking a day off and then turned her phone off. After finishing a quick shower, she put on one of the T-shirts she'd stolen from Simon, and crawled into her own bed when she heard the connecting door open with a soft creak.

Simon's broad shoulders and tapering waist and those long legs… She drank in the outline of him as if it was her life's fuel. All the tiredness fled her body just like that, a nervous energy, a restless hum under her skin taking its place.

"I'm awake," she whispered, afraid that he would turn around and walk out.

The night lamp came on by her side of the bed, illuminating him completely. From the dark wet gleam of his jet-black hair, it was clear he'd just showered too. Dark circles straddling his eyes made it clear that he hadn't slept a wink.

Her heart ached for him.

"I'm not drunk."

"It's okay if you are."

"If you want to sleep, I'll leave."

"No, stay."

He watched her from his great height, his brows strung together as if he was trying to solve the mystery of her.

With a soft sigh, he sat down by her side on the bed, his long legs thrown in front of him. For long seconds, he stayed like that, his head buried in his hands.

Anya turned to her side and pressed her hand to the outside of his thigh.

After a few more minutes, he took her hand in his and kissed it with such reverence that she felt heat pricking her eyes.

Scooting closer to her on the bed, he ran a thumb around her eyes. Her nose. Her mouth. The hollows under her cheeks. "Did you catch any sleep at all?"

She shrugged. "We watched a movie until midnight, then she slept. I left a note saying that I'd see her in a couple of hours."

Using his hand as leverage, she pushed up until she was leaning against the headboard. When she pulled, he came closer until he was sitting next to her and she could lean her head on his shoulder. Holding his hand close to her chest, Anya started talking. "She'll be okay, Simon. The fact that I pestered her so much over the past week about the interview I was able to point out that they weave all kind of nasty lies from half truths."

"Thank you," Simon murmured without turning back to

look at her. He was staring at a picture of Rani and Meera on the nightstand that the young girl had pulled out of her backpack only three days ago to show Anya.

"Stay with me," she said, sensing his retreat again. Sensing the dark pain from earlier gathering into a cloud about him again. "I wasn't feeling well to begin with this morning. If you leave me now—"

That got him to move like nothing else had. Turning toward her until his broad chest and his handsome face filled her entire field of vision, he said, "What happened?"

"Probably just anemic again. I'll see my doctor soon." Her heart thudded at her daring but Anya made the demand anyway. "Right now, all I need is you. Get ready for bed."

Other than the languid curve of his mouth twitching, he didn't point out her demanding tone. When he started to pull off his V-necked T-shirt, relief swept through her. She shivered as he gathered her hair into one hand and lifted it. Then his warm mouth was on the nape of her neck, his stubbled jaw rasping against her skin. She jerked when he gently bit her there.

"Have you been anemic before?"

"On and off since I gave birth," she replied in a hoarse whisper.

He nuzzled into her shoulder blades and spoke so softly that she almost didn't hear him. "This is the last thing I want to hear right now."

Anya blinked. Worry lines around his eyes deepened. "What…what do you mean?"

A huge sigh pressed his chest to her back. "I've got too many things on my mind already. I don't want to worry about you too."

It was almost as if he was talking to himself than Anya. But it only pushed at the roiling pot of her own emotions. "I'm capable of looking after myself," she pointed out, stiffening in his arms. Had he any idea how hard every word of his landed on her? "I've done it for almost a decade and a half now, Simon. Even with two brothers who think they know better than I do."

Glancing down at her, he frowned. "It's not a reflection on your abilities, Angel."

"No?" she said, challenging him.

"No. I… I used to think you were fragile but I was wrong," he murmured.

"I can be both fragile and fierce, Simon. Believe me, one doesn't negate the other." _

He dropped a hard, long kiss on her lips. "I know that." His right hand moved from her neck to her belly and then his fingers played with the hem of her T-shirt in a motion that only served to inflame her senses. "This needs to come off."

Swallowing down the thick desire in her throat, Anya murmured yes. She loved it when he got demanding like that. When he shed his laid-back, easygoing layer and took what he needed from her. When he let the guilt and whatever else gripped him go and immersed himself in this, in her.

It was strange how she'd gotten so used to doing the most sexual things with him, but this…this raw demand in his voice, the small intimacies he demanded of her—like always wanting skin to skin when they went to bed, making her spell out exactly what she wanted him to do, making her give voice to the darkest fantasies she'd never thought she'd want—made her heart beat faster as much as anything else.

Because she saw a Simon no one else knew. Because with her, he was exactly who he was beneath the guilt and honor and the clutches of the past. He didn't have to be a dad, or the grieving widower or the man who'd worn a shroud of loneliness for so long.

She barely had to lift her chest before he had the T-shirt off her.

He turned her malleable body until her back was to his chest—hard, warm and taut. The hair on his chest rasped against her smooth skin, the hard ridge of his abdomen a shock against her lower back before he adjusted her to his liking. Her bottom was tucked tight against his crotch, and she could feel him hardening, lengthening. Anticipation turned her mouth dry, her limbs shaky, her sex damp and ready.

But he didn't make a move. He didn't tell her he needed to be inside her like he usually did. In the middle of the night. At the first light of dawn. Once, with her face pressed against the ceiling-length glass windows which gave her a view of the courtyard but showed nothing to the people on the other side. Everything he suggested, Anya got addicted to it.

One corded arm wound around her while the other ended up between her breasts with the tips of his fingers resting on her pulse at her neck. Sometimes, his thumb would rub her lower lip; sometimes, he'd signal for her to open her mouth until she was sucking and nipping the pad of it. Sometimes, he'd take her like this, pushing into her from behind, setting a lazy rhythm that made her very blood molten.

He did none of those things today.

Anya felt as if she was being cocooned in the warmest of blankets even as his hard body around her stoked a fire in her lower belly. His mouth rested at her temple. She closed her eyes, willing her heartbeat to slow down.

Maybe the man didn't have sex on his mind tonight.

But she did. And she wouldn't know until she told him. She wasn't going to sleep until he'd rocked her to an orgasm. Until the stress and uncertainty building to a crescendo in her head had an outlet in the form of physical release.

"Simon?"

"Hmm?" His warm breath coated her cheekbone.

"Are you sleepy?"

"Not really." But his tone made it clear that the last thing he wanted was to talk. "Are *you* sleepy, Angel?"

"Nope."

"Tell me what's on your mind, sweetheart."

"Ever since I woke up, I have this…restless hum under my skin. Like this knowing in the pit of my stomach."

He pressed a kiss to her bare arm, humming into her skin. "Like dread? Like something bad is coming?"

That he didn't laugh at her made her fall in love with him a little more. A little here and a little there and soon he was going to own all of her heart. "Not bad or good. Just a…big thing."

"What did your astrology app say?"

"It said this next period was going to be all about change and growth and…whatnot. I thought I'd seen it all already." With Meera and you, she didn't have to say.

"Are you scared?"

"A little."

"What can I do to make it better?"

His rough palm cupped her bare breast, the thumb and forefinger lazily circling the already taut nipple. Fire breathed out from where he touched through to her limbs.

"I…" Anya arched into him, begging him with her body. Begging him to give her what she needed.

"What, Angel?" he growled.

Anya gripped his wrist to stop the mind-numbing circles and thrust her nipple into his palm. A sultry groan ripped out of her as his thumb rubbed the plumply dark bud in butterfly strokes. "I'd like you inside me," Anya whispered, turning all kinds of pink. "As soon as you can manage."

Raising himself on an elbow, he kissed her mouth. Naked want shimmered in his eyes. "I admit to sneaking in here, even knowing you'd be tired, hoping I could do just this. Especially now that there's not a lot of time to spare."

Anya moved to her back and searched his face. "What happened?"

He played with a lock of her hair. "Meera and I are going to leave at three o'clock tomorrow. I mean, today."

Anya wondered if he could feel the small fissure that had cracked across her heart. Would it always be "Meera and I"? Was she always going to feel like an outsider when it came to them both?

Never "Meera and us" or "you and me and Meera." It was irrational how much it hurt.

"When were you going to tell me?" she demanded, before she could curb the words.

"I did just now."

"Where are you going?"

"I have a meeting in Seychelles. I thought it would be good to get Meera out of here for a while so I'm taking her with me. So that the two of us can spend some quality time together." He drew a line from her neck to her belly button and then back up again. "I talked to Virat and Vikram. They looked at her call sheets and were able to move some dates. Her calendar's free for two weeks. Vikram also told me that he thought I'd known Rani had signed with Raawal but seeing as she died shortly afterward, he hadn't discussed it with me out of respect for my loss. He felt it would have been like rubbing salt into a wound. The information was confidential and he has no idea how it leaked, but he'll be investigating the interviewer's sources."

"Oh, that's good you sorted things out with him. Really

good," she said, swallowing the lump in her throat. Two weeks of not seeing Meera or him…it felt like a lifetime.

This isn't goodbye, she reminded herself and yet it felt like that.

"Vikram was feeling guilty enough about the interview, so I pushed my advantage and also got the dates extended for the second project Meera's signed with Raawal House," he continued, unaware of the tumult of her emotions. "This way, she can take more than a year off after this. Decide if she really wants to do the second one. I should never have agreed to the two-project contract in the first place. She was so damned excited, for the first time in months after Rani's death, that I just gave in."

It was clear he was examining all the choices he'd made after the leak about his private life. Making all the necessary routes clear for Meera's exit from the industry, if that's what she wanted. For him and Meera to leave as easily as possible. To move on from this life that he had never really wanted for either his wife back then or his daughter now, even though he'd supported both.

The sensible part of Anya's brain pointed out that this was good for the teenager. So much exposure to what could sometimes be a toxic culture at such a young age, so much pressure to always be at her best in front of the hungry media, her every mistake examined under an unforgiving microscope…it wasn't healthy, despite all the measures Simon could choose to take.

And yet, all she could think of was that it meant distance for her—from Meera and from Simon. All she could worry about was that he was retreating from this world in which she lived because of the news about his marriage. Because a wound that had never fully healed had been cracked open again.

But what else might drive him away from her then?

What could come up that would tell him she was getting too close to him?

And God, was she forever going to wait for that moment to come? Wonder if that heavy burden of guilt he carried without fully sharing might fracture the fragile wings of their own relationship? For all that she teased him, Anya didn't need marriage or promises of forever. She just didn't want to constantly live in fear for their relationship. Didn't want to feed the monster that was her anxiety any more fuel.

A warm kiss at the corner of her mouth brought her attention back to him. "Anya?"

"I think that's a great idea," she said, mustering false enthusiasm. Questions hovered over her lips, demanding, probing, and yet she couldn't give them voice. Not when his wandering hands created pockets of pleasure all over her skin, stole her breath and her mind.

His upper body hovered over her while his fingers fiddled with the seam of her panties. "Virat said you're incredibly busy all of next week."

Anya gave another nod, a small part of her taking that as some kind of explanation for why he wasn't inviting her on their trip. God, she was really clutching at straws.

"Anya, all this has made me—"

Anya pressed her hand to his mouth. "I don't want to talk anymore. Especially if you're leaving in a few hours." Especially if he was going to break up with her.

Maybe she was a coward but right now she didn't want to face her emotions or his decisions. Her T-shirt and panties disappeared and in the blink of an eye, he flipped them both over until Anya was straddling his hard thighs. She'd gotten used to being naked in front of him but with his dark eyes and roving hands, she felt completely exposed right now.

Not just because of how open she was in this position.

There was nowhere to hide, no chance he wouldn't see her heart in her eyes. And from the hungry look in his, she wondered if it was exactly what he wanted. If he wanted to take the little she hadn't already offered him yet—the rest of her heart, her love. Her everything.

Any token protest she could have mustered drifted off her lips as Simon cupped her breasts with his hands, and this time, he gave her exactly what she needed. From her neck to her breasts to her belly to her sex, he played her nerve endings like the strings of a guitar. Her spine rose and fell in tune to his demands, her skin so heated that Anya gave herself over to the sensations he strummed through her.

"Bend down, Angel."

Anya did, her body fluid under his command.

His mouth closed over a hard nipple and she jerked at the sharp, stinging pleasure at her sex. One hand on his rock-hard shoulder, she panted. With his other hand, he separated her folds, his fingers feathery and gentle. He stroked her own dampness over her before he thrust first one finger and then two into her.

Even wet and ready, the intrusion speared Anya.

"Look at me, Angel. Open your eyes."

Anya flicked her gaze open to find him watching her with a devouring intensity that brought on a fresh wave of sensation. From that first time since she'd told him she didn't come easily, he'd always given her what she needed. With words—sometimes sweet, sometimes filthy—with caresses—soft and wicked—with his hands and mouth, and fingers and his body.

Pulling out of her, he sent his wet fingers up her bare flesh in an unholy trail, until his finger reached her mouth. Anya opened her mouth and licked it, tasting herself.

"Will you give me whatever I ask, Angel?" he asked in

a ragged, hoarse tone that said this was about more than just sex.

Anya licked his finger and released it with a pop. And for the first time since they'd met, she lied. "I will, Simon."

Dark satisfaction flared in his eyes. Anya heard the rasp of the condom wrapper and then he was rubbing the swollen head of his erection at her center. Flickers of flame went up and down her spine, flooding back down into her lower belly and tightening into a feral knot.

"Ready?"

Anya looked down into his eyes and nodded.

One hand on her hip, he slowly pushed himself inside her. "Don't close your eyes, Angel. Watch this. Watch how you swallow me whole. God, Anya…" His groan as he settled himself all the way in made her shiver.

Anya jerked at how achy and invasive it felt like this. How full he made her feel.

"You okay?"

"You feel so deep like this, Simon. As if you're everywhere." Her back arched of its own accord and she braced her hands on his hips.

"You feel like heaven, Angel." Keeping his thumb on her bud, Simon urged her to find her own rhythm. Heartbeat thundering, skin flushed, Anya used her knees to push up and thrust down in time to meet the jut of his hips. On and on she rode him, gently at first, and then finding the perfect countermotion to his thrusts. And all the while, he told her how good she felt, all the while, he kept that thumb where it was needed, driving her wild.

Soon, Anya was toppling into her climax, his name on her lips. Pleasure fractured in her lower belly in deep, concentric circles, so acute that tears lashed down her cheeks.

Hands on her waist, Simon pushed up. Then she was turned onto her back while he balanced himself on his elbows and knees, his erection still hard inside her. Even in the languorous haze of her orgasm, Anya noted the flare of his nostrils, the corded strength of his shoulders, the damp sheen on his skin and the…raw ache in his eyes.

"Simon?" she whispered, fear already fluttering through her.

Gathering her hips upward, holding her gaze in guarded silence, he started moving inside her again. His thrusts were hard and short and then he climaxed with a soft grunt. He was instantly off her, even though she loved being crushed into the mattress by his powerful body.

Nuzzling into her neck, he peppered a trail of kisses up her chin and cheek. "You're very quiet."

Anya closed her eyes, afraid he would see everything even now. That maybe it was already too late. Wondering if there was going to be any part of her left that he didn't claim, that he didn't take. "I'm just tired."

And when he wrapped his arm around her and kissed her and held her as if he would cocoon her with his body, after gently cleaning her up, she shed the silent tears that had been building for a while.

This trip he was taking with Meera… He wasn't breaking up with her.

But it had made her own heart crystal clear to her. And this person she'd become—this woman who could see her daughter and love her but not acknowledge her, this woman who so boldly went after the man she wanted—she couldn't hide from the truth anymore.

CHAPTER ELEVEN

THANKFULLY, SIMON WAS out when Anya bid an emotional
Meera goodbye with a quick hug and a kiss. Of course
Meera had asked her why she wasn't coming along. Blink-
ing back tears—God, she was leaking tears these days—
Anya had said there was no way she could get away from
work. Not for two whole weeks.

With fervent promises to chat every day, the teenager
had let her leave.

Now, Anya was hiding in the empty studio near the set.

Lunch had come and gone but she'd barely touched the
sandwich or the soup. Her appetite had gone from bad to
nonexistent this morning and she knew she'd pay with
one hell of a headache later but right then, nothing could
hold her attention.

Nothing but the fact that time was passing and Simon
and Meera would leave, and for the first time in several
weeks, she was going to be utterly alone again.

In her head. In her heart. In every way that mattered.

Her astrology app kept spewing some version of "Trust
your instincts" and it made her furious.

She just wanted the hours to pass fast. Until she knew,
her body knew, that he had left and she could give up on
this…strange feverish anticipation coursing through her.
When she could go back to her room and hide for the rest

of the day. Pushing the sketches she'd been working on aside, she pressed her fingers to her temples when she heard the door open behind her.

Her breath stuttered. She didn't have to turn to know that it was Simon.

"Hey."

Bracing herself for the impact, Anya turned. As always, her entire being came awake at the sight of his ruggedly handsome face. In a white linen shirt and dark denim, he took up all the space in the small room. And all the oxygen. Hope fluttered through her, half keeping her functioning, half choking her. "I thought you'd have left by now."

"Something came up at the last minute, and I pushed our departure back by half an hour."

"Oh… Does Meera need something?"

"No, she's talking to your brothers and sisters-in-law."

Her heart was beginning to pick up pace, the tight jut of his jaw making butterflies dance nervously in her stomach. "Did she forget something?"

His head jerked up, as if she'd shouted at him. "You talk as if Meera could be the only possible reason I'd come to see you."

Gripping the wooden desk behind her, Anya stared at him. "No, that's not what I meant," she said, frowning.

"And yet you would do anything I ask just to be close to her, wouldn't you? Give me anything?"

His question pierced her, again carrying that note of something she couldn't quite put her finger on.

"Anything within reason, yes," she said, trying to inject humor into it but failing utterly. "Simon, what's going on? Why are you angry?"

"Meera let it slip that you might not be here when we come back. Is that true?"

Anya blinked, and searched for an answer. She

should've known Meera wouldn't keep it to herself. "I was just thinking that out loud when she brought up our schedules over the next few months."

"So will you be here or not, Anya?"

"Probably not," Anya said, tired beyond measure. "I don't think Virat's going to need me after the coming week and I... I want to get away from it all for a while."

"From Meera or from me?" Anger resonated in the last bit. "Have we become too much for you?"

"I would never abandon Meera like that," she said, hot color sweeping up her cheeks at his disbelieving expression. "Do you truly think me that fickle, Simon?"

"I don't know what to think because you conveniently forgot to tell me your plan to leave, Anya. And I don't believe for a second that it's simple oversight."

"Didn't Meera tell you that I said that she's more than welcome to visit me wherever I will be?"

That only made his scowl deepen, "And me, Anya?" he said, taking a step into the small room. "Would I be welcome?"

"All I meant was that I need to lay low for a while," she said, knowing that it was a non-answer. "I usually retreat after...after a big project like this."

For the first time since they'd met, Simon looked at her as if she was a complete stranger. There was a hardness to his mouth that she was afraid was there because of her. And yet, he didn't come out and say what angered him. "I don't believe you. I think you meant to run away and hide the moment my back was turned."

"That's not true."

But the truth hung there between them, waiting to strike out if either uttered a wrong word. He rubbed both hands over his face and groaned—a sound that seemed to be wrenched from the depths of his soul. "If you want this to be over, all you have to do is say it, Anya. I can't bear silences and walls and hiding behind reason. Just…"

"What?" she said, aghast that she'd hurt him.

"I put up with Rani's fluctuating moods for so long, thinking she needed space. Thinking she needed me to be just there for her. Thinking she would eventually come to me. But all that did was breed resentment between us because ultimately I couldn't give her what she wanted. I can't go down that path. Not ever again. So please, just tell me the truth."

"Fine, you want to know the truth?"

"Yes," he said, his focus all on her now. He didn't sound angry anymore. He just sounded tired. "Because that's what you and I have always dealt in. From the first moment we met. Whatever you say to me, it won't affect your relationship with Meera."

"Not everything I do with you is because of Meera," she threw at him, her chest rising and falling. "I'm upset that you didn't tell me *before* you made plans to take Meera away for a fortnight. I'm upset that you didn't ask me along on your trip, even though I can't come anyway, so it's totally irrational. I'm upset that you…won't share your pain with me, what haunts you about your marriage."

A shutter fell over his gaze. "Why do you want to know what happened in my marriage?"

"Because I want to understand you, Simon. Because… I see the grief and guilt in your eyes and I wonder if you'll ever let it go. I see you retreat from this, from us every time you think of her or your marriage. Because I'm starting to feel resentment for a woman I didn't even know."

Simon stared down at her. But his mouth gave away his shock. "Rani wasn't a bad person, Anya. She wasn't the sole reason our marriage fell apart. I was the one who let her down."

His defense of his late wife felt like a slap to Anya's emotions. "You keep saying that but not explaining it to me. You keep punishing yourself for whatever it is you think you did and now it feels like you're punishing me too."

Now it was his turn to look as if she'd dealt him a punch. "Hurting you is the last thing I want. I... I couldn't live with myself if I did, Angel. That's the entire reason..." A curse flew from his mouth.

"Then tell me what it is that you denied her. What...did she want, Simon, that you couldn't give?"

"She wanted us to try for another baby. She wanted to go through IVF, even though it failed the first time and left her body a mess, even though this time she was a decade older and was already unwell. She wanted to have my child and I said no. I refused to even indulge in a discussion. After that, she retreated from me completely. Just put up a wall I couldn't break through no matter what I said or did. And that only sent her into a spiral.

The evening before her accident, she asked me one last time and I... I got so angry I let the resentment of two years rip through. She died an hour later."

Anya stared at him, her heart aching. He was clearly submerged in guilt, in thinking himself responsible for Rani's lack of happiness. How could she ever hope to break through that? How could she continue with him in the present when he was still so caught up in the past?

"Why did you...?" Her question hovered on her lips, unformed, her throat full of a sadness. "I'm so sorry, Simon."

He only stared at her, his mouth set into an uncompromising line. "Now tell me the truth, Anya."

She nodded.

"Tell me that the fact that you might not be here when I get back was just an impulse talking."

"It wasn't."

His mouth tightened. "Tell me that you weren't going to simply withdraw from me without even giving me a reason."

"I can't."

His question when it came was soft and quiet. As if it was wrenched from the depths of him. "What *do* you want from me, Anya?"

Anya stared at him, his face as familiar to her now as her own. At the rugged terrain of his face, his square chin, his broad chest...

"I want—" she rubbed her chest with her hand, feeling as if the ache there might never go away "—I want you to see yourself as I see you—a kind, decent man who's punishing himself for something he didn't do. I want you to include me in your plans—even the smallest ones—because you can't bear to part with me even for a few days. I want you to take this chance on a future with me, even if there are no guarantees. I want...you to let me love you, Simon, because I do...so much."

Simon simply stared at her, his eyes glittering, his nostrils flaring, his entire body radiating such tension that she thought she should feel it in the air around her like hisses and sparks. Then he glanced away and her heart broke.

And still, she couldn't stop her words.

She pressed a hand to her head, the headache she'd worried about suddenly materializing with a hard pounding behind her temples. "I'm sorry. I didn't mean to put you on the spot like that. Especially when Meera needs you more right now." Her mouth curved into an inane smile as if she hadn't already acted completely bonkers in front of him. "You know the astrology app did say something about endings being new beginnings or some such nonsense. Guess now we both know what I've been so worried about."

"Anya—"

"No, please, Simon. Let me keep some dignity intact." Collecting her portfolio and her watch, this time she shied her gaze away from him. "I'm late for a meeting."

The week after Simon and Meera left, Anya called Zara and begged her to acquire a pregnancy test for her without anyone else being the wiser.

Her period was late.

In the thirteen years since she'd given birth to Meera, it had always been unpredictable and late. But this was different in a way she couldn't verbalize. Of course, there was the fact that she'd gained weight in the last few weeks.

The very day they had left, Simon—half asleep and completely wiped out—had wrapped his big palm over her lower belly and whispered, "I can't tell you how glad I am that you've lost the waif look, sweetheart." His palm had possessively cupped her hip, fingers spreading over the small curve of her belly as if to highlight the fact. Then those long fingers moved up her body and did the same to her breasts before rubbing against her ultrasensitive nipples. "And these, these were my favorite even before they became a little bigger."

The fact that her bras had started becoming uncomfortable should have told her. But she had attributed her increased appetite and weight gain to the fact that her therapist had reduced the dosage of her anxiety medication.

But now, now she couldn't bury her head in the sand anymore. Now, it was sheer stupidity to not face the fact that was staring her in the mirror.

Thankfully, Zara didn't ask her a single question and Anya also knew she wouldn't whisper a word to Virat unless Anya said it was okay to share. And that Virat, unlike Vikram, would simply let her chew through it all first before he made a big fuss. Not that she could go on for a lot longer without everyone knowing.

And yet, even before Zara handed her the pregnancy test and waited outside her bathroom, Anya knew. She knew what the universe had been screaming at her and she'd tried to blunder her way through—calling it anemia, or dehydration or her body simply doing its own thing.

The two pink lines on the test stared back at her as she washed her hands at the vanity. Her emotions resembled the sheet of instructions she'd wadded up into a ball as soon as she'd opened the box.

She was pregnant, Anya repeated to herself.

With Simon's child.

Her and Simon's baby.

She would be a mother again. And this time, she was strong enough, mentally and physically, to look after the baby and herself, to love the baby as she'd always wanted to love Meera.

Leaning her forehead against the bathroom door, she forced herself to count her breaths slowly. The last thing she needed right now was a panic attack.

The thought of facing Simon after the way she'd blurted out her love without him responding in kind, of telling him that she was carrying his child when he'd made it clear so many times that he didn't want another child, made her chest ache.

He wouldn't blame her for this; she knew that. But he wouldn't be happy either. And his honor, his heart…would force him into only one choice.

Anya shuddered at the thought of marrying Simon just for the sake of her baby. No, she was never going there.

The clarity of her thoughts held off the fingers of panic.

Placing a hand on her belly, Anya stared at her reflection.

However Simon reacted to this news, whatever shape their future took, this baby had been conceived in love. She believed that with her whole heart, with every breath in her. And she would continue to hold on to that.

She'd wanted a second chance at so many things—at love, at making her own family, at another child, at…doing things right. And she had it.

She would love this baby as she'd always love its father. And that was the thing to hold on to, even if the rest of her life didn't fall into a more traditional future she'd never imagined for herself anyway.

But first, she needed time. Time to adjust her expectations, time to strengthen herself, time before she told Simon the truth about this baby.

CHAPTER TWELVE

THIS TIME AROUND, Anya had chosen to hide herself away from the public and her own family at Raawal Mahal.

Once it had been her grandparents' home—a cocoon of love and escape for her and her brothers growing up. The place where she had the happiest memories of her childhood. Now Virat and Zara lived here with their toddler son. And since they were on-site in Udaipur and wouldn't be home for a while, along with Vikram and his family, it was the perfect hideout for her.

Anya had worried that the feel of the house would've changed for her, not that she didn't love all the small changes Zara had made to upgrade it. Instead, Virat and Zara's love and the new memories they were making in their home seemed to have just occupied a space alongside the old ones. And Anya knew that's how true love worked. It made space for warmth and connections and joy amid whatever was broken or damaged before. Right alongside past hurts and unfinished healing.

She loved wandering through the sprawling mansion, talking to the child in her belly endlessly, pointing out the art and keepsakes Raawals had gathered for generations. And she hoped the baby felt the love, security and happiness the walls carried within them.

This time, she wasn't going to hide her pregnancy. Not for anyone.

However, her solitude, she knew, was coming to a swift end. Because as much as Simon had a right to know first, her brothers had figured it out. Even without Anya confirming or denying it. She had, in the end, warned them to stay out of the entire affair between Simon and her if they ever wanted to have an active role in her child's life.

The word *affair* had sounded small and finite in its scope when what she felt for Simon was so expansive that it defied words. There was no doubt in her mind he'd suggest that they marry. But there was also no doubt in her mind that she wanted all or nothing. Even if that meant explaining to Meera why her brother or sister was going to be born out of wedlock and convincing her that Anya wasn't abandoning Meera, that she still absolutely adored her and always would.

Her cell phone's ping brought Anya back to reality.

Every day for the past week, Simon had been texting her. As if they hadn't argued before he'd left. As if she hadn't blurted out like a naive fool how much she loved him only to get no response. Not that she'd change her words or the sentiment. Just their delivery.

She'd been so emotional, like a pressure cooker with no whistle to let off the building pressure. So unbalanced by both the emotional and physical changes rushing into the very landscape of her life.

Instead of looking at his latest text, Anya scrolled up to read the whole lot. As she did several times a day. And twice before falling asleep.

The first text had arrived a week ago just as Anya had settled into a routine at Raawal Mahal.

I'm back in Udaipur with Meera. Which I'm pretty sure you're aware of since she texts you like thousand times a day. She missed you terribly on the trip. I don't know how your generation does things but we're not done, Angel. That was just a disagreement we had. Not a breakup.

She'd laughed first at his lengthy texts, remembering how relentlessly Meera teased him about his perfect grammar. But she loved receiving them. Loved knowing that he was sending them so that she could look at them over and over again. Loved that he'd remembered that she'd told him she hated confrontations. Loved that he was building a bridge between them slowly. Even though he'd admitted that Rani's silences had tormented him.

Loved that she knew her so well. That he loved her so well even though he was so gun-shy he'd probably never admit it.

Her heart had crawled into her throat as Anya waited for more. Mouth half-open, fingers clutched tightly around the phone, she'd finally fallen asleep.

Her phone had pinged around midnight.

I miss you. I miss how you cuddle into me in your sleep. I miss how you tuck your ice-cold feet between my calves and steal all my heat. I miss the sounds you make when I'm deep inside you. Seychelles was damn cold without you. Who am I kidding? Even blazing hot, Udaipur is cold without you to warm me up. I hope you're looking after yourself. I know I messed up but I'm not giving up on us.

In the dark, the words had blurred in front of her sleep-mussed eyes, before she'd realized that she was crying. She'd wanted to reply like her breath depended on it. But she'd held back. Not because she was angry with him or because she wanted to force some kind of announcement from him. She wanted so desperately to tell him her news. And she just couldn't, not over a text. She knew if she messaged him back, she'd end up blurting it out. She wanted to wait until she could see him face-to-face calmly, rationally, with her plan for her and the baby's future laid out so he didn't have to worry about them.

The next text popped up the next morning as Anya had just finished a session of meditation with an online class.

Meera got her first period. She's made it clear that she wishes you were here to help her instead of her bumbling Dad. God, Angel, I need you here. And not just to soothe Meera.

The next morning one more:

I stole a piece of chocolate from the delivery you sent for Meera. So I'm the only one you're still ignoring? You know the only reason I'm not there with you right now is because I can't leave Meera alone, right?

The next day, two more texts arrived:

Even Virat won't tell me where you are. I think I prefer his no-nonsense approach to Vikram's arrogance. Who died and made him king of the world?

You know what's freaking me out though? How weirdly silent Vikram is right now.

Two more texts the next day:

Meera asked me what I'd done to mess this up with you. I told her that her dad was an old coward.

She glared at me and then told me to fix it.

Three more the next day, like clockwork. Simon's texts had become the highlight of her day.

I think I've given you enough space now, Angel.

Zara's offered to look after Meera.

I want to see you. If you think I won't use Meera to find out where you are...you underestimate me.

Finally, Anya circled back to the unread texts she'd received a few minutes ago.

Are you free, Angel? Because I'm close. Actually, I don't care if you are free or not. I'm done trying to tiptoe around this.

Her heart crawled into her throat as Anya heard the front bell ring. As she heard their once oldest servant and now a family member, Ramu Kaaka, open the door. She could hear Simon's voice filtering up from the main lounge, up the stairs and finally his steps outside her bedroom. The fact that Ramu Kaaka had simply invited him in meant her brother—probably Vikram—had given up her location.

Anya had barely a second to brace herself when the door opened and Simon walked in. Into her childhood bedroom where he dwarfed everything all over again. Where she'd once dreamed of a man just like him—tall and kind and so...achingly handsome.

A dark blue sweatshirt spanned the breadth of his chest and Anya had to force herself to keep breathing at the sight of him. From his hard, powerful thighs to the gray at his temples, he was like a fist to her heart. Dark stubble decorated his sculptured cheekbones and his square jaw, giving him a bit of a roguish look.

He said nothing, as if he'd used up everything he had to say in those texts.

His hands went to her messy sketching table and all the free paper she'd left floating around. Head bent, he studied some of the sketches until his fingers touched on one she'd done of him.

She wasn't a portrait artist by any means—not a good one. But it was all she'd been doodling for the past two weeks. The man had a thoroughly masculine face that had drawn her interest from the first moment she'd seen him. Even before he'd asked her if he could help.

He held up another sketch of him, frowned and then he put it down.

Only then—after what felt like the longest three minutes in the history of time—his gaze moved to her. As if he'd needed time to brace himself.

Whatever he saw in her face, his big body came to a stillness. It was like a predator slowing down, all the tense muscles and tendons coming to a standstill. Anxiety rippled through Anya's belly as if there was a swarm of stampeding elephants in there instead of the usual butterflies. Her hand instantly went to her slightly rounded belly, as if to soothe the baby from her swirling thoughts.

Simon's gaze followed her hand and the frown on his face broke into such an anguished expression that Anya felt it like a lash against her skin. "You're pregnant. That's why you've been hiding from me."

Her knees shook under her.

A curse flew from his mouth, filling the air between them. His big body settled into her chair, his face buried in his hands. "There's no rhyme or reason to what the universe does, is there? It's all chaos. And yet you try to make it make sense to you with all those apps and…"

"Simon?" Anya said, a thread of fear winding around her heart.

"The number of years that Rani wanted to have a child, the things she put her body through…"

Anya felt as if she'd been slapped right across her face. "I'm sorry you feel that way. That this opens up your wounds all over again."

He looked up then, as if her apology had ripped him from the past he'd been stuck in. He paled, regret etched into his every feature. "Hell, Anya, I didn't mean for that to sound as harsh and insensitive as it did. I just meant that it's quite a shock."

Anya wanted to move closer, she wanted to wrap herself around him, until his shock subsided. She did nothing of the sort. "I know."

"All those years, all those tests, Rani told me she thought it was something to do with her body but we were both tested and the problem was never conclusive. I didn't… I never realized I could still father a child. You've had weeks to come to terms with it. I've only had a few seconds."

He was right. And she had expected he'd be shocked. Hands wrapped around her midriff, Anya nodded.

"Did you know before we left for Seychelles?"

"I didn't. But I was…definitely not myself that day. Every small thing was getting to me. I thought it was anemia or dehydration or the effects of the change in my medication. I didn't realize until a couple of weeks ago. My periods have always been incredibly irregular."

Hurt pinched his features. "And you waited all this time? You told your brothers and you didn't tell me?" His voice almost broke on the last word and Anya couldn't stay away from him anymore.

She went to her knees between his legs, her fingers catching hold of his hands. "Simon, I'd never do that. They just…figured it out. I didn't want to tell you in a text. Can you imagine for a moment how I felt? You've made it so clear since we met that you never wanted to do this again. That you were done with marriage and babies and love. I just… I needed time to brace myself before I saw you. I want you to know that this is welcome news for me even if it isn't for you."

He still didn't look at her and Anya thought this might be the cruelest he'd ever been to her. Questions and thoughts came to her lips and swung away, so many of them that it was impossible to pin one down. But before she could make up her mind, Simon was lifting her and planting her ass on the edge of the bed and then moving away.

Hands clasped in her lap, Anya watched as he paced the confines of the bedroom, agitation written into every line of his body. Time ticked slowly in seconds…but her heart was doing its own thing. Finally he came to his knees in front of her, mirroring her very pose of a few minutes ago.

The look in his eyes made her insides ache even though she wasn't sure what it was. So Anya went on the defensive. "Before you ask, yes, I'm definitely going to have the baby."

"Okay."

"And I'm not going to hide it from anyone—not the industry, not the media, not Meera. I'm not going to treat my pregnancy or my child as if it was some kind of bizarre mistake or sordid secret. I want this baby. Very much so."

"Okay."

"And I need your help in figuring out how we're…going to break the news to Meera that we won't be getting married. I mean, I understand that it might…make her feel insecure after everything she's been through, but I can't marry you. Not even to give this baby legitimacy."

"Okay," he agreed readily.

Perversely, his not insisting that they should marry made her want to cry. God, she was a contrary mess right now.

"So I guess your proposal is finally off the table then?" he asked with such mock seriousness that Anya wanted to kick him in that hard stomach.

"Yes."

"Other than those important announcements you just gave like a bloody queen, you're good? Your anxiety, your...tiredness?"

"Yes. I don't have nausea, or morning sickness or anything. My doctor already put me on the lowest dosage of anxiety medication for a while now and she said it won't cause any harm to the baby. I'm perfectly healthy—mostly hungry and horny, actually. Like all the time."

His mouth twitched and Anya felt as if she'd won a grand prize. One blunt-nailed finger traced her knuckles, up and down, side to side. A great, shuddering sigh left him. "I've dug us an even bigger pit to crawl out of, haven't I?"

"Well, it took two of us and a wall to make this baby, so it's a bit arrogant to think it's all on you."

"It was our first time then?"

"By my calculations, yes. I guess I should have told you that that condom in my bag was a few years old. I... I just wanted you...needed you so much that night that I didn't even think it might be out of date."

This time, the corner of his mouth quirked up in that crooked smile of his that she adored so much. "I needed you too."

He pushed a slightly shaky hand through his hair before

looking up at her again. "Will you listen to me if I tell you what happened between Rani and me?" Before she could say either way, he pressed a hand to her mouth. "I want to tell you because I want you to know. To see why it took me so long to realize what I have in you. To realize what a blessing you are to me.

"Because you were absolutely right. I was using everything that happened with Rani as a grand reason to not move forward in life. I was letting guilt corrode everything. Letting fear control me. To not admit, even to myself, how hopelessly in love I was with you."

Her lower lip trembled, hot liquid rushing to her eyes as if there was a geyser waiting to erupt behind them. "Simon…you don't have to…"

"Although you have to give me some allowance for not seeing the truth when it was staring me in the face, Anya. I haven't been in love for so long, not since I first met Rani over two decades ago. I'm rusty as hell and Rani's death took away my trust in myself. That's the worst part. I lost myself—my dreams, my desires, my joy for life. When we met, I was simply going through the motions for Meera's sake. Even she could see that."

Anya understood exactly what he meant about losing faith in oneself.

Her silence however made him draw in a deep breath. "Have I ever lied to you, Angel?"

Anya took a deep, shuddering breath. "No."

Simon pushed to his feet and wrapped his arms around her. "Shh…sweetheart. No more tears, please. I can't bear to see it." But more than his words, the scent of him was like a kick to her heart. Everything within her settled.

Anya patted the space next to her on the bed. While her feet dangled, his legs kicked into a long sprawl. While they weren't looking at each other, she smiled as Simon took her hand and laced their fingers together. As if he didn't want their connection to be lost even for a second.

"Meera coming into our lives at the time she did…was a saving grace. Not just for our marriage, but for Rani. She'd already been through a lot trying to conceive. We'd been married for a decade and our marriage was at its weakest. Her career—even though she was at the top—had already lost some of its allure for her. Rani, you see," he added with a long sigh, "used to thrive on challenge, on new things to be conquered, on being needed and adored. It took me a long time to see that about her."

Anya waited, knowing that this was hard for him.

"So when Meera came, it was as if Rani got a new lease on life. She wrapped up projects she couldn't get out of, got her lawyer to break contracts on a couple and threw herself into motherhood. But when Meera turned ten, things started changing. Rani raised her to be strong and independent and that's exactly how Meera turned out. But Rani… grew restless then, started saying Meera didn't need her as much anymore. I was traveling a lot and I didn't take her seriously."

He turned to face her then, and the ache in his eyes made Anya's chest ache. "It's not that she didn't love Meera or being a mother."

Anya shook her head. "You don't have to clarify that, Simon. You really don't. Some women are happy with just being mothers. Some need more challenges. There's no wrong or right."

Simon nodded. "Rani had those low periods before. She'd complain about being in a rut, that she needed a new hobby, that her body and her brain were vegetating. When I realized it continued to bother her, I reminded her that it had been her dream once to start an acting school. We went to dinner that night, just the two of us. She was glowing when she said she knew what she wanted. What would give her a new lease on life again."

"Another baby?" Anya whispered.

"Yes." He rubbed a hand over his face, his mouth tight and pinched. "To say that I was shocked would be an understatement."

"Did you argue?"

"Not that day, no. I thought she'd listen to reason. I told her we should be glad that Meera was ten now. Tried to remind her that we'd been waiting for her to grow up so that they could both travel more with me. That there was no way, even if we could conceive by some miracle, that either of us wanted to go through the nappies-and-formula stage again. She seemed to agree with me and with usual masculine obliviousness—" his voice rang with bitterness "—I thought that was that."

Anya tightened her grip on his fingers and leaned her body against his to remind him she was there. That she was listening.

"A month later, she told me she'd made an appointment with a new fertility expert. I refused to even indulge in the idea of IVF again. I didn't want any more children and I definitely didn't want them at the cost of Rani putting her mind and body through all those hormone shots and pain again when it didn't work when we were younger. She retreated from me after that argument. For months and months, all I got from her was silence. It corroded everything good between us, killed what little we still had in common. She wouldn't talk or engage, only wanted a yes from me. And the damned good actress she was, she made it look like nothing was wrong in front of Meera."

He looked at his hands, as if he couldn't bear to hold Anya's gaze. As if he still felt shame over his actions. Anya's heart ached.

"I thought she'd get over it in the end, see reason. I was busy launching a new hotel in Seychelles and I was traveling a lot. I even asked her if she and Meera would like to join me. She said she had plans with some old friends in Mumbai. She sounded so excited that I thought she was through the low. That she was finding her feet again. I was so happy that we'd made it to the other side of this rough patch too." A shuddering sigh left him. "I was a damned fool. She took Meera with her to Mumbai. When I came back from Seychelles, she told me she'd signed on to the movie project and that must be when she visited a divorce lawyer too. She told me if I didn't give her what she needed in our marriage, she could at least revive her career. As if I had ever stopped her before."

"What happened?"

"I got mad...not because she wanted to go back to acting. But that she was so adamant about trying to conceive that she was giving me no choice at all. That she held that as some kind of sword over my head to prove that I still loved her, that I wanted the marriage. We got into a huge argument. She was furious with me and drove off. Her car totaled an hour later and she died. I don't even know where she was going. The last thing she heard from me was an accusation that she had destroyed our whole marriage and everything I had ever felt for her." A broken smile curved his mouth.

"I'm so sorry, Simon. Those words must have haunted you."

"They have, ever since she died. I don't want to paint her as some kind of villain, Angel. Because she wasn't. She adored Meera."

Anya searched for the right words, knowing that there might not be any. "I would never think that of her. No one who knows Meera's confidence, Meera's faith in the mere memory of her mother, would think that."

"One minute we were arguing, the next she was gone. I started seeing myself as a monster. I was the one who'd denied her what she so desperately wanted. I was the one who'd blindly decided we'd ride it out if I just ignored her demands. If I had agreed to the IVF, maybe she'd have conceived this time. Maybe it wouldn't have pushed her into that restlessness again. Maybe she wouldn't have been driving so recklessly that day. Maybe she wouldn't have felt so alone. The truth was, we didn't love each other anymore. Guilt ravaged me after her death, not grief, and that realization made it even worse, like a vicious cycle."

"You can't just assume that she was driving recklessly, Simon. It could simply have been a ghastly accident. You can't go down that way of thinking—it'll end up destroying you."

"How can I not, Anya?"

"Because you yourself told me how much she loved Meera. I've seen that love in every word Meera speaks. You know, in your heart, Simon, that Rani would have never endangered her life like that. Not when she knew how it might affect Meera." Anya took his hands, willing him to see her. "You have to remember that she loved Meera. That while your marriage might have been irretrievably broken, she wasn't, Simon. You have to remember her as a capable, brilliant woman. The woman you once admired and respected and loved. Just because things fell apart between you two doesn't mean her verve for life was over."

"I do, now." Sadness lingered in his eyes but there was also acceptance. "It took me all this time to see that. That guilt will make you see horrible things, corrupt everything that's good and right too. That Rani lived a full, wonderful life that got cut short brutally. I know she would have thrived whatever new direction life took her in. It just wouldn't have been as my wife."

He pulled her up and into his lap before Anya could draw another breath. "Something Virat said at your birthday party made me take stock of the fear I was clinging to in the name of guilt. And sweetheart, I've been so in awe of you…and how bravely you've reached for life, how full of love and generosity and courage you are. How you decided that you'd just love Meera whether she knew who you were or not. How you made me come alive. Made me see I was denying myself happiness because of useless guilt. God, if Rani were here, even she'd have told me I'd become a foolish old man. That I was lucky to have another chance at love."

Anya hid her face in his throat. "I'm sorry for being so disrespectful toward her memory by saying I resented her. I was just miserable that you seemed to be leaving me when I was in love with you, and I know now that my body was also putting me through a hormonal wringer… I was at my worst. I'm sorry, Simon."

"Hush, sweetheart. The Rani I once knew would've never asked me to live a false life, bound to her. Not when my heart wasn't in it anymore. You're the most real thing I've ever seen, Angel, even when you think you're at your worst."

"You've made it easy for me to be brave, Simon. You make it so…easy to love you. You gave me everything I needed before I even knew I needed it."

"Then is it that hard to believe I feel the same about you, Anya?" His mouth peppered soft, butterfly kisses over her eyes, her nose, her cheeks and then the corner of her mouth. "I'm so absolutely in love with you, Angel." His palm moved to her belly and Anya felt his shuddering gasp as he felt the small but distinct swell of her belly. "And this baby…"

She shook her head, feeling as if she was being cleaved in two. "Please, don't lie to me, Simon. I can take anything but lies. You never wanted another child. You've said that enough times. I know you'd never resent an innocent child but he or she deserves more. I deserve more."

"You do," he said, rubbing the lone tear on her cheek. "Absolutely. You and this baby deserve to be loved and cherished. And I'd never lie to you. But will you hear the truth in my words? Will you give me that much, Angel?"

Anya nodded, every cell in her wanting him, wanting a future with him.

His gaze was steady, full of faith in her, full of love and affection that was like a balm to her soul. "Our marriage was already damaged even before Rani decided having a child would fix her. Would fix us. I couldn't imagine bringing a baby into that kind of unstable atmosphere. But you…you came into my life when I never expected to have another chance at love. I had all but given up on myself. I never expected to fall so madly in love with you, Anya. I fought it every inch. But God, now, I can't imagine life without you by my side. Can I not feel the same about this baby? How could I not fall in love with an innocent child that's a part of you and me? How could I not want a future with you and this baby and Meera, as a family?"

"I'd hate for you to resent me. For you to feel caught up in this without having had a say."

His fingers banding around the nape of her neck, he tilted her until she looked at him. "If you don't want to marry me, that's fine. I'm not at all worried about Meera because she knows how much I adore you. I don't care what the world or your brothers think. I only want you to know that I'm more than happy if you'll just let me be a part of your life and this baby's." He took her hand and kissed the knuckles, his gaze full of love. "All I want is a host of tomorrows with you, Anya."

Anya pulled her hand away and swatted his arm.

He froze, his heart in his eyes. How had she not seen it before? "Tell me what you need, Angel. Anything you want," he murmured, repeating the words he'd said to her that first evening.

Anya buried her fingers in his thick hair and tugged. "I mean, yes, I'm a modern woman but still... For once, Simon De Acosta, I want to be asked. I want to be cajoled. I want to be...persuaded into being your wife."

He was on his knees in a heartbeat and Anya laughed. In his big broad palm was the exact replica of a stunning ring they'd seen in his friend's collection which Anya had fallen in love with.

A giant ruby nestled among tiny diamonds and the whole thing was set in antique gold...a king's symbol of love for the girl he'd adored his entire life. "That's so beautiful. When did you have it made?"

"I saw how your eyes popped that night when Malik let us see his collection. I asked him if I could borrow it to get a replica made and he agreed. On the condition that we don't advertise where we got the design from. I was happy to reassure him that you would absolutely respect his need to keep the collection and all its valuable designs private."

"Oh...but that was weeks ago and you didn't even... know you were in love with me then."

Raising a brow, Simon made a mock bow. "Glad to know you have the timeline right in your head, Angel."

"Why did you have it made then?"

"Because even when I didn't understand it, or admit it, in my heart, I knew you were precious to me. I wanted to gift it to you because I knew how much you'd appreciate it. How much you'd adore it. And I wanted to make you happy. I wanted to give something to the girl who was strong and beautiful and as precious as this design."

Anya fell to the floor in an awkward movement, laughing and crying. Simon caught her, his arms tight around her, his embrace warm and everything she'd ever asked for. "You did give me something. My own heart back to me so that I could start living again. And it's now yours, to keep. I love you, Simon."

His mouth pressed to her temple, he dangled the ring in front of her. "I was also hoping that the ring might convince you, if my meager heart couldn't. I told myself that at least the artist in you might be tempted."

She swatted him and whispered against his mouth. "You still haven't asked me."

He took her mouth in a hard, demanding kiss that left her panting before he whispered, "Anya Raawal, will you marry me and put me out of my lonely misery? Will you and this baby be mine forever and ever? Will you give me a chance to make a family with you and Meera and this baby that I promise to love and cherish for the rest of my life?"

Anya looked into his steady brown eyes and said, "Yes."

He slid the ring onto her finger, his grin wicked and bright. And then he picked her up, closed the door to her bedroom, bolted it and then threw her on the bed, gently. And then he was covering her body with his and kissing her as if he couldn't last another second without it, and her legs fell apart to form a cradle for him and he was so hard and perfect against her core that Anya moaned into his mouth.

"Is this okay?" he asked, even though he hadn't let all his weight fall onto her.

Anya tugged at his hair and rubbed her cheek against

his rough one. "It's perfect. And I missed you too. I missed this."

"You said you were horny, and I take my duties as your fiancé very seriously so we're going to find you relief and release very soon."

Anya giggled and he kissed her again, his eyes dancing with unholy delight. He continued kissing her while one busy hand gathered the hem of her long dress and his fingers were delving into her folds and Anya arched into his touch with a greediness she knew was never going to abate. "I hate to rush you, sweetheart, but since you're ready for me— Damn it, you are *so* ready for me," he mumbled the words into her neck. "I have a feeling the entire world is going to descend on us shortly and I'd love to give us both a release before they're all here."

Anya's shock turned into a raw moan when he thrust one finger into her and sensation pooled in her belly. "Who's coming?"

"You are," he whispered, licking at her pebbled nipple through the cotton of her dress.

Anya arched into his warm mouth before she pulled back. "I meant who's descending on us as you very well know, you beast."

He pushed her T-shirt out of his way, dragged his teeth over her plump, oversensitive nipple oh so gently, cursed at how her body greedily clutched his finger inside her and then he answered with a lazy grin. "Meera and your brothers and their wives and their children. And, oh, maybe your parents too."

"Oh, God. Hurry, please," Anya said, her climax already flickering so, so close.

Anya busied her hands with his trousers, and then he was inside her and her world felt right. Balancing his weight on his elbows, Simon thrust into her slow and deep, hitting her in exactly the right spot with such dev- ilish intent that Anya thought she might die of the fast, rushing pleasure.

Lacing his fingers with her, Simon kissed the valley between her breasts, each swivel of his hips pushing her higher and higher. But it was his words, whispered warmly into her skin that flung Anya out of her own body. "I think I fell in love with you the first time you came for me."

Anya opened her eyes and held his gaze as his climax followed and she didn't stop whispering his name for a long time.

Just as Simon gathered her to him in a lazy cuddle, her phone pinged. They turned their heads together to see it was the astrology app telling her she was going to find love and she laughed and Simon laughed, and Anya thought that maybe the universe had finally gotten it right.

EPILOGUE

Eighteen months later

ANYA HAD FINALLY put her infant son, Rahul, down for a nap and stepped out into the main sitting lounge in the house Simon had built for them—close to her brothers' residences—only to find father and daughter shouting at each other.

"If either of you wakes that fussy son of mine with your argument, I swear I'm walking out the door and never returning. Then you two can fend for yourself and that cranky little guy. And the entire family that's descending on us in exactly…two hours."

Argument halted mid-words, Simon and Meera jerked their heads toward her, a guilty flush creeping up both their cheeks.

"Dad's saying I can't go to the party tonight, even though you both agreed I could like a month ago, and I promised to be back by ten."

Anya sighed, searching for the words where she didn't cut Simon's authority in front of Meera but also knowing that the girl was right. It didn't help that in the last eighteen months, Meera had lost all awkwardness and blossomed into such an achingly beautiful girl that Simon went a lit-

tle berserk at the thought of the gangly teenage boys that
surrounded her wherever she went.

Even now, as she stared at the teenager's stunning
beauty, Anya's heart beat rapidly. Thank God they'd told
Meera that she was her birth mother a few months after
Rahul had been born.

Meera had listened to all of Anya's recounting of the
past with a mature patience that had tugged at her. Her
strong, fierce daughter had cried at first, had retreated
for a few hours, even from Simon. That she'd gone into
her baby brother's nursery and held him, which had made
Anya cry even harder than Meera. After what had felt like
an eternity and yet was only an hour, Meera had emerged
brighter and braver if that was possible.

With fat tears in those wide eyes, she'd asked Anya if
she'd be hurt if she didn't call her Mama. Because she'd
wanted to reserve that for the woman who had raised her.

Anya had promised faithfully she'd never try to take
Rani's place.

So they'd settled simply on Anya. Because that's what
Meera was used to.

Not for a second did Anya begrudge Rani her place
in Meera's memories or in her heart. And through it all,
Simon had been there—patient, kind, loving, holding
space for both Anya and Meera and then baby Rahul in
his heart. Keeping every promise he'd ever made to cherish her, to cherish their family.

Of course, whatever small awkwardness Meera might
have felt in her new relationship with Anya had been oblit-
erated once she'd realized Vikram and Virat were really
her uncles, that Zara and Naina were her aunts and that
she had two little cousins to adore. Not that it had been
completely smooth sailing.

Learning that the two most powerful men in Bollywood, two men she'd had a crush on for months, were her uncles had blown the teenager's mind and she was forever hanging around them.

Until she'd learned that they'd only been keeping their distance from her because of her dad's dictates that they give her time. Until she'd seen firsthand how overprotective those two uncles could get over their niece, given a half inch.

It had sent her beautiful daughter running screaming back into Anya's and Simon's arms, more than appreciative of her own parents, who believed in boundaries and open communication and treating her like an adult. Even her parents, Anya knew, had already lost a piece of their heart to this young woman who brought laughter and joy wherever she went.

For the first time in forever, her family had come together to protect Meera. They'd all rallied around her when it had been time to break the news to the media so that they could control the story. The promos of her first movie had begun to hit the press and eighteen months had changed her daughter a lot. Especially since with her tall, athletic build and distinctively strong features, Meera had begun to look more and more like Anya's mother.

Simon's stalwart support and her own innate confidence had helped Meera swim through that too.

Now, Meera adored her extended family—particularly her aunts and her little cousins, Zayn, Virat and Zara's son; Raima, Vikram and Naina's daughter; and her own little brother, Rahul. Especially since sometimes the little ones kept everyone's attention away from her own escapades.

"Anya, sweetheart, what is it?" Simon said, enfolding her in his embrace from behind, pulling her back into the present.

Even Meera stared at her, concern in her eyes. "Anya... I'm sorry I yelled at Dad. Are you okay?"

"I'm fine," Anya said, forcing a smile to her lips. Turning, she kissed Simon to the background noise of her teenage daughter making barfing sounds. When Simon watched her with concerned eyes, she smiled. "I'm just... so happy, Simon. So much has happened and sometimes the sheer joy catches me unawares."

Dropping his forehead to hers, Simon kissed her again. But this time, slowly, lazily, pouring everything he felt into the kiss.

"Anya, you have to talk to him about letting me go to the party. You're the only he'll listen to," Meera interrupted.

Simon and she laughed amid their kiss.

"We did agree to let her go, Simon," Anya said, patting the broad chest that had been her haven from the first moment they'd met. "And before you blame past us for making that decision, Vikram promised to keep an eye on her, remember? The party's being thrown by his friend's nephew."

"Ugh... Vikram uncle's going to be at the party? He's so much worse than Dad," muttered Meera. "I can't wait until Raima grows up and he's off my back. Although poor Raima deserves better than her overprotective dad hovering over her every minute."

"See, now your dad isn't looking so bad, is he?" Simon said, forever trying to pit himself favorably against Vikram.

"A little better. Very little," Meera finally relented with a small smile.

Anya raised a brow and suppressed a smile. "So you want to stay home and catch a movie with us then?"

"God, no. I don't want to see you two making cow eyes at each other."

"Hey!"

"What? Dad only returned from his trip yesterday. That's all you guys do anytime he's back. Why do you think I was so determined to go to this party in the first place?"

Anya burst out laughing. "Go then, before he changes his mind."

Despite all the attitude she gave them, Meera made a point to kiss Anya's cheek. Then she went up the stairs even though she was already dressed in ripped jeans and a crop top.

"Where's she going?" Simon asked, frowning. "Is she staying home? Did I win?"

Anya shook her head. "No, she never goes anywhere without kissing Rahul first."

Anya stayed in Simon's arms as Meera came back down, reluctantly kissed her dad's cheek and left out the front door. "We're going to the premiere tomorrow. Are you nervous?"

Meera stilled and bit her lip. "I am, yes. Terrified to be honest. But Virat uncle said it's one of his best and Vikram uncle said that's saying something because everything Virat uncle makes is brilliant and they both said... I did a good job."

Simon squeezed her shoulder. "You trust their judgment, right?"

"I do," Meera said, nuzzling her head into her dad's chest. One of those very rare happenings now that she'd just turned fifteen. She wrapped her arm around his waist and then turned a hesitant gaze up at Anya. "But even if I didn't...even if I sucked, that's okay, right?"

Anya opened her arms and Meera flew into them. "Is that why you've been acting extra-cranky around here lately?"

Meera's muffled "Maybe" made her laugh.

Simon wrapped his own arms around both of them, ignoring Meera's fake protest. "I'm sure you were brilliant, Meera. But even if you weren't, even if this is your first or last movie, it doesn't matter to us. We'll love you, support you in everything you do."

Sniffling, but refusing to show her face, Meera ran out of the living room.

The moment the door closed behind her, Simon lifted Anya in his arms and settled into a recliner with her on his lap. His fingers played with the hem of her shirt while he buried his mouth in her neck. Anya arched into his caresses, nowhere near satisfied even after all these months. In fact, after giving birth to Rahul and the long hours with a newborn, all she wanted now was to spend every waking minute kissing and making love with Simon.

"You watched the movie already, didn't you?"

Anya tried to lie but she'd never been the actress in the family. It was her daughter who'd caught the gene. "Yes. I thought I should be prepared a bit."

"And?" Simon asked, arching a brow. While he'd made peace with the fact that her family was Bollywood royalty, as was Meera's mother, he was still the same protective dad she'd met on day one.

Anya laughed, then covered her mouth. "She's brilliant, Simon. I mean I knew it because Virat doesn't lie. She even outshines Zara...and that's saying something."

Simon groaned dramatically and Anya nipped his lower lip in retaliation. Lacing her fingers through his, he kissed each knuckle. "I wish I could say I'm surprised."

"We'll be there with her every step of the way, Simon," she said. In this matter, she was always the one who gave the reassurance.

"I know. And now that we have a teenager-free house, how long before your family descends on us again?"

"Hey… I guess I should tell Zara then that she shouldn't take Rahul along with them for the night, as we planned."

His eyes glittered with desire that was never far away. "I missed you."

Clasping his face, Anya kissed him sweet and deep and long. "I missed you too. And I want a full night with you, with no interruptions from our teething son."

"But let's not waste the two hours we have now, Angel," he said, before lifting her and carrying her to their bed-room. Where he applied himself dedicatedly to proving his love to her very thoroughly.

Or at least for the forty-five minutes before their son woke up and demanded to be cuddled.

* * * * *

A CINDERELLA FOR THE PRINCE'S REVENGE

EMMY GRAYSON

MILLS & BOON

CHAPTER ONE

It had to be a sin to be that handsome.

Briony Smith watched Cass Morgan walk through the rowdy crowd of cowboys, ranch hands and the occasional tourist singing along with the Thursday night band. Normally on nights like this, she could barely hear herself think.

But as Cass flashed her a sexy smile, white against the dark tan of his skin, all she could hear was her own heartbeat thundering in her ears. His caramel-colored eyes locked on hers. She shivered. Every time his intense gaze landed on her, slowly sliding up and down her body, she was amazed that her clothes didn't melt off beneath the onslaught of his burning intensity.

The sensual feelings warred with her brain, had ever since Cass had walked into the Ledge a week ago, sat at the bar and kicked her newly discovered desires into overdrive. Her mother had drummed it into her for years that she didn't need a man to survive. But, she'd added with a cheeky wink as Briony had gotten older, that didn't mean you couldn't enjoy yourself.

"How'd negotiations go today?" she asked as Cass leaned on the bar. Jet-black hair curled over his collar. She threaded her fingers together so she didn't impulsively reach across the bar and run them through the thick, soft-looking waves.

Cass grimaced. Ever since he'd shown up last Thursday and ordered an old-fashioned, he'd been dropping hints at some business deal that had brought him to Kansas. One of the other bartenders, Katelyn, guessed it had something to do with a resort. Simon, the cook, was convinced Cass was opening his own cattle farm.

Briony glanced at him out of the corner of her eye, keeping her looking to a subtle glimpse instead of the flat-out ogling the other women of Nowhere had done all week. Although who could blame them? In a black polo fitted perfectly to his muscular torso and tan slacks, his cool confidence and blatant I-don't-give-a-damn attitude, he looked right at home among the dusty boots, torn jeans and plaid shirts favored by the locals who called this former logging town home.

"They went."

She arched a brow at the cryptic answer.

"So a double today?"

His grin returned and sent a jolt of electricity through her veins.

"Just a single."

She poured the expensive Scotch whiskey that had languished behind the bar for years, added an oversize ice cube and passed him the glass. She sucked in a breath as their fingers brushed. Judging by the devilish gleam in his eyes, he knew exactly what kind of effect he inflicted on her.

"How was your day?"

The magic of the moment disappeared. Her day had gone much as any day. She'd woken up early to make breakfast and drag her stepsisters out of bed. Once adorable little twins with blond curls, cherub cheeks and the sweetest dispositions, they'd morphed into sullen teenagers with a penchant for leaving dirty laundry around the house and responding to Bri's questions about school with grunts.

Small wonder, when they'd just lost the stepmother who'd loved them as her own to cancer six months ago, the same disease that had claimed their birth mother when they were just three years old. Toss in a depressed father who spent his days parked in front of the TV with a beer clutched in his hand and the small house that had once been packed with love and laughter but now groaned under the weight of their family's despair.

Cheery.

"Briony?"

Cass's voice yanked her out of her melancholy state. She loved the way he said her name, the syllables rolling off his tongue in an exotic accent.

"Sorry." She gave him a quick smile. "It was fine."

Most people accepted that answer, didn't press for more out of courtesy or disinterest. But Cass stared at her, eyes probing. Her smile slipped as she shifted on her feet.

"What?"

"You're an open book."

She frowned. "Oh?"

He leaned across the bar. The scarred countertop still separated them. All she had to do was lean back to keep space between them.

But she didn't. No, she just stood there as he laid a finger on her rapidly beating pulse at the base of her throat. Amazing how much fire one graze of a fingertip could ignite, she thought desperately past the swirling rush of blood roaring in her ears. The first time he'd ever touched her, a mere tap of his finger, and she could barely stop from swooning like a teenager with her first crush.

"The pulse in your throat. Your tongue darting out to

touch your lips." Despite the uptick in volume as the band transitioned into a raucous rendition of the latest country song, his words wound around her, a seductive spell. His eyes dropped down to her mouth. A wild temptation seized her, made her sway forward before common sense yanked her back. Had she truly almost kissed a customer? A most likely very wealthy, very handsome customer who would be leaving any day now?

Flustered, she grabbed one of the glasses she'd set out to dry as she stepped back from the bar and wiped it with the towel draped over her belt.

"Did something happen with your sisters? Or your step-father?"

Her lips thinned. He'd overheard one of her phone con-versations with Trey yesterday. He hadn't asked questions, but he'd heard enough of her side to glean that Trey had run up another astronomical bill that she was still trying to figure out how to pay without getting their electricity shut off.

"Maybe it was the polite version of 'I had a rough day but I don't want to talk about it.'"

When she looked back up, it was to see the intensity of Cass's gaze replaced with empathy. Her stomach dropped. Everyone in Nowhere knew her story, looked at her with drawn-down lips and crinkled eyes filled with pity. How could they look at her with anything else when just a week before Cass's arrival she'd had to drag her own stepfather out of the Ledge, drunk as a skunk and leaning on her as he'd sobbed her mother's name over and over again.

As much as she craved the help her neighbors some-times offered, it wasn't worth the shame that would come when they saw how much of a hell her home had turned into. The sidelong glances she got now, the clucked tongues she overheard in the grocery store about how much suffering the Smith family had endured, all of it pressed on her, added to the pressure of being the sole provider for three broken people. She hated the darkness Trey had retreated into, the apathy her stepsisters had pulled around themselves like armor from the cruelties of the world.

Although, she acknowledged to herself, *they're not the only ones.* Despite her attempts to maintain a sunny facade in front of Trey and the girls, she had pulled back, too. She'd always existed on the fringes of the world created by her mother and Trey's marriage, putting on a face for her mother so Marie would never guess the depth of distance between her husband and daughter. Sometimes, if Briony had pretended hard enough, she had felt like they were all actually family.

Now she didn't even want to be a part of it all.

She winced. Just thinking that made her feel guilty.

She looked away from Cass. She didn't want pity from her neighbors, and especially not him. She'd wanted a flirtation and the chance to pretend that maybe, just for a little while, she could have a fairy tale instead of the nightmare her life had turned into.

"You can talk to me, Briony."

The words hung in the air, spoken in that seductive, honeyed voice. Her lips parted. What would it be like to confide in someone, especially someone like Cass who looked at her as if he saw her, truly saw her, and not just the persona she presented to the rest of the world?

Justin Lee and his sister Michelle wandered up to the bar, singing off-key.

"Bri!" Justin hollered. "Aren't you a sight for sore eyes."

"I'm surprised you can see straight," she retorted good-naturedly.

"Two more?"

"You got a ride?"

"Walking tonight." Justin clapped Michelle on the shoulder, who rolled her eyes. "My sweet baby sister is letting me crash on her couch."

Briony nodded to Cass.

"Be right back."

As she walked away, she felt Cass's gaze burning into her back. Their casual flirtation had deepened in the blink of an eye. She didn't know what to make of it, or him, for that matter. That she had almost slipped and confided in him should worry her. The fact that it didn't was even more concerning.

Perhaps she was just exhausted. Yes, exhausted and lonely. Otherwise she wouldn't be acting like this.

Because really, she thought with another quick glance at his dark profile, what did she actually know about him?

Cassius Morgan Adama prince of Tulay, watched his future wife pour beer into two frosted glasses. Fate had gifted him not only with a means to finally right the wrongs against his family and his homeland, but a stunning instrument with which to exact justice.

He'd seen photographs of her. None had done her fiery red locks, her bright emerald eyes or the cut of her stunning cheekbones justice. *Elfin* was a good word to describe her beauty, although *warrior* would also be appropriate, her arms slender yet muscular as she lugged trays and crates around the bar.

Yet what had stood out most to him was her smile. When he'd first walked into the dark interior of the Ledge last Thursday at three o'clock in the afternoon, Briony had turned around, flashed him a sunny grin and kindly yet firmly said, "Sorry, sir, we're closed until four. Be happy to serve you then."

When was the last time he hadn't been recognized?

Fawned over? The brief flash of irritation had vanished, replaced by unexpected excitement and anticipation. He hadn't planned on revealing who he was to Briony, not yet, but he hadn't anticipated how satisfying it would be to be nobody for a while.

Briony's sassy sweetness had been an added bonus to her physical attractiveness. He'd known when he'd set upon this course that he risked being married to someone of unknown personality. Timid, vapid or even cruel; he'd dated plenty to be familiar with the negative qualities he might expect in a spouse.

But Briony was none of those things, at least not that he had seen in the last week. Judging by how easily she'd handled the crowds streaming through the bar, the occasional drunk or mouthy vacationer, Briony was anything but submissive. Yet she never made anyone feel small or set out to ridicule or embarrass them. She was just doing her job.

Satisfaction settled like a warm blanket over his shoulders. Yes, she would make an excellent wife and princess. The kind of woman his people could look up to and follow.

Unfortunately, he wasn't the only man to be drawn in by her. Judging by the sappy expression on the drunken Justin's face, he had also been attracted by her sparkling magic.

Among other attributes, he thought testily as Justin's eyes dropped down to Briony's chest. His fingers tightened on his glass. If that clown had any idea who he was, who Briony was, he'd pick his jaw up off the floor, turn his eyes away from her stunning figure and slink off before Cass had him thrown in prison.

Steady. He was in America, not Tulay. And as much as the sight of that buffoon ogling Briony's backside, shown off to curvy perfection in slim-fitting blue jeans, irritated

him, he had no desire to sink to the depths his future fa-
ther-in-law, the King of Linnaea, had so frequently descended to. The man was a tyrant, like his father before
him. The heir apparent, Alaric Van Ambrose, wasn't the
despot his sire had been in his younger years. But the
prince of Linnaea had a heart of ice that rivaled the freezing temperatures outside.

What would Briony think when she met her half brother
and father for the first time? Two men who couldn't be
more unlike her in every conceivable way, and from what
the king had said, Briony had no idea they even existed.
Her mother had concealed everything about her royal origins from her.

A slight smile curved his lips. He wished he could have
met the woman who defied King Daxon Van Ambrose before she'd passed. Although judging by how firmly Briony handled the customers who got a little rowdy, the late
Marie Smith, formerly Carmichael before she'd gone into
hiding from her past lover, had taught her daughter well.

He pretended not to see Briony's green gaze flicker his
way as she mopped up some beer Justin had splashed on
the bar top. He'd accepted that once he'd discovered Briony's existence, he would be wed to the woman who would
provide both revenge and salvation. It was his destiny.

The looming question, however, was whether or not
Briony would accept hers.

CHAPTER TWO

BRIONY CLOSED THE door of the Ledge behind the last of the patrons and released a sigh that echoed in the cavernous room. The couple had hung on until the bitter end, well past the eleven o'clock closing time. She glanced down at her phone and sighed again.

Nearly midnight. And she had to get the twins up at six.

"You're nicer than I am."

Briony whirled around, wielding her phone above her head. Cass moved with lightning speed, one arm circling around her waist and drawing her flush against him as he grabbed her wrist and deflected the blow.

"Not the greeting I was expecting," he said, an amused smirk crossing his face.

"Why did you sneak up on me?" she demanded. She had intended to sound firm. Instead, she sounded breathless and husky. Her body had gone from fear to heightened awareness in the span of a heartbeat. Hard not to be aware when she could feel the hard muscles of his chest pressed against her breasts, his woodsy scent filling her senses as she inhaled sharply.

"I thought you saw me. I was sitting in the back corner."

She glanced in the direction he'd gestured. The corner booth was shrouded in shadow. Wariness flickered through her. Had he deliberately sat there so she wouldn't see him? So that he could stay undetected until the last guest left?

She shook off her sense of foreboding. It was late, and she was letting her imagination run wild.

"No, I didn't."

She'd been more disappointed than she should have been when she'd turned around after serving a group of hunters and found Cass's barstool empty. But she'd pushed through, focusing on filling drinks and not on glowing caramel-colored eyes that made her deliciously warm.

Slowly, Cass released his grip and stepped back, giving her space. She swayed forward before she caught herself. What was wrong with her? She never reacted like this to a man.

"I saw that you were the last one here." His voice carried a thread of steel, as if he was angry on her behalf. The thought touched her and filled her with a different, cozier kind of warmth. When had someone cared about her?

Not since Mom. The knowledge that he had stayed to make sure she was safe was like a balm to her bruised and battered heart.

"Gus, the owner, normally stays," she said past the lump in her throat. "But his wife just had a baby and she isn't sleeping well, so I told him to go home." She gestured to the snow-covered prairie outside the windows. "Not like we live in a dangerous city."

"You never know when danger might strike." With the way Cass was looking at her, she had a feeling that the biggest threat was standing less than three feet away. Not dangerous, she realized, at least not in that she feared he would harm her. But dangerous in that he was the kind of man who could make her throw her inhibitions to the wind and do something spontaneous.

"Anyway," he continued, "I thought you could use a hand."

She stared at him for a moment. "What?"

He gestured to the glasses lined up on the bar waiting to be cleaned and the bags of trash by the door.

"Help."

Her eyes slid from the crisp black polo molded perfectly to his broad shoulders down to his tan slacks and leather shoes. She'd bet his ensemble equaled a few nights' worth of tips at least. Not to mention he was a very mysterious, very wealthy businessman. Why on earth was he offering to help a lowly barmaid?

Before she could reply, he stepped forward and took her hand in his. Her lips parted on a gasp as he brought her fingers up and paused, his mouth a breath away from her skin.

"I get the impression that you excel at taking care of others." Could he feel the vibration that hummed through her body as he brushed a featherlight kiss across her knuckles? "But I'd like to help. Please, Briony."

The simple plea, combined with the way her name rolled off his tongue, crumbled her defenses as swiftly as if he'd wielded a battering ram. She should question the attention he was paying her.

Not just yet.

She wanted to enjoy the fantasy he offered, even if it was just for a night. Tomorrow would come soon enough, with its endless cycles of servitude and heartache. Tonight her world looked a little less bleak with Cass smiling at her with such warmth it made heat spread across her skin.

"Are you always so persuasive, Mr. Morgan?"

His eyes gleamed with promise. "When I see something I want, I'm relentless."

She blinked, her heart skipping a beat. Did he want *her*? Someone with his looks and obvious wealth could have anyone. But the way he was gazing at her, caramel-colored eyes smoldering, spoke volumes.

If he wanted just a short fling, what would she say? Her body very clearly screamed its answer, from her thundering pulse to the roaring in her ears. But her mind infiltrated the haze of want, reminding her that she didn't just feel physical attraction for this man. No, he had sparked something else, emotions that, even though she had never gone to bed with anyone, she was fairly certain she would struggle to keep out of any encounter with Cass.

"All right." She slowly withdrew her hand from his and focused on the safer topic. "Chairs on top of tables would be helpful. And trash goes in the dumpsters out back."

Judging by the quirk of his lips, her authoritative tone didn't mask the effect he had on her.

"Yes, ma'am."

Between the two of them, they made quick work of cleaning to the backdrop of jazz playing on the radio. Within thirty minutes, the bar was sparkling. She surveyed the freshly mopped floors and gleaming glasses with satisfaction.

"I can't believe how quickly we got that done."

"We make a good team."

She ducked her head to hide her blush. "Probably not what you were expecting to do on your trip."

Before he could respond, the soft strains of classical instruments filtered through the speakers. Briony smiled.

"I love this song."

Cass arched a brow. "Classical music?"

A moment later a woman's husky voice filled the bar, the lyrics spinning a seductive tale of spells and love.

Cass's eyes gleamed. He stepped toward her once more, his movements slow but intentional. She should run, before she did something stupid like let him touch her and drive the need that had seized her to a fever pitch she may not be able to pull away from him. Was the fantasy worth risking her heart when it was already so fragile?

But she didn't run. No, she let him slide an arm around her waist once more as her body leaned into him, molding to his muscular physique as if they'd been made for each other. He captured her hand in his, tan fingers threading through hers. The intimacy of his touch robbed the air from her lungs.

They started to sway, his other hand settling at the base of her back, his fingertips burning through the fabric of her shirt. When he leaned down and pressed his forehead to hers, the world shifted. His fingers slid up her spine, a gentle caress; it still made her arch deeper into his embrace. A thrill shot through her at his shaky intake of breath. Knowing she affected him emboldened her to slide her hand from his shoulder to the strong column of his neck. Heat radiated off his skin as his muscles tensed beneath her touch.

The singer's voice washed over them both, declaring her lover to be hers and hers alone. Cass's hands tightened on her as the words wrapped around them. The remaining thoughts at the edge of her conscience, to-dos and worries about the future, drifted away as she basked in the knowledge that after so long, someone wanted her again.

Her eyes drifted shut as her desire shifted, became clearer as her fear dropped away. She had never pictured her first lover as someone she'd known for such a short period of time, let alone someone she had no future with. She'd dreamed of that first joining being with a man she loved and who loved her just as deeply. While she certainly had strong feelings for Cass, she hadn't known him nearly long enough to be in love.

If Cass asked her to be with him tonight, what would she say? Was it worth turning him down to cling to her dream?

She opened her eyes as the last of the song faded, the

only sound left their mingled breathing and the pounding of her heart. With his body pressed against hers, his heat seeping through her clothes, her dream barely held a candle to the sensual possibilities she glimpsed in his eyes.

Please kiss me.

Their gazes connected. Heat crackled between them. His eyes gleamed as a small smile tilted up the corner of his full lips.

"Can I buy you a drink?"

She laughed. "The bar's closed, sir."

He released her and walked back to her corner, circling around the counter as he grabbed one of her towels and tossed it over his shoulder. Normally she loathed anyone being in her space. But as she watched him survey the bottles on her shelf, she felt only a languid warmth. Being with him, letting down her guard and sharing herself with him, felt right.

Curiosity drew her closer.

"What are you making?"

"It's a surprise."

She tried to peek as he bent down to grab something out of the mini fridge. The sight of his perfectly sculpted rear distracted her. He straightened and resumed his secretive mixing. Judging by the smirk he shot over his shoulder, he knew exactly what part of his anatomy she'd been ogling.

"*Pour vous, mademoiselle*," he said as he turned and set a glass in front of her. She picked it up and sniffed, the scent of brandy mixed with nutmeg relaxing her.

"I can't remember the last time I had a cocktail." She took a sip, closed her eyes and moaned as the creamy, chocolaty drink hit her tongue. "What is this?" she asked as she opened her eyes,

"A Brandy Alexander." Cass gestured to a dusty bottle

behind him. "You had a passable cognac back here. Didn't want it to languish any longer."

"Thank you, Cass." She glanced down at the shavings of nutmeg nestled on the frothy surface of her drink. One drink shouldn't matter so much.

But it did. Between working double shifts and cooking, cleaning and managing her stepfamily's existence, she couldn't remember the last time someone had done something just for her.

Warm fingertips grazed her cheek. Her head jerked up as Cass tucked a lock of hair behind her ear, a tender gesture she leaned into before she could stop herself.

"You strike me as the kind of woman who takes care of everyone. But," he whispered as he leaned in, his lips a breath away from hers, "who takes care of you, Briony?"

Me.

In a split second, she found herself caught between two worlds. Hopeless loneliness and a want so fierce it made her whole body ache.

A grim look settled on Cass's handsome face.

"That's what I thought."

She jerked back, then tried to cover her movement with a casual sip of her drink.

"I'm very good at taking care of myself," she said with a flippancy she didn't feel.

"You are."

"And tonight you made me a drink." She shot him an appreciative smile, trying to recapture some of their flirtatious chemistry. "After a long shift, I'd count that as being taken care of."

His gaze sharpened. She suddenly had the sensation she imagined one did when they realized they were in the sights of a predator.

Stop being melodramatic.

Yet she couldn't shake the sense that something was off. It wasn't just her horribly battered self-esteem talking, either. Why was a man of Cass's obvious wealth and sophistication in Nowhere, Kansas? Why had he taken an interest in her? And really, what did she know about him other than that he was from some country in the Mediterranean and liked high-end liqueur?

Cass leaned a little closer, so close she could see dark flecks in his eyes. It made them glitter in a way that was both erotic and unnerving.

"What if I could help you, Briony?"

"What?" she sputtered.

"Not just you," he continued as if they were having a normal conversation, "but your stepfather and stepsisters, too."

Slowly, she set her drink down so she didn't toss the contents in his face.

"In exchange for what?" she asked coolly. "Because it sounds like you're about to offer to make me your mistress or whatever they're calling it these days."

The intensity that had settled over Cass darkened as his eyes crackled with mahogany sparks of anger.

"I would never dishonor you that way." Her own anger dissipated as quickly as it had risen.

"Okay, then what are you suggesting?"

"What do you know about your father?"

The swift change in subject left her reeling.

"My father?"

"Yes."

A memory rose up, vivid and bitter. The one time she remembered her mother raising her voice. She'd been ten and had asked about her father for a school project.

There's nothing to tell, Mom said with an overly bright, brittle smile.

But—

Drop it, Briony. He never was, and never will be, a part of our lives.

At the time, she'd thought the emotion in her mother's voice had been anger. Mom's refusal to talk had hurt deeply and driven a wedge between them. While they had recovered, that conversation had lingered in the background of the remainder of their relationship. It had taken Mom's illness to make Briony conscious of the fact that she had been pushing her mother away, creating a distance as a shield against the hurt of not knowing that piece of her history. The realization had come in time for her and her mother to have a frank conversation, one that still hadn't resulted in her father's identity, but had left her feeling more connected to her mom than she had in years.

But as Briony reexamined the initial memory of her mother's refusal, she realized the truth: her mother had been afraid. She'd been so angry that she'd projected her own emotions onto her mother. It wasn't until now, revisiting the memory with the emotional maturity of an adult instead of the volatile feelings of a young girl, that she understood. It had been fear, not anger, that had made her mother's voice pitch up. Dread that made the tendons in her neck tense, the pulse in her throat pound so hard it was visible to the naked eye.

Warning whispered in her ear.

"What does my birth father have to do with this?"

Cass's smile flashed again, a cruel twist of his lips that made her feel cold. But she blinked, and it was gone. Had she imagined it?

"Your father has everything to do with what I'm about to propose." He reached over to a black briefcase sitting on the edge of the counter. He popped the lid and pulled out a folder. He slid it over to her. "Van Ambrose" had been written in bold black script across the top.

She swallowed hard. Intuition told her that whatever was in this folder had the power to change the course of her life. Mom had gone to great lengths to keep her father's identity a secret.

Yet her mother's unwillingness to talk about her birth father had left a void, a missing piece in Briony's life. Once her mom had married Trey and welcomed his daughters, Stacy and Ella, into the family, Briony had felt that emptiness even more acutely. Trey had been friendly, but the few moments of affection he'd displayed had felt like hard-won battles instead of fatherly love. She'd taken a shop class in high school because Trey had loved woodworking. The first time he'd spontaneously hugged her had been when she'd presented him with an end table she'd made for his birthday. When she'd overheard her mother and Trey arguing about his lack of involvement with Briony, she'd doubled her efforts to show her mom that everything was wonderful and see, she and Trey got along just fine.

The twins had been slightly better, coming into her room for slumber parties and going shopping with her up until she'd left for the university in Missoula. When she'd returned to help care for Mom, Stacy and Ella had been excited to see her.

But now...now there was nothing meaningful left in her life. Nothing but her father's true identity.

She tore open the envelope, not caring if Cass saw her shaking fingers or heard her shuddering breath. She pulled out a sheaf of photos. It took a moment for her to realize she was looking at pictures of her mom.

Tears pricked her eyes. Judging by her mother's long red hair and smooth face, the photographs had to be at least twenty years old. In every photo, she was in the company of a man who had to be in his mid-to late forties. Silver-haired with hawkish features, a smug smile and a lean figure dressed in expensive-looking suits, the expression on his face said he knew the world was his and dared anyone to tell him differently.

Yet in the few where he looked down at her mother, his thin lips were softened at the corners, his arm wrapped possessively yet gently around Marie's waist.

Briony peered closer. His eyes were green. A vivid, almost unnatural emerald green. She knew without a doubt that she was finally seeing a photo of her father.

Blood roared in her ears as time slammed to a halt. She traced a finger over his face, happiness flooding her as she soaked in the matching eye color, the same pointed chin. Her mother and her had shared the same vivid red hair, but every time she'd seen a picture of the two of them together, the differences in their faces, it had been yet another reminder of the missing piece of her life.

Mom, why didn't you tell me?

Confusion swamped her happiness and sank it faster than she could catch her breath. Her eyes flickered to Cass as she felt herself drifting out to sea, unanchored and awash in grief and bewilderment. This man—a complete stranger—knew more about her past than she did.

She set the photos aside, reached back into the envelope and pulled out a sheaf of papers. Her mother's entire life was in her hands: her hospital records from when she gave birth to Briony in Kansas City, her college degree, her teaching contract for Nowhere's elementary school, the deed to their house, her and Trey's marriage certificate.

The last piece of paper made Briony's eyes grow hot. Her mother's death certificate. Had her father planned on finding Marie, making amends, only to find out too late that his lover had died?

Slowly, she looked up at Cass. "How did you get all this? Who are you?"

"Your half brother put together the file. He and your father gave it to me last month."

The photo edges crinkled as her fingers tightened. "You've met them? I have a half brother?"

"Yes, and yes."

"What's my brother's name?" she whispered.

"Alaric Van Ambrose."

"Alaric." She dropped the papers, grabbed the cocktail and tossed back half the contents. The warm slide of liqueur and cream took some of the edge off the whirlwind swirling inside her chest. She had a brother. A father. A family. Why had they never met? Had her father not wanted her? Had Mom known about her half brother?

"How long have they known about me?"

"Your father only found out about your existence last month. I expect your half brother only knew for slightly longer than that, as he conducted his research."

Relief made her knees weak. If her father had known about her all along and not sought her out, she wouldn't have been able to bear the pain.

"Where are they?"

"In Linnaea."

She frowned. "I've never heard of it."

"It's a small country that lies on the coast of the North Sea, wedged between Belgium and the Netherlands."

Pride rang in his voice.

"You're from there."

Cass blinked in surprise before his handsome features settled into a blank mask. "Originally, yes. I've lived in the country of Tulay since I was eight."

"I haven't heard of Tulay, either."

"Another small kingdom, a principality, between Spain and France along the shores of the Mediterranean."

"Ah. Maybe you can draw a map of all these countries I haven't heard of before sometime." She winced. "Sorry. That sounded snarky. I'm just...this is a lot to take in."

Cass reached over and grasped her hand, wrapped his fingers around hers. For a moment she resisted, her fingers stiff. But as she looked back down at the photos and papers scattered across the bar, she relaxed and accepted his offer of comfort.

She breathed out. "Okay. So my father gave you this?"

The hesitation was so slight she almost missed it. "Yes."

Her earlier wariness returned. Cass wasn't being entirely honest with her. "Why?"

"Because he needs your help."

"My help?" she repeated.

He handed her another envelope. This one was made of heavy cream material, an emblem of a key and sword crossed over a crown imprinted in the red wax seal on the back. Her fingers drifted over it. She'd seen this before once...an old envelope she'd found in the attic. The seal had been broken, the letters inside written in French. When she'd brought it to her mother, her mother had turned without hesitation and tossed it into the fire.

"Just old letters," she'd said casually. But Briony hadn't missed the tightness about her mother's mouth, nor the tense set of her shoulders.

"This seal...what is it?"

"The royal seal of Linnaea."

Her mind screeched to a halt. "Royal seal?"

"Your father is King Daxon Van Ambrose of the country of Linnaea. Your mother was his lover during the summer after her semester at Oxford."

Laughter bubbled up inside her. Once she started laughing, she couldn't stop, laughing so hard that tears threatened to roll down her cheeks. Cass watched her with an unblinking gaze, but she didn't care. He'd put so much into pulling an elaborate, albeit extremely cruel, prank on her.

"Who put you up to this?" she finally asked as her laughter subsided. "Did Gus do this? Or Jacques? Is this to get back at me for the shaving cream?"

"While I look forward to one day hearing about the shaving cream, I can assure you this is all very real."

She held up one of the photographs of her mother. "So my father is a ruler of a principality I've never heard of—"

"Country. He's a king, so Linnaea is designated as a country. Tulay is a principality overseen by a prince."

She waved his interruption aside. "Country, kingdom, whatever, which makes my mysterious brother a prince, too, and me...what? A princess? Heiress to a beautiful castle?"

Cass sighed. Her mirth and attempt at maintaining good humor despite the nastiness of whatever joke he was playing on her was swiftly replaced by anger.

"It sounds incredible, I know—"

"No," she said before she tossed back the rest of the cocktail and set the glass on the bar. "It sounds like the most awful joke someone has every played on me. I'm curious to know who gave you my mom's photo." She picked up another picture of her mom and the older man, arm in arm in front of the Eiffel Tower. "Seriously, this is some great Photoshop work."

Cass's eyes glittered dangerously. A shiver traced its way down her spine.

"This is no joke." His glacial voice rivaled the winter winds tearing across the prairie outside. "Thousands of people are depending on us."

"On us?" she repeated. "Who are you? Is your name even Cass?"

"It is. Short for Cassius Morgan Adama, a prince of the country of Tulay."

Her hand drifted back toward the glass. Maybe he was actually unhinged and believed everything he was saying. It would certainly explain the conviction with which he spoke.

"The country of Linnaea is in dire financial straits. If you accept my proposal, you can help them, and I can help your family."

She stared at him for a long moment. He didn't give off a crazy vibe. But then how could any of this be true? Little girls dreamed of being secret princesses and one day being whisked off by their own Prince Charming.

But this was reality. Real life where fathers disappeared and mothers died and stepfamilies treated you like the scum on the bottom of their shoe.

"Fine. Humor me, and then I'm leaving. What exactly are you proposing?"

Cass reached down, then straightened and placed a blue velvet box on the counter. Briony stared at the box as her heart started to pound.

"Cass…"

He flipped the lid open to reveal a stunning diamond encircled by sapphires set in a silver band that screamed it was an antique. She didn't know how long she stared at the ring before she raised her shocked gaze to Cass's face. His eyes glinted once more with that predatory gleam, as if he'd cornered his prize.

"Marriage."

CHAPTER THREE

CASS RETURNED BRIONY'S stare with his own. Her emerald gaze dropped back to the ring, then up to him. The shock etched on her pale face would have been comical if there wasn't so much riding on this moment.

"Marriage," she finally repeated.

"Yes."

She whirled away from the bar, the scrunchie that had held her hair on top of her head giving way to the ferocity of her movements. Her fire-red curls tumbled over her shoulders and down her back.

God, she was glorious. Anticipation hummed in his veins as he circled the bar and followed her through a narrow doorway into a poorly lit room with lockers stacked against one wall.

What are you doing? He stopped, keeping distance between himself and Briony. He had indulged in the fantasy Briony had presented him when she'd flashed that grin, savored their flirtations and entertained vivid images of her spread naked across his bed.

But he was no longer Cass Morgan. No, he was back to being Prince Cassius Adama, and he had a job to do, a duty to fulfill. While sex would one day play a part in his and Briony's marriage, lust and any other chaotic emotions tied to love would only clutter up what he had to do.

He would not make the same mistakes his father and Aunt Alecine had by succumbing to their feelings.

Briony stalked to one locker with a sunshine sticker peeling off the metal door, twirled the combination on the lock and wrenched it open. She yanked a threadbare green coat out and shoved her arms into the sleeves.

"Do you truly have no interest in who your birth father is?"

She spun to face him. Emerald fire snapped in her eyes. When he'd overheard Daxon and Alaric's argument and realized that Daxon not only had a secret daughter but was angry that one of his paramours had given birth to an illegitimate child, he'd known that marrying Daxon's daughter would cement his plan of revenge. Yet he'd also been confronted with what he'd known since he was ten years old: that his marriage would be a formal business arrangement. Aunt Alecine had told him plenty of times how her one attempt at love had resulted in his family's banishment.

A childhood memory clawed at him: Alecine hanging a red gingham blanket over the cracked window of the dingy one-bedroom apartment they'd barely managed to afford after fleeing Linnaea with nothing but the clothes on their back. It had been both a cheery splash of color against the drab walls and a stark reminder of what little they'd had. It had only lasted for a year, but it had been the hardest year of his life. Going hungry some nights had paled in comparison to knowing his mother had chosen her life of luxury over her husband and son, that their great love story had failed the test.

That year had been the catalyst for his nearly two decades of planning, of building up wealth as he watched Linnaea crumble into poverty. He'd resolved that on his thirtieth birthday he would go to Daxon and make him an offer, a financial agreement that would elevate Linnaea out of its looming economic depression while making Daxon beholden to the man he had banished as a child. Given that Daxon had not only forced Alecine, his former mistress, and her family to flee their home but had cut off their access to their finances and spread the word as far as Vienna that Alecine was a thief not to be trusted, putting a financial spin to his revenge had seemed appropriate. Still, Cass had always known that there was a risk that Daxon, whose pride was as legendary as his numerous affairs, would turn him down out of spite.

Enter Briony. He had been at a political summit in Paris, unaware that Daxon and Alaric had been invited until he'd arrived to represent his adopted country on behalf of Aunt Alecine's husband. He'd taken a call out in the hallway and seen Daxon and Alaric stalk by, their faces dark, voices low and heavy with anger. He'd followed and, once they'd disappeared into a small conference room, stationed himself outside the door.

"…the right thing to do. By all accounts, she's in dire financial straits."

"I didn't even know she existed until you did your little pet project."

Daxon's voice had roughened with his illness, the angelic quality that had supposedly seduced scores of women now a harsh rasp as he snapped at his son.

"That's not my problem," Alaric had replied in a tone that could have frozen hell. "But if you—"

"Tell you what, *son*. If she can save the country from financial ruin or find me a cure, I'll reach out. Otherwise, I want nothing to do with a bastard child."

Just like, that puzzle pieces had fallen into place. A week later, Cass had instructed his plane to land at the private airport near the Linnaean palace. He'd been greeted by a contingency of Daxon's palace guards and taken straight to the king himself. Every time he remembered the selfish buzzard's face dissolving from smug satisfaction at having arrested a member of the Adamos family to fury mixed with grudging acceptance that what Cass was offering was a deal he couldn't afford to pass up, he savored the thrill of having finally bested the man who had ruined not only his life, but his father's and aunt's lives as well.

Cass had known there was a good chance Daxon would say no, convince himself he could somehow still drag the country out of the hole he'd dug for it with his relentless spending.

But it was that same pride that made Daxon say yes when Cass presented his offer. If Daxon didn't accept Cass's financing and offer of marriage, not only would Linnaea continue to march toward an economic depression, but word would eventually leak of Briony's existence. How, Cass had asked, would Daxon handle the press fallout, that he'd known about his daughter struggling to make ends meet in some godforsaken little town while he dined in the lap of luxury?

"You're blackmailing me?" Daxon had demanded before he collapsed into coughing.

"I don't have to," Cass had replied silkily. "Your son is already furious that you would deny her. How long do you think it will take before he reaches out to her if you don't? What if he leaks it to the press? Or she does, once she learns the truth? Compare that to not only embracing your long-lost child but forming an alliance that will save the people of your country?"

He'd arched a brow as Daxon's reply was lost in another hacking cough. Slowly he'd advanced on the old man. For a brief moment, as a child, he'd feared the legendary Daxon Van Ambrose, the man with so much power he'd driven

Cass's father from his own home and sent his mother fleeing to her wealthy relatives in Paris.

But every step he'd taken toward the throne, toward the hunched figure of a dying coward, had emboldened him until he'd been less than a foot away.

"How long do you have left, my king? A year, maybe less?"

The glare Daxon had thrown at him had confirmed that the disease was spreading faster than any doctor could contain.

"How will you be remembered? As a savior? Or as the devil?"

Briony would help Cass not only achieve his revenge but bring Linnaean back from the brink of ruin. In turn, he would rescue her and her family from looming poverty.

Besides, what woman wouldn't jump at the chance to become a princess?

He'd never once been tempted by notions of love or romance. Family, duty and honor mattered above all.

"Who the hell do you think you are?" she demanded. He stood his ground as she advanced on him and jabbed a finger at his chest. "You waltz into my bar, flash your money and make me feel…"

"Make you feel what, Briony?"

"Special," she finally snapped. "Like you were interested in me and found me attractive."

"I am interested, and I do find you attractive."

She snorted. "Sure. And I'm a long-lost princess, my birth father is a king, and you're a prince who can rescue my home country by marrying me."

"You truly think I would make up an elaborate joke like this, propose marriage to you, just to hurt you?"

It may not be a joke, but you're still lying to her. Using her.

He pushed the unexpected thought away. There was too

much at stake for him to suffer an attack of conscience now. Besides, it wasn't just his own personal vendetta on the line. The fate of thousands of Linnaeans rested on his shoulders.

"People I've cared about have done worse things."

The pain in her voice tugged at him. He took a cautious step forward. His arm came up, his fingers reaching out to caress her shoulder, do something to offer a modicum of comfort.

Stop.

His arm dropped back to his side.

"I'm not. This is real. You can trust me, Briony."

Doubt flickered through him as she hesitated. He had never not succeeded. Victory came to him as naturally as breathing.

"Look me up, Briony. I assure you, I speak the truth about my background and yours. My offers of marriage and helping your family are genuine."

Slowly, she pulled her phone out.

"Prince Cassius Morgan…"

"Adama. Of Tulay."

Her fingers flew over her phone. Then she froze. Her eyes flickered back and forth over the screen. Had she found the numerous articles detailing his life? The gossip columns hazarding guesses as to who he was dating? Or had she found the website that was his aunt's pride and joy, the official site of the royal family of Tulay?

At last, she looked at him, her eyes opaque.

"So am I supposed to curtsy or what?"

The curt yet sassy response startled a laugh from him.

"A curtsy is not necessary."

A harsh breath escaped her as she ran her fingers through her hair, further tousling the curls. He had a sudden vibrant image of her laid naked across his bed at the palace in Tulay, the setting sun painting his suite with rose-gold light as he buried his fingers in her hair and kissed that pert mouth.

"So…this is real."

"It's real."

She typed something else into her phone. A moment later she blew out another breath that bordered on a growl.

"What?"

"Just looked up 'Daxon,' 'Alaric' and 'Linnaea.' It…it all checks out." She glanced up at him and frowned. "You don't need to look so smug."

"Don't I?"

She sank down onto a bench and shoved her phone into her coat pocket.

"You can't blame me for being suspicious."

"I don't."

"Just because you have photos of my mother with…*him* doesn't mean I'm actually his daughter. And you could have forged the letter."

"And if you agree to accompany me tomorrow, we will have a DNA test performed immediately. But," he added, "when you see his eyes, will you be able to deny what your heart already knows?"

She swallowed hard.

"There is a…slight resemblance."

More like a carbon copy. Daxon and Alaric both possessed the emerald-colored eyes of the Van Ambrose royals. Once Briony was standing next to her father and brother, there would be no question about her parentage.

"You said if I accompany you tomorrow. What are you talking about?"

He eased himself down onto the bench across from her. This was a step in the right direction, but he had to tread carefully. One wrong move and he could lose his chance.

"The letter from your father asks if you will become my wife to ensure a financial alliance that will rescue Linnaea from an economic depression. If you agree, you'll accompany me to Linnaea to meet your father and brother, as well as formally announce our engagement."

Her laugh this time came out strangled.

"Our engagement? You barely know me."

"I know enough."

"Right. That I'm the daughter of a king."

The bitterness in her voice crept under his skin.

"That's part of it," he said honestly. "But as I said, this would be a mutually beneficial arrangement, and not just for Linnaea. I have paperwork ready to establish trust funds for both of your stepsisters that would ensure their financial security and a private counselor who would be available to them as long as they need to process their grief over your mother's death. Your medical and credit card debts would be wiped away. I also have a reservation on standby for Trey at an exclusive rehabilitation clinic in Kansas City with an extraordinary success rate."

She leaned forward, her hair falling in a red curtain over her face.

"You told me yesterday when I overheard your conversation that you just wanted them to get better. This is your chance to make that happen."

He knew the reminders of her home situation were calculated and heartless. But she needed to be reminded of her situation and of what he had the power to do.

"And in return I marry a stranger."

He reached out and grabbed her hand. Her head snapped up as tension crackled in the air between them. She stared down at his fingers threaded through hers, then slowly looked up at him.

He was a heartless bastard. But God help him, he couldn't stop.

"In return, I can offer you several things. Meeting the remaining family you have. A life of luxury and ease. Children. A chance to have your own family. I won't pretend that I'm capable of offering love, but I can offer a pleasant relationship between two people who are obviously attracted to each other, which bodes well for certain aspects of the marriage."

Her cheeks turned pink.

"We don't know each other well." He was treading on dangerous ground. But, he argued with himself, he was making his case, not indulging in his own attraction. "But I already know much about you."

"From your research," she whispered. He smiled. She was trying to keep him at bay. But he had started this battle, and he intended to finish it.

"Yes. Research that also showed me that you're loyal to your family, although by all accounts you have every right to walk out and leave them to their own misery."

She shook her head. "I can't do that. They're grieving."

"You're compassionate."

He meant that. It was a quality he'd normally eschewed as weak. Yet on Briony it didn't seem like weakness. No, on her it came across as strength.

"And," he added with a smile, "you handle drunks with the grace of a queen."

She laughed. Desire urged him to lean forward and claim her mouth, give her a demonstration of just how compatible they could truly be.

But not yet. Patience. It had taken more than he had expected to convince her that he was in fact a prince, that her father was a king and that she was a princess. If he frightened her off now, he might lose his chance.

And, he reminded himself as he released her hand and straightened, he'd lusted after women before. As enjoyable as those encounters had been, the actual event often paled in comparison to the anticipation that preceded it. Sex had become more of a routine, the occasional sojourn into physical pleasure a way to take the edge off after a long day of running his business enterprise or supporting Aunt Alecine or his father in their political endeavors.

Bedding Briony, while pleasurable, would most likely follow the same pattern. If he could hold on to that thought, his attraction would dim, and he could once again focus on the task at hand.

"Will you come with me to Linnaea?"

Briony sighed. "When would we leave?"

"Tomorrow at ten a.m."

She blinked. "Tomorrow's Saturday. I work."

"If you agree to my proposal, you'll never have to work again."

A scowl crossed her face. "And you think that sounds appealing? To lounge around and do nothing all day?"

He shrugged. "Given your and your family's circumstances, yes."

She surged to her feet. "How dare you!"

He stood, trying to keep a lid on his own temper. He was offering her not only a solution to her every problem, but the chance to finally meet her birth father. Based on what little she'd shared over the last week, she craved knowledge of her lineage, a chance to have blood relatives once more. She didn't know the weasel was a blight on the face of the earth. So what could possibly be leading to this unexpected and frustrating last-minute display of temper and resistance?

"How dare I what, Briony? Offer you everything you and your family need? Offer you the one thing you want?"

"At the cost of marrying someone I met less than a week ago!" she cried. "Coming in and offering to rearrange my life. I've done just fine on my own."

"Have you?" he asked softly as he stood and towered over her. "Your house is one delinquent payment away from foreclosure. Just yesterday your stepfather ran up over a thousand dollars in online gaming debt." Briony blanched, but he didn't let up. Not now, not when she needed to see how much she needed him and what he could do for her. "Between caring for him and your stepsisters, when will you be able to finish your education degree? Five years, ten? Perhaps never?"

"How I manage my life and my family's life is none of your concern," Briony bit out before she turned and fled the locker room.

He breathed in deeply, steadying himself. The hunter in him demanded that he chase her, stop her, not let her leave until he had her signature on the contract. But the planner in him knew better. To do so would only push her away. Her fierce reaction betrayed her innermost thoughts; she knew he'd spoken the truth. All he had to do was be patient. She would come around.

And if she doesn't?

His measured steps led him out into the bar just as Briony was heading for the front door. The sight of the files in her hand and his briefcase standing empty on the counter lessened some of his unease. If she was taking the papers, she was still intrigued, even if she didn't want to be.

"My plane leaves at ten a.m. tomorrow morning from the airstrip just outside of town," he said as she jerked the door open. "If you're not there by a quarter to ten, I'll assume you have rejected my offer."

"You can let yourself out the kitchen door," she retorted. "I set the alarm. If you're not out in five minutes, you'll get a personal visit from the Nowhere Police Department."

"Not very friendly to outsiders, I'm guessing?"

She stood framed in the doorway, snow swirling behind her as a winter wind teased her red curls.

"Good night, Prince Cassius. Have a safe flight."

With a final glare, she slammed the door behind her. He stared at it for a long minute before grabbing his briefcase off the counter and heading for the kitchen door. While it would be a simple matter to smooth over his presence at the bar with the local police, he'd had enough disagreements for the evening.

He glanced back at the front door of the bar, an unexpected smile lurking about his lips. Based on Alaric's file, he had anticipated a quick and breathlessly grateful "yes" to his proposal, perhaps even a few appreciative tears. Not the display of furious independence or the grand exit into the cold.

She would be there tomorrow morning, he thought as he turned the lock and let himself out the kitchen door. Without him, her family would plunge into ruin within months, if not weeks.

His mind conjured up the last image of her framed in the doorway, red curls splayed across her shoulders, emerald eyes flashing fire, lush lips set into a firm line as the snow swirled behind her. Even in her worn coat and jeans, she'd exuded a regal fortitude befitting the descendants of royalty and a frustrating yet admirable stubbornness.

She might not show. A possibility he had not accounted for. But the thought didn't fill him with anger or concern. His smile grew as he walked around the bar toward the snow-covered parking lot.

The possibility of going deeper into battle to make Briony Van Ambrose his wife filled him with a heated excitement. No matter what happened tomorrow morning, she would be his.

CHAPTER FOUR

BRIONY APPROACHED Nowhere Regional Airport at 9:46 a.m., a scowl on her face and a duffel bag slung over her shoulder. Resigned anger churned in her gut as she walked toward the tiny building and the plane looming behind it. When she'd walked out of the bar last night, it had been with every intention of never seeing Cass again.

But as her rush of adrenaline had abated on her walk home, doubt had crept in as the winter wind pierced her cloak and chilled her skin. What could she do on her own? Trey was still gambling. She wouldn't be able to work enough shifts to cover both his debts and the bills. A move to a larger city and a better-paying job was out of the question. The twins would fight her tooth and nail, and Trey probably wouldn't be much better.

She could just leave on her own. She'd dreamed of it more than once. But every time she seriously contemplated it, she knew she could never just leave her stepfather and stepsisters to drown in their own misery. The guilt alone would plague her the rest of her life.

And it wouldn't be what her mother would have wanted.

Although, she'd conceded with sorrow as she'd trudged through snowdrifts piling up on the sidewalks, did she really know what her mother would have wanted? Marie Smith had had an entirely different life before she'd fled

Europe, one she'd concealed from Briony and most likely from Trey, too. And if Cass's story was to be believed, she'd hidden Briony's birth from her father.

Out of everything that had been revealed last night, that had cut the deepest of all. Her mother had always been a proponent of honesty and tough conversations. Even when they had been uncomfortable, she'd preferred to be up-front and truthful.

So why, when she'd known how much Briony had longed to know more about her history, when she'd seen Briony and Trey struggle to form a relationship, had she concealed so much? What had frightened her so much? Had she been scared of her former lover? Or worried that if Briony knew the truth she'd be hurt, even angry?

She remembered the moment she'd confided to her mother when she'd come home how much the conversation about her father all those years ago had hurt, how Mom had cried and said she was sorry that she'd hurt her and that if Briony could just trust her, it had been done out of love. Briony had accepted it, grateful that they were putting the pain behind them and savoring the few months they had left.

That bittersweet memory was now tainted.

Those thoughts had been swirling around in her head as she'd let herself into the house at two in the morning. Dishes had been piled in the sink. Dirty clothes had been tossed in a heap outside the laundry room. The twins had tracked in snow that had melted into slushy gray puddles on the scarred hardwood floors.

And Trey... Trey had been snoring in the armchair, multiple empty beer cans littering the floor around him. The family computer in the den had been open to an on-line poker site. She'd tried to haul Trey out of his chair. At first, he'd just snored, the stench of stale beer making her sick to her stomach. Finally, after she'd pulled him to his feet, he'd opened bloodshot eyes.

"Marie?" he'd whispered.

Briony's heart had clenched. She'd started to respond when suddenly his eyes had narrowed in anger.

"It's just you. God, I wish you had died instead."

Perhaps she'd just grown numb enough that his words hadn't initially hit. She'd managed to drag him down the hall to his bedroom and lay him on the bed, where he'd promptly passed out again. She'd made it out into the hallway where she'd slid down against the wall, tears slipping down her face.

The final straw. Just in time for a dark-haired, amber-eyed seducer to come along and offer her a deal. A deal that, as she'd sucked in a shuddering breath and wiped away her tears, finally started to sink in.

She'd read and reread the contract, then read it once more before she'd walked out the door. The wedding would take place in the next eight weeks.

Eight weeks, she thought, trepidation mixed with a dash of nervous excitement. She'd always dreamed of getting married, of having a family. Even after the lackluster ending to her one college relationship, she'd still imagined her marriage having roots in love and companionship.

But without Cass's offer, she wouldn't be getting married anytime soon, much less living her life outside the tiny little circle she existed in now. Cass had a plan and the money to help not just her, but Trey and the twins, make a fresh start. He was also offering her the chance her mother never had, to meet not just her birth father but a brother who had been interested enough in her existence to search for her. Even though it stung that neither had come to Kansas, it probably wouldn't have been easy for the king or the prince of a country to suddenly travel to America. Not if things were as dire as Cass had depicted them. What little news she'd found had painted a similarly grim picture. While Alaric and Daxon mostly kept to themselves and were rarely photographed outside of Linnaea, the most recent articles had speculated on the rising inflation, labor strikes and a recent layoff of teachers.

Linnaea was in trouble. But as she'd flipped through the articles, then the photos as the sky had lightened and night had given way to early morning, she'd found herself feeling…hopeful. There had even been a touch of excitement as she'd packed her bag. A new adventure loomed on the horizon, a chance to find herself and learn more about who she was.

Not to mention marriage to a man who had frustrated her to no end last night but still sparked the most intense attraction she'd ever experienced.

She swallowed past the sudden lump in her throat. She'd been ready to give herself to Cass last night, to suggest they head back to his hotel or wherever he was staying. Last night it had been sexy, a sensual fantasy. Now, even though the thought of him still sent a frisson of awareness down her spine, the contractual nature of what would become their future relationship tempered the romance.

She hadn't just dreamed of marrying for love. No, she had dreamed of her first time being with a man who adored her. Cass had made it clear that he wouldn't be feeling much of anything for her.

There was a measure of sorrow that she would never have the fairy-tale love. But, she reminded herself, she was gaining so much. The chance to know the other half of her family. The chance to be free from the crushing weight of debt. The chance to start her life anew. And anytime she started to feel too much sadness or regret, she just replayed Cass's words over and over again in her mind:

I won't pretend I'm capable of offering love...

Each replay helped her bury any emotions she had felt for Cass Morgan deep down and focus her attentions on other things.

A gust of wind barreled across the prairie and hit her in the face as she walked around the airport. She burrowed her chin deeper into her scarf. Time to focus on the positives. At least she would be marrying a man she got along with and was physically attracted to. She might not have the love story, but her wedding would do something few marriages could ever do: make a difference.

Everything Cass had told her last night had checked out, at least with what she'd been able to find online. Numerous articles touted Cass and his family, royalty of the Mediterranean state of Tulay. Their origins were murky, barely touched on in what she'd read aside from a vague reference about them having lived in Linnaea in the past. But since Cass's aunt Alecine had married the prince of Tulay, the family seemed to have gained the Midas touch. Everything from oil and manufacturing to shipping and banking. Their estimated wealth was in the billions.

That spark of suspicion she'd felt last night crackled across the back of her neck again. If Cass was so wealthy, why did he need to marry her? Why not just give the money to Daxon? One of many questions she had for Cass on their flight to wherever it was he was taking her.

She'd pored over Daxon's letter so many times she nearly had it memorized. Written in a strong, bold script, Daxon had written out the exact same situation Cass had described: a country on the brink of ruin, a financial alliance by marriage and a chance for her to get to know the other half of her family. He had also explained that her mother had become overwhelmed by life in the spotlight and hadn't told him about her existence. It hadn't been until

Alaric, her half brother, had come across a letter from an old palace physician noting Marie's positive pregnancy test that they had even suspected Marie had had a child after she'd left Linnaea and returned to the States.

Daxon's letter had been polite but friendly, the kind of cautious wording she would expect from a man who had never met his long-lost daughter. Perhaps it was Daxon's own tempered voice that had tamped down some of her own excitement at finally meeting her father. Or perhaps she'd just had enough of getting her hopes up only to have them dashed.

Or, she acknowledged with a frown, perhaps it was the unease that invaded every time she remembered her mother's fear. Daxon's claim that life in the spotlight had scared her mother off seemed plausible. But she had a hard time envisioning that as the cause behind Marie's flight from Europe. Had the stresses of royal life truly spooked her mother so badly that she'd not only moved back to America but changed her last name?

So many unanswered questions, Briony thought with a sigh.

Her boots crunched in the snow as she neared the tarmac. The runway had been cleared of any snow—a feat, given that it had still been snowing at 6:00 a.m. when she'd roused the twins from bed for school. When she'd told them she was leaving to take care of some family business and that Trey's sister Debra would be coming to stay with them awhile, they had barely even looked at her.

"Fine," Stacy had grumbled.

"Whatever," Ella had echoed.

They hadn't even asked how long she'd been gone.

She approached a man dressed in black pants and a burgundy winter coat standing guard over the plane's stairs.

He bowed so low she nearly jumped back so his military-style hat didn't smack her in the face.

"Good morning, Your Highness."

"Um…you can just call me Briony."

The man didn't bat an eye. "Welcome, Princess Briony."

"Just Briony," she repeated with a smile to soften the edge in her voice. "Being called a princess is a little weird at the moment."

"It's who you are. Might as well get used to it, Your Highness."

She stiffened as the familiar husky voice drifted down to her. Slowly she looked up to see Cass framed in the door of the plane, a smile of satisfaction on his handsome face. Her fingers tightened around the strap of her duffel bag. She was grateful for everything he was offering. But the smugness in his expression rankled. What would he do if she turned and walked away? Chase her down? Throw her in the dungeon?

Or perhaps worse, let her walk all the way home back to her living nightmare of loneliness and rejection?

She lifted her chin. She was making the right decision.

"Good morning to you, too, *Prince* Cass." She dipped into a deep, overexaggerated curtsy. The guard made a noise that almost sounded like a suppressed laugh. But when she glanced at him, his face was as smooth as alabaster.

Cass came down the steps. Dressed in black pants and a long matching peacoat, the collar pulled up against the cold, he exuded a dark mystique that froze her in place.

He stopped just inches away from her, amber eyes fixed on her face. The same woodsy scent that had made her sway on her feet last night as he'd cradled her in his arms during their dance wound about her and filled her with warmth that not even a winter's chill could steal.

"Let me help you with that."

His voice wrapped around her, slipped into her blood and left her dazed as he took the duffel bag off her shoulder and gestured for her to go up the stairs.

Stay detached. Don't fall for him just because he's hotter than sin.

"After you, Briony."

She stared at the first step. As soon as she walked up, there would be no going back. She would be sealing her fate, traveling outside of the country for the first time, meeting her father and the brother she never knew she had, and agreeing to marry a man she'd known for barely a week. Not just any man, but a prince, an actual real-life prince, with secrets.

She glanced back once more at Nowhere a mile or so in the distance, the buildings like tiny dollhouses dusted with snow surrounded by the endless prairie. She should feel something, a sense of loss, sadness, homesickness.

But this place hadn't been home for a very long time.

She turned away and walked into the plane.

Cass watched with satisfaction as Briony gaped at the luxury laid out in front of her. Oval windows marched down either side of the plane and let in bright afternoon sunlight that lit up the creamy interior. Four white leather seats were clustered around a tabletop. Across the aisle, a flat-screen TV displayed a news channel. The second half of the main area boasted two more seats and a long sofa, complete with bright red and blue pillows to make the interior more welcoming. A partition concealed the rest.

"People actually live like this?"

Cass chuckled. She moved farther into the plane, stepping gingerly on the plush carpeting.

"They do. Soon you will, too."

"Sir, we're preparing for takeoff," a voice crackled over a speaker in the ceiling.

Cass pressed a button on his armrest. "Five minutes, Martin."

"Yes, sir."

Cass reached into his briefcase and pulled out a copy of the contract Briony had taken with her last night. He set it on the table and laid a pen on top.

"What is that?"

"The contract stating that you will enter into an engagement with me and that we'll be married within eight weeks."

He watched as she sucked in a deep breath and ran a hand through her hair.

"What if something changes?"

"Like if you change your mind?"

"Yes."

He shrugged. "There is a clause in there stipulating the agreement can be nullified if both parties agree and sign an addendum. Then I return you to Nowhere and your life goes back to the way it was."

Those green eyes narrowed, hardened. "But Trey gets kicked out of the facility and the girls lose their trust funds?"

"Why you would want anything good for them after the way they've treated you is beyond me," he retorted with an edge to his voice. Did she truly think him so callous that he would pull a grieving alcoholic out of his treatment program? "But no. Regardless of how things progress between us, Trey's stay will be paid for and your stepsisters will have trust funds established."

She blinked in surprise. "Really?"

He gritted his teeth as he stretched his lips into a small, benevolent smile. "Really."

Some of the worry eased from her face. But he still detected a couple tense lines about her eyes as she glanced down at the contract again.

"Briony…"

Slowly, she looked up at him. The uncertainty in her gaze tugged at him once more.

"This is your choice."

Her eyes gleamed for a moment before she blinked rapidly and looked down.

"I know it is."

Pain roughened her voice. He hadn't missed the look she'd cast her hometown before she'd climbed on the plane. What thoughts had gone through her mind? What dreams had she had before they'd been snatched away by death and loss?

Before he could respond, she grabbed the pen. The nib dashed across the paper with a ferocious swirl. She tossed the pen down and brushed past him.

He stared down at her signature. He'd expected to feel pride, excitement, something. One more hurdle had been cleared in the goal he'd been working toward for as long as he could remember.

Yet all he felt as he turned to see Briony sit toward the back of the plane and stare out the window was a hollow sensation in his chest.

When the clock had hit nine forty-five this morning, he'd felt an unexpected wave of disappointment. He'd anticipated a last show of resistance. But a flat-out refusal? The tightness around his lungs had eased a minute later when he'd seen the tangle of red curls and that faded green coat against the stark white of a winter prairie landscape moving toward the plane. It had confirmed one of his talents, that of reading people and sometimes knowing them better than they knew themselves.

However, he conceded, as he took a seat farther down the plane to give her space, in this case he'd only been partially right. Judging by the tense set of her shoulders and the fierce line of her jaw, Briony wasn't completely confident in her decision. Just signing the contract wasn't enough to ensure she'd follow through. Technically he could hold her to the terms all the way until they said "I do."

But he wasn't a monster. If she truly changed her mind, he wouldn't carry her kicking and screaming down the aisle.

His eyes drifted down her body, lingering on the swells of her breasts beneath her sweater and her long legs encased in blue jeans. He steepled his fingers as a slight smile tugged at his lips. Between the luxury he had to offer her, taking care of her family and the chance to be reunited with her father and brother, he had plenty of weapons at his disposal. He knew, too, judging by the way she'd reacted to him on the steps, that her attraction to him hadn't been completely destroyed by last night's revelations. No, it simmered just below the surface. Something he could use if necessary.

The door to the plane was shut as the engines hummed. His smile grew as the plane taxied down the runway and took off, soaring above the snow-dusted fields. He had Briony exactly where he needed her. In eight weeks, she would be his wife.

And he would finally have his revenge on the Van Ambrose royals.

CHAPTER FIVE

AN HOUR LATER, Briony had barely moved. Cass had conducted some business on his laptop, expecting her to pepper him with questions about her family, royal life, anything but the silence that permeated the cabin.

It bothered him, he realized with some annoyance. Yes, he was getting something out of their arrangement, but didn't she realize that he was rescuing her and her ungrateful stepfamily? That between his wealth and social standing he could literally offer the fairy tale that so many were raised on yet never got to experience?

One of his flight attendants, Sarah, entered with glasses of sparkling water. Briony stirred long enough to accept a glass and thank Sarah with a gracious smile. But as soon as the flight attendant disappeared, she went back to being stone-faced.

He sighed. "Are you going to sulk the whole flight?"

She glanced at him from beneath her lashes. "I just left the only home I've ever really known and am flying into an unknown future. I think I'm allowed some time to 'sulk,' as you put it, although I thought of it more as taking time to process the monumental changes in my life."

Of course she would need time. Irritated at himself for taking her silence so personally and jumping to erroneous conclusions, he opened his mouth to apologize.

"Not to mention I signed a contract to marry someone I've known less than a week. Actually," she said as she leaned forward, "make that less than twelve hours. I thought I was getting to know Cass Morgan. You still haven't apologized for lying to me."

His regret disappeared.

"I didn't lie."

It was ridiculous that her statement should cause a tensing of his muscles, especially since he was keeping secrets from her. He hadn't outright lied, but he had certainly played a game with the words he'd spoken last night. She didn't know that he had been the one to offer the solution to Daxon, instead of the other way around. She didn't know about his personal vendetta against the Van Ambrose royals. And she had no idea that not only was her father a self-absorbed monster, but he didn't care about her existence unless it benefited him.

Something in his chest twisted as he watched the woman across from him. He hadn't told her of Daxon's illness, and judging by her lack of questions, Daxon hadn't addressed it in the letter he'd included with the file. Even if Daxon was a monster, what would it do to Briony learning that her father was most likely going to die within a couple years of her mother? Was he doing the right thing, exposing her both to the pain of yet another loss and Daxon's horrid, selfish nature?

You'll be with her. Even though theirs would be a marriage of convenience, and it would obviously take some time to regain the camaraderie they had enjoyed when he had simply been Cass Morgan, he would protect her from Daxon, be there to support her with whatever the future dealt.

He would never be able to love her. Love, as he'd observed, could make a person deliriously happy...until it didn't. It could twist into something dark and angry, like it had with Aunt Alecine and Daxon, so-called love turning to hatred. Or it could be enough until it wasn't, like it had with his mother. It had been much easier for his mother to go against her parents' wishes as a young woman with stars in her eyes and marry an aspiring lawyer from a decent family than to flee with a king's accusations of betrayal hanging above her head.

Even if love didn't destroy, it didn't last. When he told Briony he would never be able to love her, he meant it. But that didn't mean he would leave her at the mercy of Daxon. In less than sixty days, she would be his wife. She would be family. And he protected family.

"Understandable after the numerous bombshells I've dropped on you."

Surprise flashed in her eyes, followed by a tiny smile of thanks.

"It's a lot to take in. And I don't like that you misrepresented yourself."

He tamped down his guilt and spread his hands in a gesture of openness. "Ask away. What do you want to know?"

"Why do you want to marry into the royal family so badly?"

He covered his surprise at her bold question with a sip of water. He turned her words over in his mind, trying to decide how best to address a natural yet loaded query.

No matter what, he couldn't tell her the whole truth yet. Would she have any interest in meeting her father once she learned how cruel he could be? Or would she decide that life with her selfish stepfamily would be at least marginally better?

Cass had been eleven years old when he, his father and his aunt had fled Linnaea under cover of darkness before King Daxon had tossed them in prison. Cass's father, Leopold Adama, had committed only one crime: he'd been the brother of Alecine Adama, Daxon's latest mistress. Alecine may have fallen for the king, but she'd also seen the signs that her time as lover was coming to an end. Unlike her predecessors, Alecine had prepared for the inevitable breakup by preparing a dossier of secrets that would have brought the king to his knees, records of payoffs to less-than-respectable individuals, under-the-table contracts for exorbitant quotes on construction projects that left royal accounts empty and Daxon's personal accounts full. When she'd given in to her anger and agony at being rejected for a younger woman, she'd threatened the king. A sympathetic maid had warned Alecine that the police were coming to arrest her and her family for treason. When Alecine had tried to withdraw money for their escape, she'd found their accounts frozen.

The slam of the door against the wall as Alecine had rushed into his family's home still woke him up some nights, her frantic cry of "Leo!" making his heart pound. His mother's sobs as she'd learned that her privileged life as wife of one of the most revered members of Linnaea's court was coming to an end still echoed, too. At the time it had terrified him even as he'd patted his mother's back, trying to tell her it would be okay. But now he looked on the memory with disgust for how quickly she'd abandoned him and his father, her hope that disassociating herself from the Adamas would help her salvage her own future more important than the man she had once gone against her family to marry.

Catapulted from the luxury of a wealthy household to the dirty, unforgiving streets of Europe, Cass, his father and Alecine had lived a harsh life that first year while his mother had returned to her family in France.

Grief hit so fast he barely masked it. He could still

remember his mother walking out the front door with a Prada suitcase in hand, ignoring her husband's desperate pleas. She'd whirled around, told Cass he could come with her but would never be able to see his father again, not if they were to recover from the destruction Aunt Alecine had brought down upon them. He'd chosen to stay. She'd walked away without a backward glance. It had taken Cass nearly a month to stop crying himself to sleep.

"I was born in Linnaea. My family lived there for generations. My aunt had a falling-out with the king, your father. We were asked to leave."

Briony frowned. "That seems harsh. What did they fight about?"

"My father was the former treasurer. My aunt had strong views on how the government was spending money and made her opinions known. It turned ugly." His shrug masked the banked coals of a slow-burning anger that had been torturing him for nineteen years. Just like his significantly pared-down version of events was so sparse it bordered on a lie. "But political differences are a part of life. Your father is still not partial to my family. But things have changed drastically in the last few years."

"The country's on the verge of financial disaster."

"Done some reading?" he asked with a slight smile.

"A lot," she confessed. "I don't understand all of it, but it sounds like they're steps away from a depression."

Somehow Daxon's public relations team had managed to cover the true reason for the country's situation. The king liked to spend money, regardless of the state of the country's finances. Rumors abounded, but few had proof.

Unlike Cass. Another incentive for Daxon to agree to his terms.

"They are. A marital alliance between Tulay and Linnaea will solidify their future."

Briony cocked an eyebrow. "Why can't you just give them the money?"

Cass chuckled. "It would certainly be easier if things worked that way. Have you heard of the term 'marriage of state'?"

Briony shook her head.

"It refers to a diplomatic marriage or union. Yes, I could just lend money to your father. But would you lend money to someone with no agreement? Consider this the same, but multiplied by billions of dollars."

"What do you get out of it?" She sat back and crossed her arms. "It sounds like other than marriage, you're just lending a bunch of money for nothing."

Your father loathes that I'm marrying into his family.

"Not nothing. My family and I are being reestablished into Linnaean society. While I'm being very generous with the terms of the loan, a five percent return on my investment over the next ten years will elevate my fortune even further. Trade agreements are being established between Linnaea and my adopted country, Tulay, agreements that would never happen without a union like ours."

She stared at him for a long moment. Valid reasons, all. But would she accept them? Or would she sense something else lurking beneath the surface?

"This is truly a strategic move for you?"

Danger lurked in her tone, anger and possibly even hurt. But he had no time for such emotions.

"Yes."

She blinked, then looked away. Tension settled between them. He continued to regard her with an unblinking gaze, waiting, biding his time. His patience was legendary.

"Stop staring."

"Why would I stop staring? You're beautiful."

Her lips twitched, a gesture he marked as a point in his favor.

"Let's not fight, Briony. You asked a question and I answered. We're on one of the most exclusive, luxurious private planes in the world. You should enjoy yourself."

Her fingers stroked up and down the leather armrest. His eyes followed the sensual movement for a heartbeat before he forced his gaze back to her face.

"I know I'm doing the right thing. For me. For them." Her shoulders sagged. "But it's hard not to have regrets. To wonder if I could have done something to prevent all this."

"With your stepfamily?"

She looked back out the window, the sun falling across her skin and highlighting the freckles on her nose.

"I hate his drinking."

Those words cost her, judging by the downward pull of her lips and the tensing of her shoulders. He already knew everything, from Trey's six-figure gambling debt to how Briony had been the only person present at her stepsisters' teacher conferences last month. From what he knew, Trey Smith was a failure. If the luxurious lifestyle he had to offer didn't persuade Briony to leave, the chance to escape the role of servant would.

"He didn't used to be like that."

"They rarely start out that way," he replied drily.

By Alecine's account, Daxon had been a generous benefactor and adoring suitor. He'd kept up his pretense with her longer than his previous lovers.

But inevitably, the mask had slipped and the monster had appeared.

"Trey was a decent stepfather," Briony said, a hint of defense hardening her voice. "He treated me well, especially since I wasn't really his daughter."

"After all he's done, you still defend him."

"He is…was family. You love family no matter what."

Cass swore in French. "Loving family isn't a requirement, especially when someone treats you the way he did. Your mother never should have married him if he didn't show himself capable of that."

Briony looked away. "Trey was more involved when they dated. He wanted to be what my mother wanted him to be. It wasn't until after they were married that he realized he couldn't. I heard him and my mom arguing about it once, so I told her things were better."

"To protect your mother?"

She nodded once. "I wanted her to have her fairy tale."

"What if her fairy tale didn't have to involve a Prince Charming? What if it meant her daughter was happy?"

Judging by Briony's wide eyes, the possibility had never occurred to her. Part of him wished he had left her stepfather in his decrepit house to drown himself in beer and debt.

"He should have treated you like his daughter, regardless of genetics, Briony. That is a failing on his part."

The tremulous smile she gave him warmed his chest.

"Thank you."

He leaned back in his seat, this time allowing silence to fill the space between them. Briony surprised him by not rushing to fill the gap with inane chatter. Instead, she focused on the scenery they were rushing over thirty thousand feet below.

His father, Leo, had taught him patience. Patience was a valuable asset that, despite their family's billions now, could not be bought and few possessed. Yet Briony's quiet dignity stirred him in a way that was both new and unsettling.

The plane shuddered. The captain's voice filled the cabin.

"Sir, we're experiencing some minor turbulence. Please fasten your seat belts."

Briony rode out the bout of shaking with a slight tightening of her lips and a firm grip on her armrests. Another point in her favor. The last woman he'd traveled with, an actress, had shrieked and afterward sought solace in his arms, big crocodile tears sliding down her face as she'd pressed her ample and barely covered bosom against his chest.

Once the turbulence abated, Cass leaned back in his seat.

"Do you have any other questions for me?"

"Where will we live?"

"Linnaea. We'll stay in Tulay for extended periods, and of course we can visit Kansas as often as you'd like, or anywhere else you'd like to go. But there's too much to be done, especially in these first few years, to be away for long."

"So we'll raise our children in Linnaea?" she asked softly.

An image flared in his mind of a little redheaded girl with brown eyes, or perhaps a little boy with eyes the same vivid green as his mother. He'd known children were in his future. But knowing who their mother would be made the concept more real. And, he acknowledged as his eyes caressed Briony's face, more enticing. Briony had already proven herself to be a strong and patient woman. While she overindulged those two bratty stepsisters of hers, he had no doubt she would excel as a mother. And she had proven that she wouldn't abandon her family when things got rough.

"At least two."

"Truly?"

"Yes. That wasn't just a ploy to get you to say yes."

She nodded, but a frown still lurked on her face.

"What is it?"

"It's just…weird. Talking about this lifelong commitment so factually."

"More marriages would be successful if the parties involved approached it pragmatically."

A chuckle escaped her, but it wasn't a pleasant sound. It was resigned, bleak. He didn't like it on her. He reached over and, when she didn't pull away, took her hand in his. He savored the bloom of color in her cheeks as he wrapped his fingers around hers. Fortunately, she couldn't see the effect she had on him—the uptick in his pulse, the tightening of his muscles as he skimmed his thumb over the back of her hand.

"Ours is not, nor will it ever be, a love match. However," he continued on before she could object, "it can be a partnership. A union based on mutual respect, companionship and, eventually, a family."

He released her hand, a physical reminder to himself to not push too far. She was softening; that was the most important thing right now.

He pressed the button to summon a flight attendant.

"Two glasses of champagne and a bowl of strawberries, please." At Briony's quizzical look, he shot her a smile. "We're celebrating your first trip beyond the Midwest."

Most women of his past acquaintance would have giggled or thanked him in a physically demonstrative manner. Briony, however, rolled her eyes as she chuckled.

"I don't think I've ever had champagne before five o'clock."

"Then I'm happy to be your first." She didn't even bat an eye at the innuendo, just shook her head and stood.

"I'll be right back."

He stood, as manners dictated. Briony started to walk

past. The plane quaked again, then pitched to the right. Briony cried out as she tumbled into him. He anchored himself and wrapped his arms around her. The plane steadied a moment later.

"Apologies, Your Highnesses," the captain said over the speaker. "Should be clear sailing for a while now."

The speaker fell silent. The soft instrumental music still played in the background. The engines of the plane hummed in the background. But the loudest sound of all was the thudding of his pulse. It didn't just thunder in his ears; he could feel the rush of blood pumping through his veins, the awareness crackling across his skin as he held Briony in his arms once more.

Her scent curled around him, sandalwood mixed with something light and floral that conjured images of flowering trees and the brilliant blue skies of spring. His hand skimmed up her back, grazing the silky curls that tumbled down nearly to her waist. He wanted to bury his hands in her hair, inhale the scent of her as he trailed his lips up her neck—

"Cass?"

He blinked. Briony sucked in a shuddering breath as her chest rose and fell.

Damn it. He had nearly given in, all because of one accidental touch. If he let lust rule his decision-making, he would be just like his aunt, just like his father.

Don't give in.

He gently released her, returned her oblique stare without a word, then watched as she disappeared into the back of the plane. Moments later, Julie, one of the flight attendants, bustled out with a friendly smile, a bowl of bright red strawberries and two glasses of champagne. He nodded his thanks, his gaze affixed to the bubbles rising to the top of the golden liquid.

The genuine interest in his future bride was an unexpected and unwelcome conundrum. He had heard enough of what Daxon's wandering eye had done to Alecine and countless other women to know he would never indulge in an affair after he took his vows. What little Alecine had said on the subject over the years had been the driving force for his adding a fidelity clause to the marriage contract. His own liaisons up to this point had been indulgences for the sake of pleasure, always with the knowledge that one day he would be tied in matrimony to a faceless bride. Sex would be a part of that relationship. Heirs were needed.

But he hadn't anticipated that the brief fantasy he'd entertained in his week of being Cass Morgan would not only continue, but flare up into something he struggled to control.

Which left him at a crossroads, he acknowledged as Briony walked back out and sat across from him, her face turned away from him. He needed to stay objective when it came to his future wife. But he couldn't withdraw too much and risk her becoming dissatisfied with their arrangement. If he could keep himself under control, then he could woo her as he'd wooed countless other women without surrendering himself to dangerous emotions.

He raised his champagne flute. When she followed suit, he clinked his glass to hers.

"To new adventures."

She narrowed her gaze as she took as a cautious sip. "To the unknown."

CHAPTER SIX

CASS SPUN HER around an elegant ballroom, crystal chandeliers twinkling overhead. She laughed up at him as she savored the warm appreciation in his eyes.

But then the warmth faded, replaced by cold calculation. She started to pull away. But as she turned, Stacy and Ella confronted her, yelling about homework and dirty rooms and laundry. Trey stood behind them, belly bloated, eyes bloodshot and a can of beer dangling listlessly from his fingers...

Briony woke with a gasp. She blinked against the bright light filtering in through the plane's windows. The plane's engines hummed beneath her.

Cass. She was on Cass's plane flying toward a new country and a new life. Trey and the twins were behind her, in the past. It was as if every mile they flew farther away from Kansas, the more the scales fell from her eyes that had blinded her to how bad things had truly gotten. How long had she given her entire self, her whole identity, to the purpose of supporting her family? How long would she have gone on doing so if Cass hadn't shown up in her bar?

She brushed hair out of her face with trembling hands. She could picture the sneer on Trey's face the last time she'd seen him, smell the alcohol on his breath the numerous nights she'd dragged him to his bed. She could feel the heat of his tears soaking through her shirt when she'd held him as he'd cried for her mother. She could hear her own desperate pleas falling on deaf ears as she opened yet another statement from an online gambling site with Trey's increasing debts.

Other memories rushed through. Trey asking her to call him by his name, not "Papa" or "Dad." Trey giving her a pat on the back before he swooped Stacy and Ella up into a boisterous hug. Marie, quietly asking Trey to be more affectionate with Briony and Trey assuring her he just needed more time.

Loving family isn't a requirement.

Cass's words returned, circled around in her mind. At first, she'd been excited to love Trey and the twins, to have a complete family like the other kids at school. But then, as it had become apparent that she would be treated more like the daughter of a friend than an actual daughter, she'd continued to hold out that maybe, one day, she would do enough, be enough, to be loved in return.

It would never have been enough, she realized. There was truly nothing left for her in Kansas, a thought that should have been depressing but instead felt like the shackles of her own making were falling off, leaving her feeling lighter than she had in years. She turned, pulled up one of the window shades and looked out across fluffy white clouds hanging against a beautiful blue sky. She could almost believe it was a foretelling of what was to come. The chance to start anew, to make something of herself and support the recovery of a country.

And her father. He hadn't come to visit her personally, but he'd still come after her in his own way, still put in the effort to find out about her life and invited her to become a part of his. It was more than Trey had ever done for her.

"We're forty-five minutes out."

His voice slid over her body, husky and dark. It called to her, awoke something deep inside her and filled her with an intense longing.

Don't.

Cass had stated multiple times that love was off the table, that their relationship would be similar to what she'd known so far: an association built on what she could do for him. What he sparked inside her was physical. But beneath the burning desire that had slowly been building since he walked into her bar was something far more dangerous—emotion.

Forty-eight hours ago, she would have leaned into him, sought comfort from the man she was slowly falling for.

Except now she knew the truth. He didn't want her. Everything he did, from the champagne and strawberries to any other grand gestures, would have to be taken with a grain of salt. He didn't love her. Yet knowing that had almost been freeing. Unlike the one other serious relationship she'd been in and the handful of dates, there was no wondering, no questioning of where things were headed.

She turned from the window and met Cass's amber gaze.

"I'm excited to see Linnaea in person."

She kept her voice neutral, her attraction suppressed. There had been that one moment yesterday when she'd fallen into his arms after the unexpected bout of turbulence and she'd been clutched against him, certain—her traitorous body even hopeful—that he would kiss her. But the look of heat in his eyes had disappeared so quickly she must have imagined it or even projected her own foolish desire onto him. Aside from that one moment, he'd been noticeably less flirtatious and more businesslike, a stark contrast to their week of dancing around each other with veiled innuendos and seductive glances. She hadn't just been acting confident when she'd flirted with him. She'd *felt* confident, sexy, even beautiful.

Remember that, she reminded herself. Even if he had been acting, she hadn't. She had glimpsed a view of who she could be without the trappings of her narrow-minded family focus. She could be a confident, independent woman all on her own.

Doubt trickled in. Some of her excitement was for the adventure ahead, of moving to a new country on the spur of the moment, of becoming involved in something bigger than herself. But a large part of her enthusiasm rested on meeting her father and brother. Was she still pinning too much of herself on family? She'd been picturing a beautiful reunion, the kind she saw in movies where the father looked at his long-lost child with tears in his eyes as he drew her into his arms. But what if it didn't turn out like that? What if her father was kind but distant, the way he'd been in his letter? What if her brother was resentful of her presence? Trey had once accused her of seeing the world through rose-colored glasses, of not accepting the bad with the good and putting people on a pedestal so high they couldn't help but fall off.

She swallowed hard. At the time his words had cut deep as he'd tied his biting remarks into a lecture on the boy she'd been seeing. But now…she was doing exactly that. Combining her fictional dreams of her birth father with the actual man himself and idealizing him before she even met him.

What if she hadn't left her former life for a better one? What if her father and brother rejected her and she was left alone in a foreign country tied for life to a man she barely knew? She wasn't just embarking on some grand adventure. She was getting married. For life.

The sun disappeared behind a cloud, and the interior of

the plane darkened. The unease that had lingered beneath the surface since she'd made her decision returned with a vengeance and left her adrift once more, ensnared in a tangled mess of loneliness, doubt and exhaustion.

"I took the liberty of purchasing some clothing for your visit to the palace."

Cass's words yanked her out of the storm swirling around in her head. She forced a small smile.

"Jeans and T-shirt won't cut it for my first trip to see the king?"

His lips twitched. "Something more formal would be appropriate."

With a quick nod, she passed through the doorway into a bedroom. *His bedroom*, she realized as she glanced around the small space. A full-size bed occupied one side, covered in a vibrant red comforter. Three dresses were draped across it. Her mouth dropped open. She'd never seen such beautiful gowns in person. Each one was a work of art.

"Anna Vega."

She whirled to see Cass lounging in the doorway, hands in his pockets, a smug smile on his face that said he knew he had impressed her with his choices.

"Who?"

"Anna Vega. A very talented and sought-after designer."

Briony swallowed hard. The most expensive thing she'd worn was a prom dress she and her mother had found at half price at a thrift store.

"So…expensive?"

Cass's face hardened. "Don't worry about the cost, Briony."

His casual dismissal of what she could only assume was an astronomical price irritated her.

"If I just wear my jeans and shirt, could I sell the dresses and pay off some of my family's debt without having to marry you?"

The words had barely left her lips before she regretted saying them. She was overreacting because of her own fears and self-doubt.

Cass's face sharpened into granite, his amber eyes so hard she couldn't help but shiver.

"I'm sorry," he said silkily as he advanced into the room. If she'd thought it an intimate space before, it was downright claustrophobic as his sensual presence filled every nook and cranny. She stepped back into the mirrored wall, the coolness of the glass belying the heat that traitorously flashed through her veins as he loomed over her. "Perhaps our memories differ as to what transpired yesterday. I don't recall forcing you to sign that contract."

"I didn't really have much of a choice," she retorted.

"You had choices, Briony." He leaned down, bracing one arm against the wall as he caged her in with his body. "Three of them, in fact. You chose to come to the airfield. You chose to get on my plane. And you chose to sign that contract."

White-hot anger warred with her awareness of just how close Cass was, how it would take just one slight move to press her mouth to his.

As if sensing her thoughts, his lips turned up into a cold, calculating smile.

"I know people better than they know themselves."

With that pronouncement hanging in the air between them, he leaned down and kissed her. It wasn't the sweet kiss she'd dreamed of back when he'd just been Cass Morgan. No, this was the kiss of a prince who was used to getting his way, a fierce kiss that assaulted her senses and made clear who was in charge. Despite the heat, he kept his hands on either side of her, not touching. A caress that lacked intimacy as he held himself back and kissed her on his terms.

All of the emotions from the past forty-eight hours swirled up inside her: anger, desire, hope, excitement, lust, fear. The fierce mix tore through her and propelled her up onto her toes. She wrapped her arms around his neck, returned the kiss with a fervor that surprised even herself as her fingers sank into the silky strands of his hair.

He froze for a moment. She didn't open her eyes, half terrified she'd see what she couldn't handle any more of: rejection.

Then a growl vibrated against her lips. The sound moved through her body, a hum of electricity that made her gasp. Cass's arms crushed her body to him as he took advantage of her parted lips to slip his tongue inside her mouth. Liquid heat pooled between her thighs. An ache started to pulse deep within her. Her hips arched against him, her hands tightening as she moaned.

One hand came up, fingers grazing the side of her breast, the touch burning through the thin cloth of her T-shirt. The ache shuddered, then spread through her veins like a wildfire she couldn't control. She wanted her shirt off, clothes off, his body pressed against hers, naked, hot, hard as he slid inside her and claimed her as his…

"Cass, please."

He stepped back so suddenly she nearly fell forward. He caught her arms, but as soon as she'd steadied herself, he moved away. Bewildered, she brushed her hair out of her face and looked at him. He stared back, his eyes glowing gold. He didn't bother to hide his deep breathing as his chest rose and fell, muscles outlined beneath the white material. Nor did he bother to hide the noticeable bulge between his thighs. Heat rushed into her cheeks as her gaze flickered back up to his…

...to see shock mirrored in his amber eyes for a brief second before he suddenly shut down, a mask dropping back over his face, the hint of Cass gone before she could blink and replaced with Prince Cassius, his breathing controlled once more. He was still handsome, still sexier than any man she'd ever met, but distant, regal.

Who was this man she was engaged to marry? Had the flirting, the seductive dance, the way he'd looked at her as if he couldn't bear not to touch her, all been true? The possibility that he was just affected as she was gave her some comfort.

"Cass—"

"That was careless of me."

Her mouth dropped open. "What?"

He stepped back and gestured toward the dresses. "Does one stand out to you?"

Her fingers curled into fists. "You know, my mind is elsewhere right now. I'm a little confused."

He glanced at his watch. "We're now less than forty minutes out. You should choose."

"Maybe I don't like any of them."

"Wear one of the dresses or wear your jeans. It makes no matter to me."

Before she could summon a witty retort, he turned and walked out.

The door closed behind him. Good thing, too, because she had been an inch away from grabbing one of the books and hurling it at his obnoxious head.

She sucked in a steadying breath, one meant to refocus her attention as much as it banished some of the lingering heat from her body. So they were attracted to each other. Fine. People all around the world kissed and had sex and did all of sorts of things without putting their hearts on the line. She could, too.

She had to, if this was going to work.

She ran a frustrated hand through her hair. Did she even want it to work? Could she truly accept a loveless marriage?

Her phone vibrated in her pocket. She pulled it out to see an email from her bank. A quick glance revealed that it was just one of several that must have come through when she was sleeping. Credit card balances, zero. Mortgage balance, zero. Confirmation of two new accounts established in Stacy's and Ella's names, both with six-figure statements.

She slipped her phone back into her pocket. Whether she wanted it or not was beside the point. She would make it work.

She surveyed the gowns on the bed. Part of her wanted to stalk out of the bedroom in her jeans and shirt just to spite him. Except, she acknowledged irritably, the only person she would be hurting would be herself. With another deep, cleansing breath, she shoved the kiss into the deepest recess of memory and focused on the dresses that lay before her.

The first, a deep red that reminded her of the color of wine with a short-sleeved top and a full skirt and a ribbon about the waist, was beautiful but just a tad too formal for a simple meeting. The second was sky blue but was crafted of the most delicate-looking lace she'd ever seen, threads of silver holding the intricate pieces together. Stunning, but she would probably snag it on something before she left the plane.

The last dress, though, seemed perfect. The pale lavender bodice and waist were bedecked with small jewels. Formal, but the knee-length skirt and sleeveless top lent a casual flair that made her feel more at ease.

As she slid the dress on, she couldn't help but feel a

small tingle of anticipation. In just a matter of hours, she would finally meet her father.

She focused on that and ignored the apprehension tightening the muscles in her neck.

CHAPTER SEVEN

THE CASTLE LOOKED as if it had been crafted from a fairy tale. A sparkling white palace stood against the backdrop of pine trees dusted with snow. Towering spires topped by crimson flags waved in the breeze. A cobblestoned drive wound its way in a serpentine pattern up the hillside. As the limo pulled up to a stunning marble staircase, Briony nervously smoothed the folds of her skirt.

She tore her gaze away to glance at Cass. He'd barely looked at her since she'd emerged from the bedroom dressed in her new finery. He'd murmured a "You look nice" before resuming his phone conversation. A limo had whisked them away from the airport around the outskirts of a quaint-looking city Cass had identified as the capital city, Eira. Two-and three-story buildings that looked as if they'd been crafted a couple centuries ago were interspersed with several more modern-looking towers.

With every passing mile, Cass's face had grown tense, his jaw hardening as his eyes sharpened. Was it difficult for him, being back in the country he had been torn from as a child?

An uncomfortable sensation settled in her stomach. Cass's story about his aunt and her father having a falling-out had been so vague. How could a simple disagreement over spending have led to the family being asked to leave the country? She should have pursued it more on the plane, but they'd transitioned so quickly to talking about Linnaea's financial problems that she'd forgotten.

Until now. The apprehension she'd suppressed on the plane, the feeling that she'd missed something in this rapid journey from lonely barmaid to secret princess, spread across her skin, a persistent itch she couldn't get rid of.

A guard opened her door. Cass kept a hold on her elbow, as if he were afraid she would bolt at any moment. Another guard escorted her and Cass up the stone stairs, through a set of double doors and into a stunning three-story hallway with soaring ceilings and walls covered in paintings that looked old and expensive.

It was beautiful, Briony acknowledged, but cold, more like a museum than a home she could picture growing up in. How odd, too, that the palace would maintain such an extensive collection of art when the country was in such dire financial straits.

Stop judging. For all she knew, these paintings could have been in the palace for years, decades even, long before the recession.

A young woman with pale skin and equally pale blond hair pulled into a severe bun waited for them at the top of yet another sweeping staircase. She waited until a maid dressed in traditional black with a white apron had taken their coats and disappeared into the depths of the palace before she spoke to Cass.

"Your Highness," she said in a clipped tone, bowing her head just slightly enough to have it count.

"Clara. A pleasure to see you again."

The thinning of Clara's lips suggested she was anything but pleased to see Cass.

"I received your message thirty minutes ago, Your Highness." Her ice-blue eyes drifted to Briony. Something flashed in them before she turned back to Cass. "We didn't expect you until Monday. Had you notified the palace sooner, we would have been more prepared."

"And risk not giving the king a surprise?" Cass replied with a smile so cold it rivaled the ice in Clara's glare. "You know how much he loves surprises." He glanced over her shoulder. "Besides, Alaric is expecting me."

"Prince Alaric," Clara corrected stiffly.

Cass ignored her correction and turned to Briony. "Meet your half brother's right-hand woman, Clara Stephenson. The country would fall apart without her work."

Despite his mocking tone, Briony noted a thread of genuine admiration in his voice. Judging by Clara's frigid gaze, however, she didn't pick up on it.

Clara dropped into a shallow curtsy. "It's a pleasure to meet you, Your Highness," she said, her voice a tad warmer as she addressed Briony. "Your brother has been most anxious to meet you."

And what about my father?

Her earlier worries returned in full force.

"Thank you. It's nice to meet you, too."

"Clara," Cass broke in before either woman could say anything else, "would you give Briony a tour of the palace? Just a quick one, twenty minutes or so, and then bring her to Alaric's study?"

He ignored Clara's indignant huff and kept his gaze on Briony. His eyes gleamed. Cold tendrils of suspicion sank deeper into her skin.

"Cass, what's going on?"

He gently cupped her upper arms in a surprisingly intimate gesture.

"I'm speaking with King Daxon and Prince Alaric privately before I introduce you. Is Alaric in his office?" he asked as he released her and turned to Clara.

"*Prince* Alaric," Clara snapped, "and yes—"

"Excellent." Cass started to walk away.

"After I take you to—" Clara started to say.

"I know the way. Thank you."

Cass strode confidently down one side hallway without a backward glance. Clara stared daggers at his retreating back. But when her eyes flickered to Briony, she recognized the emotion lurking in the other woman's gaze.

Pity.

Cass's blood pounded through his veins as he neared Alaric's private office. Nineteen years. Nineteen long years of biding his time, of having plan after plan dashed, only to have his archnemesis himself hand him the key he needed to unlock both Linnaea's salvation and his family's vengeance.

He'd almost ruined it, too, with that damned slipup with Briony earlier. Kissing her on the plane had been a mistake, one that had shocked him at how quickly he'd succumbed to the surge of lust. Between his anger at her accusations and the unsated passion that had been building between them for a week, he'd acted on instinct. He'd seen the look on her face. She'd been just as affected as him, which was both incredibly sexy and very concerning. He couldn't let Briony think for even a second that they could have a relationship where their attraction ruled over common sense.

But then she'd walked out and she'd looked absolutely stunning, every inch a future princess. She had picked the lavender dress, a gown that had looked almost plain to him when he'd seen them laid out across the bed. But on Briony, with her vivid red curls and bare shoulders thrown back as if she owned the palace, she was mesmerizing. Who knew elegant could be so subtly sexy?

As the limo had drawn closer to the palace, the silence between them had filled the interior, thick and oppressive. For the first time since he'd begun his quest, he knew a moment of true doubt, not just the vague morality questions that he'd brushed aside. Linnaea was in trouble. He was ensuring a steady flow of money into the country, money he could oversee and ensure went to good use instead of a worthless real estate project or kickbacks to political cronies; it was the right thing to do.

And his aunt deserved to have her revenge against the man who had driven her and her family to the point of ruin.

But as he'd looked between the approaching palace and Briony, looking so strong and lovely and yet also lost among the cavernous backdrop of the grand hall he'd guided her to, he wondered if the cost of his success was too much.

He turned down another richly carpeted hallway, this one less cluttered with marble statues and priceless paintings than the others. While Daxon insisted on featuring his most costly purchases throughout the main wing seen most by the public, Alaric had managed to slowly but surely clear the hall that housed his office.

As a child, he'd never been in this part of the palace. When he'd first stepped foot in here a month ago, he'd been escorted between two armed guards. He could still see the smug, arrogant smile on Daxon's face when the tall wooden door had swung in and revealed the nephew of his former lover-turned-enemy.

How satisfying it had been to see conceit drain from the old mongrel's face when Cass had plonked not only copies of Aunt Alecine's documentation on the table, but a file on the long-lost princess of Linnaea.

He approached the same door and knocked once. For a moment, there was silence. Then the door swung open.

"Cassius."

Cass was tall, exceptionally so, but even Alaric stood above him by an inch or two. The heir to the Linnaean throne was a larger, more masculine version of his sire. Where Daxon's face had an almost delicate quality, Alaric's was made up of hard lines and a sharpness that had enhanced his reputation as a notoriously private yet fierce leader. Daxon had tied his son's hands on many matters. But the few things he did allow his son control over, Alaric took and ran with a leadership that even Cass grudgingly admired. If there was one thing Cass was certain of, it was that Alaric hated Daxon almost as much as, if not more than, he did.

"Alaric."

Alaric's eyes, a similar emerald to that of his sister's, narrowed at the lack of formal address. Few people dared to push the buttons of a man who was rumored to be even colder than his father.

"Is she here?"

Cass nodded.

"Did she sign?"

Another nod. The tiniest quirk of Alaric's lips was the only indication that he was displeased.

"Then it's all going to your plan?"

Cass's mind conjured up the feel of Briony as she'd wrapped her lithe body around him, returned his punishing kiss with one of her own that had set his body on fire. He pushed it away, but another image replaced it; Briony, gazing out the window of the plane with hope on her face as they'd left Kansas behind. He would most definitely be able to offer her a better life. But he knew that a large part of the excitement that had sparkled in her eyes had been because of meeting her birth father.

The father he was about to introduce her to who was far worse than the stepfamily she'd left behind.

You should have told her.

He could have still persuaded her. His plan to help her stepfamily, the chance to meet Alaric, all of it could have still been enough.

But now was not the time for regrets. And regret was just another gateway to feelings that needed to stay out of their arrangement.

"Yes. It's all going according to plan."

Clara glanced irritably at her watch for the fourth time as she walked Briony down yet another hall filled with paintings.

"The east wing hallway features—"

"Clara," Briony interrupted with what she hoped was a diplomatic smile, "I know Cass sprang this on you. You probably have better things to do than walking me around the palace. If you'll just take me to Prince Alaric's study, I'm sure it will be fine."

Clara frowned, but then cast a longing glance at her watch.

"I am quite busy today. We have an important series of events with the Swiss ambassador coming up in three weeks, and assuming…" Her voice trailed off.

"Assuming I marry Cass, a wedding to plan?" Briony asked with a self-deprecating grin.

A tiny smile cracked through Clara's smooth mask.

"Yes." She grimaced. "A week after Christmas."

"Then please don't worry about this tour. Cass has inconvenienced you enough."

Clara stared at her for a moment before she let out a surprised laugh that transformed her expression from dour to startlingly beautiful.

"May I be frank, Your Highness?"

"Of course. But only if you call me Briony."

Clara glanced around the empty hall. "In private, yes. In public, however, I must adhere to protocol."

"I understand."

"Briony, when your brother, Prince Alaric, told me that you would be getting married to Prince Cassius, I worried for you," Clara confided as she led Briony down another hallway.

"Worried for me?"

"He has a reputation."

Briony thought back to the numerous photos of Cass with models, actresses and other famous women on his arm at various events over the years. Something that felt too much like jealousy curled in her stomach.

"I'm aware. Although it seems like he's kept out of the news in recent months."

"It's not just his dating history." Clara guided them around a corner and up a flight of stairs. "The history between Prince Cassius's family and the Van Ambrose family is not a positive one."

"Cass mentioned something about that."

A look of relief crossed Clara's face. "I'm glad he told you. We were surprised when he offered the marital alliance. But it will be good for... Your Highness? Briony? Are you all right?"

It sounded like Clara's voice was coming from far away, a distant echo ringing in her ears. She put out a hand to brace herself against the wall.

Cass set all of this up.

The way he'd talked Friday night, she'd assumed Daxon had come to Cass. But as she reviewed the conversation, she realized that while Cass had certainly been clever with his phrasing, he hadn't explicitly said who had requested the alliance.

Betrayal turned her blood to ice. She knew Cass had used her, but she thought he'd at least been up-front with her. Instead, he'd orchestrated this entire play. To what benefit, she couldn't be sure, but based on what little he had shared, she had a pretty good guess.

"I'm fine," she said with a wan smile. "I think just all the travel and information overload, I'm a little dizzy."

"I'll get you some water." Clara guided Briony to a chair set in a small alcove. "We're just around the corner from Prince Alaric's study. Once you're feeling better, I'll take you to him."

Clara quickly walked off. Briony waited a heartbeat before she stood and walked down the hallway. She paused at the intersection of another hallway and then turned in the direction of murmured male voices. As she drew closer to a slightly cracked door, she heard Cass's distinct voice. Just the sound of his deep tones set off a conflicting mix of desire and disgust.

"...set a date yet?" she heard a man ask, his voice deep like Cass's but flat and lacking any trace of warmth.

"We haven't discussed it yet," Cass replied smoothly. "However, the contract stipulates within sixty days, which means eight weeks from yesterday."

"What about the money?" This voice sounded much older, the raspy faintness reminding her of Trey after a night of binge drinking.

"It's all in the contract, Daxon." Cass's reply was much colder this time.

Daxon. It felt like someone reached into her chest, grabbed her lungs and squeezed. That had been her father's voice, infused with greed and disdain. Just the sound of it sent a chill skittering down her spine.

Her mind grasped at something, anything that might explain the coldness in Daxon's voice. Anything but the possibility that her birth father was just like the family she'd left behind, perhaps worse.

"You forget where you are, *Cassius*." Despite the weakness in Daxon's voice, his tone was dangerous. "You are in the royal palace of Linnaea. You will address me as Your Majesty."

"I didn't realize Linnaean families stood on ceremony in private."

Daxon's cruel chuckle made her throat tighten as her heart twisted. "Marrying my bastard child doesn't wipe away the stain of your own pathetic lineage. You will never be family."

"Not by blood. But how does it feel to know the nephew of the woman you tried to destroy will officially be a prince of Linnaea?"

She closed her eyes against the hot sting of tears. Her fears on the plane paled in comparison to the awful truths she'd just overheard. Her fiancé had had an ulterior motive: revenge. And from the sound of it, her birth father was even worse than her stepfather.

What now?

The voices in the office dimmed to angry murmurs as she closed out the world. What did she do? Leave and find a way back to the States? And return to what? Cass had said he would pay for Trey's treatment, their debt and the girls' trust funds no matter what.

But then what? She didn't have any desire to go back. So where would she go? And if she backed out of the contract, what would happen to the people of Linnaea?

Cass's voice trickled out once more. Her heart gave a painful leap in her chest. Even after all of his betrayals, she couldn't help but mourn what could have been, what she'd glimpsed on the plane just hours ago.

Her eyes opened as she lifted her head. There would be time to make her decisions later. Determination dried her tears and stiffened her spine. Right now, she needed to confront the men who had turned her life upside down again.

She didn't bother with knocking, just pushed the door open and walked in, her shoes clicking on the hardwood. Three men turned to face her. Cass's lips thinned as he took in the sight of his fiancée. She barely spared him a glance before her gaze swung to the other two men in the room.

Despite his age, King Daxon Van Ambrose was still a formidable man. His shoulders were more stooped, his slender body thinner beneath his suit and his skin ashy. But his emerald eyes, so like her own, flickered with a cold, shrewd intelligence. The black hair she'd seen in the photographs of Daxon with her mother was gone, replaced by silver that gave him a distinguished air.

The resemblance between him and his son, Prince Alaric, was clear, though Alaric was taller, burlier and colder. His face must have been carved from a glacier it was so still as he regarded her with his own green gaze. Also, unlike his sire, his hair was a dark brown, cut short on the sides and slightly longer on the top.

Cass moved to her.

"You're early."

She ignored the question in his voice and gave him a brittle smile.

"I figured it was time to meet my family."

She was done adhering to his schedule, his way of doing things.

His eyes searched her face. She stared back at him, daring him to stop her. At last, he conceded with a brief nod.

"Of course. Briony, may I introduce King Daxon Van Ambrose and his son, Prince Alaric, of Linnaea."

She turned to face her father and brother. What should have been a joyous moment was instead one full of pain, fury and perhaps worst of all, embarrassment that she had allowed herself to be duped by their machinations and her own immature hope.

"Hello."

Daxon started forward. Had she not just heard him, she probably would have been fooled by the wide smile that stretched across his face and missed the cold calculation in his eyes.

"Briony. I'm so glad to finally meet you, my dear."

Briony stepped back out of reach of his embrace and held out her hand.

"Glad I can be of service, Dad."

CHAPTER EIGHT

BRIONY STOOD ON the balcony of her private suite. The sun had already started to sink behind the snow-capped peak of the mountains in the distance. Her room overlooked the palace grounds and the hundreds of acres of forest to the west. A stunning view fit for a princess.

As was the suite Clara had led her to after her brief meeting with Daxon and Alaric. Daxon had stared at her after she'd delivered her stinging line. Alaric had stepped in and shaken her hand, introducing himself before suggesting she be shown to her suite.

"It's been a long journey," he'd said firmly as he'd steered Briony to the door. "Rest would probably be best before we talk."

Clara had appeared a moment later. Briony hadn't been able to stop herself from glancing back at Cass. For once, there had been no smug smile or hint of danger in his gaze. No, he'd looked almost regretful. She'd wanted to lash out at him, to grab the contract from his hands and rip it right in two. But she wasn't going to give him the satisfaction of seeing her fall apart.

She sighed. Cass had made no pretenses about their marriage being anything other than a contracted alliance. But she'd at least thought his intentions had been somewhat noble. To find out that he was motivated just as much by a personal vendetta as he was supposedly saving the people of Linnaea left her feeling…

Empty. Hopeless. That brief, beautiful burst of confidence and independence on the plane seemed light-years away. Her own father had used her, too. Even after hearing the words from his own lips, part of her wanted to cling to the illusion that it had all been a terrible misunderstanding. That she hadn't just left the only world she'd known to be confronted with yet another person who just wanted to use her. Remembering the sound of his voice, the disgust in his tone when he'd said "bastard child," made her sick to her stomach.

It wasn't just hopelessness. No, it was also regret that she had ever pined for a man like Daxon. If what she'd overheard was any indication, her mother had been right to run.

The regret burned brighter, tightened her throat. How many years had she wasted wishing for a dad when she'd had a mother who had loved her?

Pretty far down the road of self-pity, she thought with a disgusted sigh as she shivered in the winter cold and glanced over her shoulder. Her suite was a vision of royal luxury. A rounded bed dominated one side, raised up on a dais with a peaceful painting of the mountains on the wall. It was covered by violet silk sheets and a thick white comforter. Marble steps led down to a sitting area comprising a red fainting couch and matching chairs done up in velvet and trimmed in silver. Wood roared in a stone fireplace, flanked on either side by bookcases set into the.

Poor little rich girl. She'd heard the sentiment often enough, had done her fair share of eye-rolling when she'd read an interview with the latest actress or model who talked about the hard parts of their lives, the lack of privacy, the pervasive loneliness.

Except now she understood it all too well.

The door swung open. Her eyes narrowed even as her heartbeat sped up at the sight of Cass standing in the doorway. Clad only in his dark trousers and midnight-blue shirt, sleeves rolled up to reveal his tan forearms, he looked sinfully good.

She turned her back to him. How could the man be so manipulative and still look so handsome?

The door to the balcony clicked open.

"Cold out here."

The shiver that traveled down her spine had nothing to do with the freezing winter air tugging at her hair.

She gritted her teeth. Just because her body found Cass physically attractive didn't mean the man wasn't a manipulative snake.

"Matches the personalities of most of the people who live here."

The door shut. She felt him come up behind her, tensed, anticipated…

Nothing. He was waiting to see what she would do. She raised her chin. Two could play at that game. And she'd been letting him call the shots. Time to give Prince Cassius Morgan Adama a taste of his own medicine.

She couldn't say how long they stood out there on the balcony. The sun continued to sink behind the mountains, leaving behind peaks that glowed a dazzling array of oranges, reds and yellows. Overhead, the stars started to wink.

The wind picked up. She imagined the shooshing as the breeze darted in and out of the pine trees below, dislodging a bit of snow here or kicking up flurries there. If she focused on those details, it helped her forget the man standing less than a foot away.

"I've only said sorry once in my life."

Briony snorted. "I'm surprised you've said it even once."

Cass moved at her back, then circled around. His shoulder brushed hers as he came up to the railing and leaned forward. If the freezing temperatures bothered him, he gave no indication as he propped his forearms on the cold stone and gazed out over the landscape.

"It was when I found my aunt crying in the corner of the bedroom she, my father and I all shared." He breathed in deeply. "She blamed herself for getting us banished from Linnaea, for my mother leaving. She couldn't stop crying. She said love had destroyed not only her but her family. So I patted her on the back and told her I was sorry."

"Sorry for what?"

"Sorry for not standing up to the king. Sorry for not being the man I was supposed to be when she needed someone."

Briony's mouth dropped open in shock.

"How old were you?" she finally asked.

"Eleven."

She closed her eyes against the sudden pain as she imagined a young Cass, dark-haired with an innocent amber gaze, trying desperately to comfort his aunt.

"What did she say?"

"Told me it wasn't my fault." He looked away. "But it didn't matter. I felt like I had failed my family."

"Did…did my father force your family into that situation?"

She opened her eyes to see Cass regarding her with an opaque gaze.

"I don't know everything that transpired between my aunt and your father," he said finally. "I do know they were lovers. I know she threatened him toward the end of their relationship. And I know he in turn threatened her with prison for treason, as well as anyone who chose to stand with her over him."

Briony's hands curled around the cold marble railing as queasiness overtook her. She'd heard plenty to confirm

Daxon's true character. But hearing more evidence of her father's cruelty was almost more than she could stomach.

"I'm sorry."

"You have nothing to be sorry for," Cass said, his voice firm. "I don't blame you or Alaric in any way."

"Did my…did Daxon know what happened to you?"

"I doubt he knew or cared. He only cared about getting rid of her and slandering her to the point that no one would believe any stories she might tell about his nefarious activities."

His words to her father replayed in her head: *How does it feel to know the nephew of the woman you tried to destroy will officially be a prince of Linnaea?*

"So marrying me…it was never about Linnaea, was it? Just revenge."

"Do you think so little of me?"

His voice was steady. But his eyes were a mix of regal hardness and a hint of sorrow, a combination that seeped past her defenses straight into her bones. Part of her wanted to reach out and lay a comforting hand on his shoulder. But she couldn't just let go of everything he'd done: the deception, the subterfuge, the manipulation.

"Revenge can make good people do bad things."

He stared at her for a long moment before he stretched out his hand. "Would you come with me? There's something I want to show you."

"What?"

He sighed. "Will you trust me? One more time?"

Was she a fool to even consider saying yes? What could he possibly show her that would make any of this okay?

"Please, Briony."

Whether it was the "please" or the way he uttered her name in that deep, velvety voice of his, she couldn't say. Her rational mind screamed at her to say no, to demand that he rip up their engagement contract and take her home. Her body, however, had other ideas because her gloved hand slowly came up. Cass seized it in his before she could change her mind.

"We're going for a drive."

Ten minutes later, Cass steered the little black car he'd taken from the palace's motor pool off the lantern-lined lane of one of Eira's fashionable districts and onto a narrow street. He kept both hands on the wheel, his eyes focused on the increasingly pitted road and off the woman in the seat next to him.

When Briony had taken his hand, he released the breath he'd been holding. Seeing the look of betrayal on her face when she'd walked into Alaric's office, watching how cold she'd become as she'd processed what she'd heard, had bothered him more than he cared to admit.

He'd expected Briony to seek him out after she'd been shown to her rooms. But as the minutes had ticked by, he'd found himself pacing, checking his phone and watching the door every time he heard footsteps in the hall. Finally, fed up with his own lack of self-control and a morbid need to find out what Briony was thinking, he'd stalked through the halls to her room.

Yes, he hadn't been entirely honest with her. Yes, he'd had ulterior motives. But it wasn't just about revenge. He needed her to understand why. Otherwise, he might as well tear up the contract right now because there was no chance in hell she would walk down the aisle to be wedded to him.

He brought the car to a stop at the edge of an attractive square ringed on all three sides by white town houses with green shutters. The fourth side contained a strip of shops and cafés, from a small bookstore to an art gallery. In the middle lay a park with swings and a few benches. With the light of the lanterns casting a golden glow on the snow, it looked like a postcard. Daxon might have been a selfish bastard, but when it came to image, the man knew how to make an impact.

"Only one row of those town houses is occupied." He felt more than saw Briony turn to look at him, but he kept his gaze focused on the buildings. "Van Ambrose Tower, the latest high-rise, only has twenty percent of its offices filled."

He pressed on the gas and kept driving. A few blocks later, the elegant town houses gave way to brick apartments smooshed together. The farther he drove, the more decrepit the buildings became. Gone were the fashionable black lanterns and cobblestoned streets. Here the roads were made of simple asphalt, cracked and in desperate need of repair. The few streetlights that were working cast only weak pockets of light on streets choked with refuse. Underneath one cracked light, a teenager dug in a trash can.

"This is what I want to fix, Briony. I did not lie to you about that. Eira has at least some fashionable districts that cater to the few wealthy families left and the smattering of tourists that come through. But the rest of the country lives like this. The internet, social media—all of it's kept under lock and key to hide what's going on beyond the capital. The only reason I knew all these years is because my father still has friends here who managed to get letters out that it continued to get worse after our banishment."

He turned down another street, one filled with old houses. He parked in front of a two-story brick home that, despite its crumbling exterior and weed-choked yard, still clung to some of its old glamour. Double doors with stained glass guarded the entrance. Even though a rock had been thrown through one long ago, the craftsmanship was still evident.

"I used to stare at the floor in the morning and watch the

sun come through the doors," he said quietly. "There were so many colors."

In the darkness, Briony shifted.

"For the longest time, I dreamed of coming back here, of raising my own children in the house I grew up in." He nodded to the other once-elegant homes now sagging under the weight of abandonment and disrepair. "That dream is gone. The houses have been condemned, and the entire street will be razed in the spring." He turned and speared her with his gaze. He needed her to understand. "But progress can still be made, Briony."

For a moment, all he could make out was her profile; the slight curve of her nose, the graceful line of her jaw. Even in the dim light of the streetlight, her red hair glowed.

"You lied to me."

"I did not lie. However," he interjected as her head snapped about and her lips parted, "I won't deny that I could have handled things better. I provided only the vaguest details about my family's history with yours."

"What happened? What did my father do that made all of this deception worth it?"

Cass's hands tightened on the wheel. "He broke apart my family."

For a moment the only sounds were the distant wail of a siren and his own heartbeat. It was the first time he had spoken the words out loud. He didn't look at Briony, couldn't if he was going to finally share what had happened.

"My aunt was his mistress. I imagine not long after your mother fled."

The rest of the story came tumbling out. How his father's position as assistant to the minister of the treasury had given him access to documents on how King Daxon's frivolous spending was plunging the country into economic chaos, information he had shared with his sister, Alecine. How Alecine had used that information and other intelligence she'd gathered to threaten Daxon when he'd tried to dismiss her for his next lover. And how Daxon had retaliated by telling Alecine she had twenty-four hours to leave with her family and never return or be thrown in prison for treason.

"He froze our finances. Slandered our name to anyone who would listen and made it impossible for my aunt and father to find work."

"What about your mother?" Briony asked softly.

"My mother chose to return to her family in France." His knuckles turned almost as white as the snow on the ground as his fingers wrapped even tighter around the leather. "She knew the struggles we would face with no money and Daxon's vitriol following us throughout Europe. She preferred the comfort and ease her family could offer."

"And they didn't offer to take you in, too?"

"They did. If I agreed to never see my father again."

Briony's gasp sounded like a gunshot inside the car.

"How awful."

"My mother was furious with my aunt, and angry with my father for siding with Aunt Alecine. She told him he could go to Daxon, pledge his loyalty and turn my aunt in to keep us safe and keep our standing in society. But Father refused."

"Family duty," Briony murmured softly.

"Family honor," Cass corrected. "My father and aunt had plenty. My mother had none."

"So you fled."

"We fled. We made our way to Rome. It took a year for us to climb out of the little hovel of an apartment we lived in. My father and aunt crafted new identities for themselves, worked whatever jobs they could find to slowly build their way back up while trying to stay under the radar in case Daxon caught wind of where we were and changed his mind about coming after us." The gingham hanging over the cracked window flashed in his mind. "One night my aunt came home with this red gingham tablecloth. She hung it over a window that had cracked when some boys threw rocks at our window. Every time she tried to hang it, wind would come through the crack and blow it down. She finally started to cry and kept telling me over and over how sorry she was." He could still see her face, eyes puffy as tears ran down her cheeks. "She told me how she wished she could have stood up to Daxon and saved my father and me from everything."

"So you decided one day you would stand up to Daxon for her."

Cass's head snapped around as he faced Briony, surprised that she had so quickly seized on the moment he'd decided to get revenge.

"Yes."

"Cass, you were eleven," she said quietly. "That was too much to take on."

"It wasn't. My father lost my mother, a woman he had loved and who, when she was younger, loved him enough to defy her family and marry him when he was just a lowly lawyer versus the trust-fund prince they had picked out for her. My mother made her own choices," he acknowledged, "but without Daxon's labeling my aunt and father traitors, their marriage wouldn't have ended."

"You don't know that," Briony argued. "A woman who would leave her husband when he needed her the most could have left for any number of other reasons later on in life."

"But she didn't," Cass ground out. "She left because Daxon threatened to throw my aunt in prison for treason, as well as anyone who aligned with her."

"And your father chose your aunt."

"Not over my mother." Cass's voice vibrated with anger.

"She accused him of the same thing. But he knew it was only a matter of time before our family would be targeted, too. It wasn't just choosing to support his sister. He was the first one to mention to my aunt that he had found some troubling inaccuracies in some financial documents. My aunt is smart, very smart, when it comes to finances. Her relationship with Daxon was turning ugly. So she started compiling evidence." A vein began to throb in his neck. "My aunt lost her whole life. She lost everything, as did my father, and no one bothered to stand up to a tyrant."

Briony didn't back down from his anger. She just continued to watch him with those eyes so like his oppressor's, yet so different. Where Daxon's were hard, flinty chips of green, Briony's were warm and vibrant, a window into her soul.

"Obviously your aunt had a change in fortune, at least."

A quick smile flashed. "My aunt made her way up from cleaning bathrooms in a hotel to working as a blackjack dealer in the hotel's casino. One night she dealt cards for the reigning prince of Tulay, Daniel Callas. She beat him every hand that first night. He came back every night for a week, then proposed on his last night in Rome."

"That sounds romantic."

"More like the result of loneliness. Daniel was a widower. He married my aunt because he liked her and she didn't kowtow to him. The papers termed it a 'whirlwind courtship,' dug up her past with your father and labeled her a crown-seeking gold digger. But after a year of making significant improvements in everything from Tulay's tourism industry to housing reform, the rumors faded and the people embraced her."

"And you became a billionaire."

He shrugged. "Not without help. Daniel sent me to university. He placed me in charge of one of his holdings, a shipping company. I invested the money I made, diversified into real estate, tourism and transportation. My investments paid off. I told myself one day I would return to Linnaea and offer your father a loan to rebuild the country."

"From what little I overheard this evening, I take it accepting a loan from someone related to his former mistress who almost destroyed him angered him?"

"Enraged is more like it," said Cass with a small smile. "But Daxon is not without his pride, either. I knew that just the financial offer, even though almost no one else would be willing to put so much money on the line with the country's economic history, would not be enough to sway him."

"But I was." Briony's voice was small, shock and understanding as the last piece of the puzzle fell into place.

"Yes. Daxon has made no secret about his reputation as a womanizer. But aside from getting photographed with his date of the month on his arm, he's kept most of the sordid details private. He'd made no secret that aside from Alaric, he didn't want any more children. For an illegitimate child to be revealed, and for it to be known that he had done nothing to support that child once he found out about its existence, would have been a death sentence for him publicly. He's sick. From what the doctors say, he has less than a year to live. He knows his legacy as a leader is in tatters. The financial offer, combined with his chance to be seen as righting the wrongs of his past and doing right by his child, were more important than rejecting me. Marital alliances still serve a purpose in many parts of the world, and it acts as insurance that Daxon won't back out."

"And you have your revenge by being the sole savior of Linnaea, getting your family's banishment reversed and marrying into the very family that rejected you."

Briony's voice was flat, her face emotionless. Coldness swept through Cass. He had had those almost exact same thoughts. But when stated out loud, they sounded truly heartless.

Briony frowned. "But why did Daxon not have Alaric marry someone for financial support, or even Daxon himself get married?"

"Alaric has been engaged to some heiress for years. I don't know the details, only that every attempt he's made to finalize the marriage has been rebuffed. I don't think he has high hopes for it ever happening, but he's trapped by a contract. As for Daxon, his reputation is so well-known in the right circles that no woman with the financial resources he needs would agree to a marriage with him."

"Leaving you as the only savior in sight." One corner of her mouth twisted up into half of a sardonic smile. "And here you are."

"And here I am." He released the steering wheel and spread his hands out. "That's the whole sordid story."

She tilted her head to the side. "Was what my father did worth the lies?"

Anger spiked. "Did you not just hear what I told you he did? How he tore apart my family? And how, exactly did I lie? I told you that night at the Ledge exactly what the marriage contract would entail."

"Yes, you offered to marry me in exchange for giving money to the country." Briony's eyes flashed with anger. "But you also insinuated that my father wanted to see me knowing full well he didn't care about my existence. You lied to me. And," she said as she held up a hand to stop his reply, "don't say you didn't outright lie. You deliberately misled me. That counts as a lie."

He couldn't have picked a better future wife if he'd tried. Briony didn't capitulate, didn't back down. She was too fierce, too determined. A far cry from his own mother, who had turned weak at the first sign of not having a luxurious life.

And if he didn't own up to his mistakes now, he would be no better than her. No better than Daxon, even, who had lied and manipulated his entire life.

That thought stopped him cold. When had he become so blind, so focused on fulfilling his sense of duty to his family and his revenge that he ignored the tactics he'd used to achieve his goals?

He looked at Briony, truly looked at her, for the first time since their kiss on the plane. She was backed against the door of the car, not out of fear, but to put as much distance between them. A woman who had come from almost nothing, left behind her entire life for the promise of something better, a promise he had falsely portrayed.

"Make that three."

She frowned. "Three what?"

"Three times in my life I've apologized. I'm sorry, Briony. I did lie." He hated saying the words out loud, hated himself in that moment for who he had become. "I lied and I used you. Just like your stepfather, your stepsisters and your birth father."

She stared at him for so long he wondered if she would ever say anything. If she said nothing, if she made a scene and demanded he fly her back to the States or anywhere else in the world, it would be no less than he deserved. He should have been honest, should have stuck to what he could do for her and her family instead of adding the spin of being reunited with a father who wanted nothing to do with her.

At last, she sighed.

"I'm still angry with you. But no, Cass, you're not as bad as my family. Especially," she added with disgust dripping from her tone, "not as bad as my *father*."

"While I'm pleased to hear that, how did you arrive at that conclusion?"

"Aside from not telling me who you were at first and suggesting my father wanted to see me, you've been up-front about everything else. Especially about your expectations for our marriage."

"I never wanted to lie about that," he said firmly. "But you can help me help this country. You can help me help your brother. I can help your stepfamily. And we can still have a pleasant life together."

Silence descended once more. Briony stared at him for a long moment before she turned to look at his childhood home. He glanced at the front porch. He'd spent hours on the porch swing with his father, listened in rapt attention to his father's stories about what had happened at work, took pride in his father's hard work at helping the country take steps to become stronger.

Cass looked away. That time was past.

"I want children. So do you. They'll want for nothing."

"What about love?"

The words were spoken so softly he almost didn't hear them.

"What about it?" he asked. Hadn't she just heard him?

"Will you love your children?" She pinned him with a bleak gaze effused with a sorrow so deep he almost had to look away. "Or will you be like my stepfather and withhold the one thing they need?"

He barely swallowed his anger. She had a right to ask.

"Romantic love is off the table for me. But loving one's children…that's another matter entirely. I will love any children you bring into this world."

He'd expected something more from her, a smile or some other confirmation. But she merely nodded and looked back at the house. The seconds ticked by, each one longer than the last, as he waited for her answer.

"All right."

He hadn't expected excitement. But neither had he expected to hear her sounding so listless.

"All right?"

"All right," she repeated softly as she leaned her head back against the car seat and closed her eyes. "Will you take me back now?"

The rest of the car ride was spent in utter silence. Briony didn't open her eyes until he pulled the car back into the garage beneath the palace. He had barely put the car in Park before she had unbuckled her seat belt and gotten out. He swore under his breath and got out. She'd almost made it to the elevator.

"Briony."

She paused, shoulders rigid, hands balled into fists. Slowly, she turned but kept her head down, that curtain of red obscuring most of her face.

"I am sorry. For hurting you."

Then she turned and disappeared inside the elevator. The doors swished shut, leaving Cass alone in the garage.

He didn't know how long he stared at the closed doors. When had his perfectly laid plans, his years of plotting, become more important than his honor? When had his revenge become more important than his true duty, using his wealth to support Linnaea's recovery?

Marrying Briony was still a crucial part of the plan. A marital alliance would cement relations between Linnaea and Tulay. It would also make it much harder for Daxon to renege on their agreement.

As long as he could refocus his attention where it belonged and rein in his complicated emotions for his future wife.

CHAPTER NINE

BRIONY STARED AT her reflection in the mirror. She didn't look like herself. Her hair had been straightened, the waist of her white cap-sleeved dress cinched with an emerald belt that matched the petticoat peeking out from beneath the knee-length skirt. Matching green earrings sparkled at her ears.

She sucked in a deep breath. The cosmetologist Clara had ushered inside her room just after dawn had managed to conceal the deep shadows beneath her eyes. She had crawled underneath the thick, warm blanket and silk sheets of her king-size bed...and mourned. Mourned the death of the dream she'd held on to as a girl of who her father was. She'd envisioned him a hero, a firefighter, perhaps, or an adventurer, an astronaut who looked down on the planet on one of his trips to the space station and wondered where his daughter was.

Fanciful. Foolish.

She'd heard those adjectives from Trey often enough. Unfortunately, she was proving him right more times than she cared to admit.

By the time she'd woken up that morning, her grief had morphed into anger. Anger at the powers that be that had bestowed upon her an unloving stepfather and an even more unloving birth father. Anger at Daxon for being such a callous brute. Even knowing his diagnosis didn't alter her feelings. Just a day ago, hearing that her birth father would most likely not see next Christmas would have made her world tilt on its axis.

But last night, her world had simply shuddered for a moment. She didn't wish death on anyone. But it was hard to summon more than a vague remorse for a life cut short. Not when she had not only witnessed his cruel nature but heard about how he had treated everyone in his life, from a former lover to a child whose family had been ripped apart.

Cass had lied to her. But, she acknowledged grudgingly as she smoothed a wrinkle out of her skirt, unlike anyone else in her life, he'd come clean. He'd apologized, twice. And he'd stuck to his original offer. How many men would have continued to lie, would have manipulated her even further to get what they wanted? How many would have tried to play up a love angle, even tried to seduce her to secure what they wanted?

It didn't excuse what he'd done. But it did let her know that despite his mistakes, her original evaluation of his character had been accurate. He was a good man trying to do the right thing both for the country he remembered and loved and for his family.

Could she be strong enough to enter into a loveless marriage? Even if it was for the greater good?

But, she reminded herself, *that still didn't explain the kiss*. He'd emphasized the professional nature of their relationship multiple times. Could he remain so detached when it came to making heirs? Just the thought of his body pressed against hers, heated skin growing hotter still as they explored each other, made her breath catch.

Fanciful. Foolish.

She yanked on the zipper of her dress and groaned when

it snagged on her bra. That's what she got for fantasizing. She should have let Clara stay to help her with the dress.

A knock on the door had her hurrying to the door.

"Oh, Clara, thank good—"

She came up hard against a solid wall of muscle. She stumbled back, her legs becoming tangled in the voluminous folds of the petticoat. An arm wrapped around her waist and hauled her against a very strong body. A spicy, woodsy scent wrapped around her.

"Where's the fire?"

She tilted her chin up to look into Cass's eyes. His teasing smirk disappeared as his hand moved up and came to rest on her bare back.

"Uh…my zipper got stuck."

His fingers drifted down, lightly skimming over her skin and setting every nerve ending on fire until he reached the zipper.

"Turn around."

Was it just her imagination or did his voice sound husky? She followed his order and turned, catching sight of her reflection in the mirror across the room. His black hair and tan skin stood out against the white of her dress, his broad shoulders dwarfing her frame.

With a deft twist, he freed the zipper and slid it the rest of the way up.

"Thank you."

"You're welcome."

He stepped back as she turned around.

"You're going to give other European royals a run for their money on the best-dressed list."

A different type of warmth suffused her body, pleasant and cozy at his compliment and admiring gaze.

"Thank you. Clara picked it out." She surveyed his impeccable gray suit and navy tie. "You look good, too."

His lips twitched. "Thanks."

She wrapped her arms around her waist. "So what are you doing here?"

"The conference starts in forty-five minutes. Clara will have a heart attack if we're not there at least thirty minutes ahead of time."

He rattled off the remainder of the schedule as Briony grabbed her coat and gloves off the bed: the conference, followed by a carriage ride through the streets that would take them to lunch with members of the Linnaean government. She shrugged into her coat as she swallowed hard.

She'd said yes last night because she'd wanted to break free of her past, to stop doing things for her family and start looking to the future. She had the chance to do something with her life, not just for her but for a whole country.

Except she hadn't thought too much about appearing in the public eye until now.

"Briony."

She looked up to see Cass watching her with an opaque gaze, his handsome face smooth.

"If you've changed your mind—"

"No," she interrupted. "It's not that. It's just the thought of being on display in front of all those people." She swallowed hard. "What if I make a mistake?"

Cass's lips tilted up into a full-blown smile as he chuckled, a rich, warm sound that calmed some of the nerves fluttering around inside her chest.

"You will make mistakes, Briony. But don't forget that yesterday you stood in front of your birth father, who's also a king, and essentially told him you weren't falling for any of his lies."

He closed the distance between them and captured one of her hands in his, bringing it up to his lips. The kiss he brushed across her fingers wasn't the seductive caress he'd bestowed upon her in the Ledge. It didn't make the touch any less provocative.

"You are a worthy princess, Briony. More worthy of the title than any other woman I've met."

Her chest constricted at his words and the admiration in his caramel eyes. It was just as intoxicating, if not more so, than the attraction between them.

"Cass—"

"Your Highnesses!" Clara appeared in the doorway, tablet in one hand, cell phone in the other. "Are you ready? It takes approximately ten minutes to reach the front of the palace from this wing."

Briony looked back at Cass, but his face had smoothed once more as he turned to face Alaric's right-hand woman.

"Of course, Clara. I admire your attention to detail."

Clara snorted. "I'm sure." Her gaze slid to Briony and she actually smiled, her eyes softening. "You look beautiful, Princess Briony. If I may be so bold, Your Highness," she said to Cass, "you're very fortunate."

Cass acknowledged the comment with a nod but said nothing as he held out his arm to Briony. She accepted it and kept her gaze averted. If she was going to make their arranged relationship successful at all, she needed to put distance between the two of them now. She'd done it fairly well last night, and that had been after a transatlantic flight and numerous heart-wrenching revelations. She could do it again.

She had to if she was going to survive the choice she'd made with her heart intact.

Cass glanced at Briony out of the corner of his eye as she leaned over to better hear what Linnaea's minister of the treasury was saying. A smile crossed her face, and she laughed. Judging by the smitten look on the minister's face, he was as besotted with Briony as the rest of the people she'd met.

He'd wondered for a moment if Briony was going to be able to handle the day. She'd kept her head down on the elevator ride from her wing to the main floor. She hadn't said a word on the walk to the front of the palace. And when it had been time to step out onto the main staircase landing where the press conference was being held, Briony had stopped, her face pale.

But before he'd been able to swoop in and rescue her with a platitude, she'd inhaled deeply, squared her shoulders and walked out, one hand laid elegantly on his arm.

She'd handled the conference like a pro. Clara had avoided giving her anything to say in public, but she'd smiled at the press and gathered crowds with a genuine sweetness he knew would reflect well in tomorrow's papers. That she had stopped to accept a flower from a little girl and given her a hug on their way to the carriage had made an entire country fall in love in the span of a heartbeat.

It had also made his earlier admiration flare into a fierce pride. His fiancée was a strong woman who was poised to become an exceptional leader.

Unfortunately, his esteem had opened the gateway for his suppressed attraction to also flame up. The carriage ride to the hotel had been pure hell. They'd sat next to each other, the cold winter day making the heat of her leg pressed against his even more intense.

And now he was experiencing...jealousy. Ever since they'd been escorted into the hotel's ballroom, there had been a nonstop parade of people walking up to be introduced to Briony and congratulate her on her engagement, welcome her to Linnaea or, for a few calculating individuals, attempts to try to ferret out details about Briony's lineage.

Briony handled it all like she'd been doing this for years.

The spotlight being focused on her had given him plenty of time to observe. Unfortunately, it also gave him plenty of time to think. He'd gone up to her suite to ensure she hadn't changed her mind before the conference. He hadn't expected to find her looking so stunningly beautiful. And he most certainly had not anticipated a mere graze of his fingers on bare skin would make his muscles lock up as he fought the thundering pound of his pulse demanding that he slide the zipper not up but down, baring her body for him and him alone to see.

Now that everything was official and Briony had been introduced to the public, now that she wore an emerald engagement ring on her finger and there were no immediate obstacles to their impending marriage, he was faced with the growing conundrum of his attraction to his fiancée.

If it was just simple sexual interest, that would be easy, even welcome. But the problem that had developed with Briony and didn't show any signs of letting up was the strength of his attraction and how it had become interwoven with the emotions that surged forth no matter how much he tried to stifle them.

Why had he shown Briony his family's house? He had seen shock, compassion, even begrudging acceptance of what their union could do for the people of Linnaea when he'd shown her the trash-ridden slums of Eira's seedier underbelly. There had been no need to bare one of the most painful parts of his life.

But he had. A compulsion had seized him, a burning need for her to see him not as a spoiled prince wanting to get his own way, but as a man who had a duty to fulfill.

So why? That question had haunted him all night. Perhaps it had been the betrayal in her eyes when she'd walked into the study and confronted him, Daxon and Alaric. Or maybe it had been seeing the coldness she'd wielded like a shield last night, a stark contrast to her usual warmth.

Daxon approached, dressed in an impeccably tailored dark green suit with a light brown tie and brown shoes. He shook hands and smiled along the way. But his gaze stayed laser-focused on Briony.

Cass's hackles rose as he stood and intercepted the king.

"Daxon," he said with a smile for the cameras even as he gripped the older man's hand in a tight grip. "What do you want?"

"I want to see my daughter," Daxon replied with his own smile, clapping Cass on the back like they were old friends even as he winced under the pressure of Cass's fingers.

"Your daughter?" Cass chuckled and leaned down so that no one else could hear. "Don't you mean your bargaining chip?"

Daxon's mask slipped a moment as his thin lips stretched into a taut line.

"You're the one who proposed this, Cassius. You backed us into a corner."

"You backed your entire country into a corner with your irresponsible spending—"

"Gentlemen."

Both men turned to see Briony smiling at them with worry in her eyes.

"What's going on? People are starting to look this way," she said quietly as she slipped her hand into the crook of Cass's elbow as if they'd been touching each other intimately for months.

"A reporter has asked for a photo of the two of us, but your fiancé has decided I'm not allowed to be around you," Daxon said stiffly. "I don't recall seeing that in the contract."

Briony glanced up at Cass.

"You have enough going on today," he replied in a low voice, ignoring Daxon's snort. "I didn't want him to add more stress."

Something softened in her eyes, an appreciation that suddenly made him feel like a conquering warrior.

"Thank you." She squeezed his arm. "I can handle him."

As she walked away, Cass watched them for a long moment before he slowly sat back down. If today was any indicator, Briony truly didn't need him. She would be more than capable of handling her royal duties and living a life separate from his aside from duties that required their joint presence or the raising of their children.

It was what he had wanted, what he had been concerned she couldn't handle. So why, when presented with evidence that he was getting everything he had hoped for and more, was he feeling so bereft, like he'd just lost something incredible?

This was why emotions were better left out of arrangements like this, he thought crossly. They screwed everything up.

CHAPTER TEN

BRIONY WALKED THROUGH what in the spring would no doubt
be an incredible rose garden. The bushes had been expertly
trimmed back, the remaining branches now covered in a
light layer of snow. But the trellises that ran between the elegant stone pillars evoked images of flowers bursting into
bloom and creating a walkway lined on either side by the
most beautifully colored roses. Come late spring, this would
probably be one of her favorite places.

It was thoughts like those that kept her going on days
like today. That and, she thought with a small smile as she
glanced over her shoulder at the sled trailing behind her,
simple joys.

The week since the press conference had flown by. Every
morning she'd awoken, eaten in her room and then joined
Alaric for a brief meeting in his study at his invitation. She'd
been pleasantly surprised to find him a warmer person when
he wasn't around their father. Perhaps one day, they could
even be friends.

Daxon, on the other hand, had shown no interest, a blessing given how just the sight of him made her stomach tighten
in disgust. The few times she saw him, he greeted her with
a brisk nod. If others were around, he would pat her on the
back or press a cool kiss to her cheek. She tolerated those
brief interactions, but she ensured they were brief. By un-

spoken agreement, they each had acknowledged that they wanted nothing to do with the other outside the necessary public engagements.

As the days passed, the anger that had manifested that night after her drive with Cass had dimmed. Perhaps it was because she'd spent so many years wishing things could be different with Trey that she accepted the reality of her situation quicker. Or perhaps it was because Daxon was so far from the idealized father she had built up in her head that it was easier to distance herself from the cold, vain man he was revealing himself to be. She wasn't completely over his rejection or her own disappointment. There had still been moments of pain throughout the week. There would be more to come, of that she had no doubt.

But she was stronger than she had been. And, she thought with a smile, she finally had something to focus on besides family or the relationships that would never be. Something that was hers and hers alone.

During one of her morning meetings with Alaric, she'd shared what she wanted to focus on as a princess of Linnaea: restoring the country's education system. Alaric had been surprisingly supportive of her ideas, which is why the last few days had been consumed with setting up a council of former teachers, administrators and other professionals who could use their experience to start rebuilding Linnaea's schools.

It had been thrilling to throw herself into something she loved, to exchange ideas and have a goal to focus on. It also kept her mind off her fiancé.

Her footsteps fell harder as she moved off the path and tromped through the deeper drifts of snow, each stomp of her boots an effort to drive his face from her memory. The next round of royal events would start this weekend, kicking off with a visit to a hospital and ending with a gala exhibition of a new museum in Eira. She'd only seeing him in passing or at dinner with Alaric. They were polite, formal and barely spoke. After their encounter in her suite with the zipper and his moment of chivalry in trying to protect her from Daxon, he'd withdrawn once more into the chilly, distant prince who had emerged after their kiss on the plane.

Unfortunately, their distance didn't stop her body from responding to his presence. The low rumble of his voice rippled through her veins. A glimpse of his slow smile at dinner made her heart beat faster. The insightful questions he asked about the work she was doing reminded her of the blissful week of ignorance she'd spent flirting with Cass Morgan.

She'd known when she'd signed the contract that she was signing away her chance to love and be loved by the man she'd give herself to. A fact she'd struggled with after clinging to that idea for so long.

Yet after seeing how her vision of meeting her birth father had gone up in flames, what was the point in dwelling on what she used to want? Unfortunately, letting go of the past had resulted in even more lurid dreams of what it would be like when they finally explored the passion that had been simmering between them since the moment he'd walked into her bar.

Enough of that.

She traipsed up a hill behind the palace and stopped at the top. She sucked in a deep breath of crisp, cold air before she sat in the toboggan, planted her gloved hands in the snow and pushed off.

The sled flew down the hill, skimming so fast the wintry landscape flew by. She threw back her head and laughed as the sled reached the bottom and continued for quite a distance across the flat plain that stretched for what seemed like miles before giving way to the forest in the distance.

At last, the sled came to a stop. She sat there for a moment, then slowly rolled off the sled into the embrace of the cold snow. She wiggled around a bit, then spread out her arms and legs and swept them up and down. When had she last made a snow angel? At least a couple of years, maybe even more.

Her movements slowed as she gazed up at the crystal-blue sky. The meetings and endless to-dos of royal life, not to mention the never-ending questions Clara peppered her with about the wedding, all faded away to the simple pleasures of playing in the snow.

A noise registered. She paused, listened, then heard it again: a distant shout. Slowly she sat up in time to see a figure racing down the hill. As the figure drew nearer, it turned from a dark blur of arms and legs into the tall frame of a man dressed in a black winter coat with a matching head of equally black hair.

Cass.

"Briony!"

She started to push herself up out of the snow, but Cass was at her side faster than she had anticipated.

"Don't move," Cass ordered as he knelt down next to her. "Lie back. If you fell, you could have injured something."

"I didn't—"

"I'll call the medical team and—"

"Cassius!"

Cass blinked and stared at her as if no one in the world had raised their voice to him before. No one probably had, she thought grumpily.

"I'm fine. I went sledding, I rolled off and I made a snow angel." She gestured to the imprint behind her. "See?"

Cass let out a harsh breath and scrubbed a gloved hand over his face. "I saw you lying on the ground and thought..." He shook his head.

"I'm fine," she said again, but gentled her voice. "I can take care of myself."

"I'm fully aware that."

Was he irritated with her? Before she could question his cryptic remark, he grabbed her hands and pulled her to her feet.

"Regardless of whether your tumble in the snow was intentional or not, you shouldn't lie in the snow for too long. You could get frostbite."

She rolled her eyes as she picked up the rope attached to the toboggan and started trekking back toward the hill.

"I did grow up on the prairies of Kansas. I'm well aware of frostbite."

Cass didn't respond, but fell into step beside her. For a moment they walked in silence, the crunch of their boots in the snow surprisingly pleasant given the tension between them.

"Why did you come out here?" Briony finally asked.

"I went to your suite to confirm tomorrow's plans. The maid said you had decided to go sledding behind the rose garden."

"And you couldn't have confirmed the plans by text?"

Cass shrugged. "I've been up to my ears in financial statements and planning committees all week. I figured a walk would do me some good."

He reached down and grabbed the rope from her as they started up the hill, towing the sled behind him. Briony rolled her eyes again.

"Does your sense of duty and honor apply to pulling sleds?"

He surprised her with a small chuckle. "Perhaps."

A question rose to her lips, but she bit it back. Despite his overbearing attitude and need to protect, the walk itself was pleasant. She didn't want to ruin the first alone time they'd had in over a week.

"Something's on your mind."

Startled, she glanced over at him.

"When you're thinking about something but not sure you want to say it out loud, you get this little crease between your eyebrows and bite down on your lower lip."

She laughed. "I didn't realize I was that transparent. But yes, you're right. I was just wondering if sometimes you focus too much on your sense of duty and not enough on your life."

For several long moments, Cass said nothing. Briony inwardly cursed. Yes, she was engaged to the man and yes, they'd shared an intense, soul-stirring kiss. But that didn't give her the right to pry into the man's personal life. Not when their engagement was based entirely on business.

"What makes you ask that?" Cass finally asked as they neared the top of the hill.

"It's just that here you've been focusing on getting revenge and getting your family's banishment rescinded. You've accomplished that. But the few times I've seen you, you don't seem very happy."

Cass stared ahead as they reached the top, then turned to look back over the plain.

"I'm not."

She stared at him. She hadn't expected an answer to her question, much less an honest one.

"Why?"

"At first I thought it was the letdown that comes after something you've been anticipating or working toward for a long time. Almost like the aftermath of a holiday or celebration. But now..." His voice trailed off as he stared at the trees in the distance, his dark profile standing out in stark contrast to the pale walls of the palace behind him. "Most of my life has focused on achieving revenge against Daxon. The night I came back to Linnaea and was brought before your father,

I felt powerful. It was as if that moment in the apartment in Rome when I felt so helpless and cowardly and the moment I stood before him merged. I righted the wrongs done to my family and I stood up to an oppressor." He turned to look at her. "Except there was nothing after that. I had focused so much on that moment that not even restoring Linnaea had become a focus. That anticlimactic emptiness has only grown since I acknowledged how I've treated you."

Briony reached out and laid a tentative hand on his arm. "I forgive you, Cass. It wasn't the best way to go about things, but I know your heart was in the right place."

Cass shrugged her hand off and stepped back.

"Don't."

"Don't what?"

"Don't make excuses for me," Cass snarled. "My heart was focused solely on making your father feel backed into a corner, to make him feel the way my aunt did and as if he had no choice left but to do what I said." He leaned in, his eyes no longer golden but dark and hard. "I wanted to bring you before him so that he could be reminded every day that he had messed up. Your very existence damages his pride."

Each word landed like a punch to the stomach. But Briony didn't back down. She went toe to toe with him.

"And how about now?" she challenged. "Or are you just so determined to keep me at arm's length that you're telling me all this?"

"I'm telling you because it's the truth," he snapped back.

"Yes, but you're missing the other half of the truth!" she cried. Dear God, could the man be any more pigheaded? "You apologized. You told me everything. You offered me choices."

"I never should have put you in that position in the first place."

"No, you shouldn't have," she agreed. "But everyone

makes mistakes, Cass. It's how we react to the people we've hurt with those mistakes and how we respond moving forward that matters. From what I've seen, Daxon is stuck in an endless loop of selfishness. Agreeing to the contract was more about his own pride than saving the country he hurt. My stepfather and stepsisters cared more about wallowing in their own grief than overcoming our loss as a family. I'm working on accepting that it's not me who's to blame for any of it. They are who they are—self-absorbed people who don't bother to look beyond themselves." She poked him in the chest. "But you aren't like that!"

Cass met her gaze, his jaw tense, eyes blazing. The tension in the air between them crackled, shifted from anger to that electrifying intensity that always seemed to be just out of reach.

Please kiss me again.

Cass jerked back as if she'd spoken the words out loud.

"You have a good heart, Briony. But you make far too many excuses for the people who hurt you."

He started to walk off. She blew out a frustrated breath.

"You know what I think the other part of your problem is?" she called after him. "You're a stuffed shirt."

Cass's steps faltered, then stopped. She watched his shoulders rise up toward his ears then fall. Had she said too much?

No, she told herself. *You never say enough.*

Slowly, he turned.

"A stuffed what?"

"A stuffed shirt."

He frowned. "Is that like a stuffed bird?"

Briony groaned. "No. It's an expression. It means formal, boring, pompous."

A glower darkened his face as he took a step in her direction.

"I can assure you no one has described me as boring."

"You spent how many years focused on getting revenge? And then once you have it, all you do is feel guilty for achieving what you've been working on for so long and attend meetings. What else do you want out of your life, Cass? When are you going to start living?"

Would it be rude to dig out her cell phone and snap a picture of the thunderstruck expression on his face?

"This coming from the woman who spent six months being a servant to her abusive family?"

She raised her chin, determined not to let him see how much the cruel but accurate comment hurt.

"And I made a choice to get away from that. What are you doing?"

"I'm working to make this country a better place."

"If you count reviewing financial statements and talking with committees as fun, then you're missing out." She gestured toward the sled. "When's the last time you went sledding?"

"When I was six."

Her mouth dropped open. "When you were six?"

"Yes."

"Okay, you want to prove you're not a stuffed shirt?" She knocked her boot against the sled. "Then go sledding."

"No."

"Ah, I see." She turned her back on him and swung one leg over the toboggan. "You're scared."

"You're not teasing me into going sledding."

"It's okay if you're scared. I won't tell anyone," she said as she looked over her shoulder and winked at his thunderous face before turning around to grab the rope. "But I still think—"

Her words ended on a squeak as a solid wall of warmth pressed against her back. A moment later Cass's legs caged her in on the sled, his arms wrapped around her to snatch the rope from her hands. She sat straight up, but a quick tug sent her falling back against his chest.

"All right, Briony," he murmured in her ear, sending a careening ache through her body that made her thighs tighten as her core grew hot. "Let's go sledding."

Before she could retort, he pushed off. Their combined weight elevated them to speeds she hadn't been able to achieve on her own. She laughed as they whipped down the hillside, savoring the rush of the sled, the icy air, the contrasting warmth of the man who cradled her so firmly yet so gently against his incredible body.

They reached the flat plain, the sled continuing to churn across the snow.

Until the sled hit something concealed beneath the snow. One moment Briony was cocooned safely in Cass's arms. The next she was sailing into the air, her body propelled forward by the momentum of their crash. A second later she hit the snow with a gasp. Cass followed a moment later, his muscular frame landing directly on top of her.

"Briony!" Cass lifted himself up on his forearms, one hand brushing the hair out of her eyes. "Briony, are you all right…"

His voice trailed off, and he frowned as she started laughing.

"I've never gone that fast before!"

"Your idea of living is very different from mine."

Briony's laugh died as the weight of Cass's body registered. The blanket of snow softened the world around them, making her more acutely aware of the pounding of her heart as Cass's eyes darkened.

"Have you thought about what it will be like between us?"

His question made heat bloom across her skin, the roughness of his voice sinking deep inside her and making her restless. She wanted to tell him no, wanted to say making love had never even crossed her mind.

But it would be a lie.

"Yes," she whispered.

Slowly, he lowered his head. She gasped as her gaze met his, amber eyes flashing with desire as he drew closer. Her eyes drifted shut just before his lips touched her.

I'm in trouble.

The fleeting thought disappeared as Cass kissed her with a slow, smoldering intensity. The contact made her gasp and arch into his body as she wound her arms around his neck. His lips left hers, moved over her cheek in a caress as light as butterfly wings, then down her neck. He placed an open-mouthed kiss at the base of her throat that made her moan his name.

Even if there was never any love between them, at least she would have this, a passion she'd never known was possible.

His hand found the zipper of her coat and pulled it down. The cold air kissed her chest, enhancing the heat of his touch. When his lips kissed the swell of her breast revealed by the parted fabric, she moaned.

"Cass!"

He stopped.

"Cass?" She opened her eyes as he lifted his head.

"If I don't stop now, I'll pick you up, carry you into the palace to my rooms and..." He leaned down and grazed another kiss across her lips, lightning fast. "I won't stop."

She swallowed hard. She wanted him, wanted him more than she had ever wanted anyone.

But if she went to bed with Cass, if she made herself vulnerable to him in any way, she would be surrendering her control. She'd risked, and suffered, rejection over and over again, from Trey and her stepsisters to Daxon. Was taking this step worth the risk? Not to mention she would be truly closing the door on the possibility of having her first time be with a man who loved her.

The thought stopped her cold.

Something flickered in Cass's eyes. Before she could gather her thoughts or reply, he pushed himself off her, then held out a hand.

She accepted it, allowed him to pull her to her feet. Before she could say anything he turned, grabbed the rope of the sled and started off toward the castle.

Wait!

Her heart cried out, urging her to stop him. But the sight of his retreating back stopped the words in her throat. She had been about to make a split-second decision based on emotion. Cass had told her multiple times emotion had no place in their upcoming marriage.

She couldn't say how long she stood watching Cass walk across the plain. He stopped at the base of the hill, arched a brow and nodded toward the castle. Slowly, she followed. When she reached his side, they walked up the hill together. Once they reached the rose garden, he broke off and headed toward the stables without another word.

Once in her room, she drew herself a scalding bath. When she eased her body into the Jacuzzi tub, she imagined the hot water burning away all traces of Cass's touch from her skin.

Eventually they would have to be intimate. They both wanted children. But she had several years before she would be ready for a family of her own. Perhaps it would be better to postpone any intimacies until they'd gotten to know each other better.

Because if just a kiss was an indication of how quickly she could fall under the spell of physical passion, she needed time to fortify herself.

She would not risk losing her heart to her husband.

CHAPTER ELEVEN

CASS WATCHED BRIONY out of the corner of his eye as she surveyed a painting on the gallery wall. His fingers tightened on his champagne glass as his gaze drifted over the dark green gown, laced and fitted to her slender body like a glove.

He took a sip of his drink and grimaced as the bubbles hit his tongue. Where was a good whiskey when you needed one?

The last week had been perfect. He'd only seen Briony in public settings, in the dining room or Alaric's office. He had kept all temptation off the table. He'd focused on his committees, on working with Alaric to distribute funds, and had kept his interactions with his fiancée professional and brief.

Until he'd screwed it up. Again.

When she'd challenged him to go sledding, he'd been raw inside, not thinking straight when he'd decided to show her that he wasn't a stuffed shirt or whatever idiom she'd used. The moment he'd sat down behind her, felt her incredible body relax against him, heard her sparkling laugh as they'd raced down the hillside, he'd felt more alive than he had in years.

And then he'd landed on top of her, she'd whispered "Yes…" and the world had exploded. He hadn't been able to stop touching her, kissing her, tasting her. If they had been somewhere private and not surrounded by snow, he wouldn't have been able to stop himself from stripping her naked and sliding inside her incredible body.

His eyes narrowed as he watched Briony walk over to another painting, her head tilted to one side. It was better that he had walked away, for both their sakes. His past sexual encounters had been enjoyable. But no woman had inspired such lust in him. Before they had sex—*not made love*—he would have to find a way to támp down the physical passion he felt for Briony. He wanted to enjoy his marriage, yes.

But too much of such raging intensity could lead into territory he wanted no part of.

Out of the corner of his eye, he saw Briony drift toward an open door with a sign above that read Artistes Linnaea. Her strong, confident movements were offset by the voluminous skirts, which gave her the appearance of gliding into the gallery. Her red curls had been wound into an intricate updo on top of her head, baring her neck to his gaze.

For a moment, he entertained the notion of loosening his self-control just a bit, allowing himself to embrace some of the feelings Briony inspired.

But like a well-tuned weapon, the image of Aunt Alecine sprang to mind, her shoulders shaking as she cried into her hands and told him over and over again that she was sorry for ever being stupid enough to fall in love.

As he took another sip of champagne and steeled himself to rejoin his fiancée, his aunt's sobs echoed in his mind, each remembered cry strengthening his resolve to not make the same mistake.

She couldn't take her eyes off the painting in front of her. A dirt road meandered through fields of golden grain.

In the distance, against purple-blue mountains and trees tinged red, the palace of Linnaea stood tall and proud. A little girl stood off to the side, hair tossed in the wind as she kept one arm wrapped around the neck of a brown dog.

"What do you think?"

She turned to see a thin man, sporting round spectacles and a nervous smile. Dressed in a faded but clean collared shirt and dark pants, he looked out of place among the sea of costly clothes and jewels worn by the other guests.

She liked him immediately.

"It's beautiful. I was never good at art, but this is spectacular. And unlike some of the other art here, I can..." She paused, searching for the right words. "I don't know, it's like I can feel the painting. Feel the wind, the autumn chill."

The man flushed as his smile grew. "That's so good to hear."

She returned his smile. "I'm assuming you're the artist?"

"Hugo Verne, ma'am. Yes, it's my first work to be hung anywhere other than my living room or a local fair."

"You certainly earned it." She glanced back at the painting. "Is the little girl your daughter?"

His flush deepened with pleasure. "*Oui*, my daughter, Lorraine. She spends a lot more time with me at home since the school closed."

"I'm so sorry. Not having a school must be hard."

Sadness crossed Hugo's face.

"Most of the schools outside Eira closed within the last few years. We were told it was too expensive to operate."

The uncomfortable sensation that had settled in Briony's stomach when she'd walked into the museum and seen the opulent spending on everything from the mahogany floors to the white marble columns burst into full-blown anger. What had Daxon been thinking with constructing something this grand when the country couldn't even offer schooling?

"I'm so sorry."

"It's not your fault, ma'am. It could be worse."

"Still, something's being done."

Hugo's expression brightened a little. "I'm a little more hopeful after I heard about the marriage between King Daxon's daughter and a prince. I wasn't able to come into the city last week, but I've heard wonderful things about her."

Briony's stomach twisted. Hearing firsthand from someone outside the palace that marrying Cass actually had the power to enact change was both gratifying and terrifying. Gratifying in that, after so many of years of drifting through life without purpose, she had the power to do something. Terrifying because if she failed, she would always remember the hopeful light in Hugo's eyes and the painting of a little girl with her arm wrapped around her dog.

She sipped on her drink before she answered.

"I hope the marriage makes things better for everyone."

Hugo nodded eagerly. "I'm sure there will be some positive changes." He leaned in, dropping his voice to a conspirator's whisper. "I just hope she isn't like King Daxon. The man likes to spend money."

Briony chuckled. "I've heard she's nothing like him."

Awareness pricked the back of her neck. Without turning, she knew Cass had entered the room.

"Ah, Princess Briony." Cass's deep voice echoed in the cavernous room. "Admiring the local talent?"

Hugo's mouth dropped open before he clapped it shut and bowed so quickly at the waist Briony feared he would snap in half.

"Prince Cassius, may I introduce Hugo Verne, the artist behind this beautiful watercolor," Briony said as she turned to greet her fiancé.

Dear Lord, he's handsome. Dressed in a tuxedo cut perfectly for his muscular frame, midnight-black hair combed back to show the carved architecture of his face, just laying eyes on him after less than thirty minutes apart made her heart beat faster.

Cass stopped next to her and observed the poor painter with an arched brow.

"Your Highness," he gasped, "I beg your forgiveness, I meant no disrespect, I just—"

"Hugo," Briony broke in as she grasped his hand and gently urged him to straighten, "you're fine. I'm still getting used to all this royal business anyway."

"But...but I insulted—"

"On the subject of how money is spent in this country, you and I are in total agreement," Briony said with a reassuring smile. "And on that note, my suite is unfortunately bare. Do you have any other paintings of the Linnaean countryside I could purchase?"

Hugo's mouth dropped open again. "You want...my painting...in the *palace*?"

"Yes, please."

"Of—of course! I can't believe..." His voice trailed off, and he ran a hand through this pale hair. "How shall I...?"

"Why don't you stop by the palace tomorrow afternoon? I'd love to see more pictures of your work and learn more about what the education needs are in Linnaea. The council I'm assembling has a lot of experience to offer, but I'd enjoy hearing firsthand from parents."

She felt Cass tense beside her, but she ignored him.

"Yes, Your Highness," Hugo gushed.

"Now that that's settled, Hugo, how about you go grab

yourself a glass of champagne before you keel over," Cass suggested.

"I will, sir. I mean, Your Highness. Your Highnesses," Hugo stuttered before he gave them both another bow and departed the room, excitement vibrating off his skeleton-thin frame.

"You've already managed to snag one fan, it appears."

Briony shot Cass a teasing glance. "Do I detect jealousy, sir?"

"From a starving artist who could barely talk to you once he realized who you were? Not likely."

"Unfortunately 'starving' sounds all too accurate," Briony murmured as she resumed studying the painting.

She started when Cass laid a hand on her waist. But then slowly she relaxed, allowing herself to enjoy the small contact and draw strength from his touch.

"He told you about his daughter's school."

She nodded. "He did. I knew they'd closed from the members of the council. But hearing it from a parent who was affected…" Her voice trailed off as she looked up at the carvings crisscrossing the ceiling, the elegant chandelier in the next room. "What on earth was Daxon thinking?"

"I don't think he was."

Before she could question him further, a small group of people entered the gallery. They curtsied and congratulated Briony and Cass on their engagement. More people filled the room as they realized the long-lost princess of Linnaea was inside. Questions started to fly, everything from whether Briony had really been a bartender to queries on the wedding.

"Thank you for coming tonight," Cass finally said diplomatically, raising his voice just enough to command the attention of the room. Briony watched as he took control of the crowd. The sensation in her chest when he stepped into the role of confident leader had nothing to do with physical desire and everything to do with admiration.

"After a long day, you'll understand if I escort the princess back to the palace," Cass finished with a winning smile.

He snaked an arm around Briony's waist and navigated through the crowds. They paused near a beautiful silver sculpture of a tree. Briony inhaled deeply before taking the last sip of her drink.

"That doesn't look like champagne."

Briony shot Cass a smug grin. "Brandy old-fashioned."

"Where did you get that?"

"It helps to get acquainted with the bartender."

Cass huffed. "Next time, perhaps you would be so courteous as to get me one, too, so I'm not drinking this sparkling stuff."

She rolled her eyes and held out her glass. She'd expected him to take it. But instead, he cupped her hand in his and brought the glass to his lips, keeping his eyes trained on her as he drank. Her heart hammered in her chest. The intimacy of the act left her breathless.

"That tastes very good," Cass murmured as he released his grip.

"Um…yes…yes, it does."

This time he didn't put an arm around her waist as they continued on through the museum. But he did stay close, whispering the names of dignitaries and members of the Linnaean parliament in her ear as they came up to meet her and congratulate her on the engagement. Each subtle murmur of support calmed some of her nervousness. She was much more at ease conversing with someone like Hugo than the well-dressed masses before her.

"You're doing great."

Cass's whisper made her spine straighten as her smile widened. His encouragement and support sent a much-needed jolt of confidence through her veins. She was, she realized, enjoying her time with him, despite feeling like a fish out of water among the gilded crowd of Linnaea's upper crust.

Perhaps Cass was right, she thought with a small, relieved smile. Perhaps she could enjoy her marriage.

At last, they reached the grand entrance.

"Ready to go home?"

A small smile tugged at Briony's lips. Even though she still got turned around fairly regularly in the palace's corridors, the upstairs hallway that housed the royal family, the family dining room and the library had quickly become familiar and comforting to her. It was nice to have a home again.

"Yes."

Cass's gaze lingered on her for a moment before he helped her into her snow-white coat. He grabbed her hand and guided her down the red carpeted steps out into the snowy night.

Briony barely registered the crowd rushing at her before a light bulb went off in her face.

"Princess Briony, how do you feel about the closure of the hospital in Levrouz?"

"Did you know about the shutdown of the rural schools?"

"Do you think art is more important than paying the wages of national employees?"

The questions flew at her like barbed arrows, each one landing with a piercing blow. Shame washed over her as she looked down to blink the light from her eyes and saw the skirt of her dress. The dress that most likely cost thousands of dollars. How many people could that have helped?

Cass swore beside her before he stepped protectively between her and the photographers and reporters.

"Go back inside," he ordered over his shoulder.

"I'm not leaving you alone to deal with this," Briony retorted. "Can't I say something to—"

Her words were cut off as one of the ropes keeping the crowd back gave way. People surged forward, pushing past the overwhelmed security guards lining the aisle in their zest to get up close and personal with the mysterious princess. She took a step back, one heel catching in the voluminous folds of her skirt. Her arms pinwheeled in the air as she fell backward. A moment later she fell against the stairs, a startled cry escaping her lips.

A horrified silence descended on the crowd. Cass whirled around and knelt down next to her.

"Briony," he breathed, his voice strained. "God, Briony, stay still."

A flashbulb went off. Cass started to turn, murderous intent gleaming in his eyes, but Briony put a hand on his arm.

"Don't." Slowly, she sat up, wincing at the pain in her back. "I didn't hit too hard, and I didn't even hit my head."

"You're seeing a doctor when we get back to the palace," Cass said firmly.

Briony held her tongue. Arguing in front of reporters armed with cameras was not the best strategy.

More security guards poured out of the museum and pushed the crowds back. Cass scooped Briony up into his arms, stalked down the aisle and set her gently in the back of the limo waiting for them. He circled around, gave the driver a terse order in French as he got inside and then turned his attention back to Briony.

"You're certain you didn't hit your head?"

"Yes, I'm sure. Stop treating me like a child."

Cass's face was grim. "I never would have escorted you out the front had I known that would happen."

"But you didn't know, so stop blaming yourself."

"You still have a lot to learn about me, Briony." He leaned closer, his fingers sliding into her hair as he gently felt the back of her head. Her eyes drifted shut as she savored the feel of his touch.

"Such as?"

"Such as when I make a mistake, I ensure it's corrected." Her eyes flew open.

"What do you mean?" she asked warily.

Cass's smile flashed white in the darkness of the limo.

"It means that until the palace doctor gives you a clean bill of health, I won't be leaving your side tonight."

CHAPTER TWELVE

CASS CAST ANOTHER glance toward the closed door of the bathroom. After the palace doctor had given her a thorough physical examination and pronounced her healthy aside from a few bruises, she'd told Cass she was going to take a hot bath.

That had been over an hour ago.

Where had his legendary patience disappeared to? He wanted to check on her, make sure she was okay not just physically but also emotionally. Being attacked by reporters in such a callous manner couldn't have been easy.

The door to the bathroom creaked open. Briony emerged, her body wrapped in a fluffy white bathrobe and her hair caught up in an equally fluffy towel.

"You're still here."

"You sound disappointed," Cass replied as he looked back at the book he'd plucked from one of her shelves. He'd barely read five pages of it.

"More just wondering why."

She sat in a chair near the fireplace and held out her hands to the flames. With her makeup washed off and her skin bare, she still looked beautiful, but more innocent, ethereal.

Guilt returned in full force. He'd dragged her into this

life. If it hadn't been for his grand scheme, she wouldn't have been anywhere near that museum tonight.

"I'm still here because I needed to say I'm sorry."

Her head whipped around, her eyes widening in surprise.

"Sorry?" she repeated.

"If it hadn't been for me, you wouldn't have been at the museum tonight."

"Okay."

"And you wouldn't have been attacked."

She stared at him for a long moment.

"Do you feel…guilty?"

There was an odd note in her voice, but he ignored it, plowing forward with what he knew needed to be said.

"I do. Most of my thoughts were focused on the treaty and reclaiming my family's standing. Incidents like what happened tonight didn't even cross my mind."

"Cass, you couldn't have predicted this."

"I should have predicted this," he snapped back. "I should have anticipated something like this happening."

He'd spent the majority of the last nineteen years planning, ensuring that things would go right. When there was a plan, little could go wrong. When the details took center stage instead of emotions, there was little risk of failure. Even though so many people saw him as a playboy prince, in truth, he was a meticulous businessman who kept himself and those he allowed into his close circle in check.

But not tonight. Tonight he had been so focused on the stunning woman who had listened to a poor painter and finagled a brandy cocktail out of the bartender that he hadn't sensed the anger and resentment seething in the crowd outside until it had nearly been too late.

Yes, she was all right. But she could have not been.

Those bruises could have been on her face if someone in the crowd had given in to their rage....

"Cass!"

He jerked out of the dark hole he'd descended into as one warm hand settled on his and another settled on his face.

"Are you okay?"

Briony's face came into focus, her eyes concerned, her brows drawn together in a worried frown.

"Yes." He started to push her away, but when he laid his hand on top of hers, his fingers slid across her skin. God help him, he couldn't pull away.

He wasn't sure who moved first. He didn't really care. All he knew was that one moment they were staring at each other and the next their lips were fused together in the most incredible kiss he'd ever experienced. He stood and pulled Briony to her feet, their mouths never parting as he gently unwound the towel from her hair and sank his hands into the damp tresses. She moaned, her lips parting beneath his as her hands slid under his jacket, her fingers splaying across his chest and burning through the material of his shirt.

His hand drifted down her neck, eliciting a sigh that filled him with an ecstasy he couldn't even begin to describe. His fingers drifted over the softness of her robe, grazed the base of her throat, then went lower still...until he paused. He wanted to feel her, all of her, finally claim what he had been dreaming about for weeks. But did he deserve it? She may have forgiven him for his deception, but she had one of the most innocent natures he'd ever encountered, despite the hardship life had dealt her. If he touched her, claimed her body after what he'd done, would that make him like the other monsters who had taken advantage of her?

Her back arched. One corner of her robe slid off her shoulder, and his fingers fell onto the full swell of her breast. He groaned as he cupped her in his hand, a finger sliding gently over her nipple and savoring the tightening as her hips thrust against his. Torn between wanting to relish the moment and wanting to see her naked, he wrenched his lips from hers. Her frustrated growl slid into a satisfied sigh as he pressed his mouth to her cheekbone, trailed his way down her neck and then captured one taut nipple in his mouth. Each suck, each delicate nibble, each moan made his blood burn so hot he was amazed they didn't both burst into flames.

As he turned his attention to her other breast, her own hands made quick work of the buttons on his shirt. He nearly came undone when her fingers found his bare chest.

"You feel so good," she murmured into his hair as she struggled to tug his jacket, then his shirt off.

He lifted his head, ripped the clothes off his torso, then yanked the robe completely off her shoulders before he captured her in his arms once more. As her naked breasts pressed against his chest, he kissed her. Each press of his lips to hers spoke what he couldn't admit to himself…

You are mine.

When her hand drifted lower and slid down the growing bulge in his trousers, he groaned. Somehow, he summoned enough will to pull back.

"Briony…are you sure?"

She surged forward, throwing her arms around his neck as she kissed him again. He leaned down, slid his arms beneath her thighs and picked her up. He nearly lost it when she wrapped her long legs around his waist and pressed her body against his. They moved to the bed, tongues dueling, hands caressing, hearts pounding.

His legs hit the edge of the bed. He knelt down, slowly

easing her back onto the mattress. Finally, she let go of her hold around his waist. He pulled back slightly, smoothed the hair back from her forehead. Emerald eyes glowed at him with a lust so intense he could barely stand the hardness between his thighs. He wanted to take her— *now*—but he would not rush. Not the first time he made his future wife truly his. He would erase every memory of any other man she'd ever been with. Regardless of the business nature of their arrangement, he would ensure that the intimate nature of their marriage would be more than satisfactory.

When he fully straightened, Briony let out a mewl of protest that quickly descended into a sigh of appreciation as he unzipped his pants and shoved them down his hips. Her eyes flared as he bared his body to his gaze.

At last, he was naked. Her appreciative smile made him feel like a god.

"You're beautiful." She winced. "I mean, handsome."

He chuckled as he knelt on the bed once more.

"Thank you. So are you." He slid one hand along the folds of her robe still tied about her waist. "Your turn."

Briony swallowed hard. Was she ready for this? Did she truly want tonight to be her first time? Just hours ago, she had been reminding herself to keep her distance from Cass, to not let herself get too involved.

As she looked up at Cass's magnificent body looming over hers, she knew with a certainty that yes, she wanted this. Needed this.

She smiled and nodded. Cass reached down, undid the belt of her robe and slowly parted the material. Her hands fisted in the silky sheets of the bed as she waited with bated breath.

"Stunning."

Her entire body warmed as Cass breathed out the one word. And then he moved with lightning speed to lean down, caging her between his arms as he sucked her nipple into his mouth. She arched off the bed with a little shriek as he made love to her breasts, sucking and nipping and kissing.

"Cass, please," she whispered as a tension started to build inside her, somewhere deep that made her ache.

He chuckled against her skin.

"Soon, *belle*."

His lips trailed lower, over her stomach and her hips, down farther still to the juncture of her thighs. When he kissed her *there*, she came undone, sensation spiraling through her body as she cried out and buried her hands in his hair, unable to take any more pleasure but not wanting him to stop.

Finally, her body went limp, sinking into the welcoming embrace of her bed as Cass trailed little kisses over her thighs, her hips, back up her stomach. He kissed each of her nipples, the slopes of her breasts, her neck.

"Briony."

She opened her eyes and smiled lazily at him. Was it even possible to feel so relaxed? So sated?

"That was incredible."

He smoothed her hair back from her forehead again, a simple gesture, but a tender one that made her eyes grow hot.

"Just wait."

Before she could reply, she felt his hardness press against her core. She sucked in a breath, anticipation and nervousness tangling together as she instinctively spread her thighs. When she felt him slowly start to slip in, she sighed with contentment as their bodies started to join. How amazing to feel him—

"Ow!"

She winced as he drove himself inside her. Cass froze, his eyes widening.

"Briony?"

"Mm-hmm?"

"Is there something you forgot to tell me?"

"Like what?"

"That you're a virgin?" Cass ground out.

"Was a virgin," she corrected.

"And you didn't think that was a pertinent fact?"

"I got a little distracted."

"You should have told me."

She sighed. "I wanted to give this to you."

He blinked, a subtle gesture but one that spoke volumes to her about how much her answer had surprised him.

"You what?"

She inhaled and then wiggled a little. The pain had already started to recede, leaving her with a full sensation between her legs.

Cass groaned. "Don't move."

"Isn't that what you're supposed to do?"

She couldn't tell whether he laughed or groaned.

"It is, but had I known you had never experienced this before, I would have handled things in a different manner."

She wriggled her hips once more. Not only had the pain nearly disappeared, but a little of the earlier excitement and sensation was slowly starting to return. Feeling emboldened by her new foray into the world of physical passion, she ran her fingers up over the backs of his thighs, over his rear and up his back. Cass sucked in a breath.

"Briony, if you keep that up, I might do something drastic."

She leaned up, thrilling to the sensation of the hair on his chest scraping against the delicate skin of her breasts.

"I'd love to feel something drastic," she whispered against his lips before she kissed him.

Cass didn't waste another minute. He withdrew from her, then slid back in with one long, agonizingly slow stroke. She raised her hips, trying to take him deep, deeper, deeper still as his tempo increased.

The tension returned, coiling even tighter as Cass moved inside her. Her hands drifted all over his body before coming up to frame his face.

"I love how you feel inside me."

Cass leaned down and kissed her, a raw, possessive passion that set off a chain reaction inside her. Heat burst between her thighs before spinning out through her veins, setting her nerve endings on fire as she cried out against his mouth. A few moments later, Cass groaned her name as he found his own release. He leaned down, pressed another gentle kiss to her lips and then rolled to the side.

She lay there for a moment, wondering what one did next in a situation like this. It was her room, so she wouldn't leave. Did she ask him to leave? Or would he just know to since he'd done this sort of thing before? Even if the thought of him leaving made her feel disappointed.

Cass slid an arm beneath her bare torso and pulled her across the bed. She gasped as his naked body pressed fully against her. He tucked her head into the crook of his arm, his hand drifting lazily through her hair.

"Tell me again why you decided not to mention that you had never been with another man."

"You distracted me."

She bit down on her lower lip. She was not going to make excuses or apologize for her lack of experience.

"So it's my fault?" he asked, a teasing note in his voice that relaxed her.

"Yes." She sighed again, a soft sound of satisfaction.

"I feel like the last couple years of my life, people have wanted something from me. My relationships have been more transactional, what I could do for them."

Cass stiffened at her side.

"I wasn't any better."

"You were different. You told me up-front. Mostly up-front," she amended. "But you never portrayed our marriage as anything but what it would be." She rolled over and cupped his face. He flinched, but she didn't let him pull back.

"I know we'll never be a grand love story. I've accepted that. Tonight, before we went outside, I was enjoying my time with you. I've learned so much about myself, about what I want to do with my life and how I can make a difference here. I have you to thank for that." She smiled at him. "So much of my identity was caught up in my family, in being the person I thought they wanted so I could have their love, that I never bothered to ask what I wanted. And what I wanted tonight was you."

She rolled back onto her back and stared up at the ceiling, for some inexplicable reason slightly embarrassed by what she had to say next.

"I wanted you tonight. I know you wanted me, too, but you haven't pursued it. You haven't made sex a part of our agreement. That made me want it, and you, more. It wasn't transactional. It didn't have any bearing on our contract." She inhaled deeply. "It was just…fun."

And soul-stirringly amazing. When the pain had faded and he'd started to move inside her, she felt not only the response of her body but the response of her heart. How long would she be able to keep her growing feelings for her future husband at bay?

"Fun," Cass repeated in a flat tone.

She turned her head and smiled at him.

"Very fun."

His chuckle sounded both surprised and a little non-plussed.

"I'm glad I could make your first experience fun."

They lay there for a moment in intimate silence. Her eyes drifted shut, and she was on her way to falling asleep when his voice broke the stillness.

"Why did you wait?"

"Hmm?"

"Why did you wait?"

"I was waiting for the man I would fall in love with," Briony murmured. "Since I can't have that, the next best thing is the man I'm marrying."

She registered the slight stiffening of his body. But she was too tired to ask questions, too tired to do anything but let the pull of exhaustion take her into deep slumber.

CHAPTER THIRTEEN

C ASS GLANCED AT Briony as she watched the numbers on the elevator light up, signaling their descent to the lower level of the palace. Tonight was the dinner with the ambassador from Switzerland and his family, as well as several other dignitaries. It was the final royal event not associated with the wedding. Clara had cleared their calendars next week for nothing but confirming details, completing rehearsals and keeping their time free for the "numerous last-minute things that are bound to come up," as Clara had put it.

He should be concerned that he was looking forward to spending more time with Briony. And not just time, but time confirming tablecloth colors and floral arrangements. His engagement was starting to feel all too real. He could better appreciate the emotional hell his aunt must have gone through because it was all too easy to submit to the temptation of a relationship.

It wasn't just that they'd had sex. Briony was not one to linger in the background, reserving her time for shopping and lunch dates like his mother had. The same dedication she'd exhibited when taking care of her stepfamily had shown itself once more as she had taken her conversation with Hugo at the museum and run with it. Her committee had met every day in the past two weeks. She'd hosted a town hall for parents and even invited schoolchildren to the palace to share what they wanted out of their new school.

She was thriving. And the more she accomplished, the more captivated he became.

Even now, as she looked up at him with a small smile, Cass had to force himself to look away and not stare too much at his future bride.

Almost wife. In just over a month, she would be his wife. The past twenty-one days had flown by. The nights, however…

He'd woken up in Briony's bed after that first night to find it empty. He'd finally caught up with her in the ballroom with Clara discussing the timeline of their reception. Briony had been surprisingly distant. He didn't know what bothered him more, that he was bothered by her distance or that she had done exactly what she had said she would—not have any hope about theirs being any type of a love match.

A point made even worse by her words as she'd fallen asleep. He wasn't what she wanted, a man who could never fall in love. No, he was the "next best thing."

She deserved everything she wanted and more.

That night, he'd gone to bed alone. The following night, however, he'd been preparing for bed when a soft knock had sounded on his door. He'd opened it to find Briony in the hallway.

"I want you."

He should have said no. But he didn't, telling himself it was a natural part of their relationship, that they wouldn't produce heirs by practicing abstinence. Excuses, all, for what he knew deep down was the real reason: he wanted her just as badly. As soon as the door had closed, she'd thrown herself into his arms, kissing him with an unrestricted passion that had set his body on fire.

It had been much like that every night since. Meetings during the day, each of them pursuing their own royal agendas, and wild sex at night. Just last night, she'd sunk to her knees in the shower and taken him in her mouth, her tongue flicking over him as he'd fisted his hands in her hair and willed himself to hold on long enough to sink his length deep into her willing body.

He had everything he wanted laid before him: his revenge, the glimmers of hope for Linnaea's restoration, a fiancée who involved herself in the country's operations and who enjoyed sex almost as much as, if not more than, he did.

Yet with every shared laugh, every moment spent together, every casual caress, his uneasiness at his own lack of control and his guilt at how, once more, Briony had given up something she wanted grew.

The elevator doors slid open to reveal Clara, poised and ready as usual with her phone in one hand and tablet in another. But tonight, she looked different.

"You're wearing color," Cass said with surprise.

The tiniest blush tinged Clara's cheeks as she glanced down at the deep blue gown wrapped around her frame.

"Is it too much?"

He started to respond with his usual quips, but the uncertainty in her eyes stopped him.

"No. You look beautiful, Clara."

The pink deepened into red as her mouth curved up into the first real smile he'd ever seen on her. It transformed her entire visage and made him blink in surprise.

"Thank you, Your Highness." Clara directed her smile to Briony. "And thank you. I never would have worn it without your encouragement."

Briony reached out and squeezed Clara's hand as they started to walk down the hall.

"Cass is right. You look stunning."

Clara cleared her throat and pulled up a document on her tablet. Seconds later she was back to her usual self, rattling off facts about the upcoming dinner.

"You met his wife and daughter yesterday during lunch. His daughter is a student…"

Several minutes later, they reached the main dining room. Briony slid her hand into the crook of his elbow, a gesture that had become comforting and familiar. He reached down and squeezed her fingers.

"Ready?"

"Ready."

The dinner flew by. The Swiss ambassador and Alaric spent most of their time in quiet conversation at the head of the table. Briony chatted with the ambassador's wife and daughter. Cass spoke with two members of parliament at length about the trade agreements with Tulay. From what little he could hear of Daxon's conversations with the minister of the treasury, he was trying to make a case for money being allotted for a new resort in the mountains. Every now and then, he caught Briony's narrowed eyes as she glanced at her father.

How could the man be so blind? He had a son who would be a good leader for the people, a fact Cass had learned working so closely with Alaric the last three weeks. And he had a daughter who had not just overcome the most heart-wrenching disappointments but thrived as she continued to put others first.

The courses flew by: braised endive salad, scallops with caviar cream, and roasted venison with confit potatoes.

As their servers brought out plates of ginger cake topped with creamy icing and served with cinnamon apples on the side, Daxon's words carried across the table during a lull in the conversation.

"We could capture some of the tourists that go to Amsterdam or Rotterdam. We just need to make that initial investment."

"I think that's a great idea," Briony broke in.

Daxon smiled at her across the table, a smile that reminded Cass of a shark eyeing its prey.

"Thank you, my dear."

"Especially if the resort were to be located in Dhara or Candon," she continued. "I spoke with parents from those towns and their primary sources of income have all but dried up. A resort—"

"I would prefer to keep the resort close to Eira," Daxon interrupted, his smile turning patronizing. "It's a quaint notion, but Dhara and Candon have none of the luxury Eira can offer."

"I disagree. I haven't been to Dhara or Candon personally, and I would want to ensure the people would welcome a resort, but both areas offer mountains, lakes and towns that could thrive with an influx of tourist dollars."

Daxon's expression tightened, his skin stretching even further over his skull as he attempted to keep a smile on his face.

"Daughter, you've made quite an impression on the public, and some headway on your little project with the schools. That's good. But you don't have the experience to evaluate such a big investment."

"And I disagree with that."

Heads swung around to watch Cass as he speared Daxon with an icy gaze. His fingers tightened around the stem of his wineglass, the fragile material a reminder to keep a hold on his temper.

"Your daughter has proven to have an exceptional knack for evaluating Linnaea's weaknesses and proposing reasonable solutions that don't tax the treasury."

The barb hit its mark, Daxon's eyes narrowing to slits.

"While Eira has a lot to offer tourists, diversifying would be in our best interests to fully develop the entire country. And as Her Highness has said, getting the opinion of the people is paramount to success. It's why her work on the education system has been so widely welcomed. She has not only intelligence but a genuine interest in helping others."

"Not to mention time training in education with an American university," Alaric broke in.

"All excellent points." Everyone swung their gazes down to the Swiss ambassador, who nodded approvingly at Briony. "The Federal Council has admired the initial work being done to restore Linnaea's schools. It's still early, but if progress like that continues, I foresee a prosperous future for our two nations."

Daxon was many things, but he wasn't stupid. He inclined his head to Briony.

"My apologies, my dear. I certainly didn't mean to imply that you had not accomplished a great deal during your time here. And I welcome any suggestions you have on how to better benefit our rural regions."

Conversations slowly returned to normal around the table. Cass kept his eyes trained on Daxon, waiting in case the bastard chose to say something else foolish or hurtful. But the king simply resumed finishing his dessert.

Cass started as a hand wrapped around his under the table and squeezed. He glanced over to see Briony smiling at him with such warmth and affection in her emerald depths it made his chest ache.

"Thank you," she whispered.

You're in too deep.

He knew he was. He knew he had foolishly gone down

the same path his aunt had, was succumbing too quickly to the emotions Briony created in him.

But when she made him feel like a knight in shining armor who could conquer the stars with just two simple words, how was he supposed to resist?

"You can call me Father at events like this, you know," Daxon said quietly with a smile that he probably meant to be paternal but instead looked forced. They had all gathered in the library after dinner and were enjoying cocktails as the evening wound down.

"I don't think we've spent enough time together for me to call you that just yet," Briony replied as kindly as she could manage.

Rage flashed in Daxon's eyes, an unexpected fire that transformed him from cool, distant monarch to almost unhinged. Her previous hurt over how they'd met and his cool distance in the prior weeks seemed like a faint memory. Why had she ever wanted a relationship with him?

"Don't cause a scene," he hissed.

"I'm not," she shot back. "You're the one who's about to embarrass yourself."

"At least I'm not marrying the nephew of a traitor," he spat back in a fierce whisper.

Her lips parted in shock. "From what Cass said, you spent money that wasn't yours. I would say that makes you the traitor."

"I was going to pay it back. I just needed more time." His lips tightened. "Alecine got everything she deserved and more, and so did that bastard of a brother of hers and his little brat. Cass's father fed her information, I'm sure of it. Had they stayed, I would have had them all thrown in prison for treason."

The depths of Daxon's viciousness, not to mention his complete lack of remorse, rendered her mute.

"Come now, my dear." Daxon's tight grip was no doubt leaving fingerprints on her waist. "She had to pay."

"Somehow I don't trust your version of events." She managed to push back and put some distance between them. "And even if she had, that was no reason to punish an eleven-year-old boy."

"If I had only gone after her, that wouldn't have sent a message. I needed to make it clear that no one would get away with crossing me."

Pride swelled in Bri's chest as her eyes found Cass. He stood on the edge of the room, arms crossed, eyes narrowed as he watched them talk.

"No one had the guts to stand up to you until Cass."

The rage returned, more intense than before. "He didn't stand up to me. He backed me into a corner. I had no choice but to agree."

"Agreed to use your own daughter as a bargaining chip to solve the problems you created."

"You're just like your mother," he sneered. "Idealistic. A dreamer."

"That's the best compliment anyone has ever given me." She turned, about to walk away, then paused.

"I know now why Mom never told me about you. And I have to say, I'm glad."

With that parting comment, she walked away and circled the room, bidding good-night to the ambassador, his family and the other guests. Clara had fetched Alaric earlier. Judging by the glower on his face, it had not been for anything good. But before he'd quit the room, he'd come to her side and squeezed her hand.

"You are an integral part of this family now. Do not let our sire convince you otherwise."

Tears pricked her eyes. How could she have been so blind all these years, always fantasizing about the father she never had, pinning her hopes on Trey or reminiscing about the few good times she'd had with her stepsisters? All people who only gave out love if they got something they wanted. Transactional relationships she had gone along with, always focusing on what she didn't have instead of what she did, like the love of her mother who had gone to incredible lengths to keep her child safe.

Her gaze swung to Cass. He was talking with the minister of the treasury by the door, nodding at something the minister said but watching her with an intensity that made her catch her breath. Their relationship may have started out as a political alliance, but it had changed, deepened even before they'd made love. Tonight, when he'd defended her with pride in his voice, she'd known in that moment she was well and truly lost.

She was in love. She was in love with her future husband, and she didn't know what to do about it.

CHAPTER FOURTEEN

CASS BADE GOODNIGHT to the minister and the ambassador before he followed Briony out into the hall. As she'd been saying her goodbyes, he'd seen her eyes swing to him, a shell-shocked expression in her gaze. Before he could discern what was going on, she'd left.

"Briony."

Briony paused but didn't turn to face him. His eyes dipped down to her back, her skin visible beneath the turquoise lace. His exhale came out harsh. Now was not the time to be entertaining risqué thoughts.

"Are you all right?" he asked as he circled around and looked down at her.

She slowly raised her gaze up to his. Something flickered deep in her eyes.

"I am. It was just a longer night than I had anticipated."

"He had no right to embarrass you like that."

The corners of her mouth tilted up into a faint smile. "Thank you again for defending me."

"Of course."

Her face softened, her eyes coming alive with gratitude and that affection he'd glimpsed when she'd leaned over to whisper her thanks. It was a sight that both electrified and terrified him.

"It was the right thing to do."

Her head snapped back as if she'd been slapped.

"The right thing to do?" she repeated.

"Yes." His body tensed, muscles tightening as his heart tried to resist his rational mind taking over. "We need to present a united front and ensure there is no question of the work either of us is doing."

She stared at him, her gaze opaque. He stared back. She needed to stop putting him up on a damned white horse and turning him into her knight in shining armor. He wasn't a hero. He was a strategist, a survivor.

She circled around him and continued toward the elevator. He stood for a minute, frozen in place that she would reject him in such a manner. Yes, his response had been cold. But it didn't warrant such a cutting rejection.

He turned and started after her. As she got into the elevator and saw him striding toward her, she regarded him with a burning gaze before reaching out and punching a button. The doors swished shut in his face.

He stared at the closed doors for a long moment. No one had ever walked away from him, much less closed a door in his face. He used the time the elevator traveled up and back down to breathe deeply and regain his sense of control. By the time he reached the doors to Briony's suite, he had his temper mostly back under control.

Mostly.

He knocked once.

"Go away."

He sighed as Briony's muffled voice traveled through the door.

"Briony, can we please talk?"

"There's nothing to talk about."

He tried the handle, surprised when it turned under his touch. The door swung open to reveal Briony slipping out of her dress, the material pooling about her feet and leaving her clad in nothing but black lace.

God, but she was beautiful. Slim legs, rounded hips, pert breasts straining against the cups of her bra. All he had to do was think about her and he stirred.

"Cass!"

She grabbed a blanket off the bed and wrapped it around her body.

"I did knock."

"And the door was closed!" she snapped.

"Should I go?"

She glared at him but didn't respond. He shut the door and walked into the room, taking slow, purposeful steps toward her. Judging by the blush creeping up her neck, she was just as affected as he was.

"In the Midwest, most people know a closed door means we don't want anyone coming in." Her teeth sank into her bottom lip as her gaze traveled down his body. Every step made him harder, amped up his desire until it took every ounce of willpower not to lunge forward and sweep her into his arms.

A distant warning sounded in his mind. This was what Aunt Alecine had told him about, this all-consuming passion that wiped out all rational thought and made one a fool. This was how she had fallen so low.

He pushed the warning away. He would address it later. Right now, he wanted her, his future wife, in his arms.

"You're not in the Midwest anymore, Briony." He stopped just a few inches away, not touching her, but inhaling her scent, savoring the heat from her body. Her quick inhale filled him with a want so deep he didn't know how he'd ever be able to sate it. "You're in Linnaea. And you're going to be my wife."

"A wife who will still slam the door in your face when you lie to me."

Her words were feisty, but her voice was breathy and heavy.

"I spoke the truth."

She shook her head. "I don't believe you. Why do you insist on keeping this distance between us? On trying to be the bad guy?"

He leaned down, his lips a heartbeat away from hers.

"I'm not trying, Briony. I am the bad guy."

With that, he kissed her. As soon as she started to kiss him back, he grabbed the blanket and wrenched it out of her grasp. She gasped as his hands trailed down her body, unclipping her bra in one quick movement and baring her breasts to his touch. She removed his tie with frantic grasps, then grabbed his shirt and ripped it down the middle, buttons flying across the room as she pressed her naked skin against his. He scooped her up into his arms and carried her to the thick rug in front of the fireplace. With the firelight dancing across her skin, her eyes glazed with passion as she reached up and cupped his face with her hand.

A thickness formed in his throat. When she looked at him like that, he wanted to be more than he was. He wanted to be capable of giving her what she wanted, the love story she deserved.

But since he couldn't do that, he could at least give her pleasure.

He removed the torn shirt, suit jacket and pants, then lay down next to her, sliding one arm beneath her body and cradling her against him. His fingers slid from her breasts, down her stomach to beneath the edge of the black lace panties that were driving him wild. He slid one finger down the middle of her molten heat, watching her face as her lips parted in ecstasy.

"Please!" she gasped.

He teased her, slipping one finger in and out, watching her arch and moan his name, her skin flushed as she neared the peak. Then, just before she went over the edge, he withdrew.

"Cass!" she half moaned, half laughed. He removed her panties, pressed a kiss to the sacred spot between her thighs, then moved up her body and slid inside her wet core, nearly coming undone as her body closed around him. He moved with slow, deliberate strokes, their tempo building as his body coiled, tight, tighter still. He would never get enough of her, could never have enough of the pleasure and joy she brought him.

She called out his name as she sailed into oblivion, wrapping her arms around him and hanging on as if he was her salvation instead of her curse. He whispered hers as he drove into her one last time as his release shuddered through his body.

He didn't know long they lay there, tangled in each other's bodies. When he finally raised his head, it was to see Briony looking up at him with questions in her eyes.

"What is it?"

"I've been doing a lot of thinking about my family. About Trey and the twins. My mom. Daxon."

He stroked a hand down her back, a touch designed to soothe away tension and provide comfort.

"A painful subject, I'm sure."

"I…" She sucked in a deep breath. "I have been focused on family for a long time, ever since my mom and Trey got married. At first it was trying to fit in and be who I thought Trey and the twins wanted me to be. How my mother loved me was the way all children should be loved, unconditionally."

"She should have seen that Trey wasn't being a good stepfather."

"Yes," Briony agreed with a nod. "But when she did confront him, I lied and pretended like everything was fine. I didn't want her to see how deeply Trey and I not forming a relationship hurt. After she passed, it went from trying to be who they wanted to trying to rescue them."

Cass smoothed a lock of hair out of her face, his hand lingering on her cheek. Her eyes fluttered shut as she pressed her face into his touch.

"Briony." He waited until she opened her eyes and met his gaze. He leaned down and touched his forehead to hers, the gesture somehow more intimate than many of the kisses he'd experienced in his life. "Your stepfather is a fool."

"He is," she agreed softly. "But so was I. I based myself on my family. I didn't take the time to get to know myself." She bowed her head. "And I thought that if I at least learned who my father was that it would make me whole. I was always looking for someone else to complete me."

Guilt hit him hard in the chest. His hand dropped from her face as he sat up and leaned back against the headboard, putting distance between them. He'd used her need to find out more about her family to manipulate her.

Coldness swept through him despite the warmth of the fire just feet away.

"I'm sorry things didn't turn out the way you wanted," he finally said.

Her hand came to rest on top of his. He watched with an almost horrified fascination as she wound her fingers through his, the emerald-and-topaz ring glinting in the firelight.

"I'm not."

His head jerked up. The tremulous smile on her face and the emotion brimming in her eyes set off dread in his heart that spread through his body like poison.

No. She can't possibly...

"Because your stepfamily is taken care of?" he asked with a casual indifference he didn't feel.

"No. Daxon turning out to be such a horrible person... it was freeing." She chuckled. "Learning what a horrible person he was, witnessing it for myself, it was like any desire I had to form a relationship with him just dried up. It was almost like when I made the decision to leave Kansas, as if chains had fallen off and I was suddenly free of this weight I'd created for myself. I had nothing but what I wanted out of my life. And the last couple of weeks, learning my royal duties, finding my passion again in working with the schools... I feel more like myself than I have since I was a child."

He suppressed a sigh of relief. Perhaps he had misunderstood what he'd read in her gaze. Perhaps she was just overcome with happiness at having a purpose.

"I'm glad."

"As am I." She brought his hand up, her fingers lightly dancing across his knuckles, the back of his hand in absent caresses that stoked the heat in his blood.

"Cass..." She sucked in a deep breath. "In finding my confidence, I also came to realize how important you've become to me. Not just because of what you've done for my stepfamily or because of what you're doing for Linnaea."

No. No, no, no.

"Briony—"

She placed a finger over his lips.

"Cass, please let me say this."

He watched her, not trusting himself to move. He

would either kiss her senseless or flee. Neither option was a good one.

"I want to marry you, Cass. Not because I have to, but because I want to. I feel like I belong here, like I've found my home. Part of it is Linnaea, but a large part of it is you." Her smile grew wider. "Because I—"

"Stop!"

Cass stood in one swift motion and pushed Briony's hand away as he stalked over to the window. He stared out over the frozen landscape, his chest rising and falling as his heart raced. She'd been on the verge of saying it, saying the words that would ruin everything.

He focused on the line of trees in the distance, followed their trunks and snow-covered branches with his eyes as he slowly distanced himself from the emotions waging war inside his chest. When he'd at last regained control, he slowly turned to face Briony.

She sat on her bed amid a tangle of sheets, shoulders thrown back with the confidence of royalty. Pride surged through his defenses. She was more of a royal than Daxon could ever hope to be.

She would have made an excellent partner.

He acknowledged that thought with a measure of regret before he quashed it and buried it deep.

"I regret to inform you, Briony, that I must terminate our arrangement."

To her credit, she didn't dissolve into tears or throw a fit like other past lovers had. No, she just continued to stare at him, eyes searching for answers he couldn't give.

"Why?" she finally asked, her voice low and surprisingly emotionless given that just moments ago she'd been on the verge of saying something quite emotional.

"The dynamics of our relationship have changed. We will no longer suit."

"Because of what I almost just said?"

"Yes. I cannot return the sentiments you almost shared."

She cocked her head. "I believe you already have."

His chuckle filled the room, dark and caustic.

"You're imagining things, Briony."

Her eyes narrowed. "Am I?" She tossed back the sheets and stood, crossing the room in measured steps. He tried to keep his gaze on her face and off the swells of her breasts, the nip of her waist, the curve of her thighs. Tried not to remember how perfectly she'd fit into his arms, how she'd made love to him with a trust and wild abandon he'd never experienced with any other lover.

"Your actions have spoken quite clearly in recent days."

"How so?"

"Spending time with me. Defending me in front of my father. Standing up for me to the paparazzi. Making love to me."

"Protecting my investment," he replied cruelly.

She stopped a mere foot away. Her sweet scent slid over his skin, sending a cascade of images through his head. Briony in her magnificent gown talking with a man just trying to survive. Briony refusing to back down in the face of the photographer. Briony standing up for the people of a country she hadn't even known existed a month ago. Briony, naked and shimmering beneath him as she cried out his name.

The ache of guilt was crushed beneath the weight of what he was about to do. What he had to do, he reminded himself as he summoned all of his strength. He couldn't give Briony what she wanted, what she deserved. She might consider herself in love with him now. But it wouldn't last when he couldn't return her affections. Their union would slowly dissolve from a respectful partnership to a prison of heartbreak and sorrow.

Briony had experienced enough of both to last a lifetime.

"How you held me just now," she whispered as she brought one hand up to touch his face.

He caught her wrist in an iron grasp.

"Briony, I used you. I've known for years how wretched Daxon is. I knew if I told you the truth, you'd never agree to the marriage contract."

"Why are you pushing me away?" she whispered.

"Because you love me and I don't love you."

The words had barely escaped before he longed to reach out and yank them back. Something felt wrong as he uttered them, a sense of imbalance deep in his soul.

Because you're a selfish bastard and you don't want to lose her.

Compassion and mercy blazed in her eyes, so strong and beautiful it almost hurt to look at her.

"Why can't you love me?" she asked softly.

"I've told you." He sounded ragged, torn up. The severity of his tone should have pushed her away, but damn it, she didn't back down.

"Yes, you have. Because of your aunt and your father. But you're not either of them, Cass."

She tugged her wrist free, and weakling that he was, he let her hand rest on his face, couldn't prevent the harsh exhale that escaped. Her palm warmed his skin, a simple touch but far more intimate than any liaison he'd ever experienced.

"I think your aunt and your father are just excuses."

His head snapped back, and he stepped out of her reach. "Excuses?"

She threw back her shoulders, the confident woman he'd first fallen for in the bar standing in full force before him.

"I can't imagine experiencing what you did. But I think

you're scared to be vulnerable. I think you use your aunt and father as a shield so you don't have to risk being hurt."

"Or I don't want to love you."

Silence fell. Even the crackling of the fireplace faded, overrun by the roaring in his ears that drowned out everything.

The words weren't entirely false. But they didn't tell the whole story. He didn't want to love Briony. But if he let himself, he would love her as he had never loved anyone, with his whole body and soul.

Briony was right. It wasn't just his father's and aunt's doomed relationships that held him back. It was a volatile mix of his own cowardice, guilt and a fear that he wasn't the man Briony deserved.

Briony's face shuttered, her eyes going blank. He was doing the right thing. Trapping her in a loveless marriage would be liking trapping a wild bird in a cage and watching it beats its wings against the bars day after day.

"I've enjoyed our time together, Briony. But as of tonight, our engagement is over."

"What about Linnaea?" she finally asked.

Amazingly, she still sounded calm, in control. And, of course, was thinking about others instead of herself.

"I'll figure out something."

Even if he didn't have all the answers right now, he would find them. Briony might suffer in the short term, but one day she would look back and realize that he had set her free. When she had a husband who loved her and children of her own, she would be grateful.

Just the thought of another man touching her, let alone having children with her, made his blood boil with rage.

"I will, of course, provide you with funds, too, so that you may..."

His voice trailed off as she shook her head.

"No, thank you. I will swallow my pride to accept your generosity regarding Trey's treatment, the mortgage and the twins' funds. But anything else would make me feel... bought and paid for."

"You are not a whore," he ground out.

"No, I'm not. But I appreciate your concurrence. And how much you've helped my family. Thank you, Cass."

The words were gracious, her tone soft as she turned and walked away from him. He wanted to go after her, to reach out and touch her one last time, to tell her how much she'd helped him focus on the future and let go of the past.

But he couldn't. One touch and he'd be lost.

She started to pull on her dress.

"I'll go."

"No." She held up a hand. "I need to take a walk, clear my head."

She finished dressing and went to the door. Her hand reached out, grasped the handle.

Go. Go now.

She glanced back at him, and he nearly staggered at the depth of love shining in her eyes.

"I loved you because I wanted to, Cass. Not because I had to."

And then she was gone.

CHAPTER FIFTEEN

SHE HAD ONLY known this sense of heartbreak once: the moment her mother's hand had gone limp in her grasp as she'd breathed her last. She knew the feeling all too well. The numbness at first, the mind and heart both denying the evidence that lay right in front of her eyes. Then, slowly, the pain as reality trickled in, then broke through as if a dam had burst and an ache filled her entire body.

When she'd made the decision to tell him, she'd accepted that there was a strong possibility he would say he didn't love her. But she had comforted herself with the fact that at least she had tried, that it was better to tell him how she felt and risk that rejection than to cower like she had for so many years and not share what was in her heart.

She had not anticipated him ending their engagement. Now she had not only lost Cass but lost her ability to help Linnaea as well.

The elevator dinged, the doors swishing open to reveal the hallway where the royals kept their private offices. Alaric's was on the left. Her own was just past that on the right. Daxon maintained the most luxurious office at the end, although she'd never seen him enter it.

She started down the hall. Perhaps if she focused on some work, reviewing the feedback from parents from her town hall or a building proposal for a new school in the southern region, she could keep the pain at bay.

Everything was quiet. Almost quiet, she amended as she neared the door to Alaric's office. A strip of light was visible at the bottom of the door. She could barely make out the quiet murmur of two voices. Daxon had left as she'd been saying her goodbyes. Was he in the office with Alaric? She had no desire to see him again tonight.

She picked up her skirts and started to walk faster, hoping the tapping of her heels wouldn't be audible through the thick door.

So much for hope, she thought miserably as the door swung open.

"Briony?"

She turned and flashed a brittle smile at her brother.

"Sorry. Didn't mean to disturb you. I'm just heading to my room…"

Her voice trailed off as she caught sight of Clara standing behind Alaric. She drooped in relief.

"Where's Cassius?"

She blinked. "Cass? Oh, he's…um…well, that is to say…"

Clara surprised her by brushing past Alaric and coming up to lay a comforting hand on her shoulder. Her eyes were surprisingly kind.

"Did something happen?"

Briony swallowed hard.

"We…that is to say, Cass ended our engagement just now."

"What?" Alaric snapped. "Where is he? I'll—"

"Hush, Alaric," Clara said in a firm voice. "Briony, come inside, dear. Tell us what happened."

Briony let Clara lead her into the office and sit her down in one of the stiff-backed chairs in front of Alaric's desk.

Alaric circled around and sat opposite her, steepling his fingers as he stared at her with his arctic gaze. Despite his power stance, he looked decidedly unsure of himself. If she hadn't been so upset, she would have found the sight of her older brother at a loss for words humorous.

"Why did Cass end the engagement?" Clara asked as she pressed a glass of water into Briony's hands.

Briony breathed in deeply. "I fell in love."

By the time she made it through the whole story, the painful ache had eased a fraction. Clara had filled her glass once, only interrupting here and there to ask a clarifying question. Alaric had watched her with a detached gaze the whole time.

Briony forced herself to swallow the rest of the water.

"I'm sorry, Alaric."

"Sorry?" he repeated softly.

"Without Cass's money, the country—"

"Damn his money."

Unlike his father, Alaric didn't need to raise his voice to be heard. The deep tones resonated with a barely suppressed fury that made Briony shiver.

"But—"

"I detested this arrangement from the start." He paused for a moment, as if trying to formulate his words. "But when I saw how the two of you were together, it convinced me that perhaps you could also be happy."

Briony smiled weakly. "For a brief time, I was."

Clara squeezed her hand. "Take it from me, Your Highness. You do not need a man or family to be happy."

Alaric frowned in his assistant's direction before he directed his attention back to Briony.

"The ambassador was impressed by what we've started to rebuild in such a short amount of time. Switzerland is ready to offer financial aid in exchange for several things we can offer, such as building a port along our northern coast. We won't get as much done as quickly as we would have with Cassius's money," Alaric admitted, "but we can still accomplish a great deal and become independent. You have not ruined this country, Briony. Far from it."

Relief swamped her. "Thank you."

"You're welcome. Now, what will make you happy?"

She knew the answer in an instant.

"I'd like to stay in Linnaea."

Alaric nodded. The look of pride on his face touched her.

"I'm glad," he said, and he sounded as if he genuinely meant it. "I tend to do well with Linnaea's finances, laws, rules. The country could benefit from having someone who sees shades of gray, not just the black and white that has been my life."

Clara arched a brow as she tucked a long strand of white-blond hair behind her ear. "What an astute self-observation, Your Highness."

Alaric bowed his head. "Thank you."

Briony set the empty water glass on an end table.

"Thank you, Alaric. I don't know if Daxon will let me stay once the engagement is officially ended—"

"Let me worry about him."

Judging by the ice in Alaric's gaze, Daxon had a lot to answer for. There was a slight pang in Briony's chest that she had struck out twice when it came to father figures in her life. But then she released it. She may not have a father, or the man she'd fallen in love with, but she had a half brother she was coming to care for very much and, if Clara's unexpected support was anything to go by, another friend right here in the palace.

Really, she thought as a tiny seed of hope lodged in her chest, when she thought about it, she had a lot to be grateful for. The best part was she'd chosen all of it, not because she had to, not out of some misguided loyalty to family, but because she'd wanted it.

Briony stood.

"Thank you both. If you hadn't welcomed me in, I'd still be crying alone in my room."

Alaric stood and came around the desk. He grasped both her hands.

"He's a fool, Briony."

She nodded. "He is. But he's a fool who's hurting very deeply."

"No excuse," Alaric retorted.

But you don't know him like I do.

How could Cass even begin to compare himself to Daxon? Misguided, yes, and at times selfish. Yet in the time she'd come to know him, truly know him, she'd found that Prince Cassius Morgan Adama shared far more in common with Cass Morgan than probably even he himself realized. The man she'd started to fall for in Kansas had turned out to be so much more than she could have ever hoped for.

One day, she would be able to look back on that and smile knowing she had loved an incredible man.

"We'll agree to disagree," she said with a soft smile.

"For now. What else can I do?"

The idea popped into her head. At first it surprised her. But the more she thought about it, the more it felt right.

"Can you cover me for a couple days? There's someone I have to visit."

CHAPTER SIXTEEN

RAYS OF EARLY-MORNING sun filtered through the snow-covered trees. A whisper of a breeze trailed through the branches, releasing an occasional dusting that sparkled like fairy dust before it fell to the white ground. Somewhere deep in the woods, a bird tweeted a soft greeting. It was the kind of scenery painters rushed to capture and poets wrote odes to.

Cass barely noticed it as he wandered aimlessly through the snow. He didn't care about the beauty of his surroundings. If he focused on it too long, he would start to think about Briony, about how much she would love it and how she would probably lob a snowball at him when he wasn't looking.

You did the right thing.

He'd been playing that mantra in his head over and over again since last night. At first, it had done its job. It had stopped him from doing something rash like going after her. After the fourth shot of brandy had made the world tilt a little too much, he'd managed to sneak back to his room and fall into bed, his repetition providing some comfort as he drifted into a restless sleep.

But halfway through the night, when he'd awoken and reached out to touch her, only to have his hand graze the cold sheets, he'd had a moment of panic. How could he have let her go? Even if he couldn't return her love, he could have given her the world.

She doesn't want the world. She wants you. You don't deserve her after what you've done.

That reminder had made him put his phone down and lie back down. Even if he could overcome his decades-long commitment to never let himself make the same mistakes his aunt and father had, how could he begin to forgive himself for what he'd done to Briony? How had he ever thought that forcing her into marriage was better than what Daxon had done? Those thoughts had kept him tossing and turning until the first crack of dawn had finally roused him from his bed. Needing a distraction, he had donned his winter gear and traipsed out into the cold of a November morning before the majority of the palace had awakened. He'd avoided looking back, knowing his gaze would be drawn to a certain balcony and the room beyond.

Briony had fallen for a lie. She may not have realized it yet, but one day she would. And then not only would he still not be worthy of the incredible gift she had offered him, but she would leave. Leave like Daxon left Aunt Alecine. Leave like his mother had left his father.

Which just confirmed that he was a coward. That he would give in to his fear instead of take the risk like Briony had. Another confirmation that he wasn't good enough for her.

He circled around the north end of the small lake and headed back toward the palace, the sun climbing higher in the sky until it finally crested over the mountains. A golden glow bathed the landscape. It also obscured the figure moving swiftly toward him until the man was nearly upon him.

"It's difficult to kick you out of the palace when you're nowhere to be found."

Alaric's voice rang out across the field. Cass turned,

resigned to whatever punishment Alaric was prepared to deal him.

"My apologies. I was on my way back. I can be in my room within twenty minutes if you'd like to schedule my eviction around then."

Alaric's curse reached him before he was able to blink the sun out of his eyes enough to see the prince's towering figure trudging through the snow. Alaric's face was a thundercloud, his lips stretched into a tight line.

"I would prefer to punch you."

Cass spread his gloved hands out. "I'll give you the first one for free."

Alaric snorted. "That wouldn't be as satisfying. Besides, a punch can't begin to compare to how much my sister is suffering."

A different kind of pain, sharp and cold, pierced his heart. It wasn't the pain of being out in the snow for too long. No, this was heartache at knowing he had hurt the one person he cared about more than anyone.

His eyes flew open as he straightened. He did care for Briony. Deeply. So much that he was prepared to give up the one thing he'd been working toward for nearly twenty years.

"I ended our engagement because I can't give her what she deserves."

Alaric arched a thick brow. "And what is that?"

"Love."

Alaric groaned and scrubbed a gloved hand over his face. He stomped over to a tree and leaned against it.

"I've seen the way you look at her, Cassius. You care for her."

"Of course I care for her," Cass growled. "How could I not?"

"So what is the difference between caring for and loving her?"

"Love can only last for so long before reality takes over. It may work for some people, but genuine affection and friendship last far longer in most cases."

"So why not give her that instead of making both of you miserable?"

"Because your sister thinks she loves me," Cass replied softly. "And she deserves to have someone who can give her something more in return than I'm capable of."

Alaric stared at him for a long moment. Cass returned his stare. He knew he was being evaluated, measured, on the verge of most likely being banished from Linnaea forever.

Strangely, that knowledge didn't make him feel angry or even desperate to find some way to stay. Unlike Aunt Alecine, he would deserve whatever happened to him. His dream of coming home, restoring his family's honor and reclaiming what had once been theirs seemed like a pale, distant memory compared to his past few weeks with Briony. Even after she had learned of his subterfuge, she had loved him, faults and all.

"I think, unfortunately, you and I are a lot alike."

Cass laughed. "Ah, yes. The jet-setting Mediterranean prince with a slew of broken hearts in his wake and the ice-cold heir apparent to the winter country of Linnaea. We could have been separated at birth."

"You don't love because you're scared."

His laugh abated as he slanted a glare at the older man. "Sounds like you talked to your sister last night. I have been many things in my life, but I've never made a decision out of fear."

Liar.

Alaric pushed himself off the tree and stalked closer. "You did last night. Briony offered you a gift, herself and her love, and it scared you. I know about your mother. I know what my father did to your aunt." He jabbed a finger in Cass's direction. "I think you based your decisions on what are obviously horrible examples of relationships, which makes you a damned fool. You kept yourself withdrawn, didn't get too deep into emotions and focused on other things like your revenge against Daxon."

A simmering anger started in Cass's stomach. "Speaking from experience, are we?"

Alaric froze, his eyes narrowing. Then, "Perhaps."

Cass shook his head. "What about your own fiancée, the one we never hear about?"

Alaric's jaw tightened. "Ours was a business arrangement. Necessity. Affection didn't play a part."

"That was what I had envisioned for myself."

But then I got to know your sister and she turned my world upside down. She is kind and strong and passionate. She deserves everything she ever wanted.

Alaric swore again and turned away.

"I can't help you. Not if you're going to remain steadfast in your belief that you can't love her in return." He stopped and looked over his shoulder. "And if you truly can't, then she's better off without you."

Cass balled his hands into fists. Why could Alaric of all people not see that he had done the right thing in setting Briony free to find true happiness?

"I expect you to be out of the palace by noon today," Alaric called over his shoulder. "Briony encouraged me not to void your reinstated citizenship, even though I could have since you terminated the contract when you ended the engagement."

"What if we signed a new contract?"

Alaric paused, then slowly turned back to face Cass.

"I don't want or need your money."

"Linnaea does."

"Not anymore. The Swiss ambassador has offered us financial aid."

"An offer that I'm sure is nowhere near as generous as the one I offered."

"We'll make do," Alaric ground out.

"Or you could listen to my new proposal, one that won't tie anyone down to any agreements and keep Linnaea on this new path."

As he said the words, Cass was filled with a sense of rightness that had been missing when he'd signed the contracts with Daxon and Alaric last month, and when he'd signed the contract with Briony. On those days, his thirst for revenge had overridden what the focus should have been on.

But now, in this moment, he knew he was doing the right thing. Not to exact revenge, not to secure a place for his family, but because it was the right thing to do for his country.

"What are you proposing?"

Alaric's voice was cautious, his face a solemn mask.

"Everything we've discussed the past few weeks, minus the marriage. I won't force Briony into another agreement against her will. My only condition is that my arrangement be with you and not Daxon."

A grim smile crossed Alaric's face. "After all this time, you would give up your revenge?"

Cass shrugged as he started walking. "It never should have been about revenge in the first place. Once the details are taken care of, I'll be leaving for Tulay."

Alaric fell into step beside him. "You're just going to leave?"

"Yes." After last night's disaster, Linnaea no longer felt like home. Neither did Tulay. Perhaps he would never find a place to call home.

Alaric shook his head again.

"You're a fool, Cassius. A damned fool."

CHAPTER SEVENTEEN

BRIONY WALKED AROUND the interior of the Ledge as she soaked up the memories of the past eighteen months. It hadn't been her dream job, but for a long time it had been an escape. It had become one of the few constants in her life, and for that, she would always be grateful. She had spent so much time lamenting the lack of affection from her stepfather and stepsisters that she hadn't fully appreciated the people who had made that time bearable.

Time didn't erase the vivid memory of the last time she'd seen Cass as he'd tried to push her. Despite his cruel words, she'd seen his own emotions in his eyes. He loved her, of that she was certain.

But she was done waiting for people to treat her the way she deserved to be treated. If Cass preferred to deny how he felt and chose living in his emotionless world, and if she truly loved him, then she had to respect his choice. To force him to do anything would make her a monster in her own way. And it would wipe away the strength she'd discovered in herself this past week. To live her life pining for someone else and placing her entire happiness in his hands would be falling right back into a pattern she'd only just begun to break free of.

Knowing she had made significant changes would one

day bolster her spirits. But for now, it served as the most minimal of cold comforts.

Gus came out of the back, wiping his burly hands on a towel.

"Still can't believe we had an actual princess slinging drinks," he said with a gap-toothed grin that flashed white against his dark brown skin.

"I don't think I was technically a princess at the time," she replied with a small laugh.

"Kim says you better come say goodbye before you go back so she can curtsy to you. And so she can tell Lisa that she met a real princess when she was a baby."

"I'm in town through tomorrow, so I can definitely do that."

Gus's face sobered. "How's the stepfamily?"

A sense of peace filled Briony's chest. "Surprisingly decent. Trey's out of rehab and back home. He has a job interview next week with his old company."

Gus's eyebrows shot up. "Well, least it's something."

"It is. And he even apologized."

After she'd made the decision to fly back to Kansas, pack up her remaining things and say goodbye to her co-workers, she'd texted Trey and the twins to let them know. Trey had surprised her by calling her. He'd thanked her for getting him help and then surprised her even more with a heartfelt apology, not just for the months since Mom had died, but for how he'd failed her as a stepfather.

"I thought treating you nice was enough," he'd said, sorrow heavy in his voice. "After your mother died, I got angry. Angry that your mom wasn't there to see us, angry that you were so much like her. It's no excuse," he'd added quickly. "I just need you to know it wasn't you."

Even though she'd already known that, hearing it from Trey had been a balm to the wounds she'd sustained.

They would never be close. But it was better than anything they'd ever had.

Gus grunted. "Bet he's playing nice so he can try to finagle some money out of you."

"I wondered so, too. But money hasn't come up since we started talking again. Maybe I'm being naive, but I'd like to think he's becoming a better man."

It had been nice, too, hearing that Mom had actually told Trey about her history with Daxon. She'd even left a packet of letters for Briony to read, letters she hadn't quite been able to read yet. But soon.

"And the twins?"

Briony's smile grew. Ella had surprised her by throwing her arms around Briony when she'd stopped by to pick up the letters, sobbing and asking for forgiveness for her horrible behavior. Stacy had been a little more reserved, but had echoed her sister's apology and even given Briony a gift—a necklace of her mother's she'd found in the attic.

"Apparently Trey's sister Debra was just what they needed. I made too many excuses for them and let them get away with too much for far too long. Between the chores, grocery shopping and getting grounded for not doing their homework, they had a rough few weeks."

Not that Debra had done it out of any great love. As she'd told Briony as she'd thrown the last of her suitcases in the trunk, "I got sick of the whining."

Gus rolled his eyes. "How many times did I tell you that you were too easy on all of them?"

Briony held up her hands in surrender. "And you were right." She leaned up on her tiptoes and pressed a kiss to the owner's cheek. "You're a great dad, Gus."

Gus flushed with pleasure. "Thanks." He glanced at the clock. "Four o'clock. Sure I can't convince you to work one last shift?"

"No, thanks. But I'll stay for a bit."

As Gus opened the doors and a few customers poured in, Briony hung off to the side. Some of the regulars came up to her to congratulate her on her engagement. She managed to paste a smile on her face and thank them. A couple asked for selfies, which she grudgingly obliged.

Yes, things had definitely changed, she mused as the bar started to crowd up. People still waved and were friendly. But there were plenty more side glances, whispers behind hands and people trying to covertly snap her photo. Fortunately, she was leaving later that evening. It wouldn't be too long before the photos made the rounds online and an enterprising paparazzo or two came knocking.

For a moment, she thought back to that Thursday just before three o'clock when she'd been alone in the bar pulling chairs off tables. The last minute her life had been somewhat normal. Despite the yuckiness of her situation at home, she had been anonymous, just one person moving in a sea of billions worldwide.

And then Cass had walked in.

Her eyes drifted toward the door before she could stop herself. She'd been gone three days. The first day, she'd spent the plane ride back to the US grabbing her phone every time it dinged.

No text messages. No phone calls. No emails. Nothing.

The second day, she'd perused the newspapers, waiting for news of their broken engagement to circulate. Except it hadn't. Aside from photos of the ball, there had been no news of Linnaea or Cass.

She'd called Clara to ask what had happened. With the wedding just four weeks away, she thought the palace would have released a statement as far in advance as possible.

"We'll make the announcement at the appropriate time,"

had been Clara's cryptic reply. She'd then told Briony to stop worrying and enjoy her time in Kansas.

She'd tried. She'd tried very hard, but in moments like these, when she had little to distract her, it was very hard to prevent her thoughts from drifting to Cass and the last time he'd held her in his arms. To close her eyes and remember how gentle he'd been with the children when they'd toured the wing of the hospital that would be upgraded to a pediatric unit. As he'd crouched down to admire a little boy's cast and sign his name, she'd known what a wonderful father he'd make.

Stop.

Cass was out of her life. Perhaps one day she could stomach the thought of going on a date with someone else. Although whether that person would be interested in her or her new status, she would probably always wonder.

Not to mention the thought of sharing a romantic meal, let alone holding hands or, God forbid, kissing someone else made her sick to her stomach.

Maybe I could adopt. The thought gave her a much-needed boost of happiness. Between that and her work with Linnaea's schools, she could have a full life.

And the more time that passed, the more she'd be able to visit her memories of Cass and smile with nostalgic longing instead of swallowing back tears of heartache.

Gus turned the televisions on in preparation for the game. Briony glanced at one of the screens, then did a double take.

"Wait, Gus, go back!"

Gus clicked back to the first channel. A picture of her and Cass was featured in the corner. The news anchor's mouth was moving, but she could barely hear what was being said.

"Turn it up!"

Moments later, the anchor's deep voice reached her ears over the din of the bar.

"...Morgan Adama of Tulay released a joint statement with his soon-to-be brother-in-law, Prince Alaric Van Ambrose of Linnaea. Prince Cassius is engaged to Prince Alaric's long-lost half sister, Princess Briony Anne Van Ambrose."

The screen filled with an image of Cass and Alaric standing next to each other at a lectern in front of the grand entrance to the palace. Her throat tightened as her heart started to pound furiously. Despite the dark circles beneath his eyes, Cass still looked incredibly handsome in a navy suit and brown tie that brought out the amber in his gaze.

"Prince Cassius and I have renegotiated the terms of the financial agreement between Linnaea and Tulay. The previous draft was an alliance based on his marriage to my sister, Princess Briony. The provision of marriage has been struck from the contract."

Her stomach dropped. This was it. The entire bar, let alone the world, was going to learn that her engagement was over.

Someone from the audience in front of the palace shouted a question. Cass stepped up to the lectern. Briony turned away, tears blurring her vision as she started for the back. If she was going to cry, she was going to do so in private.

"Prince Alaric and I reached this agreement because I want my future wife to know that I am marrying her for her and her alone."

Briony froze. Then, slowly, she turned, her eyes riveted on the screen as a cautious hope filled her chest.

Another indiscernible question was asked. Cass looked straight at the camera.

"I am very much looking forward to an alliance between

EMMY GRAYSON 183

Tulay and Linnaea. But I would be lying if I said I wasn't looking forward to my wedding the most."

"I meant every word." She heard him speak, this time much clearer, much closer.

His voice washed over her, deep and smooth like a fine whiskey. She wanted to turn, but it was as if roots sprang from the ground and wrapped around her feet. She couldn't move, couldn't breathe.

Awareness swept over her with a crackling intensity as she felt him come closer, felt the heat of his body as he stopped mere inches away.

"I missed you, Briony."

Slowly, ever so slowly, she turned and looked up to meet Cass's smoldering golden-brown gaze.

"Did you?"

"Very much."

She swallowed hard. "I'm a surprised to see you here given the way our last conversation went."

"I imagine you are."

He breathed in and she realized Cass was nervous. The thought made a laugh rise in her throat that she barely bit back in time.

"It's rather crowded in here," Cass said as he cast an eye over the bar.

"Football game tonight."

He rolled his eyes. "I forgot how you Americans use the wrong name for your sports."

Briony arched an eyebrow as she folded her arms over her chest. "You came all this way to criticize one of our favorite pastimes?"

Before she could pull back, he cupped her cheek. The shock of his bare skin on hers after several days apart electrified her senses as she instinctively leaned into his touch. He bent down.

"No," he murmured, the warmth of his breath brushing her ear. "I came all this way for you."

CHAPTER EIGHTEEN

CASS WAITED WITH bated breath as Briony watched him with an opaque stare. She would be well within her rights to have him tossed out of the bar and tell him she never wanted to see him again. The thought made him press his hand more firmly against her cheek. If this was going to be the last time he got to touch her, he would soak up every moment he could.

"We can talk on the patio," she finally said.

Relief spiraled through him. Talking was a start.

Briony led him through the crowds. He spotted more than one curious stare, and a couple people snapping photos. He grimaced. One of the positives of living in security-tight Linnaea the past month had been not having to worry about the media or a wayward tourist snapping his photo. Who would have thought he'd have to worry about such things in the middle of a Midwestern prairie?

The patio was mercifully empty. Surrounded on three sides by a wooden privacy fence and dotted with chairs and tables, the patio was covered in snow. With a string of lights casting a glow on the snow and a lone firepit flickering in the center, it offered a cozy and intimate atmosphere. Perfect for what he had to say.

And if Briony walked out of his life after she'd listened to him, he'd have somewhere private to mourn.

Briony brushed some snow off one of the chairs and sat, holding her hands out to the fire. She kept her gaze focused on the flames. The light brought out the gold intertwined in her strands of red.

When it seemed like she had no intention of saying anything, he decided to plow forward.

"You saw the press conference."

"I did."

Her tone betrayed nothing. No anger, no sadness, no happiness. Her face remained a blank mask.

"What did you think?"

"It was surprising."

He stifled his initial irritation at her oblique answers. It was no more than he deserved.

"I did it for two reasons." He moved toward the fire and sat down in the chair next to her. When she didn't move away from him, he took it as a positive sign. "You were right, Briony."

That got her attention. She turned to look at him, a quizzical look on her beautiful face.

"Tying my offer of help to marriage wasn't a means of protecting my finances or ensuring the money was properly spent. It was part of my revenge."

The bleakness that appeared in her eyes made him hurry on.

"That was how I saw it when I made the offer to Daxon. I reasoned that because I would be helping a country, and rescuing you from a poor financial situation, it was okay for me to get some benefit, too." His voice turned bitter as he forced out the words. "I saw myself as a knight in shining armor for both you and Linnaea. I was so proud of myself for intertwining my revenge with what I saw as helping that I didn't stop to think about how my motivations tainted what I was doing."

Briony reached over and laid a hand on his knee. Just that simple touch, her gloved hand on his leg, nearly made him reach over and haul her onto his lap. But there was too much left unsaid. And if she did decide to not kick him out of her life forever, it had to be her choice, not him forcing her.

"I started to realize what I was doing was unfair when I first got to know you. Because you weren't some helpless damsel in distress. You were a living, breathing, compassionate woman who worked hard to provide for her family, harder than I ever have."

"I find that hard to believe," Briony said softly with a small but kind smile. "You wouldn't have the wealth you do without some hard work."

"Wealth that got a very generous start from my Aunt Alecine's husband." Slowly, he laid his hand on top of hers and murmured a silent prayer of thanks when she didn't pull away. "The more I got to know you, and the more I worked with your brother, the more my focus started to shift. It was no longer about punishing your father. It started to be about what it should have been all along— helping the country avoid a depression and regain its footing."

Briony's lips parted, but then she looked away.

"What is it?"

"It just…if things started to change, why did you…"

"Send you away?"

She nodded, her gaze still focused off to the side. He ached to hold her, to comfort her and wipe away all the pain he had caused her.

"Because I fell in love with you."

For a moment, he wondered if she'd heard him because she just continued to stare into the fire. But then slowly, so slowly it nearly tore him apart, she turned to look at him, her eyes wide, lips slightly parted.

"What?"

"I fell in love with you," he repeated. "And it was wonderful and terrifying. The guilt I'd been feeling since I met you took over. I felt like I was just as bad as, if not worse than, your father."

"How could you possibly be worse?"

"Because he has no conscience. I have at least somewhat of a conscience, and I still proceeded to pressure you into getting engaged and leaving your life behind."

Briony shook her head. "You offered me a choice."

"Between redemption and devastation." No longer able to stop himself from touching her, he slid his gloves off. Then, with slow movements, he slid hers off as well. Her breathing quickened as a blush crept over her cheeks. Slowly, ever so slowly, he entwined his fingers with hers, his heart racing as if he were a teenage boy on his first date. Amazing how Briony brought even the simplest of things to life.

"You're being too hard on yourself, Cass."

"I'm not, Briony. And it wasn't just how I'd treated you." He frowned, remembering Alaric's too-accurate analysis of his history. "I've never felt about anyone the way I've felt about you. The one example I've had of so-called love ended in devastation for my entire family. My aunt and father described such emotions as weakness. It's hard to rework one's lifelong views in such a short time, especially when guilt weighs you down."

"What changed?"

Cass smiled ruefully. "Your brother started me down the right path."

"My brother?" Briony repeated disbelievingly.

"After he threatened to punch me."

Her eyes swept over his face. "Did he actually hit you?"

His hand came up and cupped her cheek once more. "Not physically. But emotionally, yes. He told me how foolish I was, that it was evident how much I cared for you. I resisted at first. But I offered to rework the contract so the financial agreement would no longer be tied to our marriage."

"Why?" she whispered.

"Because it was the right thing to do. And," he added as he leaned in, "because as your brother and I were talking, all I could think about was you. Linnaea no longer felt like home. Tulay didn't, either. When I thought of home, I thought of you. Once I realized what that meant, I knew removing the marriage stipulation from the agreement not only was the right thing to do, but it would give you the true choice I never gave you in the first place."

"Oh, Cass."

"Linnaea and Tulay have officially entered into an agreement that will provide substantial funds for Linnaea's recovery. Your stepfather's treatment is paid for, including a year's worth of counseling services. Your stepsisters have full college funds, and the mortgage has been paid in full."

A single tear slid down her cheek. He released one of her hands and wiped it away.

"Please don't cry, Briony."

"You've been so generous," she said shakily as another tear fell.

"No, I haven't. It's what I should have done all along without holding an engagement ring to your head."

"Cass…"

He put a finger to her lips.

"One last thing, Briony, and then I promise to be silent for whatever you have to say." He came out of his chair, got down on one knee and reached into his pocket. Briony gasped as he pulled out a black velvet box and popped the lid. Nestled inside was her engagement ring, the emerald-and-topaz stones winking up at them.

"Briony, I love you. You've brought joy to my life. You've already made me a better man and a better leader. Would you do me the honor of becoming my wife and making me a husband?"

Tears were now cascading down her cheeks.

"Are you crying because you're happy or because I've ruined any chance I ever had?"

With a deep sob she flung herself forward and wrapped her arms around his neck. His arms flew around her and crushed her to his chest.

"Briony," he breathed into her hair, inhaling her intoxicating scent, "is that a yes?"

She pulled back and framed his face between her hands. "Yes! Yes, yes, yes!" She pressed her lips to his. Hunger and love surged through him as he buried one hand in her hair and poured all of his emotion into their embrace. His mouth moved over hers, claiming her with every touch.

At last, they emerged for a breath. Cass slipped the ring on her finger and pressed a kiss to her knuckles. But, as her gaze moved from her ring back up to his face, he realized that even though Briony had accepted his proposal, she still hadn't told him how she felt.

As if she could read his mind, she gave him the most incredible smile.

"I love you, Cass."

He swallowed hard past the thickness in his throat. "Truly?"

"Oh, yes. I had already started to fall in love with you when you were plain Cass Morgan. And when you stood up for me, and encouraged my ideas, and saw the real me, I fell in love with Prince Cassius."

He pressed a kiss to the tip of her nose, then her cheeks, then once more on her lips, savoring her sweet sigh of contentment.

"I know your brother flew you here on the royal plane. But I think it would make much more sense for you to fly home with me."

The smile that lit up her face made him feel like he could move mountains.

"Home," she echoed. "That sounds wonderful."

EPILOGUE

BRIONY STARED AT herself once more in the mirror. But today, instead of gazing at her reflection with trepidation, she felt as if she could fly, she was so happy.

The designer had fashioned a gold creation, vines intertwining over the strapless bodice before cascading down onto the full, fluffy skirt. Matching gold slippers peeped out from beneath the material. A stylist had made her curls gleam beneath the matching veil. The florist had put together burgundy and white flowers that stood out beautifully against the gown.

Her hand drifted down to her stomach, still flat beneath the dress.

But not for long, she thought with a small, secret smile. She'd taken the test that morning. Cass would be getting quite the wedding present that evening.

A brief knock sounded a moment before Clara walked in. Dressed in a midnight-blue shift dress, flats, her hair pulled back into her signature tight bun at the base of her neck and a clipboard in hand, she looked every inch the personal concierge of the prince.

Except, Briony noted with some concern, she looked awfully pale, with dark half-moons beneath her eyes.

"Are you all right, Clara?"

Clara gave her a wan smile. "Yes, just feeling a little under the weather."

One hand came off the clipboard and drifted down to land on her stomach. Briony froze, then looked away as the puzzle pieces clicked into place. The night of the dinner for the Swiss ambassador, Alaric's fiancée had ended their engagement, a fact Briony had learned about after she'd returned from Kansas.

Memories of that night flashed through her mind, details she had missed as she'd focused on her own grief. Clara's unbound hair, Alaric's slightly mussed shirt.

Apparently, Alaric and Cass were going to have even more in common.

"I appreciate all you're doing."

Clara nodded, then slipped back into planning mode.

"Ten minutes and Prince Alaric will be here to walk you down to the chapel. We'll line up outside the doors at a quarter to five. The doors will open at five exactly."

When Alaric had offered to walk her down the aisle, Briony had barely stopped herself from bursting into tears. Who would have thought that just when she started focusing on other things in her life, she would be gifted a family?

Daxon hadn't taken too kindly to her turning down his offer to walk her down the aisle. But Clara, bless her, had arranged for Daxon to welcome guests to the ceremony, a role that had assuaged his ego enough that he hadn't made a fuss since. Trey, the twins and the employees of the Ledge had even been flown in as guests.

Briony stepped down from the dais and wrapped Clara in a hug. Clara froze, then slowly hugged her back.

"Thank you, Clara." She leaned back. "For everything."

Clara's face relaxed into a genuine smile. "Of course.

Prince Cassius and Prince Alaric are both lucky to have you in their lives."

Clara hurried out, leaving Briony alone in her suite for a blessed few moments of peace and quiet. She went back up on the dais and spun in a circle. The skirt flared out before coming to rest against her legs. Her mom would have loved it.

Another knock sounded on the door. Briony stepped down and crossed the room. Perhaps Clara had forgotten something.

"Who is it?"

"Your future husband."

His voice washed over her and ignited the heat that flared to life every time she heard his voice.

"It's bad luck to see the bride before the wedding."

"My eyes are closed."

She should send him away. But that would just be spiting herself. She slowly opened the door, making sure his eyes were truly shut, before she threw herself into his arms. He caught her and wrapped her in a strong hug that made her feel cherished.

"You feel beautiful."

"How can one feel beautiful?" she asked with a laugh.

"I don't know, but you do."

She leaned into him, inhaling his scent and soaking in his warmth.

"I have a surprise for you," she whispered, unable to contain her excitement anymore.

His hands slipped down and cupped her backside.

"Does it have something to do with what's under your dress?"

She laughed. "Yes, but not what you're thinking. Promise to keep your eyes closed?"

After he nodded, she grabbed one of his hands and

guided it to her stomach. His fingers fell flat on her belly, a frown crossing his face before he froze.

"Briony…really?"

"Really."

With an exultant shout, he picked her up and spun her around in a circle as she shrieked with laughter.

"No peeking!"

"I'm not!"

He set her down and kissed her with a fervor that made her head spin.

"You're pregnant. And you're going to be my wife," he whispered reverently as his hand drifted back to her stomach, his fingers drifting across in a soft caress.

"I love you."

"And I love you, Briony. Always."

* * * * *

COMING SOON!

We really hope you enjoyed reading this book.
If you're looking for more romance, be sure to
head to the shops when new books are
available on

Thursday 9th June

To see which titles are coming soon, please visit
millsandboon.co.uk/nextmonth

MILLS & BOON®

Coming next month

CINDERELLA IN THE
BILLIONAIRE'S CASTLE
Clare Connelly

"You cannot leave."

"Why not?"

"The storm will be here within minutes." As if nature wanted to underscore his point, another bolt of lightning split the sky in two; a crack of thunder followed. "You won't make it down the mountain."

Lucinda's eyes slashed to the gates that led to the castle, and beyond them, the narrow road that had brought her here. Even in the sunshine of the morning, the drive had been somewhat hair raising. She didn't relish the prospect of skiing her way back down to civilization.

She turned to look at him, but that was a mistake, because his chest was at eye height, and she wanted to stare and lose herself in the details she saw there, the story behind his scar, the sculpted nature of his muscles. Compelling was an understatement.

"So what do you suggest?" She asked carefully.

"There's only one option." The words were laced with displeasure. "You'll have to spend the night here."

"Spend the night," she repeated breathily. "Here. With you?"

"Not with me, no. But in my home, yes."

"I'm sure I'll be fine to drive."

"Will you?" Apparently, Thirio saw through her claim. "Then go ahead." He took a step backwards, yet his eyes remained on her face and for some reason, it almost felt to Lucinda as though he were touching her.

Rain began to fall, icy and hard. Lucinda shivered.

"I – you're right," she conceded after a beat. "Are you sure it's no trouble?"

"I didn't say that."

"Maybe the storm will clear quickly."

"Perhaps by morning."

"Perhaps?"

"Who knows?"

The prospect of being marooned in this incredible castle with this man for any longer than one night loomed before her. Anticipation hummed in her veins.

Continue reading
CINDERELLA IN THE
BILLIONAIRE'S CASTLE
Clare Connelly

Available next month
www.millsandboon.co.uk

LET'S TALK

Romance

For exclusive extracts, competitions
and special offers, find us online:

f facebook.com/millsandboon

🐦 @MillsandBoon

📷 @MillsandBoonUK

Get in touch on 01413 063232

For all the latest titles coming soon, visit
millsandboon.co.uk/nextmonth

MILLS & BOON

THE HEART OF ROMANCE

A ROMANCE FOR EVERY READER

MODERN
Prepare to be swept off your feet by sophisticated, sexy and seductive heroes, in some of the world's most glamourous and romantic locations, where power and passion collide.

HISTORICAL
Escape with historical heroes from time gone by. Whether your passion is for wicked Regency Rakes, muscled Vikings or rugged Highlanders, awaken the romance of the past.

MEDICAL
Set your pulse racing with dedicated, delectable doctors in the high-pressure world of medicine, where emotions run high and passion, comfort and love are the best medicine.

True Love
Celebrate true love with tender stories of heartfelt romance, from the rush of falling in love to the joy a new baby can bring, and a focus on the emotional heart of a relationship.

Desire
Indulge in secrets and scandal, intense drama and plenty of sizzling hot action with powerful and passionate heroes who have it all: wealth, status, good looks…everything but the right woman.

HEROES
Experience all the excitement of a gripping thriller, with an intense romance at its heart. Resourceful, true-to-life women and strong, fearless men face danger and desire - a killer combination!

To see which titles are coming soon, please visit

millsandboon.co.uk/nextmonth